I0718560

Once Upon a Princess

DEMELZA CARLTON

Four tales in the Romance a Medieval Fairy Tale series

Revel: Twelve Dancing Princesses Retold

DEMELZA CARLTON

Book 4 in the Romance a Medieval Fairy Tale series

One

"We should have made the wedding this week," Dokia said, lacing her fingers through Vasco's. "Waiting eight more days is torture."

"I call it delicious anticipation," Vasco replied. "Besides, if we got married this week, we wouldn't have a house to live in. Tomorrow I'll make a start on the roof, so that when you become my bride, we'll be able to spend our wedding night under a roof."

She lifted her gaze to the sky and sighed. "Right now, I would be perfectly happy with the stars as my roof, the night I become yours. If I have you, I will have everything I ever wanted."

"Right up until it rains," Vasco said.

Dokia laughed. "And that is why you're my lord and provider, or you will be, after next week. I cannot think of rain while the sun still shines."

"Ah, but the sun is setting now. And once the sun is gone, I'll make sure that all you can think about is you and me." Vasco raced into the trees, pulling her along until they reached the clearing they had claimed as their own.

Kissing Dokia was like air – he couldn't get enough of her. Their kisses grew more heated, and their clothes began to loosen before they started removing them entirely.

Vasco laid her on the soft grass by the stream, where she gazed up at him with eyes full of love.

"With all the practice we're getting, you will

be perfect at this when our wedding night comes," she teased.

"Only because you are already perfect, my Eudocia," Vasco said, kicking off his boots.

"Flatterer," she replied, undoing the lacing of her gown to expose most of her chest. "What about these? Perfect enough for you?"

"Too perfect for me," Vasco replied. "Much like the rest of you. I don't know what madness made you accept me, but before you recover your senses, I will accept anything you offer me."

She parted her gown completely, laying herself bare. "I offer you everything I am, and everything I have. Take me, Vasco."

Vasco opened his mouth to respond, but another voice cut in, "That's a mighty pretty morsel. Too pretty for some peasant boy."

Something crashed into the side of Vasco's head and he fell lifeless to the grass. He never heard Dokia's screams pierce the air, or those from the village as it burned. When he awoke, there was nothing but silence and death to greet him.

For hours he walked the ruins of his home, looking for hope where there was none. So he did what any young man would after everything he had known was dead and buried: he joined the army, figuring that death would find him soon enough.

But fate had a different plan for Vasco.

<h1 style="text-align:center">Two</h1>

Wishing to be the fairest of them all was the worst kind of curse to visit on a princess, Bianca mused. She alone among her sisters had fair hair, so pale that in today's bright sunlight it almost seemed white. It made her stand out, drawing unwanted attention from men and women alike. The men she did not mind so much, for she knew that as a princess she was near untouchable to most of them, but when the queen's gaze landed on her one too many times, nothing good could come of it. That

Bianca was the daughter of a minor concubine, a princess in name, but not much more, who outshone the queen's own daughter, only made it worse.

So that was why the fairest of all the king's daughters now rode through the unseasonable heat into exile at the Summer Palace. A place where the king's virgin daughters would be safe, the queen had said with a vicious smile, until they were married.

Bianca knew better. The Summer Palace was where girls were sent to become old maids. No girl who had ever been sent there had returned, nor had they received word of any fortuitous marriage alliances the girls had made. That in itself was suspicious, Bianca mused. For the proposed marriage between the queen's daughter, Lagle, and the neighbouring king had been trumpeted far and wide. For one horrible moment, Bianca had worried that she would be sent as Lagle's companion to the foreign court, but the queen had taken a dislike to another minor princess instead. So poor Ava could look forward to a lifetime of servitude, while Bianca was granted the relative freedom of exile.

Right now, though, Bianca almost envied Ava. Ava would ride through shady forest all the way to her new home, while Bianca's road was just that…a road. A road tramped by thousands of marching feet, when her father's armies had been fighting to claim this place, and it was kept clear to facilitate troop movements, should they be needed in future. So the sun beat down mercilessly, with no shelter in sight.

Which brought her back to the curse of being the fairest of all the king's daughters. Her cheeks burned, though she had no reason to blush. Bianca had never experienced a sunburn before, but if this was one, she had no desire to experience one again. By the time they reached the edge of a wood and a cottage where she might take shelter, Bianca's face felt like it was on fire. She signalled for her guards to halt, and she dismounted. Praying that the owner of the cottage was home and willing to offer temporary shelter to a traveller, Bianca knocked tentatively at the door.

The door creaked open, as though she was expected. "Princess!" an elderly voice croaked. "Please, come inside." A wrinkled hand beckoned her in.

Bianca glanced at her guards, who didn't look concerned, so she accepted the old woman's invitation and followed her into the blessed cool of the cottage.

The old woman shuffled to the table where she poured two cups of liquid from a stoppered jug. Then she waved her hand and the door slammed shut. That got Bianca's attention. "I am Kun, the witch who guards these lands. Welcome, princess. I take it you're not accustomed to travel?"

Bianca shook her head, wincing as this only seemed to make her face hurt more.

"I can give you a salve to soothe that burn, if you wish. If you're anything like your sisters, you wish to stay pretty for as long as possible."

She gave a gummy grin.

"I would prefer not to be pretty," Bianca said with regret. "Pretty princesses attract unwanted attention. Much better to be unseen."

The woman cackled again. "An invisible princess, eh? That's quite a trick. Even more impressive than the day when the queen's new gown…"

"Please don't mention that," Bianca groaned. "I only wished to see how the queen's new gown was made. I had no idea what was invisible to me became invisible to everyone else, too. My mother banned me from using magic every day after that, so that the queen would not know that it was I who made her gown invisible so that she appeared naked at court. I think she suspect something, though. She has never liked me."

Kun patted Bianca's hand. "It matters not. You're far from court and the queen now, and your mother, too, I think. Mayhap you should practice your magic a little more. You never know when it might be useful to become invisible."

If Bianca didn't know better, she would think Kun knew of her desire to escape. Or perhaps Kun knew the truth about life in the Summer Palace. Surely the politics could not be worse than those in the king's harem. But where there were a lot of women… "Are there many ladies residing at the Summer Palace?" she ventured.

"Not so many. With you, there shall be twelve princesses. All about your age, and ripe for marriage. All they need are suitable husbands."

Bianca tried to hide her surprise. What, no old maids? Were the stories wrong, and the girls really would be married off? Or were the old maids taken somewhere else?

"Here's your salve," Kun said. The jar clattered to the table from her shaking hands. "You be sure to put some on now, then another coat morning and night. It should heal without a blemish."

Bianca obeyed. The salve seemed to extinguish the flames, though some of the heat remained. "Thank you," she said with feeling.

"You can come visit, any time you wish to practice your magic," Kun said.

"I… I can leave the palace? To come and visit you?" Bianca asked in surprise.

Kun snorted. "It is a palace, child, not a prison. Within the borders you will be safe. My cottage marks the edge of palace lands, so take care you do not go beyond it. The Summer Palace has its pleasures, as I'm sure you will find out, once you begin to explore. No doubt your sisters will enlighten you."

Her sisters. Bianca swallowed. Half sisters, more like. And her rivals, should her father choose to marry one of them off for an alliance. Marriage would be her only means of escape, and if the opportunity arose, Bianca intended to take it. Perhaps being the fairest of them all might not be a curse, in this case.

Three

When Bianca left Kun's cottage, she found her guards had gone. Her mare stood outside where she'd left her, along with the packhorses carrying her belongings, but no one else. When Bianca looked askance at Kun, the old woman just grinned.

"Like I said, princess, you are safe here. There is no need for guards, while you are on the grounds of the Summer Palace."

Bianca looked around nervously. "But I do not yet know where the Summer Palace is," she said.

The old woman cackled. "Neither did your guards, for none of them have been allowed to go further up the road than my cottage." She eyed Bianca. "Simply follow the road. It will lead you to your destination."

"Is it far?" Bianca asked, hating the tremor in her voice. Her instincts told her to turn her horse in the opposite direction and urge it to a gallop until she was as far away from this place as possible.

"Less than an hour's ride, I am told. But that depends on just how eager you are to reach the palace."

Bianca swallowed. Perhaps Kun truly could read her mind.

Bianca found that for a less than eager princess, on a tired mount she had no desire to kick into a faster pace than a walk, it was indeed less than an hour before the palace loomed into view. Much smaller than the women's palace in the capital, she would not have called it a palace at all, if not for the decorative stonework that marked it as a noble's residence. Her father's seal on the gate left no question as to her destination. Small though it was, this was the Summer Palace, and her home for the foreseeable future. But not, she vowed, the rest of her life.

Servants ran out to greet her, to take care of her horses and see to her things. None of them dared raise their gaze to meet the eyes of a princess. That was as it should be, Bianca supposed. Then why did she feel such a strong burst of fear from them all? Perhaps she only imagined it.

"Princess Bianca, I presume?" a booming male voice rang out, preceding a richly dressed man who bowed low before her. "I am Efe, cousin to the queen, and the steward of the Summer Palace. The king wouldn't trust anyone less with such treasured jewels from his harem such as yourself and your sisters."

A crow cawed loudly with what sounded like laughter as it took flight from the roof above.

Bianca drew herself up to her haughtiest height, which sadly fell short of this odious man's shoulder. Nevertheless, she was a princess and the king's daughter, not merely some distant relation of the queen's. "No, he would not trust a lesser noble then yourself," she said sweetly. "After all, guard duty for a group of women who are used to living a protected life in the palace is hardly a job for someone the king values highly."

The steward's nostrils flared. Her barb had indeed landed. "I would not expect such a sheltered princess as yourself to know anything of the dangers outside your father's palace in the capital." His vulpine grin said what his words did not: that he hoped Bianca would fall afoul of some of these dangers, for he would enjoy her misfortune.

Bianca suppressed a snort, for such things were unladylike. She was no ordinary princess, but let the man believe what he liked. She had learned politics from her very infancy, for no girl survived long in a harem otherwise. Let him do his worst. She would be prepared. Bianca bowed her head to hide her smile.

The steward seemed to take this as submission. More fool him. "I shall take you to your quarters, and to see your sisters." He waved her inside.

For a moment, Bianca hesitated on the threshold. Even in the evening light, it seemed much brighter outside the confines of the Summer Palace. But such fears were silly, she told herself. Taking a deep breath, she strode forward with her head held high.

Four

Bianca heard her sisters before she saw them. The sounds of women at dinner when there were no men to command restraint was a familiar song of home. Lesser wives, concubines and their daughters who didn't have the status to be entitled to a private apartment had shared a common table in the harem. Several tables, as her father prided himself on the sheer number of women under his authority.

So it was with a smile on her lips that she

entered the dining hall, taking a deep breath to greet her sisters.

Bianca's gaze swept across their faces and stopped dead.

She knew every face but one.

The ruddy face of a man beamed at her from under a hat so fluffy and floppy it looked like he wore a dead puppy on his head. If this was to be a new court fashion, Bianca was glad to be well away from it. "And who might you be?" the strange man slurred, raising a cup of wine to her.

Bianca lowered her eyes, but had to force herself not to incline her head. There could only be two men superior to a princess – her husband, and the king. As this man was neither, he must be beneath her notice. Her sisters didn't deem his question important enough to answer, either.

"This is Princess Bianca," Efe said. "Only just arrived from the palace." He made her sound like some sort of delectable dish, fresh from the kitchen.

Bianca suppressed a shiver. She'd heard children's tales of men who ate human flesh, but surely they were nothing but stories. Yet the way Efe spoke…

"You must sit beside me, princess, and tell me about your father's court," the man said.

As if by magic, her sisters slid up the bench to make space for her. For a moment, she hesitated, wondering what they knew about the stranger that she did not, but she could hardly ask them in front of the man. Better to ask him to talk about himself. Her mother and the other concubines had often said it was a man's favourite conversation topic, for the more he talked about himself, the more he liked the lady who pretended to listen.

But Bianca did not need to pretend. "I would much rather hear about you, sir. We hear little of the adventures to be had in the world outside my father's harem. The women's palace shelters us from such things. But you, I am sure, have travelled very far. How did you come here?"

He laughed so hard he spat out his wine. "By horse, of course! It isn't how I came here that matters, but why. Do you know why I am here, pretty princess?"

Bianca recognised the lust in his eyes. She lowered her gaze and shook her head. "I am just arrived, so I have not yet heard, sir."

"I am here to get myself a wife, and a palace!" he announced, grinning. The grin vanished when he reached for his wine, only to find Brenna's little dog lapping at the cup. "Wretched creature!" he shouted. The dog took fright and galloped across the table to seek refuge under Brenna's chair.

What appetite Bianca had possessed now vanished at the sight of dog footprints in every remaining platter of food. She waited for a maidservant to remove the tainted dishes, as would happen in the women's palace in the capital, but no one moved except the man beside her, who seized another chicken leg.

"More wine!" he called, raising his cup. "And a fresh cup to drink it from."

To Bianca's surprise, Hazel rose from her seat. "I will fetch it," she said, and headed out of the hall.

"You make my decision a difficult one," the man said. "Which of you will be my wife? If I can only have one of you, should I choose the prettiest, or the most obedient?"

Silence reigned at the table, broken only by the sound of mastication. No one laughed at his attempted jest, and none of them deigned to reply. Was that because they'd given up on the chance of escape from this life?

Bianca refused to give up, so she seized her chance. "You should choose the fairest, sir, the one who will best please you." She lowered her gaze and batted her eyelashes, as she'd seen the maids do to the handsome guards, when they thought no one else was looking. She felt like a complete fool, until she realised it had worked.

"You're as wise as you are beautiful, Princess Bianca," the man said. "I think you will please me very well."

Triumph welled up in her breast, but she did

her best to hide it. "I hope so, sir."

Hazel returned with a goblet of wine, which she presented to the man. He drank it off in three huge gulps, then flashed a red-lipped smile at Hazel. "Thank you, my dear."

Bianca held her breath, but she caught the sneer that curled Hazel's lips. Hazel didn't want him for a husband.

He'd evidently caught her look of distaste, too. "But I think Princess Bianca is prettier than you. If she were to fetch me more wine, I think she will capture my heart completely."

"I will show her where to find it, then. Bianca?" Hazel jerked her head imperiously toward the door.

From princess to serving wench? Bianca balked at the thought, but she could do worse things to catch a husband and secure her escape from exile. Resignedly, she rose from the bench and followed Hazel out.

"Good girl," the man slurred behind her.

Bianca gritted her teeth. She would pay a high price for her escape if she were to marry that fool, whoever he was. But weren't all men fools?

Five

Bianca followed Hazel through the house to the wine cellar, which she was surprised to find appeared bigger than the house above.

It wasn't until they were deep between the dusty barrels that Hazel spoke. "You're wasting your time with that one," she said. "Like all the others, he'll be gone in three days."

"Others?" Bianca asked, her mind whirling. The thought of better men to choose from was certainly appealing.

Hazel grinned. "Oh, so many others. The

promise of a palace and a princess's hand in marriage is quite the prize to a penniless adventurer, which most of them are. Dear Cousin Efe dresses them up in fancy clothes, but if you look closely, you can see how poorly they fit. Borrowed finery instead of the patched rags they arrive in, so that we allow them to sit at our table, but they will learn no secrets from us." She pointed at a barrel. "This is the one. This wine is stronger than anything you have ever tasted, which is why we don't. It's for men only, Cousin Efe says, which is fine by us. Here, look at the mark." She rapped her knuckle against the barrel, below a blackened smudge.

Bianca squinted at it. Now she looked more closely, she realised it was a brand, applied several times to the same barrel or just once by a particularly unsteady hand belonging to a man who'd perhaps drunk too much of his own wine. "Is it a bird of some kind?"

Hazel nodded. "This comes specially from somewhere far to the west. It's Efe's private supply, which is why we give it to his guests." She took a jug and proceeded to fill it from the barrel.

"Why didn't he dine with us tonight?" Bianca asked. Surely the queen's cousin would take every opportunity to dine with princesses, if only to make himself feel important.

Hazel laughed. "Oh, he wouldn't stoop to eat with us. We're the queen's hostages to our mothers' good behaviour. Anyone too pretty or too clever or even anyone who catches our father's eye for too long winds up here. For if another wife's daughters marry better than hers, she might lose her place as principal wife and queen. Perhaps that's why he forces us to share meals with beggars and soldiers of fortune, in the hope that we're silly enough to marry them. Disgraced daughters, disgraced mothers…that would only serve to cement her power in the capital."

Considering the idea, Bianca shook her head. "More likely she intends to leave us here to rot in spinsterhood, for any children we might have would still possess royal blood, no matter who their father was. But why would that man tonight think he had a chance to marry one of us, if he is a beggar?"

Hazel winked. "Delusions of grandeur, I'm sure. He believes he is better than any man before him, so he will be the one to solve the mystery, winning a bride and lands that he does not deserve."

"I have not heard of any mystery here."

"That's because it's no mystery to us."

Bianca opened her mouth to insist that it most definitely was a mystery to her, then closed it again as Hazel leaned in closer.

"Wait and see. Brenna has a plan that will confound even the queen. We are the king's daughters and we will not be held prisoner against our will. Not even Efe and a whole army of beggars will stop us." With another wink, Hazel led the way up the steps to the palace proper, carrying the jug of wine.

Six

Several hours later, when Bianca could barely keep her eyes open, she was startled into alertness by the clatter of metal at her feet. She peered under the table. A sword, still in its scabbard, attached to an unbuckled swordbelt, lay on the flagstones.

A snore cut through the air like a rusty saw, before something clunked to the table beside her. Bianca bumped her head painfully in her haste to see what it was this time. The man at her side had fallen face-first onto the table, and the snoring came from him.

"Finally," Brenna said, rising. The other girls followed her example, and Bianca struggled to her feet.

Bianca swayed, exhaustion conquering her as surely as it had the unknown man. The unknown, boring man she would sooner die than marry, she knew now.

"I'm going to bed," Bianca mumbled, stumbling in the direction she vaguely remembered led to the bedchamber she'd share with her sisters.

"But you must come dancing with us!" one of the other girls said.

"'Nother night," she managed to say.

"Let her rest," she heard Hazel say as someone took her arm, leading her. "She's been travelling all day. Tomorrow, she can dance."

Dance? Bianca could do many things, but dancing wasn't one of them. Grace was not one of her virtues. She opened her mouth to say so, but all that came out was an unintelligible yawn, followed by another one.

Somehow, she found herself on a soft surface. A bed, she hoped, but she was too tired to care, as sleep enticed her into a dream where dogs drank wine, beggars wore silk and princesses served their every whim as crows cawed from the heavens.

$\mathcal{S}$even

Waking in a darkened room where the only sound was the even breathing of what Bianca thought must be a dozen sleepers disoriented her at first. She had never shared a sleeping chamber before, and the tiny cubicle that had been hers in the capital had always glowed with the first light of dawn. Groggily, she rolled out of bed, dressed, and padded to the door.

As she reached to push it open, Bianca nearly tripped over something on the floor. She caught herself in time, and shoved the door open to let in enough light to investigate the obstacle. Bianca almost laughed at what appeared to be a pile of worn-out dancing slippers, so hard used the soles bore huge holes. They'd been piled artfully in a drift just inside the door, where anyone trying to enter or exit the room would certainly trip over them and wake everyone.

Bianca surveyed the room, but by some magic, she hadn't woken any of her sisters. Pushing the door open wider, she stepped out of the room, and found the reason for her sisters' makeshift security measures. The adventurer who'd been sleeping on the table last night now lay snoring on a pallet beside the entrance to their room.

Wondering whether he was supposed to be a guard or if he intended to waylay one of the girls when they emerged from their chamber, Bianca did her best to be quiet as she crossed the room and made her way to the dining hall.

The empty table bore no signs of last night's meal, or anything with which to break her fast.

Which was strange, given the sun showed it was mid-morning at least. In the women's palace at the capital, the benches would be full of minor wives, concubines and princesses, gossiping like the brightly coloured birds they resembled, as they tried to work out who was missing and hence who the king had favoured to share his bed the previous night. For it was common knowledge in the harem that he and the queen had not shared a bed since she bore his son and heir.

But there would be no such gossip here. The girls all shared a room, and would continue to do so until they died old maids. Unloved, untouched and unwanted. It was no surprise Brenna had brought her little dog along. It was a wonder no one else had pets. If she was forced to live in exile here for the rest of her days, Bianca might consider getting one. A cat, perhaps.

She found her way to the kitchen, where it sounded like the household servants were having their breakfast.

"Anyone willing to place a wager on the latest one?" Bianca heard one girl ask.

A loud snort silenced the rest of them. "That one? Guzzled his wine down like he'd never tasted it before. Probably hadn't. No one will solve the mystery, least of all these adventurers who keep showing up. When it was princes and such, maybe they had a chance, but these men? I wouldn't trust them anywhere near my daughters, and I don't know why the king does."

Someone made hushing sounds. "Don't talk treason. You never know who's listening."

The woman wouldn't be silenced. "It's no treason to speak the truth. I don't know why the king does what he does. But if he's so desperate to see this mystery solved, seems to me he'd only have to question the girls. Not send in some stranger to investigate for him. It sounds like something out of a story, from someone with too much imagination. Next thing you know, there'll be witches and curses and magical gifts, and someone will fall in love."

"You'd better hope none of the princesses falls in love with one of those men. The king would never let one of his daughters marry a nobody."

A clatter told Bianca they were clearing the table.

"But he wouldn't be a nobody any more if he solves the mystery, will he? Even if the man is a beggar, he'd become master of this house."

"Yes, but if they were to fall in love before he solved the mystery…"

Someone laughed. "Then he'd better solve the mystery, or lose his love!"

Dying to ask more about this mystery, but not wishing them to know what she'd overheard, Bianca scuffed her feet deliberately along the flagstones before she entered the kitchen. She found all eyes on her for a stunned moment before they were lowered in respect.

"Your highness," a woman murmured, and the rest chorused something similar.

"I've recently arrived," Bianca began, "so I don't know when or where meals are served here. I fear that I have missed breakfast, yet I am so hungry…"

"I'll fetch you something directly, your highness," a girl said, bobbing in such a way that Bianca wasn't sure if she was trying to bow or curtsey. Both, maybe. "Where would you like to be served?"

Bianca was stunned into silence for a moment. Never before had she been given a choice in such a thing. A minor princess ate at the common table in the harem, sitting in a spot designated by her rank. For the first time in her life, Bianca was her own mistress. The freedom both frightened and exhilarated her.

"I will eat in the hall where we dined last night," she said breathlessly.

As if reading her thoughts, the girl bobbed again and replied, "As you wish, mistress."

Bianca managed a nod in response before she left the kitchen. Her feet felt strangely light, as though she walked on air. Free. She was free of the miasma of politics she'd lived with so long in the harem. Perhaps she could even…

She returned to the kitchen. "Once I am finished eating, have someone saddle my horse. I wish to ride."

Bianca half expected someone to tell her she couldn't, or caution her against leaving the palace, but the only reply she relieved was a colourless, "Yes, mistress," from one of the people bustling about.

An hour later, when she sat astride the same horse she'd ridden yesterday, Bianca could barely believe it. No one came out to stop her. Why, she could kick the mare into a gallop and leave all this behind forever, if she chose.

For a moment, Bianca was tempted, but she resisted. She knew little of the world outside the walls of the palace. There could be wild animals or anything out there. But Kun had said she was safe inside the palace estate.

Kun. She would ride for Kun's cottage, and visit the old woman. Perhaps even practice a little magic while she was there. After all, she was free to do as she wished now.

Bianca urged the horse into a comfortable pace, feeling a smile light up her face more brightly than the morning sun. Who knew exile would feel so good?

Eight

Vasco's stomach growled, reminding him that it has been many hours since he had eaten his last crust of bread. The incessant hunger pangs were almost enough to make him forget the pain in his knee. In battle, he had scarcely felt the prick of the arrow as it worked its way between his armour, so it was a cruel twist of fate indeed that with every step he took, he had to grit his teeth as pain pierced his knee again and again. Such a small wound had yet made him unfit for war, so his commanding officer had kindly chosen to send him home.

For a married man, or one with any family at all, this would be a blessing. For Vasco, whose entire family had been slaughtered before his village was burned to the ground by the enemy, it was the worst kind of curse. No home, no family, nowhere to go, nothing to do. Vengeance had spurred him to join the army in the first place, but he lost his taste for violence as quickly as it had come. It was too late to protect those he had lost. No matter how many lives he took, he could not bring them back. So he had learned to fight for families and homes that were not his own. If he could save just one village, or someone's parents and brothers and sisters, someone's wife and children, so that no one else had to endure the emptiness inside that ate at him every day, perhaps Vasco would understand why his life had been spared.

Now, understanding eluded him. He had killed, and he had survived, but a single arrow had ended his purpose. So he wandered, doing whatever work he could to earn enough to eat, and sometimes even a place to sleep at night. Or he could, if he saw another soul he could ask for work. These woods he'd wandered into confounded him. The road stretched empty before and behind him, and he had not seen even a single dwelling for two days. If he did not find somewhere soon, he would have to hunt for food. Vasco's lips curled with distaste at the thought of having to use his bow. He was a foot soldier, not an archer, but fate seemed to wish it otherwise.

A hundred steps, he promised himself. He would walk a hundred more steps, and if he did not see any sign of civilisation, he would attempt to make camp and hunt for something for dinner.

Even if it involved… ten, eleven, twelve… archery. He grimaced. He counted forty-seven steps as he rounded a bend, but the forest hugged the road as happily as before. At seventy-nine, climbing a rise in the road, he almost considered changing it to two hundred steps or maybe even three. But the pain in his knee was growing insistent. He needed to stop, and soon. Sighing, Vasco topped the rise. And stopped.

At first, he only saw one house, tucked between the trees. But as his eyes adjusted, he realised he wasn't looking at an isolated cottage in the woods, but enough of them to count as a town. The trees had been thinned to allow space for the houses, but they still towered above them, hiding the place from watchful eyes as they kept their secrets. Though what sort of watchful eye could spy on a village from the very sky itself, Vasco did not know. In fact, he almost laughed at himself for entertaining such a strange notion. Eyes in the sky, indeed! Why, they would have to belong to birds.

Concluding that hunger had scrambled his wits, Vasco resolved to deal with that first. As was his custom when arriving at a new place, he first took stock of the businesses. After all, a thriving business was more likely to have work for him than a humble cottage. He might be lame, jobless and homeless, but Vasco was too proud to beg. As long as he could work to pay for a meal, he was not yet worthless. He squinted at the first shop sign. It showed a garish coloured woman's shoe that no woman he'd ever met could afford. Only a queen or perhaps a princess would wear something in such a bright shade of purple.

But it might tempt a woman who had heard too many fairytales and dreamed of one day being a queen. She might then choose to enter the shop, so that the shoemaker might grant her a smaller dream: that of a new pair of shoes. Perhaps it was not as silly a sign as he'd thought. And a clever shoemaker who could turn a fine profit might have need of a hard worker, and the wherewithal to pay him. This was as good a bet as any.

Vasco pushed open the door and stepped inside. A bell tinkled, announcing his presence before he could open his mouth.

"You are early, sir," a voice said. A man

appeared in a doorway behind the counter, his eyes widening when he caught sight of Vasco. "You are not one of the palace servants, unless the king has spent so much money on shoes that he can no longer clothe his servants in proper livery." He laughed as if this was some sort of joke.

Vasco's voice was grave. "I served the king as a faithful soldier, until my superiors said the wounds I had received in battle made me unfit to fight any more." He spread his hands wide. "Now, I ask if you have any work I might do, so that I might earn a meal and perhaps a bed for the night, to help me make my way home." Vasco did not say that he no longer had a home. He had already learned that it was unwise to mention the possibility of staying in a village where he was a stranger. Better to earn a place through hard work and then be invited to stay. His village had been no different. His heart tightened in his chest. At least, it had been. Now, there was no one left but strangers. For all his own people were dead.

The shoemaker squinted at him. "A soldier, eh? Have you any experience in making shoes?"

Vasco shook his head. "I wear shoes, but the making of them is a mystery to me." He managed a faint smile.

The shoemaker sighed. "Then you are out of luck, wounded soldier. I could do with a skilled assistant for I am busier than I ever believed possible. But I have no time to train an apprentice, especially one who has never shown any interest or aptitude for making ladies' shoes."

Vasco bowed his head. "I understand," he said. "Would you know of any other business in town who might be able to offer me a day's work?" He did not let desperation colour his tone yet. After all, he had gone longer without food before.

The shopkeeper grimaced. "If this were any other town, you would have more luck. But this is Slipper Town, and our trade is shoes for the palace. If you're not a shoemaker, there is no work for you here."

A whole town of shoemakers? Vasco found that hard to believe. In the capital, perhaps, but out here, in the middle of the woods? "Who buys so many shoes?" Vasco demanded.

"The king, of course," the shopkeeper replied cheerfully. "He has many wives, and many daughters. And each must have shoes befitting a lady of the court."

Vasco frowned. "But the court is far from here, surely."

The shopkeeper chuckled. "Ah, but the Summer Palace is very close. And the princesses there need more shoes than the rest of the court put together." He winked, as though they shared a secret.

A secret Vasco did not know, but what cared he for princesses? He was a lowly soldier, who would never be allowed to catch a glimpse of such a high lady. He would happily live and die with no knowledge of such strange creatures. There was but one woman he wished to see again, but as long as he lived, he would only see her in his dreams. She had perished along with the rest of his village.

The shopkeeper's voice broke through his reverie. "Perhaps you should ask at the palace." The shopkeeper coughed. "With so many of the king's precious daughters in residence, the palace is surely in need of more guards."

Vasco thanked him for his advice, and ask for directions to the palace. Vasco was surprised to hear that it was but an hour or two's travel from the village – he could reach the palace by nightfall. Thanking the man once more, Vasco returned to the road.

From the array of signs showing similarly brightly coloured slippers, he realised the truth of the shoemaker's words. This was indeed Slipper Town. A town of shoemakers and little else. The palace must be large indeed, with hundreds of female residents, to keep so many tradesmen in business. Perhaps even large enough to offer him a bed and meals for the rest of his life.

He set off up the road, a new spring in his step for the first time. For deep in his heart, Vasco felt the stirrings of hope.

Nine

Bianca settled into a new routine quickly. She woke with the dawn, while her sisters slept on until well past noon. After breaking her fast, she rode or walked to Kun's cottage. On her return, she would walk beside the lake. Some days it was mirror calm, reflecting the sky and birds above as though there were a second world below, if she but had the courage to pierce the surface. On other days, the beach vanished beneath an onslaught of waves blown up by the slightest breeze, and the lake licked at the very foundations of the Summer Palace.

She grew more skilled at making things invisible. She'd managed to vanish most things in Kun's cottage, before making them visible again. Today, Kun had insisted she bespell the cottage roof. Except she was not to make it vanish entirely – oh, no. Kun asked her to vanish patches of it so that there appeared to be holes in the roof, yet anyone looking through those holes would see nothing of what went on within her house.

The strange twist on her invisibility spell had made Bianca work harder at her magic than ever before. She'd felt worn out by the time she'd accomplished it, only to find Kun demanding proof that the spell had worked. That meant climbing on the cottage roof and peering in.

Bianca had protested at first – after all, princesses did not climb on roofs. Her mother would be horrified at the very thought – but Kun was adamant that one of them must, and the old woman was hardly spry enough to make the climb.

Bianca managed to hoist herself onto the water butt and scramble onto the roof without too much trouble, but climbing down had been her undoing. She'd hit the lid of the water butt on the way down wrong so that it tilted, and instead of landing firmly on it with both feet, she'd slid into the cold water. The butt was easily as deep as she was tall – Bianca might have drowned had Kun not witnessed her fall. As it was, the woman had reached in, seized her collar and dragged the spluttering princess to the surface where she could breathe again.

While Bianca's clothes dried in the sun, she sat in her shift before the fire with a scalding cup of tea in her hands to ward off the chill from her immersion. Kun didn't ask her to perform any more magic, so Bianca decided it was her turn to do the asking today.

"What is this mystery in the palace everyone keeps talking about?" Bianca said, blowing on her tea to cool it.

"Do you mean the shoes?" Kun asked as she poured herself some tea.

The shoes were no mystery, Bianca was sure of it. The other girls piled them up to keep adventurers out of their sleeping chamber, for she'd counted at least half a dozen different men who'd come and gone. They shared the princesses' table and slept on a pallet outside their door for three nights, before they disappeared, never to return.

More than once, Bianca had wondered whether the men were some sort of illusion she'd conjured to keep her hopes alive of finding a husband and a way out of exile, but she knew the men were real. The first adventurer, who'd dropped his sword beneath the table on her first night in the Summer Palace, had neglected to retrieve it. Bianca had found the sword, scabbard and belt several days after his departure, half-hidden under the bench where he'd sat. She'd carried it all to her bedchamber and concealed the items under her bed. The sharp steel was real enough, so the sword's bearer must have been real, too. As were all the adventurers who claimed to be able to solve the mystery. A mystery so mysterious even Bianca didn't know what it was.

"I don't know. The mystery that draws men to the palace like flies to honey," Bianca said finally. "I know men are fools when faced with a beautiful woman – we learned that with our first breath in my father's harem – but they seem taken…nay, obsessed with the notion that they can solve some mystery and claim one of us as a wife. It's not just them, either. The servants say the same. Whoever solves the mystery will become master of the Summer Palace and marry one of us. If I have to make myself invisible to avoid it, I swear his bride will not be me."

She meant it, too, Bianca realised. She would not trade her freedom in exile for marriage to some lusty brute she barely knew.

"The choice may not be up to you," Kun chided. "If the king offers a man a princess for a bride, he might also offer the man his choice of his daughters."

Bianca shuddered. To be given away as a prize, instead of a marriage alliance…as though she were a possession instead of a person…it chilled her. Her father was many things, both bad and good, but he was fiercely protective of his family. "What would make my father offer his own flesh and blood as a prize to any man?"

Kun grinned gummily. "Have you noticed anything unusual about the shoes?"

"They are worn out," Bianca replied. "My sisters pile up their worn-out dancing shoes on the threshold to our sleeping chamber, to trip the unwary adventurer if he seeks to enter without our permission." Permission that would never be granted, she was certain of it.

"So they do, and every morning, a maid comes to tidy away the broken shoes. She throws them on the refuse heap, and brings new shoes for each princess. Yet the next morning, there are more broken shoes." Kun drank deeply from her teacup. "How do you explain this?"

It was on the tip of Bianca's tongue to say that her sisters must have quite a store of broken shoes, or they retrieved them every night from the refuse heap. But that could not be. None of them would soil themselves by setting foot anywhere near the refuse heap, especially not to claim some old shoes. Instead, she said, "I can't."

"And nor can the king, or any of the adventurers who hear of this mystery. That is why the king has offered the Summer Palace and the hand of a princess in marriage to any man who can solve the mystery for him." Kun set her empty cup on the table.

Bianca still didn't understand. "All that because of some shoes?"

Kun shook her head slowly. "Not just some shoes. A dozen pairs of dancing shoes every night. Fine shoes suitable for a princess. Why, it would take a dozen craftsmen more than a day to make such shoes. And all the silk and leather that must be used to make them…why, you and your sisters will bankrupt the treasury if this keeps on much longer. What else can your father do but offer a reward to anyone who can find him a solution before you and your sisters run his treasury dry?"

"I have not had a single pair of new shoes since I arrived," Bianca objected. "Nor have I worn any out. My father cannot blame me for whatever it is my sisters do. I will not be punished for their carelessness!" She rose and stormed outside to where her clothes were almost dry. She dressed quickly, ignoring the way the still-damp cloth clung to her. It would surely dry on the ride home.

With a curt farewell to Kun, Bianca spurred her horse toward the Summer Palace.

"Not all women see marriage as a punishment," Kun called softly after her. "If you marry a good man, what feels like duty at first can be a pleasure, in time."

The horse snorted, echoing Bianca's sentiments. She might have lived a sheltered life, but she'd lived in a harem. A harem full of wives who spoke little of the pleasures of marriage. If a woman wanted pleasure of any kind, she must make it for herself. The pleasure of a refreshing ride, or a brisk walk by the lake. Such were the pleasures available to her now, and Bianca found very little enjoyment in Kun's company if the old woman intended to harp on about duty.

Instead, she would ask her sisters to let her know their secret, and protect it so fiercely no man would pry it from her. For if no man solved the mystery, no man could marry one of them. It was the perfect solution.

Ten

After an hour's journey up the road, with no signs of the palace or even a break in the woods, Vasco was ready to curse the shoemaker into oblivion for his poor directions. But, he reasoned, his steps were slower than most, what with his limp and all, so perhaps the shoemaker's directions were for a fitter man than he. Or the palace was as well hidden as the village. Neither would have surprised him, so he trudged wearily on.

This time, when he saw a cottage, he paused

to scan the woods for the rest of the village. However, this cottage truly did stand alone. From its falling down state, he doubted anyone lived there now. But an empty cottage that no one lived in was a place he could happily spend the night. Nevertheless, the door to this cottage stood shut, so he knocked tentatively on it instead of barging inside.

To his surprise, a querulous elderly voice said, "Who is it?"

Vasco wet his lips, suddenly nervous. "My name is Vasco," he said. "I am a wounded soldier, recently returned from war. I seek a meal, and perhaps a bed for the night, and, in exchange, I offer my services." He eyed the holes in the roof. "For instance, I could fix your roof so that the next time it rains, it no longer leaks."

The door creaked open and a wrinkled face peered out. "Fixing my roof is no small job," she said. "You would need a place to sleep for more than one night, and you'd more than earn your meals between."

Vasco smiled at the old woman. "Honoured grandmother, we have a deal."

She eyed him suspiciously. "I'm not your grandmother, boy. I'd remember a strapping soldier like you. You can call me Kun." She gave him another hard look before she added, "And you can sleep in the barn with the goats." She cackled. "For I've no use for a handsome soldier in my bed. Not at my age."

Vasco smiled wistfully, for now, she reminded him of his own grandmother. She had not lived to see her village slaughtered. "You must have few visitors, if you think me handsome. And I have better luck with goats than women, so the barn is a good place for me." After all, three goats had survived the massacre of his village. Three goats and one man, but no women. Goats' milk had kept him alive long enough to join the army, when he traded them for the price of his weapons and armour. None of them had been his family's goats, but he had reasoned that the spirits of the slain would have happily handed over their last livestock in order to exact vengeance from their murderers. Perhaps it would help their spirits rest. For Vasco knew it would be a long time before he would know a good night's rest.

"Come in, then," Kun said, stepping back and holding the door wide open. "There is soup in the pot, and fresh straw in the barn. It will be dark soon, and repairs can wait until morning."

Gratefully, Vasco stepped into the dark cottage, his stomach rumbling so loudly at the first whiff of soup that he hardly heard the door slam shut behind him.

Eleven

It was not to be, Bianca found when she reached home. Her sisters were already in the dining hall, studiously ignoring a new adventurer whose eye-watering pink robe fit so badly Bianca wondered whether Efe was trying to blind them.

The new man was well into his cups when his eyes fixed on her. "Well, aren't you a pretty one?" he slurred. "Mayhap I'll take you to wife, so I can see if you're as pale under that robe as you are above it."

Bianca was too tired to be courteous to this buffoon. "I assure you, I am not. Beneath this robe, I'm covered in thick fur like one of the bears from the mountains. I must shave my face every morning to stop the fur from growing. And cut my claws, lest I disembowel someone by mistake." She curled her fingers into claws and bared her teeth.

Hazel choked on her soup. Aruna had to pound her on the back as a coughing fit engulfed her, effectively ending the conversation for several minutes.

When she thought no one was looking, Brenna set her dog on the table, who scampered straight for the man's goblet. Bianca had to smother a laugh, for this wasn't the first time she'd seen Brenna set the dog on their unwanted dinner guests. She was certain her sister had trained the animal to only drink from a man's cup. Or perhaps he only drank wine, for all her sisters' cups contained water tonight.

"Cursed creature!" With a backhand blow,

he sent the little, yelping dog flying off the table to hit the wall. It slid to the floor, looking stunned, before it crawled under the table to hide from the horrible man.

"I shall fetch you some fresh wine," Bianca said through gritted teeth, wishing she could slip poison into the cup. No man who hurt a helpless animal so deserved to live, let alone marry. What if he treated his wife that way?

She swept out of the room before he could say anything more. Bianca considered heading to her bedchamber for the sword beneath her bed, but she dismissed the idea almost as soon as she'd thought of it. She'd never handled a sword, and with his greater strength, he would easily beat her in a fight. Women didn't wield swords, anyway. They fetched wine and waited for the fool to fall asleep.

The jug she carried back was so full a little slopped over the brim at every step, but grim determination drove her. Bianca would do her best to get the man to drink himself to death before he could do the dog further injury.

She filled his cup, and filled it again, until the jug was empty. To her chagrin, he seemed no closer to succumbing to sleep than he had earlier. Yet her own eyes felt heavy, what with all the climbing and spell-casting she'd done at Kun's today.

Bianca rose unsteadily to her feet. "More wine," she muttered, stumbling a little as she headed for the door.

Hazel appeared at her elbow. "Let me help you, sister," she said, prying the jug from Bianca's fingers.

Bianca gratefully accepted the other girl's arm. "I went for a long ride today. Too long, I think. So….tired," she yawned.

Hazel glanced back at the dining hall. "His boasting is enough to put anyone to sleep. Retire early. I'll fetch the wine and make your excuses." She gave Bianca a push in the direction of their sleeping chamber.

Bianca nodded and did as she was bidden. It wasn't until she was tucked in her bed that she remembered wanting to ask her sisters about the mystery. Ah, it would wait until morning. It wasn't like the mystery was going anywhere. They'd want a huge pile of shoes to guard against tonight's buffoon.

She drifted off into dreamless sleep.

$$\mathcal{T}welve$$

As Vasco slid from the roof, he tried to think of a way to tell Kun that she was lucky her house hadn't fallen down around her ears. Yet. But he was a soldier, not a diplomat.

"Well?" Kun demanded, her hands on her hips.

Vasco blew out a breath. "You were right," he said heavily. "The roof doesn't need repairing as much as it needs replacing completely. I think some of the beams are rotten, too. I noticed last night that one of the barn walls has a definite lean to it, though the roof is in better repair. If it rains, my bed with the goats might be drier than yours here in the house."

Her eyes were shrewd as she regarded him. "So how long do you propose to squash my straw and eat my larder bare, soldier boy?"

Vasco looked her in the eye. "As long as you have work you wish me to do, ma'am." He coughed. "But the repairs to your roof and the barn will likely take a week or two, depending on how long it takes me to find good timber."

Kun waved at the woods around. "There are trees aplenty, boy. Take your pick."

He nodded. "A week, then."

"A week's work for just room and board? Surely you will ask for more than that," she said.

Vasco spread his arms wide. "It is all I ask," he said carefully. "But if you choose to gift me with something more, I will not refuse."

She nodded slowly. "Very well. A bed, board, and a gift to match how good a job you do. We have a deal, though you are a fool to accept it."

He shrugged. "We are all foolish at some point in our lives. But no more foolish than necessary. Which is why I think I shall spend the morning chopping firewood for you before I take your axe into the woods, for a hard worker deserves a hot meal at the end of the day. That soup you made last night was the best I've ever tasted."

"Flatterer," Kun scoffed. "I'll wager your mother makes better."

"Alas, my mother roams the spirit world now. She has no need for soup, not that she ever did. My father hated the stuff, so she never made it." Vasco bowed his head briefly before turning away and making his way toward the chopping block. If his eyes seemed watery, and he had to blink back what felt suspiciously like tears, no one would see.

He swung the axe a little harder than necessary, but he told himself that Kun needed kindling as much as big logs to burn the night through. He could no longer cut down his enemies, but a few trees would fall to his frustration before the day was out.

The skin of his back crawled, as if someone was watching him, but Vasco ignored it. It was probably only Kun, not some enemy who would attack him. Right now his only enemy was wood, and he was more than a match for it.

Thirteen

When day dawned, Bianca stepped over the pile of shoes without a second thought. She tiptoed past the snoring adventurer and made her way to the dining hall, where she knew breakfast would be served for her. While she ate, the kitchen staff prepared a basket of provisions for her to take on her ride. Usually she gave most of it to Kun in thanks for the woman's time training her, for there was far too much for one person, but Bianca wondered what the staff would say if she returned with a basket that wasn't empty.

They might send less food with her on the morrow, she decided, which would not do. She had no other way of repaying Kun.

So, though it was the last place she wanted to go after Kun's comments yesterday, she guided her horse along the road to the old woman's house.

The sound of an axe biting into wood stopped her before she reached the cottage. Tethering her horse to a tree, out of sight of the road, Bianca paused for only a moment to render herself invisible before she continued on foot.

It was probably some villager, looking for some healing herbs or a good luck charm from Kun. It wasn't the first time Bianca had arrived when Kun had a customer, so she was content to wait until the man was gone. A princess shouldn't speak to the villagers, especially not the men. For the adventurers Efe set at their table were coarse enough, under the thin veneer of good manners they assumed, but a peasant who had no need to pretend to be polite might do anything.

Bianca's invisibility might protect her somewhat, but it did nothing to hide the sound she made. Or her scent, if the man had a dog. And if he were to bump into her…but he wouldn't get close enough for that, Bianca resolved as she crept closer.

She skirted Kun's cottage, heading to the yard where she knew the chopping block stood.

The man wielding the axe was no villager, though. Unless he was the blacksmith. She'd never seen so much muscle on a man, and there was plenty to see, for he was naked to the waist, with sweat gleaming on his broad chest. A scarred chest, she noted. If he wasn't a smith, then he had fought battles against men instead of metal. Or some horrible accident had befallen him.

The way he hammered the axe into the hapless chunks of wood spoke of some personal grudge he held against the tree. A section of trunk turned to kindling under his relentless strokes. He swept the spars up in his arms, stacked them in the woodshed, then grabbed another log to dismember. Whoever he was, he showed no sign of slowing. He must have asked for a really complicated spell from Kun, to do so much work in payment.

Bianca settled on the grass to wait.

Hours passed, but he did not slow. If anything, the furrows in his forehead only deepened as he continued to work. He allowed the timber to break into bigger pieces than kindling now before he stacked them in the woodshed, too.

He circled the chopping block, giving Bianca a clear view of his equally well-muscled back. He had fewer scars here, though they weren't entirely absent. What did that mean? That when he fought, he faced his enemy head on, and never turned his back on them?

Bianca felt the most peculiar urge to ask him. She could return to the road, dismiss her invisibility spell, and stroll into the yard as though she'd just arrived. She could offer him some of her provisions and introduce herself as Bianca. Not a princess, just…a maid from the palace. There. That would do. She rose to her feet, determined to put her plan into action.

"You've been working hard. You must be hungry. Come inside. The noon meal is ready," Kun said.

The woodcutter swiped his arm across his face, then grabbed a tunic he'd hung on the edge of the woodshed roof and pulled the garment over his head, hiding those delicious muscles from sight.

Delicious? Bianca scoffed at herself for having such thoughts. Why would she want to lick the man's sweaty skin? It would be hard and salty and…definitely unpleasant, she told herself. She was just hungry, that was all.

She rose, stretching the cramps from her legs from sitting so long, before heading back to the road in search of her horse. The mare stood exactly where she'd been left, with no sign of distress at being invisible. Bianca could see her, of course, as she could with anything she bespelled, but if she concentrated, she could also see what everyone else saw — nothing.

She grabbed the first thing she touched in the basket and bit into it. The sweetness told her it was fruit, but that's all the attention she paid to food. Her thoughts were with the scarred man in Kun's cottage.

Who was he?

Fourteen

With every limping step, Vasco reminded himself how much he hated archery. This hadn't always been the case, of course, for archery practice had been a required part of his training. He'd even been good at it once. Now, though…he hadn't been able to bring himself to fire an arrow at the enemy since he'd been wounded. Shooting someone from a distance was cowardly, especially if you couldn't give them a clean death. If they fell before you and you had a sword or an axe, it was a simple matter to deliver another blow if the first hadn't killed them. With arrows, though, it was much harder to hit someone who'd fallen. And no man, friend or foe, deserved to live with the constant pain he did. Wounds either healed or they killed you. They weren't supposed to torment you for the rest of your life.

Yet he nailed the slice of tree trunk to a tree on the edge of Kun's yard, and it became an archery target. Because while he might never shoot another man, he would undoubtedly need to hunt for his dinner one day. If he could not shoot something for the pot, then he would go hungry.

Besides, archery practice had always been his favourite part of army training. His thoughts grew clear and singular, focussed only on the target and the conditions that might affect his shot.

As if carried by a breeze from the distant past, he thought he heard the bark of some long-dead training officer shouting the drill: Stance. Nock. Draw. Aim. Loose. All followed by a bellowed, "AGAIN!"

Vasco marched to the other end of the yard in the pre-dawn light, and began to string his bow. He would shoot until he lost or broke all his arrows, or until Kun woke and he could start work on her cottage for the day.

Stance. He positioned one foot, then the other, ready to move and fire in any direction.

Nock. He'd seen men argue over the best way to do this, which side of the bow and whether to rest the arrow on one's knuckles or one's thumb. Vasco had never bothered to argue. His father had been a good archer, though he never shot an arrow in anger. And he had taught his son the only good way to do it. Vasco's arrows shot from the right side of the bow, over his thumb. He reached for the one of the arrows in the earth at his feet, and nocked it.

There was no wind in the clearing where Kun's cottage lay. Not for the first time, he wondered whether it was luck or if she was a witch. Neither would surprise him. If she was a witch, though, all the more reason not to wake her before she chose to rise.

Draw. Vasco sucked in a breath, held it, and drew the arrow back a little. The bowstring pulled as smoothly as a song.

He sighted along the arrow, aiming for the target, as he drew the arrow back further.

Breathe, he told himself. There was nothing else in the clearing but him, his bow and arrow, the target he intended to hit and the air separating him and his goal. Air he had to breathe.

One…two…three. Vasco loosed his arrow at the target.

It hit, but barely. He had aimed too low.

AGAIN.

Vasco reached for another arrow. It sped off into the trees, missing the target completely.

Vasco swore under his breath.

AGAIN.

By the time Kun called him for breakfast, he had run through his store of arrows three times, but on the third round, he'd managed to hit the target on every shot. Tomorrow, he would do better, he promised himself. If he did not, better to give Kun the bow for firewood than carry it around any longer.

His father's bow was the only thing he'd salvaged from his burned home. That and the goats, of course. His father had kept the weapon in the woodshed, the only building in the village that hadn't burned. Perhaps because it was full of green wood, not yet dry enough to burn, that Vasco and his father had cut the week before the attack.

To burn it would be to lose the last link to home. To his family. To Dokia. Though they all walked with the ancestors now, he would carry their memories with him every day. And his father's bow.

"If you don't come in now, I shall give it to the goats!" Kun threatened.

A very real threat, Vasco knew. He'd let the goats out of the barn to munch on the fresh spring grass for breakfast, but they wouldn't turn their noses up at human food.

He hurried to obey her summons. Tomorrow, he swore. Though to who, he wasn't sure.

Fifteen

After waiting most of the afternoon, during which the muscled man still didn't leave, Bianca reluctantly climbed back on her horse and headed home. It wasn't until she reached the palace that she realised she hadn't given Kun any of the food. Tomorrow, she promised herself, for the man would have gone home by then, surely.

Yet when she returned on the morrow, he was still there, cutting trees and dragging them back to the cottage. He looked bigger and brawnier than she remembered, which only made her feel worse about forgetting to give Kun her basket the previous day. So today she watched and waited, telling herself she was looking for an opportunity to sneak into the cottage unseen so she could repay Kun for her kindness.

Once again, the man did not leave the yard for long enough. He had enough timber to keep him occupied well into the afternoon, when Bianca had to return home.

Every day for a week she returned, and every day she found him still there. She wanted to resent him for keeping her from meeting Kun, but she couldn't. He took such care in his work, cutting the timber so precisely before using it to build Kun a completely new barn. Only when it was finished did she see him smile, and what a change it was. The brooding man seemed to light up from the inside. He took pride in a job well done. Something she had rarely seen in her father's palace, where servants held their positions for life and had no need to be good at their jobs to keep them.

Oh, she'd seen musicians dedicated to their craft, and cooks who cared about what their kitchen created, though the staff under them might not be quite as enthusiastic about such exacting standards, but this? The way this man built that tiny structure to house Kun's goats made her wonder how the architects and builders of the palace in the capital had felt when they regarded their handiwork.

She would never know, for the palace was completed before she was born, and definitely before she discovered she could use her invisible talents to escape the harem and roam about the palace. She fancied that she was the only princess who had ever entered the kitchens, and watched the soldiers at training in the guardhouse yard, when neither was deemed a fitting place for the king's daughters.

She could have watched the scribes and calligraphers for hours, though, for their painstaking work was akin to art. Only the knowledge that her mother would miss her and know she had escaped sent her back. Otherwise…Bianca fancied she might have joined them. If she had not been born a princess, she would have liked to choose the life of a scribe. Locking up words and whole stories in a series of symbols, so that people miles away or a hundred years into the future could see them and know what had happened. It was a kind of immortality, she supposed.

Now if she could immortalise Kun's carpenter in art, capturing the bulge of his muscles as he hefted the axe, or lifted a new beam into place, or that look of calm concentration he wore when he practiced archery in the early mornings. She'd only caught him at it once, but his makeshift target, a round slice of tree trunk, bore the signs of increasing accuracy as the week progressed.

She imagined him returning home to his lovely, loving wife – for a man like this could not go unloved – carrying fresh meat he'd caught on the point of his arrow on the way home after finishing work on Kun's cottage.

His own cottage would be immaculate inside and out, for a man who took such care on Kun's house would lavish even more attention on the home of the woman he loved.

And at night, beneath that perfectly crafted roof, he would use those skilled hands on his wife, in all the ways they'd whispered about in the harem. Bianca sighed at the thought. She envied the man's wife, for she knew a joy Bianca herself would never know.

Movement sighted out of the corner of her eye roused Bianca from her daydream, and she sat up to find Kun's eyes on her. The old woman beckoned her over, as if she could see the invisible princess as clearly as anything else in her garden.

Bianca glanced around, not seeing the man, so she dismissed the spell and hurried into the house.

"You've been so busy watching Vasco that you've forgotten about me," Kun remarked as she set some water boiling for tea.

Bianca opened her mouth to protest, but

the old woman's sharp look silenced her. Instead, she said, "How did you know?"

"I recognise the smell of your magic now, having seen you cast it so often. There is more to this world than what the eyes can see," Kun said. "Though you've been using your eyes more of late, I see."

"What sort of spell did he ask for, to repay you with a beautiful new barn?" Bianca asked. "It must be something difficult. Healing for his wife, perhaps?" The man she'd watched all week would do anything to make his wife well, if she fell ill, Bianca was certain of it.

Kun laughed. "Not all want a spell. And not all men have wives. This one shares a bed with my nanny goats every night, which might be why he built me such a stout barn. He is a soldier, injured in battle, who now wanders while he looks for work. He had thoughts to apply at the Summer Palace."

Bianca's hopes, which had soared at the thought that the man had no wife yet, plummeted to earth at the realisation that he was another adventurer. "So he will appear at our table next, swathed in ill-fitting silk, as he tries to wheedle secrets out of my sisters?"

"He had thoughts to work as a guard, but I have kept him busy here. He's not like the others. The others barely had two words for me before they hustled themselves up to the palace. Vasco is a good man who has no wish for fame and wealth. Not like the others, who would thrust a blade through my body without a second thought if the reward asked for my heart and not the palace secret."

Bianca wet her lips. "So he does not want a bride or a palace?"

Kun's forehead furrowed, then smoothed. "He is a man who keeps his feet solidly on the ground, who might look at the stars above, but will never reach for them. A man who happily shares a barn with goats knows a palace and a princess are far beyond his reach."

"What if he had help?" The words left Bianca's lips before she'd really thought them through.

Kun eyed her suspiciously. "Are you offering to help a man you do not know, and betray your sisters in the same breath?"

Bianca gaped. She, a traitor? Never. "I meant…if you mentioned the king's offer, and told Vasco what you know of the mystery so that he might have a better chance than his predecessors, and maybe encouraged him to try…"

"Do you know what happens to the men who fail to solve the mystery?" Kun demanded.

"They have three days. If they fail, they leave," Bianca said.

"Have you ever seen them leave?"

Bianca shook her head. "No, but they must. They are no longer at the palace."

"Are they?" Kun's eyes were sharp. "There are many cellars beneath the Summer Palace, much like its grander cousin in the capital. It would be easy to turn one into a dungeon to imprison them."

"But why? What would Efe have to gain in

imprisoning such men? I don't know how you could imagine such nonsense." Even as she said the words, Bianca didn't believe them. For under her bed, she still had the first adventurer's sword. No man would leave without his sword, the means to defend himself. Yet…why would anyone imprison the man? He had committed no crime. But the sword…

Kun's look was knowing. "Ah, you suspect there is more than nonsense in it. I see it in your eyes. Why should I throw a good man to the wolves? It seems to me he can do a lot more good in his life than try to solve some mystery not even the king knows the answer to. Have you solved it yet?"

Bianca forced herself to admit that she had not. Vasco – if that was indeed the man's name – had distracted her from asking her sisters about it. But if she asked them… "I could help him," she offered eagerly before adding, "Not to betray my sisters. But to stop the flow of beggars and braggarts Efe sends to our table. It is not right. He dresses them like noblemen, but beneath the veneer, I fear that they have few principles. It is only a matter of time before one of them threatens us with violence, or invades our sleeping chamber at night, or…" Bianca shuddered. She didn't want to think of anything worse, but the images crept to her mind, unbidden. She had heard stories of the things men did to unprotected women. There was a reason she hadn't left the palace grounds alone.

"If you help him, the man may stand a chance," Kun admitted. "But you will rob me of my servant, before he has fashioned a complete new cottage and furnishings for me. A project he seems to enjoy. It will take all my powers of persuasion to make him believe he wants to leave my employ for the uncertainty of a job at the palace. It will cost you more than a basket of food this time, princess."

Bianca recognised the steely look in Kun's eyes. That very same look had made her climb on the cottage roof to see her own handiwork.

"Very well," she said. "What would you ask of me in payment for such a service?"

Kun shook her head. "You would not last a day in a village marketplace, let alone the wide world, girl. You should offer a very low price, not let me name mine. That isn't how bargaining is done."

Bianca's lips lifted in a smile she did not feel. "I cut my teeth on politics. The bargaining at court is very different to a common marketplace. Both parties ask for all that they desire, before negotiations commence to whittle down the lists to some sort of compromise where neither are happy, but each gets some of what they wish for. Name your price, and then we shall bargain in earnest."

Kun's eyes widened. Perhaps she had underestimated Bianca, the girl mused. She wagered the witch did not make that mistake often. "A new cloak that is so beautiful, so stunning that no man can look at its wearer and truly see them, but nothing is hidden to the wearer."

Bianca nodded slowly. "You wish me to make you a cloak which will render you invisible, yet able to see the invisible, like I do."

"You're quick, girl."

"Would you like a cloak made of silk, wool, or something else?" Bianca asked.

Kun looked thoughtful. "Silk seems a little too grand. And besides, I already have the cloak. It is your magic I want." Her gnarled finger pointed at the hooks behind the door. Beside her own faded, worn cloak in earthy brown hung another one, much longer and thicker than the first. Dark as a raven's wing, the blackness of it seemed to steal some of the room's light.

It almost seemed alive, for it certainly held its own magic. If Bianca bespelled it so that it made the wearer invisible, it would be a valuable thing indeed.

"We have a bargain," Bianca announced. "I will cast an invisibility spell on that cloak that also works on its owner, and you shall send your servant to the palace to solve my mystery."

Kun eyed her. "Most would hesitate before making a bargain with a witch, girl. Are you sure?"

Bianca almost laughed. "But we are both witches, and you are the one asking me for a spell, in exchange for a trivial favour. Shouldn't I be asking you if you are sure?"

Kun seemed to consider for a moment, before she nodded. "We have a bargain. Cast your spell, and the man will be at the Summer Palace on the morrow."

The spell was surprisingly simple, shimmering across the cloth like so many stars. Yet when Kun donned the cloak, it hid her completely.

"That will do," Kun said, appearing again as she shrugged off the cloak, which was so long it pooled in the floor around her.

Outside, the rhythmic blows of an axe biting into wood pierced the stillness.

"Good to hear him hard at work," Kun said, jerking her chin in the direction of the yard.

"Tomorrow. You promised," Bianca said, feeling her heart beating fast. It must be the surprise at hearing axe blows, she told herself. Not the prospect of sharing the Summer Palace with Vasco. Why, she barely knew the man.

"I will hold up my end of the bargain. Ancestors help him if you don't keep up yours, though. He will need all the help he can get," Kun replied.

"I'm sure he'll succeed where the others failed," Bianca said, trying to sound more confident than she felt. He had to. Summoning a satisfied smile, she strode out of the cottage, covered her fair skin from the sun, and rode home.

That night, she could scarcely sleep from excitement. But finally she did, only to dream of ravens wheeling in a sky of invisible stars.

Sixteen

This time when Vasco climbed down from the roof, he felt the weariness of the long day's work. But a good day's work. A good week's work, truth be told. He had repaired walls, replaced beams, and Kun's cottage now had a completely new roof. She also had a year's worth of firewood — the remains of the trees Vasco had cut down which had been suitable for nothing but burning. And yes, he'd chop that into suitable lengths for her, too.

He hadn't quite shaken that prickly feeling

of being watched, but he'd learned to ignore it. Kun spent most of her time in her cottage, not outside it watching him, and as he'd seen no one else, he concluded that his watchers must be birds. For what novelty could there be in a man rebuilding a house, except for the woman who lived there?

He paused to wash his face in the water butt, and only then did he hear voices. He listened hard, for more than once he had heard Kun talking to herself. No, this was definitely two voices and only one of them was Kun's. The visitor must have arrived while he'd been working on the roof, too busy to notice her arrival.

Not wishing to disturb Kun and her visitor, he peeped through the window. Kun sat at the table, pouring tea, but the visitor had her back to the window. In the dimly lit cottage, all he could see of the visitor was her white hair, carefully braided into one long queue that hung down her back, contrasting with her dark cloak.

Another old woman, he concluded. He debated whether to go and introduce himself, in the hope that Kun's friend might have more work to keep him busy for another week or two. For Kun could not complain about his diligence or even his appetite. Vasco was a hard worker and he knew it. Perhaps it would be better to demonstrate that to the guest, rather than going into the cottage and interrupting their conversation. He headed to the chopping block, where there were still some logs uncut. He had planned to leave them for the morrow, but he was not so tired that he could not cut them now. Levering the axe out of the chopping block where he'd left it that morning, he set to work.

Vasco soon fell into a rhythm, turning one log into suitable pieces for an old woman to carry, before chipping a pile of kindling. He piled his handiwork up in the woodshed before starting on the next.

When the door opened and Kun's visitor emerged, Vasco almost dropped his axe in surprise. In the bright sunlight, her hair appeared a pale gold, not white at all. She moved like a much younger woman then Kun, with her straight back and a pert toss of her head as she stepped out fully.

When Vasco saw her face, the axe fell from his nerveless fingers. This time, he didn't notice. He had eyes only for the fair maiden before him. He had never seen a girl with such fair skin, paler even than her hair. Pink lips and bright eyes, separated by a small, pointed nose, and all lit up with a satisfied smile. A smile that would haunt his dreams for the rest of his life, he was certain. He had only a moment more to stare at the vision before him, before she pulled her hood up, and her face vanished from sight in the depths of her cloak. She mounted a horse Vasco had not seen until now, waved a pale hand at Kun, before urging her mount into a trot.

The moment she disappeared through the trees, Vasco felt the most powerful sense of loss. It was almost like losing his village all over again.

"Put your eyes back in your sockets, boy," Kun snapped. "You look like a fool who has never seen a pretty girl before."

Vasco found his voice. "I have seen pretty girls before," he said slowly. "But never a creature as beautiful as her." He swallowed. "Who is she?"

Kun cackled. "That is Princess Bianca." She paused as if to let her statement sink in before she continued, "She is one of the king's daughters who lives at the Summer Palace. She is kind enough to come and visit an old lady, and bring me supplies from the palace kitchens." She eyed him speculatively. "But the princess has not come to visit me since you arrived, perhaps scared away by the hulking brute of a soldier. A pity, for you have not tasted palace food. As it is, I was running low on well-nigh everything until she arrived."

Vasco hung his head. "If I have outstayed my welcome, then I shall depart. Your house is repaired, as promised, and I hope I have earned my board and lodging. If you know of anywhere else I might be of service –"

Kun waved him into silence. "Don't be silly, boy. If you had eaten every crumb in my larder, it would be a good bargain for the new house and barn you have built for me. And I might be able to suggest further employment for you, especially if you are interested in seeing the princess again."

Vasco was afraid to meet her eyes. "I would dearly love to see such beauty again, but I fear she is too high for me. Just a glimpse will leave me distracted from my work all day." He cleared his throat. "I had thought to ask at the palace whether they have need of more guards, but now I am certain of it. A palace that keeps such treasures as that princess within its walls can never have enough guards."

Kun smiled faintly. "I don't know about guards, but I do know of one problem the king has with keeping so many princesses in the palace. He has a mystery he wants solved. And any man who can solve this for him will be richly rewarded."

"Will the king provide a lowly soldier with a bed and a meal while he solves this mystery?" Vasco asked.

Kun laughed. "I believe so."

"Then what can you tell me about this mystery?" Vasco asked.

Kun raised her eyebrows. "You ask about the mystery and not the reward? You are a strange man."

Vasco shrugged. "There is no reward unless I can solve the mystery. And if I have a place to eat and sleep, I have little else to worry about."

"Then come inside, for royal mysteries are best discussed over tea and cakes from the palace kitchens." Kun beckoned him inside, and Vasco followed.

Seventeen

Bianca paced along the lakeshore while she waited impatiently for her sisters to wake or for Vasco to arrive. She hadn't cared about any of the previous adventurers, but she wanted to speak to him. To see if he truly was different from the others, like Kun had said.

The sun had already started to sink by the time a maid finally came to tell her that her sisters were awake.

Bianca thanked the girl, then added, "Do you know if any visitors have arrived?"

The girl frowned and shook her head. "No, mistress."

Surely Kun wouldn't have broken her bargain, would she? They had a deal. A bargain between two witches wasn't to be broken lightly, Bianca knew. But the day wasn't over yet. Perhaps Kun had kept Vasco for one more day to finish working on her roof, and he needed daylight to work. It might be dark by the time her arrived at the palace, if there was a lot of work to do.

In the meantime, she would find out all she could from her sisters, Bianca decided. She headed inside, and found her sisters seated in the dining hall, breaking their fast, though it was well into the afternoon.

Bianca slid into an empty spot on the bench. "Good day," she began.

A chorus of mumbled responses came back to her.

Bianca hid a smile. They really had just awoken. "I've been wondering for a while now, and I must ask. Why the pile of shoes at the door every morning? I have lost count of the number of times I have tripped over them."

A few of the girls shared smiles, and Brenna laughed. She set her dog down on the floor with a bowl of food she'd selected from the table for the animal. "You mean the shoes we have all danced to pieces?"

Bianca nodded. "They do look quite worn. I wonder why you would keep shoes in such a state."

Hazel laughed. "We don't keep them. We pile them up so that the servants can throw them on the refuse heap, and Cousin Efe will have new shoes made to replace them. He's been sending up new shoes for you, though you haven't danced at all since you arrived."

"I don't dance," Bianca said, ducking her head. She reached for a piece of bread.

"But you must," Aruna exclaimed. "Tonight, you will come with us. I promise you, you will feel like the most graceful dancer in the world once you have the right partner."

A vision of Vasco popped into Bianca's

head, and she blushed. "The right partner?" she echoed, trying to rid her mind of the thought of Vasco holding her in his arms.

"Oh, yes," Nera gushed. "Just wait until you see – "

A masculine cough interrupted her. All the girls fell silent.

Efe stepped into the room with a simpering smile on his face. "My dear princesses, may I present Lord Vasco?"

Lord Vasco? Bianca choked.

Eighteen

Princesses who danced their shoes to pieces? And a king who was so insistent upon knowing why that he would hire a man just to solve the mystery of the worn shoes?

Even as Vasco trudged up the road to the palace, away from the comfort of Kun's cottage, he shook his head in disbelief. He had seen the town of shoemakers, so he knew there was some truth in these princesses who wore out shoes faster than a soldier wore out boots, but there had to be more to this mystery than first appeared.

Why else would Kun have given him so much advice? She'd told him to refuse any food or wine that the princesses themselves did not consume. If he wanted to know what the girls did at night, he must enter their bedchamber before the door was locked – as though he dared enter a princess's bedchamber! Yet she'd told him to hide there, and wear the new cloak she'd given him, as though the black wool would conceal him completely in what would surely be a well-lit chamber. And to top it all off, she'd said he only had three days in which to solve the mystery, so if he ran into difficulties, he was to approach Princess Bianca, the pale beauty he'd espied at Kun's cottage, and ask her for help. As if such a highborn princess would stoop to assist someone as worthless as him.

But Kun had insisted, and he had repeated all of her advice, until she was satisfied that he remembered it all. Still, he didn't trust what he'd heard, so instead of approaching the front entrance as Kun had told him to, Vasco skirted the building until he found the servants' entrance, and knocked there, instead.

The maid who answered the door wore a dress far finer than anything the women in Vasco's village had ever owned. For a moment, his voice died in his throat as he wondered if he'd somehow arrived at a private entrance to the princesses' quarters instead.

Vasco's hands tightened around the hat he held level with his belt. "I came seeking work, and an old woman down the road told me the master of this house might have need of a man."

The girl's eyes held sympathy as she shook her head. "There is no position here that I know of. We are but a small household. I don't know why Mistress Kun would send you here. She of all people knows…" She swallowed. "Unless she sent you here to solve the mystery?"

Vasco gave a nod. "She did mention a mystery."

"Are you sure?" the girl asked. "You will only have three days, and no one else has managed to solve it in that time. You aren't like the others…"

The others being princes and lords, noblemen who were accustomed to being in the presence of princesses, Vasco assumed. Not common soldiers like him. Yet Kun had been confident he could do this thing.

"I must try," he said finally. "I have nothing else. No home, no family, and nothing to occupy me once the army had finished with me. Unless you can point me to somewhere else where I might find work, this is the only employment for miles around."

Now she looked almost pitying. "I understand. What is your name, soldier?"

"Vasco," he answered.

"I'm Gerel," she said. "I will tell the Lord Steward you are here. If there is no other suitor, he will introduce you to the princesses and you will be in their company for three days until you solve the mystery or are banished from this place. But…if you wish for company, or more plain fare than is served in the dining hall, or if the Lord Steward will not see you, I pray you will come to the kitchen. There will be a place for you at our table, for anyone who can tell us about what goes on outside the estate is welcome. We are very isolated here."

As isolated as his own village before it was wiped out, Vasco thought, though he couldn't bring himself to say the words aloud. Not to this pretty maid who had probably never seen any sort of violence in her life, much like the princesses she served. Gerel deserved to marry one of the manservants of the house and live in the shelter of such a great house, birthing babies who would grow to replace her in service once they were old enough. A life, a home and a living, with parents who would live until old age with such security. What more could anyone ask for?

It was more than Vasco could ever expect now, he told himself. A quick glance told him

Gerel was still waiting for an answer. "Tell the Lord Steward I seek work. If he turns me away, then I will gladly enjoy your hospitality for a night, and tell you all I know of battles in the borderlands." He would have to censor his tale, and make the men sound more heroic than they truly were, he knew, but it wouldn't be the first time. No one wanted to hear stories of blood and death and tragedy, tainted by the darkness in his own head. If it would fill his belly for a night and perhaps the next day, he would spin tales of heroes so that those who had died in blood and pain might be remembered as more than they were in life. Perhaps it would even ease the spirits of those he had fought with, only to lose them to a stray arrow or well-placed spear.

Gerel pushed the door open wider, and beckoned him in. "Come sit in the kitchen while you wait. Cirina, the cook, will make you some tea, and maybe spare you a cake before they are sent up to the dining hall for the princesses."

To his surprise, Cirina soon had him ensconced on a seat by the fire, tea in one hand and cake in the other. Vasco hoped that Gerel was wrong and there would be a place for him in this household. He hadn't seen a single guard yet, and he didn't understand it. Surely princesses needed protection.

"The Lord Steward will see you now," Gerel said.

Vasco hurried to swallow his mouthful of cake. "Are you sure?"

She nodded, her eyes on the flagstones at her feet, as she led him out of the kitchen and into the house proper.

Tapestries lined the passageways, the colours increasingly vibrant, until they reached a richly carved door. Gerel knocked, then pushed the door open. "The man you sent for, m'lord," she said, gesturing for Vasco to enter.

The moment Vasco's worn boots touched the carpet inside the room, Gerel closed the door quietly behind him.

The Lord Steward sat in a throne-like chair

raised up on a dais facing the door. Almost like a king, though the man's bald head bore no crown. His clothes were a mix of scarlet, purple and yellow silk, an eye-watering combination in any light, let alone a chamber filled with lit torches.

"What makes you think you can solve the mystery not even the king can solve?" the man asked.

Vasco bowed low, racking his brain for an answer that would satisfy the man. Something in Gerel's words struck him. "I am different to the others," he said.

The Lord Steward snorted. "Very well. You have three days to bring me a solution, or you die. I will present you to the princesses and – "

"Three days or die?" Vasco blurted out. Kun had neglected to mention this part.

And yet…

Since the day his village burned, he had gambled his life in every battle. At the end of each fighting day, either he or his enemies would lie on the battlefield to be food for crows. As a guard, he would need to be willing to lay down his life to defend his master and the master's family. How was this any different?

The Lord Steward made an impatient noise in his throat. "If I do not believe you are doing your best to uncover the mystery, it could be less than three days. My primary care is for the princesses, and if I hear a whisper of any untoward behaviour, or that you are wasting my time, your time will be up." He rose to his feet, smirking as though he liked the way he towered over Vasco from his high platform. "So, are you wasting my time now, or do you wish to meet the princesses? At one word from me, I can have you executed before you can draw breath to protest."

Vasco had no choice. At least his body would not become food for crows, and his death would be quick. Small comfort if he failed, but he did not mean to. "I would be honoured if you would present me to the ladies of the house," he said.

The man clapped his hands. "Excellent. But first, you must dress properly. The princesses will not allow you anywhere near them looking like some peasant." When Gerel cracked open the door, the Lord Steward said, "Take him to the guest dressing room and see that he is dressed."

Hoping he wouldn't have to wear the same garish colours as the Lord Steward, Vasco followed Gerel out.

Nineteen

The other girls didn't even glance up from their dinner, but Bianca couldn't tear her eyes away from the man who stepped into the room. Her fingers itched to stroke his black silk tunic. It certainly wasn't made for him

. The sleeves that would have been loose on any other man bulged with the muscles she'd seen in Kun's yard, making them look even bigger. He'd had to unlace it a little down the front to allow space for his broad chest without ripping the fabric, but the tantalising glimpse of flesh at his throat only made her mouth dry at the thought of touching, kissing, stroking…

Bianca mentally shook herself. If Cousin Efe had brought him here, dressed up like the lord she knew he wasn't, then he had a mystery to solve.

She patted the bench beside her, shifting over until her foot nudged the dog's furry body. "Come sit by me, Lord Vasco," she said, surprising herself with the low purr that came out of her throat.

Vasco looked even more startled. "I…I can't," he mumbled, backing away.

Cousin Efe screwed his face up in annoyance. "Why not? The princess gave you an order."

Vasco bowed deeply. "I am no lord, princess. I am just a common soldier, not worthy to share your table. Even the honour of sitting at your feet is more than I deserve."

Bianca couldn't help it. She laughed. "The place at my feet is taken by a dog. I'm afraid you must make do with the bench. We are not in the capital now, and the accommodations here at the Summer Palace are more informal." Her sisters were staring at her, and she felt blood rush to her cheeks. "Please sit here." She lowered her gaze until the other girls turned their attention back to their food. Evidently they hadn't noticed anything different about Vasco. They must be blind, she decided.

Vasco slid easily into the spot beside Bianca, who found her breath caught in her throat now he sat so close. Why, his thigh brushed her skirt, and if she moved her own leg just the slightest bit, she would be able to feel him through the fabric.

"I'll fetch you some wine," Hazel said, rising.

Bianca saw the reproach in her sister's gaze – after all, she was the newest to arrive, which meant she was the one who was supposed to head down to the cellar for their guest's wine – but Hazel was gone before Bianca could apologise.

Probably for the best, Bianca told herself. After all, what would Hazel say if her only excuse was that she was too busy admiring the man Cousin Efe had thrust among them? Hazel would think her mad. Perhaps she'd be right, too.

She glanced at Vasco. He sat, silent and motionless, not touching a crumb of the food that covered the table, as if he was somehow afraid of it.

"Eat something," Bianca said, offering him the nearest platter.

He bowed his head. "You first, princess."

Of course. She outranked him, something she'd forgotten in sharing a table with her sisters and the mannerless men who had come and gone.

She seized the nearest thing and took a bite, not really tasting it. Only then did Vasco take food for himself.

He ate in silence, his head down as though he wished he were invisible.

Bianca understood the feeling, though not

the reason for it. He seemed terribly uncomfortable.

"Where are you from, sir?" she asked.

He swallowed. "Nowhere."

She managed a smile. "No one is from nowhere. Why, we are all born somewhere, even if we no longer live there. Where were you born?"

"I was born in a small village that no longer exists. Razed to the ground by an advancing army. Or a retreating one. I am not sure. Heedless of those who lived there. So the village where I was born is no more, and nowhere."

His voice sounded so dead, like the village itself.

"What happened to those who lived there?" she asked.

"They died."

So final. And yet...

Hazel appeared with a jug of wine in hand, which she poured into Vasco's cup. He seized it and drank down the contents before holding the cup out for more.

"But you survived," Bianca began eagerly. "I imagine that must be a thrilling tale."

The eyes he turned to her were dark and haunted. Bianca's smile died on her lips and Hazel gave a cry of alarm. Somehow the whole jug of wine had slipped from her hand and smashed on the floor. The shards lay in a spreading lake beneath the table.

"I am sorry," Vasco said, rising. He bowed abruptly, then hurried out.

Bianca tried to follow him, but Brenna's dog tangled itself in her skirts in its hurry to reach the spilled wine, and by the time she managed to clamber to her feet, Vasco had vanished.

"Good riddance," Aruna said. "You can do much better, sister. And you will tonight."

Hazel seized her hand. "You must dance with us. I won't let you retire early. Not with that man about. He did not drink enough of the strong wine to sleep the night through. We'll take him another jug on our way to bed."

Twenty

The sweet princess with the expressive eyes just wouldn't give up. Again and again, she asked him about his home until he wanted to scream the truth for all of them to hear. The village bathed in blood, the smell of burned bodies and Dokia…Dokia…

Vasco downed his wine and pushed away from the table. He staggered out of the room, clamping his mouth shut to keep the horrors in. Like Gerel, she did not need his nightmares. They were his alone.

Speaking of nightmares, it was time to give in to his once more. He'd worked hard all day before walking up to the palace, and he could scarcely keep his eyes open. But he didn't know where his bed might be – if he even had one.

Vasco headed for the kitchen. Surely someone there would know where he was billeted.

He met Gerel on her way back to the kitchen, carrying a tray of half-eaten food.

"Serving the Lord Steward?" he asked, nodding at the scraps.

She nodded. "He takes his meals in his rooms."

"Too good for the company of princesses?" Vasco said.

Gerel reddened. "Actually, I believe they refuse to eat with him. The Lord Steward is not well liked." She pressed her lips together, as if she wished she could unsay her words.

"What about the princesses? Are they well liked?"

Gerel managed a nervous smile. "They are princesses. The king's beautiful daughters. You can't help but admire them, even if we see them so little. They spend most of their time abed, but when they are awake, they are not unkind."

Not unkind. What a thing to say about someone, let alone her mistresses. Better than not well liked, though. "What of the pale one who is fairer than the others?" he demanded.

"The Princess Bianca? She is our most recent arrival, only a few weeks ago." Gerel's expression brightened. "But I have seen more of her than her sisters combined. They sleep, while she rises early. Sometimes, she even enters the kitchen to ask for things. The way she speaks to you, looking in your eyes like she really sees you, and not just some invisible servant to be ordered about…such a small thing, but it truly sets her apart from the others. She likes to ride or walk down by the lake, and she takes a basket of provisions with her so she can stay out of the house for longer."

Remembering the time he'd seen her at Kun's cottage, Vasco asked, "Where does she ride to?"

Gerel shrugged. "Wherever she pleases, I am sure. She is a princess, and all the land around belongs to her father, the king. Who would dare stop her?"

Who indeed. "Do you know anything about this mystery with the shoes?" he said.

Gerel shook her head. "No more than you. That is why you sleep in the maid's room off their bedchamber, and not one of us."

He had a place to sleep. Vasco grasped at the idea. "Can you show me where?" he asked urgently.

"Of course. I have already placed your things there. You left them in the kitchen." Gerel glanced down. "Let me just take this tray to the kitchen, and I will show you up."

Gerel returned a moment later, beckoning Vasco to follow her.

Tapestries lined the walls here, too, but they

were not as grand as the ones outside the Lord Steward's rooms. They looked too old and faded to be the princesses' own work.

The décor didn't improve when they entered the princesses' receiving chamber. If anything, the walls were even more bare here, for the room held only a few benches and little else. The girls did not spend much time here.

Gerel gestured toward an open door at the other end of the chamber. This new room was full of beds – a dozen to be precise. All the princesses slept in the same room, which had a row of small windows, but only the one door in or out. Perhaps they danced around their audience chamber and that's why there was no furniture to speak of. Mystery solved.

"Your bed is there." Gerel pointed at an alcove just outside the door to the princesses' bedchamber. It contained a straw pallet and some hooks that now held his meagre belongings. "You have the most beautiful cloak."

Vasco glanced at Kun's gift. In truth, the

thick, black wool was better quality than anything he'd ever owned, but much like tonight's fancy clothes, he hadn't been able to refuse it. He didn't have to sleep in silk, though. But Gerel should go before he undressed.

"I wish to retire now," he said.

It took Gerel a moment before she understood. Then she coloured. "Of course. In the morning, when you wish to break your fast, come down to the kitchen. We have orders to serve you in the dining chamber with the princesses, but they rise so late that you might wish for something earlier." She bobbed on the spot, as if she'd almost curtsied to him before remembering she didn't need to, and hurried off.

Vasco peeled off the black silk fripperies the Lord Steward had made him wear, and donned one of his own worn tunics. Much more comfortable, he stretched out on his bed and almost instantly fell asleep.

Twenty-One

While Bianca's sisters headed for their bedchamber, she dutifully made her way down to the cellar for another jug of wine. On her way back up, she returned to the dining hall to grab Vasco's cup from the table. She peered under the table, wondering what to do about the puddle of wine. She decided to leave it for one of the servants to deal with. After all, someone would come to clear the table of the remains of their meal.

Most of the wine was gone, sunk between

the flagstones or, more likely, lapped up by the little dog that now slept under the table in the puddle that remained. Bianca smiled. Brenna's dog would probably sleep there all night.

Wine jug in one hand, cup in the other, she made her way to her bedchamber. Efe waited outside, looking irritable. "Hurry up. I must lock the door," he said, waving her in.

Lock the door? Bianca had never seen him do such a thing before. She stepped into the audience chamber, then turned to ask Efe what he meant by it. He slammed the door shut in her face and she heard the sounds of a bolt being drawn across it, effectively locking them all in. Including Vasco, she realised, who now slept soundly on the pallet beside their bedchamber door.

No wine necessary.

Nevertheless, she set the cup and jug down beside his bed. Staring at the snoring soldier, she suddenly felt very tired herself. Probably because she'd slept so little the previous night. Maybe she should climb into bed and sleep the night away. Her sisters' shoe mystery could wait for another night.

"Hurry up and dress, or we shall be late!" Nera hissed, tugging on Bianca's arm.

She allowed herself to be pulled into the bedchamber. Brenna closed the door behind her. All the other girls were in various stages of dressing not for bed but for what appeared to be a royal ball. Well, if they were going to dance, she thought wryly, why not? They might be exiled from the palace and the capital, but they could still dress like they were attending court.

Now, more than ever, she felt too tired to join them.

"Hurry!" Nera repeated as Hazel helped her lace up her gown.

Bianca shook her head. "I am too tired. Tomorrow night, maybe. I can scarcely keep my eyes open."

Nera made an exasperated noise. "Sleep, then. We'll choose the handsomest and you'll have to make do with what is left. Unless you prefer the fool outside?" She tittered, and the other girls joined in.

And what if she did? Bianca wanted to say, but she held her tongue. They were locked in their own bedchamber, with no men, handsome or otherwise. She stripped down to her shift and climbed beneath the covers of her bed. Almost as soon as her head touched the pillow, she drifted off into dreams.

What seemed like only a moment later, she was roused by the sound of hammering on her bedchamber door.

Vasco woke with a start. It took him a moment to realise that the soft weight on top of him was merely the bed coverings, and not Dokia's dead body. He wasn't sure which nightmares were worse – the ones in the heat of battle, or the ones from the night his village burned. He hoped he hadn't woken the princesses by crying out.

He rose and padded to the door to their bedchamber, pressing his ear to the closed door. Silence greeted him – they were surely asleep. Sighing in relief, he crossed to the narrow window and took a deep breath of the cool night air, hoping it would clear his head. But the view from the window made his breath catch in his throat.

A flotilla of small boats, like a flock of swans, drifted across the lake toward the misty island in the middle. Moonlight glistened on silk and he realised what he was seeing – in each boat sat a princess, wearing a shimmering silk gown and, he didn't doubt, a pair of matching slippers that would be danced to pieces by morning. He shouted, but no one seemed to hear him.

He had to follow them. Vasco dashed for the door to the passage, only to find it barred from the outside. He was locked in.

But if he was locked in…surely they had been, too. There must be another way out – through their bedchamber, perhaps.

He tried that door, but it was locked, too. He hammered on it, then threw his weight against the timber, over and over again. He had to follow them. His very life depended on it.

He heard the scrape of a bolt and the door cracked open. "What is it?" a sleepy female voice asked.

Had he imagined the boats? If the princesses were still in their bedchamber, he couldn't have seen them on the lake. Vasco pushed the door wide and strode into the room. A candle burned beside one of the empty beds, but there was not a girl to be seen.

He swore.

"What does that mean?" a female voice asked.

Vasco blinked. Beside the door stood Bianca, wearing nothing but a thin shift, as if she'd been roused from her bed. Shame welled up as he realised he'd been the one to wake her in his panic.

"Forgive me, princess," he said awkwardly. "I had a bad dream, and then I thought I saw something on the lake."

"On the lake?" Princess Bianca crossed to

the window beside his bed and peered out. "I don't see anything."

Vasco looked over her shoulder. The boats had reached the mist, which hid them from view. Yet he knew what he'd seen.

"Maybe I dreamed that, too," he admitted.

"When I had troubling dreams as a child, my mother would have one of the maids bring me milk to drink. Ice-cold from the cellars." Bianca smiled at the memory. "I can send for some, if you like?"

Vasco shook his head. "The door is bolted. We are locked in. Though how your sisters managed to get out...I don't know." He wanted to ask her what she knew, but he already felt embarrassed enough. Interrogating a princess was hardly the way to behave after he had woken her so rudely.

"Wine, then?" she asked, offering the jug.

Kun had warned him not to drink the wine. "NO!" he said, then added, "It might dull my wits. I will need all the wits I have to solve this mystery. Is there anything you can tell me about it, princess?"

Sadly, Bianca shook her head. "I don't know where they go. Until tonight, I didn't believe they went anywhere at all, yet they have gone. And tomorrow there will be a pile of shoes on the threshold of our room for me to trip over."

Vasco managed a smile. "A graceful princess like yourself would never do something so clumsy."

Bianca laughed so hard she had to sit down. "I am many things, but graceful isn't one of them. As you will soon find out, if you spend much time with me."

"I have only three days," he replied. Three days left to live, unless he found a way to follow the princesses across the lake. But he didn't tell Bianca that, for he would sound like a whining coward, when he was neither. If he would die for his failure, so be it.

She sighed. "So you do." She glanced up. "Perhaps tomorrow night you should hide in our bedchamber, so you can see where they go. Wearing your new cloak, you will be invisible in the shadows." She reached out to touch the wool cloak Kun had given him. In fact, her words echoed Kun's almost exactly.

Yet she looked the polar opposite of the old witch. Where Kun wore so many layers of clothing she appeared shapeless, Bianca wore a thin shift that clung to her curves even as it concealed them, but barely. She truly was the most beautiful woman he had ever seen, and in the moonlight shining through the window, she seemed infused with a kind of magic that turned her from a woman into a goddess. The kind armies would die for.

Yet she was still a woman, as much as he was a man. Increasingly aware of how little clothing they wore and how much his body desired her, he forced himself to shut down all such thoughts. She was a princess, which made her untouchable by one such as him. That she spoke to him at all was an honour he did not deserve.

"Perhaps I will. It's too late for that tonight, though. It appears our birds have flown," he said. He bowed. "I am sorry I woke you, princess. It will not happen again."

She rose, unwittingly giving him a glimpse down the front of her shift before she straightened. Vasco had to close his eyes, but it was too late. Those creamy breasts would haunt his dreams until the day he died.

In three days.

"Pleasant dreams, Vasco," she said.

He didn't reply.

Twenty-Three

Day dawned and Bianca rose with the sun, as usual. Her sisters had returned and they were sound asleep, having left the usual pile of shoes before the door, which she stepped over carefully. She didn't want to trip and wake Vasco.

When she reached the receiving room, she found his bed empty and the outer door ajar. She needn't have bothered being quiet. For a moment, she worried that he might have left, but his belongings still hung from the hooks over his bed. Perhaps he was simply breaking his fast, she decided. Something she should do, too.

Maybe they could speak more over the morning meal. After all, it wasn't like her sisters would be joining them. She would have him all to herself.

She fairly skipped down to the kitchen to order breakfast, before asking about Vasco's whereabouts.

"Out by the archery butts," she was told.

Bianca knew the spot, though she'd never seen anyone using them. The practice targets stood on the lakeshore, faded from long disuse.

As she approached, she heard the whistle and thunk of arrows hitting a target in quick succession. It wasn't until she stepped out onto the sand that she realised how good a marksman he was. The targets were at least a hundred yards away, maybe more, yet he never missed. In fact, one target was peppered with so many arrows it had split in two, and the one beside it looked dangerously close to sharing its fate.

"You are an exceptional shot, Vasco. Wherever did you learn to shoot?" she called.

The next arrow sheared off into the water as Vasco started in surprise. He recovered quickly. "Good morning, princess. My father taught me to shoot a bow when I was a small boy, and it became a part of daily training when I joined the army. An infantryman who cannot shoot becomes a target for those who can." He winced as if at a painful memory.

"From seeing how well you shoot, I imagine you have killed many men with your well-placed arrows," Bianca said.

Vasco sighed. "Then you imagine wrong." He set down his bow and trudged out of earshot to retrieve his arrows. He took his time, as though he hoped she might grow bored and leave, but she had learned early in her life that boredom was best chased away by a busy mind when it belonged to a girl in a harem, lest she go completely mad at the tedium of her own life. Some of her father's wives and concubines had succumbed to madness, and taken their own lives, she knew, though her mother had considered her too young to hear of such things.

Watching him walk away from her, Bianca realised he limped, favouring his left leg. For all her days of watching him, she'd never seen him limping before.

When he returned with his arms full of arrows, she asked, "Did you fall from the roof and injure yourself while you were fixing Kun's house?"

Vasco frowned. "No, I did not."

"Then why are you limping?" she persisted.

He slid his arrows back into their quiver. "Because in the heat of battle, someone shot me with an arrow that I will carry with me always." He patted his knee, shouldered both quivers and his bow, then headed for the house.

"That is hardly fair," Bianca said, hurrying to catch up. For a lame man, he moved quite fast.

He laughed without humour. "Princess, war is never fair. Good men die and bad men live on, unhurt. And then there are those like me who perhaps should have died from their wounds, who yet survive, as if fate has yet to make up its mind about me. When your business is war, you live from day to day, meal to meal, one battle to the next until it is your last. I am not a shoemaker, piecing together pretty things for your feet. My job was to destroy. Men and lives and property – whatever got in my commander's way. Perhaps I am no longer a good man at all, but a bad one, after all the things I have done."

No. She refused to believe it. "You built Kun a new barn, and rebuilt her house. That is not destruction."

"There are dozens of dead trees now filling her woodshed that would call you a liar, if they but had mouths to speak," Vasco said. "My axe no longer cuts down men, but it still thirsts for death."

Bianca stopped dead. Had she truly been so

stupid not to see it?

"You mean you've hurt women? And you will again?" she asked, hating how weak her voice sounded.

"NO! I have never intentionally hurt a woman, and I never intend to. I have made mistakes, but…" He shook his head. "Never mind. My troubles are so far beneath you as to be completely insignificant. Please forget I said it." He redoubled his pace back to the house.

"What was her name?" Bianca demanded. "The woman who was hurt because of your mistake?"

Vasco stopped so suddenly she almost ran into him. He whirled on the spot, eyeing her as if sizing her up. "Eudokia. If she had lived, she would be my wife."

Bianca's heart ached for him. "I am sorry for your loss," she said carefully. "I hope she sees the honour you do your family now that she walks among the ancestors."

Vasco's mouth twisted into a wry smile. "Given her memory disturbs my sleep and drives me to practice shooting even when I no longer have anyone to shoot at, perhaps the honour belongs to her. She was a good girl, and a kind one, who did not deserve to die the way she did."

"How did she die?" Bianca ventured.

"Horribly. Painfully. Perhaps even cursing my name. I can only guess, for I did not see her die." Vasco's eyes seemed to focus on her properly. "My apologies, princess. You do not need to hear of such things. Have you broken your fast yet? Gerel said she would summon me when the food was ready."

Horribly. Painfully. And in the next breath, he spoke of one of the palace servants, as if the death of the woman he loved was something he could easily dismiss. Palace servants he could name, though he had only arrived last night.

Bianca didn't know what to make of the man. He was certainly different to the others, but…had she made a terrible mistake and invited a killer into her home?

Twenty-Four

The princess seemed a lot more human in daylight. More like an innocent young woman who had lived a sheltered but privileged life in the palace than last night's moonlit vision.

Yet she'd managed to make him speak Dokia's name aloud for the first time since the day she died. There was just something about her…

Something that made him follow her into the house and to the dining hall, to share a meal with her instead of heading for the kitchen and the servants' table, where men of his rank belonged. She smiled at him as she sat across from him, for all the world like they were equals, and his heart warmed at her welcome.

She is a princess and I am nothing, he reminded himself, tucking his boots under the table, but they bumped into something. He peered into the shadows. "Does your dog normally sleep under the table?" he asked.

"He's not my dog. He belongs to my sister, Brenna. I don't know where he usually sleeps, but last night I think he drank too much wine, and drifted off into sleep where he lay." She broke off a piece of meat and tossed it before the animal's nose. "Wake up, boy. Food for you."

The dog didn't move.

She nudged the animal with one slippered foot, but it didn't respond. Puzzled, she reached a hand under the table to stroke the dog. The moment her fingers touched its fur, she snatched her hand back as if scalded. "He's cold," she said, her eyes widening with horror.

Vasco dragged the bench back and crawled beneath the table. He scooped up the dog's limp body and set it on the bench. After a quick examination, he confirmed his first verdict. "The dog is dead. He must have died in his sleep, he appears so peaceful."

A tear slid down Bianca's cheek as she shook her head. "Oh, I told Brenna wine was bad for dogs. He drank too much and it poisoned him, I know it!"

Poison. The thought chilled him to the bone. Poison was a woman's weapon, like an axe was his. "I've seen men die from drinking too much liquor. This looks like some other poison."

"But who would poison a defenceless dog?" the princess whispered. "It makes no sense."

"Perhaps the dog wasn't the intended victim," Vasco said gravely. "What did he eat last night?"

"I don't know," she said tearfully. "I only know he drank the wine before he fell asleep."

The wine. Wine one of the girls had poured into his cup, before he bumped her and spilled it on the floor. No wonder Kun had told him not to drink the wine, if it was poisoned.

"Who drank the wine last night?" he demanded.

Bianca stared at him. "None of us. I mean, we do not…the wine is Cousin Efe's, from the cellars. Only at very special celebrations do we have wine, but it's not the same. Ours is lighter and sweeter and…"

Vasco huffed out a breath at his own stupidity. He'd drunk poisoned wine, despite Kun's warning. He was lucky to be alive. "So just me and the dog, hm?"

Bianca's mouth dropped open. "You don't think…" She looked genuinely horrified.

Either she was very good at looking innocent, or she hadn't known about the poison. She hadn't fetched or poured the wine, though – that had been one of her sisters. One of the same sisters who had disappeared across the lake last night.

Bianca's thoughts seemed to be travelling along the same path as his own. "No, Hazel would not poison your wine. She taps it from the same barrel in the cellar. I have done it myself. It is Cousin Efe's strongest vintage, and it helps one sleep, Hazel says. If there is poison in the wine, then it is in the barrel."

Vasco said nothing.

"I'll take you down there and show you the barrel myself!" Bianca insisted. She marched to the door, then turned. "Are you coming?"

For a moment, he had forgotten that this pretty princess was the daughter of a king. A king whose desire for conquest was the reason half the world was at war. Bemused, he rose to his feet. "Of course, princess."

As he followed her into the cellars, it dawned on him that if she were to order his death, he would perish. The Lord Steward might hold more power than Vasco himself would ever possess, but Princess Bianca was one of the twelve mistresses of this palace.

He could always ask one of her sisters about

the wine but…

But Kun had told him to ask Bianca for help if he ran into trouble. None of the others.

Vasco shook his head in an attempt to clear it. Solving mysteries and playing politics were tasks for a noble courtier, not a farm boy turned soldier. If he survived the next three days, he'd beg the king for a job as a simple guardsman. One who manned the gate or the wall and did as he was told.

"That barrel!" Bianca pointed.

Vasco hid a smile. The princess couldn't tell one cask from another. The hogshead she indicated stood out among the massive tuns filling the rest of the wine cellar, for it was the only cask of its size in the place. He found a bowl and filled it with wine.

Cautiously, he sniffed it, but it smelled of…wine. He wasn't sure what poison smelled or tasted like. All he knew was that it could kill.

"Are there rats in this cellar?" he asked.

Bianca's eyes grew wide. "Rats?" She edged toward the steps.

Ah, yes. He'd forgotten how much rats had frightened the women of his village. He'd only ever brought one home as a pet and his mother had screamed herself hoarse.

"All cellars have rats," he said with what he hoped was an air of authority. He hoped he was right, too. "We'll leave this bowl out for them, and come back this evening. If the wine is poisoned, then we will know."

Bianca bit her lip and nodded.

Vasco let out a breath he hadn't known he was holding. By the ancestors, he was truly stumbling in the dark now.

He followed Bianca up into the palace proper, where they were met by Gerel. "Is there anything you wanted, mistress?" she asked Bianca.

Bianca glanced at Vasco, then said, "We were looking for the Lord Steward's wine."

Gerel smiled. "Most of the wine in this cellar is his. He drinks only wine with the Gu mark." She touched the brush marks on the lid of the nearest tun. "Like this."

Vasco traced the lines that made up the complicated symbol until he thought he could recognise it. He spotted it on several other casks, while others bore other marks he didn't know, but when he reached the hogshead, he found no mark at all. Only a bird, branded into the lid. "So the Lord Steward doesn't drink from this cask?" Vasco asked.

Gerel peered at it. "No, I have never served that to anyone."

Vasco wanted to ask more, but Bianca's cold voice silenced him.

"Thank you. You may go," Bianca said, waving the serving girl away.

Gerel bobbed on the spot and hurried off.

When the maid was out of sight, Bianca's regal stance slumped. "This is the wine my sisters told me to fetch for the men who seek to solve the shoe mystery. They believed they were siphoning it from Cousin Efe's private supplies. But if it is poisoned, and all those men have been drinking it…what happened to them?"

Three days. Three days was all they had before… "They died, princess."

She clapped her hands to her mouth. "No! Surely not. They leave. They leave the palace, never to return…" Her eyes begged him to take the words back.

"They die, because they failed. As will I." He wanted to reassure her with all his being, but he could not lie to her. "The Lord Steward said I have three days to solve your mystery, or I die. Whether they died by poison or something else, it won't change the result. Men are dying to protect your sisters' secret. Is it worth their lives, princess?"

"No," she whispered, tears running down her cheeks.

"So tell me where they go," he said.

She shook her head. "I can't. Ancestors help me, Vasco, but I cannot tell you what I do not know!" She broke into a run, dashing up the steps and away.

Vasco was tempted to follow her, but he resisted. If she wanted him, she could send a servant to summon him, and he would obey.

Or he could wait until tonight, don his new cloak, and hide in the princesses' bedchamber. When they opened their secret entrance, he would follow them across the lake and uncover their secret. His life depended on it.

Twenty-Five

Bianca walked the lake trails without seeing them, her mind roiling with more and more terrible possibilities. Her sisters were poisoning people. The adventurers they'd sneered at might have been fools, but that didn't mean they deserved to die for it.

Brenna would be heartbroken when she learned of her dog's death.

Vasco would die if Bianca didn't help him. And his death would be her fault, because she had insisted on inviting him to the palace.

When she thought it was late enough to wake her sisters, she headed into the house. Afternoon sun filtered through the windows in their bedchamber, and the girls showed signs of stirring.

"Brenna's dog is dead," Bianca announced.

"My…what?" Brenna mumbled.

"Your dog is dead. We think the wine is poisoned," Bianca said.

Nera peered at her blearily. "Who's we?"

Bianca cursed her ill-chosen words. "I do. And…Vasco. The man who arrived last night."

Nera sat up suddenly. "You stayed here to flirt with one of Cousin Efe's adventurers? Ugh. Tonight, if we have to drag you all the way there, you are coming dancing with us."

Dancing. The one thing Bianca hated most. But if it would save Vasco's life…she must do it.

"All right," she said.

"How could the wine be poisoned?" Hazel asked. "I took it from the barrel myself. No one touched it but me. You don't think that I tried to kill Brenna's dog, do you?"

"Of course not," Bianca said. "If anything, the whole barrel is poisoned."

"Then why hasn't Cousin Efe expired yet?" Aruna grumbled.

"He doesn't drink from that barrel. I checked with the servants. The wine we've been giving those poor fools was poisoned," Bianca said.

"But it hasn't killed any of them," Hazel objected. "They drink it down like it was water, and you can hear them snoring all night. Only Brenna's dear little dog has died. Perhaps it is only deadly to dogs."

Bianca doubted it, but, "Perhaps," she admitted. Best not to argue with her sisters now. Not when she would soon have to betray them to save a man's life.

Twenty-Six

When he heard the babble of female voices approaching, Vasco's courage failed. Instead of huddling in the corner of their bedchamber under his cloak, he dived under the nearest bed. A bed with a sword beneath it, of all things.

Trying to keep himself concealed and quiet while the princesses bustled about was bad enough, until the purple gown he'd seen Bianca wearing only hours before puddled on the floor inches from his face. He couldn't help himself. A glance upwards revealed pale, shapely legs and the underside of the sweetest pair of breasts he'd ever seen. Ancestors help him, but even Dokia's couldn't compare.

Vasco squeezed his eyes shut, but it was too late. The image of Princess Bianca's naked body was branded to the inside of his eyelids. Princess or not, the burning desire that coursed through his body didn't care – he wanted her in every way a man wanted a woman.

He forced himself to think of the dead rats he'd found in the cellar this evening. Rats that had drunk the poisoned wine and died for their crimes.

The slither of silk made him open his eyes again. The purple gown was replaced by one as blue as a summer sky, covering those beautiful legs to the ankle. A pair of matching slippers, embroidered in gold so pale it matched her hair, slapped to the floor. She carefully slid her feet into them.

"Have you seen tonight's fool? He's not in

his bed," one of the girls said.

"Not since last night. Perhaps he has given up." The second girl giggled.

A third voice piped up: "Or perhaps he is hiding in this very chamber, thinking to follow us. Search the room!"

Bianca bent over, her face so close to Vasco's that he could feel her breath on his face. Then she brushed his hood forward, covering his face entirely. "Melania, where would he hide? He would need some sort of magic in order to conceal himself in here. If you want to search the room, suit yourself. The rest of us have more important things to do. Like dressing our hair."

"Let me do yours, Bianca!" one of the girls begged.

To Vasco's surprise, he found he could see through the cloak as though it were gossamer thin, instead of thick wool. When an angry face framed with dark hair peered under the bed, he saw her as clearly as he'd seen Bianca. Yet she shook her head in annoyance and moved to the next bed as if she hadn't seen him.

Vasco breathed a sigh of relief.

"Come on, girls. I can see the boats!" a princess called imperiously.

A dozen pairs of feet clad in dancing slippers stampeded to the corner of the room furthest from the windows, where a section of the stone floor tilted up at a strange angle. It was a trapdoor, Vasco realised, with a thin veneer of stone on top to make it look like a normal part of the flagstones. One by one, the girls descended through the hole in the floor.

Crawling out from under the bed, he tried to stay low so they wouldn't see him. He rounded the end of the last bed, only to see the trapdoor closing behind the last princess.

He dived for it, hands outstretched, but he wasn't quick enough. The trapdoor settled among the flagstones as if it had never been. Vasco raked his nails across the stones, to no avail. He didn't know the trick to opening the secret door.

He sat back on his heels, anger and despair

warring within him. He should have been faster. Now he would waste another night.

As if by magic, the trapdoor rose.

"What are you doing?" Melania's voice demanded.

"I forgot my fan," Bianca said.

That was all the warning Vasco got before the trapdoor was thrown open and she burst out of the hole in the floor. She raced past him as if she couldn't see him, presumably in search of her fan.

Vasco took his chance and propelled himself through the hole in the floor. Rough steps had been cut into the stone, leading down into the darkness. With one hand on the damp, stone wall, he followed them down to where he could see a light flickering.

One of the princesses held a torch aloft, her face scrunched up in annoyance. "Do we have to wait for her?" the dark-haired girl, Melania, asked.

Another girl put a hand on her shoulder. "Yes, we do. It will take all of us to break the curse. Without her, we are only eleven. The spell calls for twelve princesses to free the twelve princes. Any fewer and they will still be trapped."

Melania grumbled something under her breath, then fell silent.

"I'm coming!" Bianca called from above.

All eyes suddenly turned toward Vasco, too quickly for him to hide, yet none of the girls reacted to the sight of him. They continued to stare expectantly at the steps behind him.

Figuring that the torch had blinded them so much that they couldn't see him, Vasco relaxed. It was only a moment before Bianca came down the steps, painted fan in one hand and a candle in the other. She walked to his side, so close she brushed his cloak, and waved the fan at her sisters. "See? I told you I would be quick. Ooh, are those the boats?"

As one, the girls turned away from her to stare at the lake.

Vasco couldn't believe none of the girls had seen him. Not even Bianca, and she'd touched him. Perhaps the cloak truly did make him invisible, like Kun had said. Still, it wouldn't do to be reckless. He waited for Bianca and her candle to lead the way before he followed, several steps behind.

The stone path was uneven and he stumbled frequently, wishing he dared to walk closer to the light she held. If only the world were a different place, where a soldier could walk arm in arm with a princess as equals. But it was not to be.

His distraction was almost his undoing. The path curved, but he had not seen it, and he fell headlong over a pile of rocks. The cloak's hood slipped from his head.

A moment later, Bianca cried out, "My light!"

The candle rolled down the path toward Vasco. Impossibly, the flame hadn't been extinguished. Which meant that if Bianca came chasing it, she would spot him instantly.

Vasco forced himself to his feet, pulling the cloak closed around him once more, as the candle came to a stop where he had lain only moments before. He edged along the path, which was scarcely wide enough for one, let alone two.

Bianca rounded the corner, too intent on her candle to notice her cloak brushing against his.

Vasco experienced a mad desire to reach out and wrap his arms around her, bringing her body against his and…then what? She would hardly consent to a kiss. He clenched his hands at his sides to stop himself from doing something else stupid.

"Must hurry…don't want to miss the boat," she murmured to herself as she passed.

Though he was certain the words weren't for him, Vasco obeyed them anyway, stumbling down the path to reach the other girls. More confident in his invisibility, he dared to stand closer than before.

"What is she doing? They are almost here!" Melania muttered.

Vasco followed the girl's gaze to the lake.

The same boats he had seen vanish into the mist the previous night now approached the shore. A lantern hung at one end, while a dark-cloaked figure poled the boat at the other end.

The hair on the back of Vasco's neck prickled. Whoever was concealed by those cloaks brought an ill wind with them.

The first of the boats reached the shore and its captain leaped onto the sand, holding onto the lantern post so that the boat did not drift away. He let his hood fall back, revealing hair as long and pale as Bianca's. "Good evening, my beautiful princesses." He flashed a brilliant smile before bowing low. "Is it true that there are twelve of you this evening?" The eagerness in his tone set Vasco's teeth on edge.

"We were twelve, but Bianca ran back to get something," Melania grumbled.

"I am here!" Bianca's voice called.

Vasco wanted to move to the middle of the path to bar her way. Nothing good would come of this, he was certain of it. He must protect her.

The other girls closed around her, a gaggle of impenetrable geese, until they delivered her to the cloaked man.

"This is Bianca, newly arrived among us," Brenna said, pushing her forward. "With her, we are twelve."

"Such beauty," the man breathed, reaching for Bianca's hand. He bowed low over it. "Princess Bianca, I am Prince Corbin, and it would be my honour to be your escort tonight."

"But I thought I was going to – " Melania protested before Brenna hushed her.

"She would be delighted," Brenna said. "You have rendered her speechless, Prince Corbin. Bianca has spent all her life in the women's palace, where we see few men, but I am sure you will help her find her voice again."

Bianca had no trouble speaking to men, Vasco wanted to say, incensed at her sister's presumption, but once again, he was silenced by Bianca herself.

"I thank you, sir," she said, accepting his

assistance into the boat.

More boats had come ashore during the exchange, and the girls spread out along the beach, one to a boat.

Corbin had already poled Bianca's boat away from shore – too far for Vasco to reach them. He cast about for another boat to board.

"You'll do as you're told," Brenna hissed as she shoved Melania toward one of the boats. "Prince Fiachra is just as handsome as his brother. You should consider yourself lucky to have a suitor at all. Why, your mother was a slave before my father took her for a concubine."

While Melania struggled and whined about her mother, Vasco crept into the boat Brenna evidently had in mind for the irritating girl. The cloaked man who stood beside it – Fiachra, Vasco presumed – only had eyes for Melania. The hunger in his gaze made Vasco feel queasy.

At a nod from Brenna, Fiachra seized the slight girl and deposited her in the boat, narrowly missing Vasco. Fiachra stepped aboard after her and quickly poled the boat out into deeper water.

Once again, the boats headed for the small, mist-shrouded island in the middle of the lake. Only this time, Vasco was with them.

Twenty-Seven

Bianca wasn't entirely sure what to make of Prince Corbin. Between his perfect manners, outrageous compliments and the glittering coronet he wore on his head beneath the hood, he appeared to be the sort of prince only found in fairytales.

He was the complete opposite of all the men who'd come to the Summer Palace, trying to solve her sisters' mystery. Yes, even the opposite of Vasco. Where Vasco said little and behaved as though he felt he was out of place,

Corbin smiled and laughed as if he was completely comfortable.

On a misty lake, late at night, carrying off a princess whose father would probably skin him alive if he caught Corbin, the man's smile never wavered until they reached their destination – the small island in the middle of the lake.

As he helped her out of the boat, Bianca glanced back. The Summer Palace wasn't visible through the mist. So close, and yet so far. She shivered.

"I should get you inside. It is warmer there," Corbin said, offering his arm. In his free hand, he held the lantern from the boat.

Without his help and the light, she was bound to trip again, Bianca knew, so she tucked her hand into the crook of his elbow and allowed him to lead her away from the water.

Another boat crunched into the shore behind her, but Bianca's attention was drawn to the path ahead. Corbin led her up a slight rise to the bare peak of a hill, the highest point on the island. Torches glowed and danced in a circle around them as Corbin set down his lantern.

He reached down, grasped a ring set in a stone and heaved. It came up easily, tilting up to reveal that the slice of rock was fixed to a wooden trapdoor, the twin of the one in her bedchamber. Almost as though the same person had constructed them both. Though to what end?

"You look intrigued, princess. Wait until you see what awaits you downstairs," Corbin declared, gesturing for her to precede him.

Descending into a dark cellar with a stranger didn't seem like the wisest thing to do, but a glance back told Bianca that her sisters and their cloaked escorts were on their way here. They didn't look worried.

She stepped inside, holding tight to the railing as she followed the steep spiral staircase down, down, down until she was certain she was below the surface of the lake. Yet the deeper she descended, the brighter it became. The mystery was solved when she rounded the last twist into a small subterranean chamber filled with candles.

Corbin was only a few steps behind her. "Let me take your cloak, princess."

As he spoke, she was already unfastening the clasp, so it was a simple matter to shrug the garment off into his waiting arms. Bianca patted her hair carefully and straightened her dress, wishing she had thought to bring a mirror instead of a fan.

Corbin finished hanging her cloak up next to his, and turned to face her. He immediately dropped to his knees. "Princess Bianca, never have I seen such radiant beauty. You are an angel come to earth to tempt me, surely. I will not rest until you agree to be my wife."

What? Bianca searched his expression for some hint that he was joking, for surely this was a jest. No man declared his love for a girl the moment he met her. And no sane woman would accept the proposal of such a fool.

And yet…the look in his eyes was so earnest, she was forced to believe he meant every word.

"I…am speechless once more," she faltered.

"Beautiful Bianca, I understand. Take all the time you wish. But do not torture me for too long. I will not be willing to let you go tonight until I have received your answer." Something flickered in his eyes so quickly Bianca wasn't sure whether she'd imagined it or not. Whatever it was, it chilled her, for his words definitely carried a threat.

What would he do if she refused him? Would he hold her prisoner here until she changed her mind?

Aruna stepped off the bottom stair and allowed her princely escort – he wore a circlet, too, though of a different design to Corbin's – to divest her of her cloak. She received no marriage proposal. Her escort merely extended his arm to her and they walked together through the arched doorway at the other end of the room.

More people spilled down the stairs, crowding the tiny room.

"Allow me to show you our humble home," Corbin said with a wry smile.

He led her through the arch Aruna had entered. Only, it wasn't just an arch – it was an arched passageway that extended a considerable distance. From what Bianca had seen of the island above, she was certain this passage extended under the lake itself. Why, it felt like they were walking back to the palace, it was so long.

Finally, they stepped out into a much wider space. Bianca's breath caught in her throat.

The domed ballroom stretched high above them, the ceiling made of… "Is that glass?" she asked eagerly, craning her neck to stare up at it. Each pane was no bigger than her mirror at home, but each pane was a slightly different colour, turning the ceiling into a marvellous mosaic that shone in the moonlight filtering through the lake.

"It is," Corbin replied, grinning. "Brought

from Arabia just to build this ballroom. I swear some magic must have gone into its construction, for it is only by some miracle that the lake doesn't try to claim our home for its own."

As if by magic, music began to play.

"Shall we dance, princess?" Corbin asked.

Now Bianca truly was speechless. At her father's court, the only dances she'd heard of were performed by women, for the pleasure of men, and no man ever danced with a woman. It was unheard of. "I…don't know how," she said.

He laughed. "I will soon teach you. You will see. Your sisters said the same thing to my brothers, and watch them now!"

Brenna, then Aruna, Nera, Hazel…all of her sisters had entered the ballroom while she'd been admiring the ceiling, and each stood in the embrace of a different prince, moving about the dance floor in what looked like synchronised steps. Well, nearly synchronised. Melania kept twisting in her partner's arms so that she could glare at Bianca.

Bianca sighed. She hoped when Corbin lost patience with her for her lack of dancing skills, he would rescind his marriage proposal and consent to let her go home.

Twenty-Eight

"Something pulled on my cloak, I swear it!" Nera cried.

Vasco swore under his breath and lifted his foot off her cloak. If she hadn't let it trail on the ground behind her, he would not have trodden on it.

"You must have caught it on a branch or something," Brenna advised her. Even though she looked in Vasco's direction, he was certain she could not see him. None of the girls could, and none of their mysterious princes, either.

Nera seemed satisfied by Brenna's explanation, but it drew Vasco's attention to the well-worn path at their feet, which had no branches to catch anyone's clothes, and the trees that grew on either side. Their leaves shone silver in the moonlight, as though made of metal and not living wood. He hadn't seen any such trees when he was cutting timber for Kun's cottage. Without thinking, he broke off a small branch so that he might study it later, in daylight.

"What was that?" Hazel whispered. "I heard something crack."

"Someone stepped on a stick, is all," Brenna replied. "Why, I think I felt one crunch under my shoe just a moment ago."

One by one, the young couples disappeared into a hole at the top of the hill. Fortunately for Vasco, the last one left the trapdoor open, so he climbed in after them.

At the bottom of the stairs, they were too preoccupied with uncloaking and flirting to notice him slipping through the crowd, though he brushed against more than one person on his way through. He passed through the passage, marvelling that he cast no shadow. He truly was invisible.

More confident now, he strode into the ballroom, keeping close to the walls. He watched Bianca talking and laughing with the prince as easily as she'd done with him that morning. What he didn't like was the adoration in the prince's eyes, burning brighter every moment he spent with her.

When the prince asked her to dance and actually dared to hold her in his arms, Vasco felt his fury rise. How dare any man put his hands on her? He wasn't worthy to touch her!

Even as he started forward to yank the man away from her, Vasco's own mind ventured a traitorous thought: why couldn't a prince touch a princess? Vasco might not be worthy of her, but she belonged with a prince, a man of her own rank. Reluctantly, he shrank back against the wall, forcing himself to watch but not interfere.

Even if it killed him.

After some time dancing, the prince led Bianca to a table where food and wine was laid out. He poured the wine into what looked like a golden goblet, before handing it to her.

After last night's poisoned wine, he wanted to leap forward and dash the cup from her hands, but she simply sipped from it and smiled.

Vasco crept closer, in order to hear their conversation.

Another couple joined them before he could reach them.

"So how are you two getting along?" Brenna asked as her prince poured her wine.

"I don't think I have ever done so much dancing in my life!" Bianca said.

"She dances as well on the dance floor as she does around my heart. I have made her an offer of marriage, but she will not give me an answer." Corbin gave a melancholy sigh.

Vasco's heart stuttered. Surely he hadn't heard correctly. The prince had proposed to marry her?

"You will say yes, won't you?" Brenna implored. "We have all agreed to marry one of the princes. Once you accept Corbin, that will be all of us." She beamed.

Bianca lowered her gaze. "But I scarcely know him."

Vasco's heart began to beat again. The man might have asked, but her heart was still her own.

Brenna grabbed Bianca's arm. "I think we need some air. Excuse us, sirs." She dragged her sister across the room, toward the stairs.

Vasco took a step away from the table, intending to follow the princesses.

"So will she do it?" Brenna's prince asked Corbin.

"By the time I am done seducing her, of course she will," Corbin said easily, pouring himself some wine. "She'll make a sweet wife, that one. I'll enjoy the wedding night."

The other prince laughed. "I wager Fiachra won't. He will not forgive you for foisting the slave's daughter on him while you kept the jewel for yourself."

Corbin drained his cup. "You know, you might be right, Raban. I know we only need them for one night to break the curse, but I might just keep that one. She'd make a fine mistress of Beacon Isle."

Raban laughed even harder. "I'll wager you tire of her in a week, or you'll give her to Fiachra to silence his complaints. By the time we reach Beacon Isle, we'll have all had her so many times she won't be able to close her legs. She won't be fit for a whorehouse, let alone our father's house."

Corbin shrugged. "Mayhap you're right. Who cares? The curse will be broken, and there are more women in the world than we could bed in a lifetime." He reached for Bianca's goblet, which she'd left on the table, and downed the contents. Wiping his mouth with the back of his hand, he added, "But the next woman I bed will be that one. Tomorrow, if I am any judge. Come, let's go find them. I must have her answer."

Let it be no, Vasco prayed. Bianca deserved better. A prince he might be, but he and his brothers were kin to toads, not kings, if they thought to treat her that way. She was far too precious to be thrown away on such men who were so far beneath her they did not deserve to even look at her.

He snatched up the empty goblet and tucked it under his cloak with the tree branch. This would end tonight.

Vasco marched through the dancers, taking the stairs two at a time in his hurry to leave. Choosing the nearest boat, he jumped in and poled himself back through the mists to shore. Dawn was whispering her way into the sky already, but the sun wasn't up yet.

When he reached the beach, he leaped onto the sand and shoved the boat back out onto the lake. If he was lucky, the princes would assume it had drifted away on its own.

Only when he was outside the palace proper did he remove his cloak, using it to wrap the goblet and branch as he strode to the Lord Steward's chambers. He had solved the mystery of the princesses' shoes, and it was far more sinister than he'd thought.

Twenty-Nine

Brenna didn't release Bianca's arm until they'd reached the surface. "What are you thinking?" Brenna hissed.

Bianca folded her arms across her chest. "I'm thinking of my future. I don't know that man!"

"Who cares? Do you think our father would let you get to know a man if he promised you in marriage?"

Still Bianca didn't budge. "If he intended to use us to forge a marriage alliance, we wouldn't be here. We'd be in the women's palace still, under the queen's watchful eyes. He sent us here to become spinsters. He will never let us marry."

"So take your life in your own hands! Now you have a chance to make your own choices. To marry, have children. Don't you want children?" Brenna demanded. "Or do you want to have a succession of dogs that die too soon?" She swiped at her tears.

"I'm sorry about your dog, Brenna, and yes, I would like to marry and have children," Bianca said carefully. "But…"

But…what? Corbin was everything a prince should be. Charming, courteous…handsome, even. She could do worse.

"You have known the freedom of the Summer Palace for many months. I have scarcely tasted it in my few weeks here. Why, this is my first night dancing with all of you. I would like a little more time," she finished.

Brenna closed her eyes. "I understand. Truly, I do. But you must understand that there is far more at stake. At any time, our father might recall one of us back to the palace, to marry the man he chooses. And the princes themselves…they are cursed, and they suffer so. They are confined to these chambers during daylight hours, only venturing out at night under the light of the moon. They need our help to break the curse. All of our help. There are a dozen princes, and twelve of us. In order to break the curse, they must each find a maiden willing to pledge her love and life to them. All at the same time. Only then will they be free."

Bianca couldn't seem to close her mouth. "Why didn't you tell me this earlier?" she demanded. "The princes are prisoners? Who would do such a thing?"

Brenna shook her head. "A wicked witch cursed them for some imagined slight. She did not bother to tell them her name. But we can release them, sister. And take them as husbands. Princes – our father cannot object when we marry princes! Tell me you will accept his offer, Bianca. All of our futures depend on it."

Bianca turned away, not wanting Brenna to see how torn she was. On the one hand sat Corbin and his brothers, trapped by a terrible curse that she alone had the power to free them from. Yet on the other hand stood Vasco, who would die if he did not share the secret of the princes with Cousin Efe.

She bowed her head. "Very well. I shall marry Prince Corbin."

"Did you hear that? She says yes!"

Bianca whirled to find Corbin and one of his brothers only a few yards away. She and Brenna were led back into the ballroom, where Corbin announced what he'd overheard to everyone, prince and princess alike.

A rousing cheer erupted, and Bianca began to believe she had made the right choice. What was one man's life compared to the fate of a dozen men, not to mention her sisters?

"Tomorrow, we will be wed. What say you?" Corbin boomed.

More cheering, drowning out Bianca's surprised exclamation. Tomorrow? She would marry the man tomorrow?

She swallowed. Why wait? If she had made her choice, there was no sense in delaying the inevitable. Summoning a watery smile, she joined in the celebration.

Thirty

"…And that's how the girls dance their shoes to pieces every night," Vasco finished triumphantly.

The Lord Steward continued to stroke the golden goblet. "So let me get this straight. They have a secret trapdoor in their bedchamber, which is how they escape to the lake where a pack of ruffians claiming to be princes carry them to a secret underground ballroom where they dance all night until their shoes are destroyed. Then the ruffians bring them back, so the girls can get some sleep and new shoes before doing it all again the following night."

Vasco nodded. "I think they mean to carry them off, but they haven't yet. I heard two of them talking, but I didn't hear enough to be certain."

The Lord Steward rose, setting the cup on his desk. "Very good, soldier. You have earned a reward. I shall send these with a note to the king this very morning. I will have a flagon of my best wine sent up to help you sleep, for I am sure you need rest."

Vasco tried and failed to smother a yawn. "Yes." He gave a perfunctory bow and left the Lord Steward's chambers. He limped all the way up to his pallet and struggled to remove his boots so he could sleep.

Gentle laughter made him look up. Gerel stood in the princesses' audience chamber, holding what Vasco presumed was the promised flagon. "I can help you, if you wish."

Vasco grunted and with one final effort

managed to pull off one boot. The other took even longer.

He stared longingly at the flagon. "What's in it?"

Gerel set his boots neatly side by side at the end of his bed, then smoothed the folds of his cloak as she hung it on its customary hook. "Wine from the hogshead you were so interested in yesterday morning."

Vasco had almost managed to lie down, but he shot up again. "The one with the crow?"

Gerel wrinkled her nose. "The one with a bowl of dead rats in front of it."

Vasco swore, then apologised. "Why did you draw the wine from that cask, and not one of the others?"

"Lord Steward's orders. Otherwise, I would've chosen any cask but the one with the rats."

Absently, he thanked her and dismissed her.

Did the Lord Steward know it was poisoned? And if he did, why would he want to poison Vasco, after he'd finally solved the mystery?

Movement outside caught his eye. Vasco crept to the window, peering out carefully so that he could see without being seen.

On the beach, he saw the Lord Steward standing by the water's edge. He drew something out of his pocket that glinted in the morning sun, then pitched it into the lake. The golden goblet flew in a glittering arc for a moment before it plopped into the depths.

All thoughts of sleep fled. The Lord Steward wasn't sending anything to the king. Instead, he'd destroyed the evidence Vasco brought him and tried to poison him. Did he want the girls to be carried off by these mysterious princes to dishonour and who knew what else?

Well, Vasco wouldn't let them. He might not be a prince or even a lord, but he knew where his duty lay. He had to protect the princesses, even if it cost him his life. Except...he didn't know how he could possibly do that now.

He needed someone who understood intrigues and politics to tell him what to do. So he did the only thing he could think of.

It was time to ask Princess Bianca for help.

Thirty-One

It felt like Bianca's head had barely touched the pillow before she was awake again. Someone was calling her name.

"Mm?" she said, hoping this was a dream.

"Princess Bianca, I'm sorry to wake you, but I need your help. Mistress Kun told me if I ran into trouble, I must ask you. Please, Princess Bianca." Vasco's voice was far too earnest for this to be a dream.

"Give me a moment to dress. I shall meet you outside," she mumbled, prying her eyes open. The light streaming through the open door told her it was dawn. Ugh. She shouldn't have drunk so much wine last night. Surely it had only been two cups. Perhaps three. Surely not four or five. Her sisters had drunk more, she was certain of it. They would sleep for hours yet, while she had a promise to Kun to keep.

The moment her feet touched the floor, she regretted it. Her head ached, but it was nothing to the tenderness of her feet. Dancing all night, dancing so much she wore through the soles of her shoes, was not something she ever wanted to do again. She'd taken her ruined shoes off in the boat, letting her feet soak in the surprisingly warm lake water, but the walk up to the palace from the lake had been tortuous. The path had been littered with so many sharp rocks she feared her feet had been cut to ribbons. She would not be dancing tonight, that was for certain.

Shielding her eyes from the far too bright light in the audience chamber, she could barely make out Vasco, silhouetted against the window. "What is it?"

"I followed you last night. I now know the answer to how you and your sisters dance your shoes to pieces every night," he said gravely.

Good, she thought muzzily. Then she had no need to venture to the island or dance until dawn ever again.

"I brought back some items from the island, and showed them to the Lord Steward when I told him my story."

Bianca nodded, then winced as the movement only made her head ache more. She'd wager Cousin Efe had been shocked by Vasco's discovery. Now he could claim the palace and his bride and…

Bride. Her memories of last night threw up an image she'd forgotten until now. Tonight, there would be a wedding in the underwater ballroom. Someone called Corbin was going to be married, or was it one of her sisters? More than one, maybe. Bianca wished it weren't so foggy in her head. There'd been much celebration and cheering, hence the wine, and…

"He promised to send the evidence with a note to the king, then gave me a flagon of wine, before he threw all my evidence in the lake. It was poisoned wine. The Lord Steward doesn't want the mystery solved. He wants me dead, and you and your sisters carried off to dishonour. I need your help to stop him."

Vasco's words started to sink in, and Bianca stared at him. Surely she hadn't heard right. "You think Cousin Efe is a traitor, who would deliberately withhold information from my father, the king?"

Vasco looked scared. "Perhaps. That is why I need your help. If the Lord Steward is not to be trusted, the king will never know I solved his mystery, and you will be…those princes have plans for you and your sisters, princess. They mean to use you to break some sort of curse, but they will discard you the moment the spell is broken."

"I know about the curse," she said absently.

She did. She couldn't remember what she knew about it, but it certainly sounded familiar. It didn't matter, though. What mattered was saving Vasco's life. Vasco shouldn't die if he'd solved the mystery. He should present his case to the king in person. "You must tell the king what you know."

Vasco laughed mirthlessly. "The king will not listen to a common soldier."

Bianca knew he was right. Her father was a busy man.

"Then we must return to the island on the lake and gather as much proof as we can." Bianca surprised herself by the vehemence in her tone.

"Thank you, princess. I will find us a boat." Vasco sketched a hasty bow and hurried away.

"And I will find the kitchens, and some willow bark tea," she muttered to herself, vowing never to drink wine again.

Thirty-Two

Vasco asked a manservant whose name he did not know where he might find a boat.

"There is a whole fleet of pleasure boats in the boatshed, usually," the man said, pointing. "But the Lord Steward went out on the lake this morning. The boat he used should still be on the beach, as he hasn't asked me to put it away yet."

Vasco thanked the man, offering to return the boat to the boatshed when he was finished with it. That way, no one would know when he and Bianca returned from their errand – or see what evidence they carried. Vasco trusted no one now, except perhaps Gerel. Bianca…that remained to be seen.

He paused by the kitchen to ask for a basket of provisions for the day. Gerel smiled broadly when she heard him ask for food and drink for two, but she didn't ask questions. Perhaps she already knew his partner in the day's activities would be Princess Bianca, and she fancied some sort of romance between the two of them. Vasco suppressed a snort. As though a princess would stoop so low as to fall in love with a soldier. He should be thankful she had agreed to help him at all.

Her life depended on the outcome of today's expedition just as much as his did. He couldn't forget that. Still, that didn't mean she needed to put herself in danger. He could easily go to the island and return while she stayed in the safety of the palace. More than anything, he wanted to protect her.

Lifting his chin and straightening his spine,

he marched to the dining hall to tell her what he'd decided.

"You should have some breakfast, Vasco," she greeted him, gesturing for him to sit down.

Obediently, he sat, and reached for some fruit. "I've been thinking, and it seems to me that it is too dangerous for a princess to be haring about across the lake. You should stay here, where you will be safe."

"Where the Lord Steward is cousin to the queen, a woman who likes me so little she exiled me out here? To a man who poisons people." She sipped from her cup and set it down. "It seems to me that I will be safer outside the palace than in it."

"But – " he began.

She interrupted, "Last night seems like little more than a fever dream, with boats in the mist, charming fairy princes, and dancing until dawn. I need to see where it all happened in daylight, to know I did not dream it. I need the evidence of my eyes as much as you want items you can take to prove what you have seen."

"But Princess Bianca…"

She waved him into silence. "If we are to sneak around the island, I cannot be a princess today. I am merely Bee, as my mother liked to call me. Buzzing around, butting my head into matters that do not concern me. Though today, they most certainly do concern me."

Curiosity got the better of him. "What does your father call you?"

Bianca sighed heavily. "I do not know. I'm not sure my father even knows my name. He has so many children, so many daughters, that I am just one in a multitude." She flashed a rueful smile. "So while you call me princess, the pampered daughter of a king, which I am, were anything to happen to me…I'm not sure my father would know, or even care."

"I would know, and I would care a great deal," Vasco said gravely.

"Truly?"

He nodded. "I have no right to give you orders, though I wish you would stay here. But if you will not…then it is my duty to go with you and protect you."

She drained her cup and set it on the table. "I'm ready when you are. You might want your cloak, though." Bianca winked. "It might be helpful for sneaking around."

It sounded almost as though she knew its magical properties. Had Kun told her? Or had she glimpsed him last night and said nothing?

"As you wish," he said. He rose, bowed, and went to retrieve his cloak.

Thirty-Three

Bianca caught Vasco stealing glances at her last night when she wore the ornate silk dress her sisters had insisted upon, but today he'd gone back to not meeting her eyes again. As though he fancied himself a servant, and not the rightful lord of the Summer Palace. Which he was, now, by her father's own conditions. Never mind that Cousin Efe had rejected his claim to have solved the mystery – Bianca knew he had.

Even the drab clothes she'd donned today

did little to dispel his servility. Sure, she was a princess, but she was a woman first. Last night, he'd looked like he recognised that. Now, she wasn't so certain. Still, if he called her Bee, just the once…

He took her down to the beach that last night had been littered with lantern-lit pleasure boats, but now only held one aging boat in need of fresh paint, which had oars instead of a pole. Unlike the pleasure boats, this one could have held at least half a dozen people comfortably – maybe more if they were as slim as her sisters.

He said little as he rowed out to the island, except to comment on the absence of last night's mist.

That meant that anyone could see them on the lake. Bianca felt the hair rise on the back of her neck, as though hostile eyes watched her.

"Put on the cloak," she ordered.

"There is no point. It won't cover the boat," he said, rowing steadily.

"Put it on anyway," she insisted, biting her

lip as she started to cast a spell that would hide the boat from sight as well.

"If you sit here beside me, it will cover us both," he said.

Bianca considered telling him she was quite capable of taking care of herself, thank you, but something in the way he held out his arm, ready to pull her to his side, melted something inside of her. Instead she said, "Thank you," and carefully shifted to the bench beside him.

The prickling sensation was gone almost instantly, replaced with the warm presence of the man beside her. She could feel the hardness of his muscles as he rowed, the lulling sensation as they contracted and relaxed around her. His chest, his arm…oh, it was everything she'd imagined as she watched him work on Kun's house.

When her father asked Vasco to choose one of his daughters to be his bride, Bianca wanted it to be her.

The boat grated on sand, jolting her out of her fantasies.

"We're here," Vasco said.

He helped her out of the boat and they both stood on the shore, surveying the island.

"What sort of evidence did you give to Efe?" Bianca asked.

"I broke off a branch from one of the trees. They only grow here on this island." Vasco stepped forward and seized a branch. This time, he tossed it into the boat, then threw several more on top of it. "I also had a goblet from the banquet table in the ballroom."

"But we can't go into the ballroom. That's where the princes will be. They won't help us," Bianca said, then stopped. How did she know that?

Vasco didn't question her knowledge, though. He merely nodded and said, "So we sneak in under my cloak?"

Would invisibility be enough? Bianca had to hope so. After all, no one but she had seen Vasco last night. She nodded.

At the top of the hill, Bianca stood back while Vasco raised the trapdoor.

The spiral staircase disappeared into the darkness. "I'll go first," Vasco said. "You keep close behind me, and stay under the cloak as much as you can."

If she hadn't been fighting the rising dread of what awaited her in the underground chamber, Bianca might have refused. As it was, she wrapped one arm around his waist and slipped under the woollen folds. Vasco was a comforting bulk in front of her as they made their way slowly down the steps.

"There's no one here," Vasco whispered.

Even in the darkness, Bianca could see that he was right. The antechamber where they'd left their cloaks last night was empty. Yet light shimmered at the end of the passage, tempting her to enter.

"No goblets, either," she whispered back.

That was enough to impel him forward. What could Bianca do but follow?

Together, they shuffled along the passage to the ballroom.

She heard his gasp as he stepped out of the

passage, but she couldn't see past his bulk to work out what had elicited such a response. Before she could struggle free of his cloak, he let it slide off his shoulders, and draped it over his arm.

"The whole place is empty. There's no one here. No princes, nothing. Just the remains of last night's revelry," he said.

"What startled you, then?" she asked.

"There are no torches, yet it's as bright in here as it was last night. Look up, princess." Vasco caught her around the waist and pointed up.

Bianca lifted her eyes to the ceiling and it was her turn to gasp. Last night's moonlight was nothing to the sun filtering through the water now. Shades of blue and green, even rainbows, shimmered across the glass.

"It's beautiful," she breathed.

"Not as beautiful as...never mind," he muttered, half under his breath. The arm around her middle released her.

"You've seen a place more beautiful than

this?" Bianca asked. "It must be a great thing, to have travelled and seen so much."

Vasco chuckled. The sound echoed strangely around the underground room. "I was thinking of you. You looked beautiful last night. The perfect marriage of summer sky and moonlight."

She stared at him, and for the first time today, he met her gaze. He seemed a little embarrassed by his admission, but the look in his eyes was honest. Unlike all the other fools with their empty compliments, he truly meant his.

And if she didn't tear her gaze away from his, she was going to throw her arms around his neck and kiss him until she couldn't breathe.

Bianca closed her eyes. "Summer sky and moonlight. I wish I could be as free as both of those things. I might even dance…"

Another chuckle. "I bet your prince from last night has sore feet this morning. I lost count of the number of times you stepped on his feet while you were dancing."

Perhaps his honesty wasn't quite as attractive as she'd first thought. It certainly broke the spell between them, allowing Bianca to seize two of the goblets from the table. "Here. These should replace the one you gave to Efe."

Vasco tucked them in a fold of his cloak. "Thank you. Now we have what we came for, shall we head back to shore?"

Bianca wanted to say yes, for this beautiful place frightened her more than she was willing to admit. Yet she was so certain the princes would be here. They couldn't leave the island, she was sure, because of something half-remembered that she'd heard last night. Something about the curse. "We should finish exploring the island. The princes must be here, and the food and wine has to come from somewhere."

"As you wish." Vasco led the way back to the surface.

The hilltop clearing where the trapdoor lay

had only the one path leading off it – the one which led back to the boat, so they followed that to the beach and trudged through the sand, looking for signs of another path.

The beach ended in a collection of tumbled rocks before they were a quarter of the way around the island. Vasco helped her climb up the slope. Bianca wasn't sure whether it was a path or simply the fact that nothing grew on the bare rock, but she glimpsed another beach through the rocks. Without waiting for Vasco, she trudged on until she stood on a cliff overlooking a beach like nothing she'd ever seen before.

The sand was black, with occasional pieces of bleached wood scattered along it. Then something moved, exposing a flash of pink and red, before it was hidden from sight once more. One flash was enough.

Bianca blinked, her mouth falling open in horror. Deep within her, she felt a scream fighting to escape.

Thirty-Four

When Vasco reached Bianca's side, it was already too late to stop her from seeing the horror no one should ever be subjected to. The corpse-strewn beach had bodies in various states of decay, from scattered bones to a cadaver so fresh the flesh the crows ripped off it was still red and moist. No, not crows — ravens, he corrected himself. He counted a dozen of them picking at the corpse, which still wore the tatters of clothing in a particularly brilliant shade of pink.

He knew the expression on her face all too well. Every soldier viewing a battlefield for the first time looked like that. But she was no soldier. Why, the princess had probably never seen blood that was not her own until today.

"Princess," he whispered.

No response. Her mouth gaped, but no sound came out.

He prayed she would forgive him for the liberty. "Bee. Look away."

She blinked. Once. Twice. Then she turned and flung herself into his arms, pressing her face against his chest. Sobs shook her body. "No. All those men."

He eyed the pink-clad body. "Women, too, I think. One of them wore pink silk."

Bianca shook her head violently. "No. I remember that tunic. The foolish adventurer who came before you wore that. He's dead, Vasco. Dead because my sisters wanted to go dancing! And if we do not stop it, you will be next!"

"I should have died when the rest of my

village was slaughtered. Yet here I stand. We all must die sometime." The words slipped out before he could stop them.

She squinted up at him. "How can you be so calm? There are dead bodies on that beach. Have you killed so many people that you no longer care when someone dies?"

Vasco sighed. "I do care. In my dreams, I see the faces of everyone I knew who has died, while I yet live. Every enemy soldier I have killed. Every brother in arms who died at my side when an enemy sword took them instead of me. Every man, woman and child in my village, whose bodies burned with the village itself. Eudokia…my Dokia…who agreed to meet me one evening by the river. We were betrothed, but the wedding could not come soon enough for us, and there was no privacy in the village. A scouting party found us, too engrossed in each other to notice the men until they were upon us. One knocked me out, and the others…" Vasco swallowed, blinking back tears. "They left me for dead, and when I woke, they had thrown her body atop mine. She was naked, and they had done unspeakable things to her before they killed her while I lay senseless and useless. I should have saved her."

Bianca clapped a hand to her mouth. "Ancestors, I am so sorry! That poor girl. What did you do then?"

"I took what little was left in the village of value, and traded it for arms and equipment when I joined the army. I trained hard and vowed to fight for those who still had their homes and their families, because I could not fight for my own. I became a soldier, living only for vengeance, until one day that was not enough. That day, I took an arrow in the knee that dwells there still." He shook his head. "I should not have let you see this. No woman should see this. Dokia's spirit would never forgive me if I let you and your sisters join this graveyard. I will do anything I have to in order to save you from this fate."

As though the creature had heard him, one of the ravens lifted its head and fixed a beady eye on Vasco. The creature appeared to have a band of greyish feathers around its head, like a kind of crown. It made a menacing sound low in its throat. The other birds looked up from their meal, their beaks still red with gore. As one, they turned to stare at Vasco. The menace emanating from them was unmistakeable.

"Bianca…" he said softly. "Princess, we need to go."

One of the birds extended its wings and started to run toward them.

"Now." Vasco threw his cloak around his shoulders, scooped her up in his arms, and ran. "Fasten the cloak," he urged her. "Then they won't be able to see us."

The first bird had made it into the air, and it took advantage of its height to dive at them. Vasco felt claws scrabble at his hood, but they didn't seem to be able to grab a hold of it.

Bianca's pale arm rose up, her hand clenched into a fist, and she punched the raven. The bird squawked and fell away, but not without raking its claws over her hand.

She didn't cry out. Instead, she brought her bleeding finger to her mouth. "Get us to the boat. I'll take care of the birds."

Vasco didn't have the breath to argue. His wounded leg screamed at him, but nothing mattered more than keeping Bianca safe.

He set her down on the bench, wrapped his cloak around her, and shoved the boat away from the beach. He jumped in, taking a seat on the bench beside her, and plied the oars.

Only when they reached open water did she seem to recover a little. She arranged the cloak over them both, tucking herself against his side. "The boat might be visible, but they won't see us," she said with quiet confidence.

Vasco scanned the sky, but he couldn't see the birds any more. "I think they're gone."

"Not gone. They just can't find us while we travel unseen. Did you see the crowns on their heads?" She sounded so calm.

"You mean the light coloured feathers?"

"Crowns," she corrected. "Each one was slightly different. Just like the ones the princes wore last night. And there were twelve of them. Dark magic clings to them like mist. Those were not normal birds."

"Ravens are meant to be very intelligent. I have heard tales of wise men who kept them as pets. Perhaps your princes do the same." Vasco didn't believe a word of it. Those ravens were on the beach for the carrion feast spread across the black sand.

"Those birds are not pets," she said. "They knew you would be their next meal." She swallowed. "Vasco, what if those birds are the princes? Carrion crows by day, and charming men by night? My sisters…my sisters are in danger. You must go to the king and tell him. Tell him what you have found. Cursed princes trying to seduce his daughters to their deaths. Take the ring from my finger, and take my horse. Ride to the capital. You must." She swallowed again, fighting to keep her eyes open. "I will warn my sisters and try to keep them away from the island. You must tell my father."

Vasco glanced down. She slumped against him. Asleep or unconscious, he wasn't sure, but it mattered little. However crazy her thoughts sounded, they tallied with his own. He must ride for the capital, trusting no one but the king himself. For Bianca, he would do anything.

He rowed the boat to the boatshed, where he dragged it out of the water. In the shadows, he saw the shapes of many small boats – the pleasure boats they'd used last night. The princes used the palace's own boats! Then that meant…

The Lord Steward truly was in league with them.

"Princess, you must wake. I can't leave you here with him. Not if he is at the heart of this," Vasco said, but Bianca's eyes stayed shut. Frustrated, he lifted her in his arms and carried her up to the house. She did not even wake when he laid her on her own bed, and pulled off her boots. He didn't dare remove anything else.

He watched her for a moment, but there was nothing he could do here. It would be a long, hard ride to the capital – and it would take much longer if he carried the unconscious princess with him. He must go now, alone, for it was the fastest way to save her from the clutches of the Lord Steward and his pet ravens, or princes, or whatever they were. Demons, surely.

"Stay safe, princess, and don't leave this room until I return," he whispered. Planting a quick kiss on her forehead, he turned and strode out of the room.

Thirty-Five

"You can't go dancing tonight," Bianca insisted for what felt like the hundredth time. Her head had started to ache again, but this was too important to wait. When they listened to her, then she could ask the kitchen for some more willow tea to ease the pain.

"Of course we can, and we will," Brenna said smoothly. "Don't be silly. Tonight is too important to miss. Tonight, we shall be free." Her face glowed. "Do you think I should wear the white or the pink?" She held up both gowns.

Bianca shuddered. White bones and pink silk, as the raven princes pecked at a bloody corpse that had once been a man. "Neither. Don't you see? They will kill us and strip the flesh from our bones!"

"Who will?" Melania asked.

"The cursed princes, of course! By night, they look like handsome men, but in truth, they are carrion crows. I have seen them!" Bianca said.

Hazel patted her shoulder. "Just a dream, sister. You went to bed when we did, just before dawn, and I shook you awake myself not an hour ago. Whatever you thought you saw, it was a nightmare brought on by too much wine and excitement. Do not drink so much tonight, for you will not want to alarm your new husband on your wedding night."

The thought of a wedding night with Vasco sent blood rushing to Bianca's cheeks. But that would not be tonight, surely. He hadn't returned from the capital yet, but he should be there by now. Hopefully telling her father all about the princes and Efe. If all went well, he would return by this time tomorrow, and he'd choose her for his bride, surely. He'd barely noticed the other girls, but he'd watched her so closely he knew she'd stepped on Corbin's feet when they danced.

Corbin…wedding…Bianca's memory itched, but she'd had too little sleep to understand what it was trying to tell her.

"What dress are you wearing tonight?" Hazel asked, opening the chest that contained Bianca's clothes. "That blue you wore last night was so lovely."

"Black," Bianca said absently. What other colour could she wear when her thoughts were as dark as ravens' wings?

"Ooh, I love the embroidery on this one. You should wear your hair loose tonight, cascading over it," Hazel gushed, helping Bianca into the black gown. Her mother had embroidered it with fish in silver thread which seemed to move if they caught the light right.

"Corbin won't be able to take his eyes off you."

Bianca didn't care what Corbin did. He wouldn't see her, because… "I'm not going," she said flatly.

Brenna stormed across the room and slapped Bianca's face hard. "What is wrong with you? Stop this madness!"

Bianca rubbed her cheek and glared back. "What is wrong with you? Don't you hear what I'm saying? The princes are cursed!"

"I told you about the curse last night," Brenna returned. "And how it could be broken, which is when you agreed to become Corbin's wife while the rest of us marry his brothers. Together, we will break the curse and we will all be free!"

"We will be dead!" Bianca insisted.

Brenna raised her hand to slap her again, but Bianca caught it this time before the blow could land.

"You're a fool if you think the princes have any love for us. They only want us to break the curse, and after that, we are expendable. You'll see," Bianca said. "I'll go with you to the island tonight. And I'll show you what they truly are."

"Princes who want to marry us!" Nera giggled.

Bianca gave up. While her sisters busied themselves about their toilette, she opened the trapdoor and headed down to the beach. She left her torch in a bracket at the bottom of the stairs, preferring to use just the moonlight to make her way to the lake. There was no need to pretend to stumble so that Vasco could catch up tonight – he had all the proof he needed.

The fog hadn't engulfed the lake yet, so when she heard a commotion by the boathouse, she could clearly see the little pleasure boats making their way out of it.

"You fool! You nearly capsized me. For that, you, Ronne and Guntram can take the food to the island. Set it up as quickly as you can, and hurry back. Our brides will be here soon, and everything must be perfect!"

Bianca recognised Corbin's voice from the previous night, but it hadn't sounded so imperious then. Was he the eldest of the raven princes? Had he led the attack against them this morning? Her blood froze in her veins at the thought that she'd let him touch her. A carrion-pecking crow. She would not allow him the same liberty tonight. The moment she reached the island, she would take her sisters to the cove full of corpses and show them the princes' handiwork. They might not believe her words, but they would believe their eyes. Better to see a corpse than to become one before your time, she thought grimly.

She hid behind a rock as the boats sailed past, headed for the island and the fog bank that only now crept over the lake, as if by some magical command. Yet there was no magic in it. If there was, she would sense it, she was sure of it.

The magic around the princes was there, though she'd been too busy to notice it last night. It was less noticeable on them when they were human — more concentrated when they were birds.

When the lake returned to its normal, glassy calm, showing no sign of the boats that had rippled its surface only moments before, Bianca heard the cheerful chatter of her sisters coming down the stairs to join her. If only they knew what awaited them tonight...but they hadn't listened, so they did not.

The boats arrived through the mist once more and they boarded them. Bianca managed to do so without Corbin's assistance, to her delight and his annoyance, though he smoothed his face back into a smile so quickly she almost doubted what she'd seen.

"You look so beautiful in that gown, it will be a pity to take it off for our wedding night," he said as he wrapped his hands around his pole and plied it vigorously. The boat set off so abruptly that a wave of water splashed over the side, soaking her shoes. "Forgive me, Bianca. I am so eager to make you mine that I forgot myself."

She suspected that it was more likely he'd forgotten anything but himself and his own desires, but she forced herself to smile and say nothing.

His eagerness got them across the lake in record time. By the time they'd reached the island, the others had only made it halfway.

Bianca climbed out of the boat before Corbin could offer his hand, and just as she was congratulating herself on managing to keep him from touching her, she felt his arms close around her waist like the cinch of a saddle.

He inhaled deeply as his lips grazed her throat. "By all that's holy, you're beautiful. I can scarcely wait to find out what you taste like."

Ravens with red-stained beaks, dripping gobbets of flesh. Bianca gave a delicate shudder. He would never taste her, alive or dead.

She twisted out of his grasp, bit down hard on her lip, and vanished from sight.

Thirty-Six

For what Vasco knew was the thirteenth time, though it wouldn't be the last, he said, "I already told you. I've come to speak to the king. He offered a reward for anyone who can solve the mystery of the shoes danced to pieces, and I have his answer."

But the guards at the palace laughed, taunted him, or bluntly told him they'd heard nothing about any such thing, and that he would never be granted entry to the palace, let alone the king's court.

Worse, Vasco knew how crazy he sounded. Were he a guard, he would probably behave much like these men were doing. But that didn't change the fact that Bianca was in danger, and he needed to speak to the king in order to keep her safe. Nothing else mattered.

Finally, he gusted a huge, sorrowful sigh and thanked the guards for their patience. He trudged across the courtyard and rounded a corner where he figured he'd be out of their line of sight. In a practiced motion, he swung his cloak around his shoulders and fastened it, before bring the hood up over his head. A moment passed and he could see through the thick wool as if it didn't exist, yet he knew he was invisible to everyone else. Kun had used powerful magic when she cast the invisibility spell on this cloak. He wished he'd had a second one to give Bianca to keep her safe from those raven princes.

As it was, he needed to hurry. Time was of the essence.

He strode past the guards, then a second

set, and a third. Though he had never been to the capital before, the king's court was the subject of legend – everyone knew it was in the highest hall, in the very heart of the palace. So up he went, sweeping past anyone who might have stopped him if they could see him, until he stood at bottom of the steps to the very doors themselves.

Which swung shut before he could set his foot on the first step.

"There will be no further audience with the king today. If you have a petition, return tomorrow," a guard in a fancy uniform shouted to the crowd.

People grumbled and slowly dispersed.

Vasco hesitated for a moment, but the thought of Bianca spurred him on. The king was her father. It was his responsibility, nay, his duty to keep her safe. The king would see him. And if there was no audience, then there would be no one to interrupt him before he told his tale.

His knee was stiff from riding and walking

so far, so he laboured up the steps like an old man. When he reached the top, he had to push against the doors with his whole weight, for they were heavier than he'd thought. The stories about the doors were true, then – they were made of solid gold, or at least solid metal, for no timber was that heavy.

"I told you, no more petitioners!" a man roared from the opposite end of the huge hall that was the king's court. A look of puzzlement crossed his face as he rose from his ornate throne. This man was the king, and Bianca's father.

Vasco continued until he reached the foot of the dais that held the king's throne. Only then did he fall to one knee as he whipped off his cloak. "Forgive me, your majesty, but your daughters are in great danger."

The king jumped a foot off the ground. Given the man was wearing enough metal to make armour for three men, that was quite a feat. "Where did you come from?"

"The Summer Palace, where your daughter,

Princess Bianca, bade me give you this." Vasco held out the ring he'd pulled from her finger. "Your steward has made a deal with demons, who even now are trying to seduce your daughters so that they might kill and eat them."

These words started an uproar among the crowd of people who remained in what Vasco realised wasn't an empty court after all.

The king held up his hands for silence. "Silence! I will hear what this man has to say!" he roared. In a slightly quieter tone, he added, "Where are my daughters now?"

"The Summer Palace still, I hope, but if the demons have succeeded, then they are on an island in the middle of the lake beside the palace. There is an underground chamber beneath the lake where – "

The king cut him off. "We will leave for the Summer Palace at once. No demon will steal my daughters from me." He snapped his fingers. "Have every soldier in the capital assembled on the training grounds outside the city before the sun sets. Let it be known that the man who kills the most demons may choose one of my daughters as his bride!"

Vasco had a vision of himself slaughtering every one of those raven princes, before asking the king for Bianca. He almost laughed at the vision.

"What is funny?" the king demanded. "Why do you smile so?"

Vasco lifted his gaze to meet that of the king. "No part of this is funny, your majesty. But the thought of killing demons to save your daughters brings a fierce joy to my breast that I cannot help but smile at. No demon can withstand the might you will bring to bear on them. They will be crushed, as they should be."

"Yes, they will," the king said darkly.

Thirty-Seven

"Princess? Bianca, where are you?" Corbin called.

Pressed against the trunk of the nearest tree, Bianca suppressed the urge to shout back that she was out of reach, so he would never touch her again. She had first discovered her magical talents when playing hide and seek with her sisters. If she stayed still and made no sound, they would never find her.

Other boats landed on the beach, spilling out their passengers.

"Where is Bianca?" Hazel asked.

"I don't know," Corbin said. "One moment she was in my arms, begging for a kiss, and the next…she was stolen from me. I saw a shadow and then she just…disappeared. Whoever took her, I will hunt him down and make him pay!"

Liar, Bianca thought furiously. Corbin hadn't seen any shadow. With a chill, she realised his anger wasn't directed at some imagined captor, but at her. If he caught her, he intended to make her pay.

Never.

"She can't have left the island," one of the other princes said reasonably. "If we spread out and search, we will find her, and whoever has taken her."

"I'll take the princesses to the ballroom, where they will be safe. No need to risk losing anyone else this night," another man said.

"No." This time the voice was female — Brenna's. She continued, "Our sister is missing. She knows us, and will answer our calls. We can help you search, so that she will be found faster. The sooner she is found, the sooner we will all be married."

Bianca wasn't sure whether Brenna or her other sisters knew about her magical abilities. Her mother had insisted she keep it a secret in the harem, but in a place where secrets were the highest form of currency, even the most carefully whispered confidence could be betrayed.

A brief argument ensued between Corbin and Brenna, but when the other girls weighed in, the princes were forced to concede.

They didn't want to lose all their brides. One was bad enough, but a dozen rebellious princesses spelled disaster for their plot. Bianca couldn't have planned this better if she'd tried. If only she had a plan at all.

"Fiachra, you search the ballroom. Cormac and Guntram, take the west thicket. Raban and Ronne…" Corbin divided them into six search parties that set off across the island. That left just him and Bianca on the beach.

"Where are you, princess?" he whispered. "I

know you can't have gone far. You are dressed for a ball, not a walk in the woods. It will go easier if you show yourself. The longer I have to hunt for you, the worse it will be for you when I do find you. And I will. Of all my brothers, I have always been the best hunter. It is fitting that the curse that began with a hunt will end with the best one of all, for the sweetest quarry in the world is a woman."

He had done this before, Bianca realised in horror. The bleached bones on the beach…did some of them belong to women? Or did he mean he'd been cursed for hunting women in the woods for sport?

Not just him. His brothers, too. For they were all cursed, not just him.

She couldn't let him find her. She would die, as would all her sisters, and no one would ever know how it had happened. The princes could kill again, and again, and there would be no one to stop them.

Why hadn't her magic included fireballs or the ability to kill just by looking at someone?

Then she could fight and defend her sisters, ending these wicked princes forever. Not hug trees and hide, which is all she could do with her invisibility.

If she weren't so clumsy, she might have moved to a better spot, but all it would take was one sound and Corbin would know where she was, invisible or not.

A shrill scream ripped through the air, before a second joined it.

Two of her sisters had found the black beach, Bianca guessed.

Corbin swore and dashed in the direction of the screams.

Bianca took her chance, climbing into the nearest boat. They were all drawn up on shore so close to one another that it was almost easy to move from one to the other without needing to touch the ground. Or leave footprints, which she knew would be her undoing. She chose a boat that was closest to the water, hemmed in by other vessels that the princes would have to climb over in order to reach her. That would take time, and hopefully allow her to get away if they found her. Not that she knew how to paddle a boat, but it hadn't looked that hard when Corbin did it. If only she could make the boat invisible the way she'd done with Vasco for a moment before she lost consciousness. Because it wasn't just the boat she had to make invisible. It was the boat and the surface of the water beneath it and…

"Take her down to the ballroom and make her drink some wine," one of the men said.

Bianca ducked low, so only her eyes were above the gunwale of the boat. One of the princes tramped past, carrying a woman in his arms. She thought it might be Aruna, who'd been wearing a golden dress. He was followed by another pair. Nera's eyes stared at nothing as she walked like a woman in a dream. The prince beside her gripped her arm, tugging her along like she was a dawdling child.

Bianca ached to help them, but if she revealed herself, there was little she could do.

No, her strength lay in hiding. If she could hide until dawn, the princes would turn back into birds and then she could help her sisters escape. Until then…she had to stay concealed.

Bianca settled in the bottom of the boat, out of sight even if she wasn't invisible. She liked the way the waves lapped at the boat, rocking it. So soothing. One day, when all this was over, she'd like to sleep in a boat. She'd heard of an ancient queen who had a pleasure barge that she sailed up and down the river. Bianca didn't need a whole barge. Just a boat big enough for her to lie down in. Just let it drift…

"She's escaping in the boat!"

Jolted from sleep, Bianca sat up. How had she fallen asleep? She stretched, knowing the stiffness in her limbs and the lightening sky meant she'd slept for several hours. And while she'd slumbered, as if responding to her unspoken command, the boat had drifted away from the shore with her in it. Now, she floated halfway between the island and the shore. That meant only half the distance to pole, she thought to herself, searching for the long paddle she'd seen the princes use.

Only…it wasn't in the boat. No pole or paddle or anything. Just the empty boat with her in it, while the princes had all the others at their disposal. They would catch up to her in minutes, drag her back to the island, and force her to marry that hateful man.

Bianca peered at the island. Through the mist, she couldn't tell if they were following her or not. It looked like the boats were still pulled up on shore.

The sun peeked above the horizon, blinding her as it turned the mist into blazing gold.

Then out of the mist flew a murder of crows.

Thirty-Eight

The king maintained a slow but steady pace that drove Vasco mad. Every moment, Bianca could be in more danger, yet the king seemed to be in no hurry. More than once, Vasco found himself drifting off to sleep, but he knew he could not. Bianca depended on him to bring help, and he would. He rode with an army at his back and her father, the king…well, he didn't ride precisely at his side, for the king's personal guard surrounded him, but Vasco was still close.

Finally, Vasco started to recognise the trees along the way. He knew they were near the Summer Palace when they passed Kun's cottage. Night was draining away, as the predawn light began to illuminate their path. One by one, they extinguished their torches, but still they rode. There would be no stopping until they reached the Summer Palace and saved the princesses.

What the king would say when he saw the demons were merely ravens, Vasco did not know, but nor did he care. The king could do whatever he liked with him, as long as Bianca was safe.

The Summer Palace loomed into view, a shadow between them and the lake.

"Summon the Lord Steward," the king commanded. A squad of soldiers dismounted and marched toward the door.

Vasco shook his head. The Lord Steward didn't matter. It was the princes who were the problem. "They will be on the lake," he said, directing his horse on a different path that led to the beach, or so he thought. Instead, he emerged beside the deserted archery range.

A single boat drifted into view, ominously empty.

Vasco heard shouts, but he wasn't sure whether they came from the island or the army behind him. He didn't care.

A chill breeze rippled the water of the lake, sending the boat in a lazy circle.

Shivering, Vasco pulled his cloak around him.

He glimpsed movement and then, a figure rose from the boat. Though he could only see her head and shoulders, he would know Bianca's pale hair anywhere. She was alive and unharmed. He was not too late.

Dawn kissed the horizon, setting her hair ablaze and turning the mist behind her into a glorious halo.

Yet in the light, there were shadows. First one, then two, then a dozen crows came flying out of the mist, arrowing straight for her.

No.

Vasco reached for his bow and strung it like a man in a dream. Nock, draw, aim, loose, the wind seemed to whisper, and he obeyed, like the good soldier he was.

"That's impossible!"

"It must be five hundred feet!"

"No one can shoot that far."

"Why is he shooting birds on an empty boat?"

Vasco paid no heed to the men behind him. His first arrow hit its target, a bird extending its talons toward Bianca's face. The bird flipped over and over before landing in the water with a splash.

All at once, a great wind ruffled the water, making it rise up in waves that carried the boat away from the stricken bird.

The ravens converged on their injured fellow, hiding it from sight for a moment before they rose up in one flock, flying over the lake and away across the forest. The body of the bird Vasco had shot had vanished.

Vasco paid no attention to the birds. His

gaze was fixed on the boat making its way steadily to shore. It grounded on the bank just below him, and he ran to meet it, catching the edge of it so that the boat would not drift away again, no matter how the waves sucked at it.

Huddled in the bottom, her arms covered with cuts as they shielded her head, was Bianca.

Gently, Vasco reached for her, wrapping her in his cloak as he lifted her from the boat. "You're safe, princess," he murmured.

Bianca blinked. "Vasco?" She bit her lip, then seemed to shimmer like sun on the water.

"He has one of the princesses! She was hiding in the boat!" A great shout went up, carried by a multitude of throats.

"But where are the others?"

"Underground." Bianca cleared her throat, then tried again, louder this time. "They are in a chamber under the island. They needed all of us to break the curse. But they didn't get me. I'll show you where they are."

Vasco's arms tightened around her. "No. I

will show them. You will stay here in the palace, safe under your father's care." There were few men he trusted, but the king was Bianca's father. If anyone could keep her safe, he could.

Reluctantly, he surrendered the woman he loved to her father, and set off to save her sisters.

Thirty-Nine

By the time the sun had burned away the mist, Bianca stood with her sisters beside the archery range. No other space was big enough to hold all of the warriors the king had brought with him. She'd never seen so many men in one place, but she had eyes only for one. Vasco stood beside the king, looking as tired as she felt, but none of that mattered. Sleep could wait, for her future hung in the balance. Hers, and Vasco's.

Efe lay at her father's feet in chains,

shouting about liars and traitors and all manner of insults that Bianca had never heard of, but they evidently offended someone, because one of the men guarding him pounded him with the butt of his spear until the steward fell silent.

"You spoke of demons, but my men have found none. My steward says you imprisoned my daughters, but you insist upon blaming these demons. I will have the truth!" the king boomed.

Brenna stumbled forward. Her pink dress was smudged with black, as though she had fallen on the black beach. "The demons looked like men, claiming to be handsome princes who were our rightful bridegrooms, but they were beset by a terrible curse. By night, they danced and laughed and seduced us with lies. And by day…they turned into great black birds that ate corpses. I saw the bodies of those they had killed. And I saw with my own eyes as the sun rose…the men turned into birds and flew away."

"And what of this man?" The king pointed at Vasco.

Brenna shrugged. "He is some fool the Lord Steward employed to amuse us at dinner."

The king began to laugh. "A fool who sees true while my own daughters are foolish enough to fall for the lies told by demons?"

"Not all your daughters, sire. One fought them, and very nearly escaped, too." Vasco smiled at Bianca. "Perhaps I am a fool, but I was once a soldier. And I would defend your daughters with my life, even from demons."

"A soldier who shot one of the demons, too. Where is the monster's body?" the king asked.

"It seems the demons took the body with them when they left, your majesty," one of his personal guard said. "We saw the bird fall, but they gathered it up. Perhaps they are cannibals."

Bianca's stomach churned. She did not want to think of the princes' eating habits. She would have nightmares about blood-smeared beaks until the day she died.

Efe started shouting about liars and traitors and whores.

The king unsheathed his sword and set it at the bastard's throat. "You dare to call my daughters whores? You, a lying traitor who sold them to demons?"

A pained gurgle was the last sound Efe made before the king silenced him forever. Bianca turned her eyes away from the blood staining the sand. She had seen enough blood and death to last her a lifetime.

"So, after punishments, we come to rewards. It seems I owe you a reward, soldier. You saved my daughters' lives, yet the demons were allowed to escape. What will stop them from returning?" the king asked.

Vasco stepped forward. "I will. I shall set up camp on the island and should they ever return, I will slaughter them all."

"It seems to me there's a perfectly good house here. A fitting reward for a hero. I shall make you Lord of Raven Lake Estate, and you and your heirs will hold it against all enemies, demon or human," the king declared.

Vasco's mouth dropped open. Bianca almost laughed. Had he truly meant to camp on the island?

It was Bianca's turn to step forward. "That is not enough. He deserves more reward than just the house. He came to the Summer Palace to solve a mystery. You promised that anyone who could discover where the princesses went at night and danced their shoes to pieces might have both the house and a bride."

The king stared at her. Bianca knew she should bow her head, as any woman in his harem would, but she had endured too much from men tonight to bow to any of them.

"I made no such promise, and I have heard of no such mystery," he declared.

Bianca opened her mouth to protest.

"But I will honour it, all the same," the king continued. "Lord Vasco, in addition to this estate, you will need heirs to maintain the vigil when you are gone. For that, you will need a wife. I give you your choice of my daughters to be your bride."

Vasco's eyes met Bianca's, and it seemed like there was no one else in the world but the two of them. She wished with all her might that he would choose her.

"I am but a soldier, though you honour me with more than I deserve," Vasco said carefully. "Your daughters are jewels indeed, worthy to be the brides of kings and princes. To them, I was but a fool at their table, not worthy of a princess for a wife, as I am sure they will tell you, if you but ask them. I will not marry a woman against her will."

The king glared at the girls. Several of them, already overcome by their ordeal, cringed away from his gaze.

Bianca stood firm. "I volunteer." She met her father's eyes once more. "He saved my life, and that of my sisters. I, Princess Bianca, would be honoured to be the wife of Lord Vasco." This time, she forced herself to drop a deep curtsey, first to her father, then to Vasco.

"I've had my fill of princes and I will be happy never to meet another. Soldiers have far more honour than any prince."

Muffled laughter came from the assembled soldiers, which quickly died when the king held up his hands for silence.

"What do you say, Lord Vasco?" the king asked.

"The honour is mine," Vasco replied.

Bianca wasn't sure whose smile beamed brighter – hers, or Vasco's.

Forty

Vasco and Bianca were married that day, so the king could return home safely with his daughters. His guards kept a close watch on the traitorous steward, as if they thought his corpse might spring back to life again, and stuck him in a cart alongside the barrel of poisoned wine.

The girls huddled together in a second cart, barely saying a word, aside from a listless farewell to Bianca as their own cart rattled off down the road.

Leaving Bianca alone with her husband. A man she suddenly didn't know what to say to.

"Oh, good. I caught you before you dragged him off to bed," an elderly voice cackled.

Kun. Of all the things to say…Bianca felt her face grow red.

Vasco curled an arm around Bianca's waist and bowed to the old woman. "So you have heard our news, then. I couldn't have done this alone, and I will be forever grateful. You will be welcome in my home whenever you wish. Without your help – "

Kun laughed. "Without my help? You mean her help." She pointed a wrinkled finger at Bianca. "The invisibility cloak was her doing. She wanted answers, and she knew you stood a better chance of getting them than she could. After a few days of watching you work, she was itching to be your prize."

"My…prize?" Vasco stared at Bianca, before understanding dawned on his face. "So you truly did want to marry me? Not out of pity, or duty?" His eyes held so much hope.

No matter how brightly her face burned, Bianca forced herself to tell him the truth. "Every day you worked on Kun's house, I watched, invisible," she confessed. "Until one day when you were outside, I asked Kun to send you up to the palace to solve the mystery. I cast the spell on your cloak that rendered you invisible. I hoped that if I helped you, you might choose me." She frowned. "I had no idea that Kun didn't tell you that part of the reward."

Kun cackled. "It would have distracted him. Thinking about his house and which girl he wanted for his wife. That's what killed the others. Distracted by a pretty girl who brings him a cup of wine, sending him dreaming of all the things he might do to her when they are married..." She flashed a gummy grin. "Oh, but I forgot. You two are married, and ready to do something about those dreams, I am sure. But humour an old lady for a moment. I have something to show you." She led them through the house to the room where the girls had once slept, now home to their discarded finery that would have to be sent up to the capital after them.

The trapdoor creaked open, moving without anyone touching the lever that normally worked the mechanism.

"How did you..." Bianca began, but Kun waved her into silence, beckoning them to follow her down the steps. Swallowing, Bianca did as she was bidden. It was daylight now, and there were no raven princes to attack or attempt to seduce her, but she couldn't suppress the thought that last night, she'd almost...

Vasco's arms wrapped reassuringly around her waist as if he could read her thoughts. "Don't you worry at all. If those accursed birds come anywhere near us again, I will pepper them so full of arrows, they'll look like they've grown a second set of feathers. I might not be accustomed to owning lands and being the lord responsible for them, but I have plenty of experience in defending them. I promised to keep you safe, Bianca, and I will."

She relaxed into his embrace, for she believed every word. And it felt good to be in his arms, his hard body pressed against hers, his breath on her neck…she wanted to turn around, take him back up the steps and do all the things married women did to the husband they loved. Maybe even let him do some things to her, too.

"I don't have all day!" Kun said. "You have all night to get naked, and the rest of your lives to work out what to do with each other. Can't an old lady ask for a few minutes of your time?"

Red-faced once more, Bianca continued down the steps with Vasco not far behind.

Kun led them down the path to the lake. Bianca didn't feel self-conscious at all as she grabbed Vasco's hand. After last night, she never wanted to walk this way alone. He squeezed her fingers gently and limped on at her side.

They reached the spot where Vasco had

tripped that first night, almost giving himself away, and Kun stopped.

"This is it," she muttered, biting down on her lip. She waved her hands, an intense look of concentration on her face as she stared at the pile of rocks.

To Bianca's surprise, the topmost boulder rolled down, settling to the side of the road. The pile that had stretched higher than Bianca's head now arranged themselves in a rough ring. Around them, a small stream of water trickled, which had been hidden by the rocks before. As she watched, one of the tall, narrow stones toppled over, forming a natural drawbridge across the stream into the small fort.

Kun settled on a rock by the side of the path, a satisfied look on her face. "Go in and see."

When Bianca hesitated, Vasco stepped forward. A heartbeat later, she followed. Inside the stone circle was a pool, which was rapidly filling with water. Water that sent up wisps of mist or steam. Magic, surely.

"It's a hot spring," Kun said. "The earth has spots like this around, and if I'd left it alone, this one might have built enough pressure to blow some of the rocks off one day. Maybe not this week, but when your children take over the estate. Or their children. If you ever get around to having any."

"I have heard of places like this," Vasco said slowly. "They say the hot water works miracles. Healing old wounds, taking away stiffness and pain…"

"Yes," Kun said. "It relaxes you, too. Consider it a wedding present to the two of you." She bit her lip again. "Which reminds me…seeing as that new cloak was really a gift from your new bride, I still owe you a bonus for the service you did me." She bent over before Vasco and made a mysterious gesture with her hand beside his injured leg.

Vasco gave a cry of pain and Bianca's heart leapt into her throat. "What did you do to him?" Bianca demanded.

Kun turned her hand palm-up. Nestled among the wrinkles was a barbed arrowhead, glistening with blood. Vasco's blood, judging by the way he clutched at his knee. "I am no healer, for my talents lie with the earth. Yet what is metal but the bones of earth? Without the arrowhead buried in your knee, your body should heal itself. You may lose that limp and have no need to lean on your lady, as you do now."

Vasco straightened. He stayed that way for barely a moment before Bianca managed to get under his shoulder to take some of his weight off his injured leg again. "I am his support as much as he is mine," Bianca declared.

"A little pain wouldn't stop me from protecting my princess," Vasco added, gazing into Bianca's eyes.

It seemed she stood with him in the underwater ballroom again, drawn to one another like moths to the same flame. Yet Vasco's eyes seemed to burn when he gazed her at her, in a way that kindled a strange heat in Bianca's chest.

"Vasco," she breathed, reaching a hand up to his cheek.

He pulled her hard against him, and kissed her. The fire in her heart blazed, shooting down to curl at her toes. It could burn her to cinders, and she wouldn't care, as long as Vasco didn't stop kissing her.

Several minutes later, Kun's coughing became too alarming to ignore, and they broke off their kiss to stare at the old woman.

"Now, I have other things to take care of." Kun straightened, and it seemed to Bianca that she stood taller all of a sudden. Her hair darkened, too, so that instead of white with strands of black, her hair now looked as sleek as a raven's wing. When she turned around, Bianca barely recognised her. Why, Kun looked younger than her own mother – not much older than Bianca herself. This strange, young Kun laughed, her voice rich and full, without any of the tremors of old age. "Did you truly think me just some weak witch, girl, like your queen? I am an enchantress, gifted in elemental magic, though my affinity has always been with the earth. At the queen's request, for she is my god daughter, for good or ill, I kept those princes prisoner here. I fed them those foolish enough to fall under their spell, or the spell of greed, in the case of those silly boys who saw an easy way to win a wife and property. But they have flown, and my vigil is ended. So, while I thank you for your kind invitation, I will not accept your hospitality at this time. I am needed elsewhere. Perhaps we will meet again, far into the future. My best wishes for your health and happiness, both of you, because I think you two truly have a good chance of living happily ever after."

With that, she traced a fiery circle in the air, stepped through it, and vanished.

Forty-One

Bianca stared after Kun, barely believing her eyes. Then Vasco's arms snaked around her waist, and she could think of no one else but her husband. She turned around. "Kiss me again, just like the first time."

The moment his lips touched hers, desire ignited her whole body once more, and she was surprised to hear her own voice moaning in pleasure.

He broke for breath and grinned at her. "You taste of paradise, princess. But you are wearing too many clothes for my liking." He tugged at the lacing of her gown, which had somehow come undone as they kissed.

She glanced around. "We should go inside for that."

He laughed. "Why? It would be a shame not to use Mistress Kun's wedding gift. And for that, you must be naked."

The hot spring. How had she forgotten?

Vasco stripped off his own clothes, laying them on a rock, then stepped into the pool. Just as she remembered it, his body was all muscle. Once again, she couldn't help staring.

"You may come and touch me instead of just looking if you take your clothes off," he teased.

Her mouth suddenly seemed dry as she fumbled to finish unlacing her gown. She laid it beside his clothes and stood before him only in her shift. "But what if someone sees us? Out here, naked like this?" she asked.

He laughed. "Then you will use your magic to make us invisible. Or I will tell them to go away. This is our estate now, and I am the lord here."

Lord Vasco. She liked the sound of it. Bianca dropped a curtsey, flaring out the hem of her shift. "My lord," she said, pulling the shift off entirely.

Now she found Vasco's eyes on her, devouring her like a starving man might with his first meal. Yet in his eyes, such hunger only inflamed her own.

She stepped cautiously into the water, which now reached just past her knees.

Vasco settled on a natural stone ledge that seemed a perfectly formed seat for two. He patted the place beside him. "Come sit with me, princess. I want you close enough to kiss."

But Bianca wanted more than a kiss. For a girl who'd lived in a harem all her life, she'd never actually touched a naked man, and she wanted to. She took a deep breath as she crossed the pool, then climbed into his lap and kissed him.

Bianca gasped as she felt him hardening

between her thighs. In the harem, the women whispered that if you rode a man just right, he could make your soul take flight. More than anything, she wanted to know what that felt like. She'd tried it on one of the statues in the palace once, but all she'd experienced was pain as she left a smear of blood on the statue's nethers. She hadn't wanted to try again, but with a living, breathing man between her thighs who could turn her whole body to flame with a kiss, she knew it would be different.

She rocked against him, and Vasco groaned. Perhaps they could fly together. She reached down and guided him inside her as she rocked again.

One moment she was empty and aching for him, and the next she was so full of the hard heat of him that she could scarcely breathe. All she knew was she did not want to stop. "More," she gasped.

"Bianca…Bee…" he groaned. "I do not wish to hurt you. This is your first time. Perhaps we should…"

"You're not hurting me. I want more," she insisted. When still he hesitated, she opened her thighs wider, sliding down his shaft until her knees touched the stone beneath him. She cried out as he filled her completely, revelling in the sheer pleasure of having him inside her as she rode him to heights of pleasure she had only dreamed of before.

All at once, he shuddered into stillness, her name on his lips until she kissed him. Then there was silence, except for their shared breathing and the bubbling of the spring around them. The water had reached her breasts, buoying them up before her.

Vasco stared at her in wonderment. "I feel like a king. No man could ask for more."

Bianca laughed. "Ah, but I am just a princess. As long as you are my husband, I will always want more."

"And I shall always give you what you desire, though perhaps not right away." Vasco kissed her again, long and lovingly, setting the pattern for the first of many nights in their long lives together.

Silence: Little Mermaid Retold

DEMELZA CARLTON

A tale in the Romance a Medieval Fairy Tale series

One

The ocean sang in harmony with the oncoming storm. Though she stood on deck, Margareta could hear the song so clearly she wanted to join in. Three times the captain had tried to persuade her to go below decks, or into his cabin at the very least, but she hadn't budged. As long as a single man stood on deck, so would she.

Besides, the cabin was crowded enough

with the young prince, his entourage and the cloying reek of seasickness.

She smelled it first, before the fine down on her bare forearms stood on end. Then blinding light erupted from the deck, consuming the mast before splashing across the sky. She clapped her hands over her ears, but it did little to quiet the thunderclap when it came.

After that, silence descended on the ship, for the thunderclap had deafened them all.

When the smoking mast cracked into pieces, smashing through the cabin and all those within, no one heard their screams, or the horrible ripping squeal as the ship's beams broke asunder, surrendering to the sea.

While panicked sailors raced around, trying to put out the fires or save themselves, Margareta sat on the deck and calmly removed her shoes and stockings. There wasn't time for more, as the deck was already awash. The ocean licked at her bare toes, enticing her in.

Margareta climbed over the railing, until there was nothing between her and the waves below. She closed her eyes and dropped, feeling the ocean's cold embrace welcoming her home.

It would be so easy to change into a more suitable form for swimming, and let her mermaid instincts take her to depths where no human could follow, but Margareta resisted. She was supposed to be on the surface, not in the sea. She was the daughter of the Master of Beacon Isle, and Beacon Isle was where she belonged right now.

The island was miles away, and it would be a much easier journey in a boat than relying on her own fins. Maybe one of the lighters had survived intact.

Margareta surfaced to survey the wreckage floating amid the waves. A hatch cover, what looked like a cabin door, barrels, corpses, the curve of an overturned boat…

Smiling, Margareta swam for the boat. A well-placed wave set it right way up. All she had to do was climb in and the ocean would take her home.

She had one hand on the gunwale when she clearly heard someone shout, "For God's sake, help me!" before the words ended in a gurgle.

Among the floating corpses was someone who wasn't dead yet, though he would be soon, if no one helped him. He clung to a splintered chunk of mast that rolled in the waves like a drunken sailor. As Margareta watched, it rolled him under the water before bringing him to the surface again, coughing and spluttering.

"Help!"

Margareta did. Guiding the boat to his side, she reached out to haul him in. He was heavier than she expected, though he was the same size as she, and the boat nearly capsized, but water was her element, so Margareta won him from the ocean.

He flopped into the bottom of the boat, the most unlikely catch ever landed. His fine clothes marked him as one of the prince's entourage, but his gasping mouth made him look more like a fish.

"You're just a girl!" he said.

She was far more than just a girl, but Margareta had more important matters to attend to than educating one of the prince's servants. "I'm the girl who saved your life, and I'd have thought you'd have learned better manners as the prince's pageboy."

"Squire," the boy corrected. "I am…I mean, I was…Prince Philip's squire." He was silent for a moment. "They're all dead now, aren't they? He asked me to fetch them some wine, so I was on deck when the mast crashed into the cabin. It must have crushed them instantly."

Margareta surveyed the corpses, then closed her eyes. "Yes, they are all dead. We are the only ones left, and to survive, we must reach the shore. Do you think you can – "

She should have kept her eyes on the ocean, for she knew how treacherous it could be. One moment they were in the boat, the next a wave sent them tumbling back into the water.

Margareta came up cursing. She'd bitten her

lip, so it was with blood on her tongue that she commanded the ocean to do her bidding. The waves brought the boat to her, but the boy was nowhere to be seen. "Find him," she said tersely, ducking under the surface to search for herself.

A glint caught her eye – metal reflecting the lightning above – and she dived, shifting to her tail to give her the power to drag the boy back to the surface. This time, she made the waves lift him into the boat as she hauled herself aboard.

"Take us home," she ordered, and the waves obeyed, parting to form a path before her as a powerful surface current pushed the boat along it.

Satisfied that the ocean would continue to do her bidding without her watching, Margareta turned her attention to the boy. There was no gasping now, nor breathing, either.

"Don't you die on me, squire, or I'll throw you back over the side," she threatened.

No response.

"I saved your life, so it belongs to me, not the ocean. You hear me? No dying on me, now!"

She pounded his chest and back until he coughed up the water he'd swallowed and began to breathe again.

"Who are you?" he croaked out.

"I'm the girl who saved your life," she said again. "So what's your name, squire?"

He mumbled something that Margareta couldn't quite make out, but before she could ask him to repeat it, he fell back against the boards, unconscious. At least he was alive.

Leaving the stormy ocean in her wake, Margareta's vessel sailed for home.

Two

The journey took so long, Margareta stretched out along the bottom of the boat with the boy to get some sleep. She didn't wake until she felt the keel scrape along the sand, and then it was to the bewildering sight of the boy's arms wrapped around her, as she embraced him. She only had a moment to reflect on it, before a wave tipped the boat over on its side and they both tumbled out onto the wet sand.

The wave retreated faster than it had advanced, taking the boat with it.

Margareta considered for a moment, then let the sea have its fun. She had no further need of the boat, for she was back at Beacon Isle. She felt refreshed by her swim and short voyage, but the boy looked the worse for wear. That he was still unconscious worried her. She dragged him further up the beach, out of reach of the playful waves, but still he didn't rouse. Perhaps he had been injured. The surgeon in Harbour Town would know what to do.

She rose, straightened her salt-dampened gown, and marched up to her father's house. Pausing only to ask a maid to have some water sent up to her chamber so that she might wash, Margareta headed for her father's chamber, where she was certain he would be at this time of the morning.

"Good morning, Father," she greeted the Master of Beacon Isle. "We have a man on the beach in need of medical attention. A boy, really, but he claimed to be the prince's squire before he nearly drowned."

"Good morning, Margareta. I – " Father

broke off to peer at her. "I thought the *Golden Eagle* wasn't due back in port until tomorrow. I didn't hear it return."

"And you won't," Margareta said bluntly. "It was more of a wallowing duck than any kind of eagle. The stupid captain sailed her into a storm and she sank."

Father sighed. "Margareta, what have I said about sinking ships? I realise it is your nature, but – "

"It wasn't me!" she protested. "I haven't sunk a ship in my life! I told the captain about the storm, but he didn't listen. Lightning struck the mast and it exploded into flaming pieces. There was little I could do but return home."

"What of the prince? The captain and his crew?"

Margareta sighed with genuine regret. "Dead. All dead. Except for the boy I left on the beach, of course. If he survives. Can you send a surgeon down there, please, and some strong men to carry him to the house?"

"What, aren't you going to carry him up

here yourself? You've played the knight in shining armour, rescuing him and all. Let him play the swooning princess while you carry him up to your chambers to seduce him." Father grinned as though he'd made the best joke.

Margareta frowned. "I don't intend to seduce him. The boy nearly died. You must think me a monster, Father, if you believe I would do such a thing. I…I'm going to wash, and change into fresh things that aren't encrusted in salt. Please have someone see to the boy." Not waiting for her father's response, she swept out of the solar.

Three

Erik drifted, dreaming of a mermaid who had saved him. A few times, he could have sworn he felt her in his arms, like one of the sirens in the stories. But sirens lured men to their deaths, just as mermaids dragged mariners to the depths of the sea. He'd never heard a tale about one who saved people.

When he awoke alone on the sand, he was disappointed. Oh, not that he wasn't dead — that he was quite relieved about, or he would be, once he worked out where the mermaid had gone.

Perhaps she had only left to get her sisters, and together they would finish him off.

"Is he dead?" a male voice asked.

Erik leaped to his feet. He found himself face to face with three fishermen, their arms full of fishing nets. "Prince Philip is dead," he said.

One of the men shrugged. "Don't know any princes. But dead men don't talk or jump, so I'd say he's not dead."

"He looked dead," one of the others said.

"Maybe he's like that miracle man who came back to life," the third ventured eagerly.

Erik didn't feel like a miracle man, nor did he deserve it, if Philip was dead and he yet lived. "Is there a town nearby? Or somewhere I might find a ship? I must go home to tell the king about Prince Philip."

"Up that way, just over the dune," the first man said, pointing. "White Harbour always has some ships coming and going."

Erik thanked them and trudged toward what

turned out to be a sizeable town, clustered around a busy harbour that he recognised as the one at Beacon Isle. Could it really have been less than a week since he sailed out of this very harbour?

He enquired at the docks, and soon found a vessel willing to carry him and his ill tidings home, though for a price.

"Do you have any coin to pay for the passage, boy?" the captain asked, squinting at him.

Erik reached for his belt, where he still carried Philip's purse. He had coin enough to pay for the passage of their entire party home, but he knew better than to say so. "Will two silvers buy me a cabin on a ship that sails on the next tide?" he asked innocently, showing the captain his two coins while palming a third.

"The next tide?" The captain's eyes widened. "I had not thought to leave until the morrow. Rounding up the crew, loading the cargo…these things take time. But for three silver coins, I might manage it." He held out his hand a little too eagerly for Erik's liking.

Erik sighed and counted the coins mournfully into the captain's outstretched hand. "Very well. Show me to my cabin."

The cabin the captain ushered him into was barely big enough to hold a bed, but Erik didn't care. He stretched out on the pallet and stared at the wooden ceiling, wishing he wasn't the one who would have to tell his parents that their favourite son was dead. Maybe that's why the mermaid had spared him: she knew a worse fate awaited him if he lived.

All too soon, the ship cast off, and he felt the lull of the waves once more. Erik surrendered to sleep, only to dream of a mermaid who rocked him in her arms.

Four

When she was dry and dressed, Margareta returned to the beach where she'd left the boy. She was surprised to find no one but a few fishermen mending their nets, like they normally did in the afternoon. Her father had heard her, after all, she marvelled.

But when she asked the servants which guest quarters he'd been given, no one could tell her anything. It was as though none of them had yet seen him. Her father would know, she was sure of it, so Margareta marched back to her father's solar to ask him.

She found him bowed over the desk, with his head in his hands.

"What's wrong, Father?" she asked. "Is he dead?"

He glanced up. "Who?"

"The boy on the beach." Margareta wished she'd thought to ask the squire's name.

"I know nothing of any boy, except my own. And they have flown." He sighed heavily. "Something terrible has happened to your brothers."

Margareta clutched the table so hard her knuckles went white. "What happened? They're not dead, are they?"

He shook his head. "No, but they may as well be. While they were hunting, they met a witch, who took offence at some imagined slight. Before they could stop her, she cursed them. All of them. She turned them into birds and made them fly far away."

Knowing her brothers, the slight was probably not imagined, Margareta knew, but she didn't say. For all her reputation for seduction as a siren, even the most chaste of her brothers could boast more romantic conquests than she. Most likely one of them had made a coarse comment, and the others had joined in, until she cursed them all.

"Is there a way the curse can be broken? Did you speak to the witch? Perhaps – " she began.

Father silenced her with a wave of his hand. "She presented herself right here in my solar, and told me she would never lift the curse. But the curse could be lifted by a maiden who loved my boys enough to make a huge sacrifice for them." He reached for her hand. "Margareta, I know you like to save people. Here is your chance. Do you love your brothers?"

She might not like them at times, but… "Yes, I love them," she said steadily.

"Are you willing to make sacrifices to save them?"

Margareta hesitated, before she finally said,

"What kind of sacrifices?"

"She said they could be saved in one of two ways. If each of them could persuade one woman to declare her love and dedicate her life to one of your brothers, a dozen girls in the same night, they might break the curse themselves."

Margareta burst out laughing. "If my brothers — all twelve of them — agreed to get married at all, let alone on the same night, to women who truly loved them…Father, that would be a greater miracle than raising a man from the dead. If that is their only chance, then my brothers are truly lost."

"There is another way."

She managed to stop laughing. "There had better be, or they shall be birds forever."

His grip tightened around her fingers. "If one maiden is willing to sacrifice her voice for as long as it takes to break the curse, they will be set free. She cannot speak or laugh or even whisper."

"One maiden. That would be me, I imagine?

You wish me to be silent for…how long, exactly?"

He shook his head. "I do not know. Weeks. Months. Maybe even years. Until the witch believes you have sacrificed enough to make her lift the curse and restore my sons to me."

"Father, find someone else. I must find the boy. He was unconscious, and needed help. I can't find him if I can't ask anyone about him."

Father captured her other hand, squeezing both in a desperate entreaty. "Margareta, my darling Meg, there is no one else. If you love me, as you love your brothers, you will do this. Save them. I will find a place for you in the priory, and tell them you have taken a vow of silence. You can roam through the rose garden, or spend all day in the library, or do whatever you please, as long as you do it in silence. I beg you to save your brothers."

The library and the rose garden were her two favourite places on the island, as her father knew well. It would mean staying longer on land, too, without returning to the ocean where instinct might take over and make a monster of her as it had so many of her mother's kind. She needed very little persuasion when he offered her such things. But… "What of the boy?" she asked sharply. She needed to know he was safe.

"I will find him, and make sure he is safe. If you will save my sons, my heirs."

Margareta took a deep breath. "All right, Father. I will do it. Silence my voice to save my brothers."

"Thank you!" He threw his arms around her, hugging her as he hadn't since she was a child.

And from that moment, not a sound passed her lips. For her father was right about one thing. If she chose to save someone – be it her brothers from some folly or some nameless squire from a shipwreck – she would not rest until she had succeeded.

Five

For a week, Margareta wandered through the house and the priory like a corporeal ghost. She avoided people she would normally acknowledge, taking her meals alone in her chambers. If it weren't for the library and the rose garden, she would have been bored out of her mind.

All right, she was ready to scream when a thin wail erupted from the other end of the rose garden. Curiosity got the better of her, so Margareta crossed the courtyard to investigate.

The wail issued from a bundle of blankets held tightly to a young woman's breast. The woman herself reclined on a bed of sorts, and she was wrapped in more blankets than her baby.

"Lady Margareta!" the nun exclaimed before dropping a deep curtsey. "Lady Margareta is the Master's daughter. She has taken a vow of silence, in the hope that her sacrifice will persuade the Lord to save her brothers."

Margareta opened her mouth to correct the woman, then remembered and closed it again.

"My lady, may I present Lady Penelope, widow to the late but valiant Sir Godfrey, who died defending the priory?"

Margareta inclined her head. She hadn't heard of any such knight, but if the baby in Lady Penelope's arms was his, he couldn't have died very long ago.

The nun fluttered her hands. "Oh, but you wouldn't have heard about Sir Godfrey's brave deeds, for you had not yet arrived. Lady Penelope, you must tell her."

It was Penelope's turn to duck her head. "Perhaps when I am recovered. I am but recently widowed and I fear the birth of my daughter…"

The nun's hands fluttered more violently. "But of course. Perhaps I should help you inside, so that you can rest?"

Penelope wrinkled her nose. "I much prefer it out here. I'm sure you have better things to do than hover around me all the time. I will be perfectly well here for a while, if Lady Margareta does not mind sharing her garden?"

For all that she wanted to be alone, Margareta knew she would look churlish if she refused. Besides, she was curious about the other woman. And she wanted a peek at the baby.

So Margareta smiled, spreading her arms wide to signify how delighted she was to share the garden her father had planted for her.

As if on cue, a bell tolled.

"Oh! That is the bell for prayers. I must go!" The nun hurried away.

When Margareta was sure the nun was out of earshot, Penelope said, "If you wish me gone, merely nod and I will ask them to take me somewhere else tomorrow. It is so different to things at home. There, I would have a private courtyard where I could sit and my sleeping chamber is just for sleeping. Here…why, the moment I arrived and they found out I was with child, they confined me to a dark room and seemed terrified that some dark spirit might harm me or the baby if a single ray of sunlight or a breath of fresh air reached us. I threatened to walk out here by myself if they did not let me out of that room."

Margareta felt a strong desire never to have children. Not that her father was likely to accept any offer of marriage that came her way, anyway. That would mean giving her a dowry and part of the island, which he would already have to divide between his twelve sons.

Of course, that only strengthened her desire to hold Penelope's child, for if she could never have one of her own…

Margareta held out her arms for the baby.

Penelope looked surprised. "You want to hold her? Sure." She settled the baby in Margareta's arms and sat back. "Her name is Melitta."

Margareta stared at the sleeping child. She weighed next to nothing, yet Melitta held more power over her than the tiny girl would ever know. The aura of magic that swirled around her marked her as a witch. Magic followed bloodlines, which meant her mother might also have some magical talent. Or it could have come from her father, though it was rare for magical ability to manifest in men.

"My husband was a fool," Penelope said. At Margareta's startled glance, she smiled, revealing a spot of blood on her lip from where she'd bitten it to cast what Margareta could only guess was a spell of some kind. "A brave, loyal fool, but no less a fool. What talent she has comes from me, though it is very faint. I thought my mother's bloodline would end with me, until a woman who is what you would call a witch joined our travelling party. Back home, we would call her an enchantress. That's a powerful kind of witch, who can cast many types of spells, not just the one or two that she is best suited to."

Margareta nodded. Penelope would call her an enchantress, too, if she knew, though Margareta's power was limited by her nature. There had never been a mermaid witch before, and it was unlikely that there would be another. She could command water in ways that sent the other merfolk whispering and wishing she were far away, but any other spell – even the slightest blessing or curse – sapped her energy for hours. Penelope's power ran to…telepathy, she thought.

"Reading minds, yes," Penelope said. "Or strong emotions. I cannot change them, but I can perceive them. You should see Melitta's thoughts. Nothing but blurs of colour…and milk." She laughed.

Margareta ached to laugh with her, but she could not. Her father and her brothers depended on her silence. Yet with Penelope, she could perhaps hold something approaching a normal conversation. For the first time in Margareta's life, she wanted a friend. And a baby like Melitta, though motherhood would have to wait.

"I would like that," Penelope said. "Though I will ask one favour. Can you invite me into the garden every day? Arguing with the nuns here nearly wore me out before I made it outside." She winked. "I still might be in my room if I hadn't squeezed out a tear or two as I invoked Saint Godfrey, which is what they'll make of him if they are given their way. A brave, foolish man who would still be alive if he weren't such a brave fool. He should have left matters to the enchantress, as I did." Penelope smiled wanly. "I know you are curious. I will tell you the whole tale one day, but not today. I promise." She reached for the baby and Margareta reluctantly handed Melitta back to her mother.

Penelope's story could wait for another day.

Six

Erik trudged into his father's throne room with his eyes on the stone floor. He didn't want to meet his father's gaze at all, so when he approached the throne, he not only fell to his knees but bowed so low his forehead touched the stone.

"Father, I bring heavy news from Beacon Isle," he said.

The courtiers hushed each other, to better listen to his news.

"Crown Prince Philip is dead, as are all who

sailed with him," Erik continued.

"How did he die?" Father demanded.

"The ship we were on ran into a storm. Lightning struck the mast, which crushed the ship's cabin when it fell. All those within perished, and the ship sank." For the first time, Erik wished he'd been inside the cabin with his brother, for he knew what the king would ask next.

"How did you survive, when your brother perished?"

Erik wished he could bow lower, so that he sank right through the stones. "Philip sent me to fetch more wine, so I wasn't in the cabin. I was thrown into the ocean with everyone else, but by some miracle, I found my way to an undamaged boat, and made my way to shore." A mermaid, not a miracle, Erik was certain, but his father would never believe him. He barely believed himself, and he'd seen her with his own eyes.

"The sea is a perilous mistress, that no man can withstand. Not even a king. Poor Philip,"

Father said gravely.

No man, maybe. But the more Erik thought about it, the more he remembered about his time on that little boat. There'd been a girl, he remembered now. She'd hauled him aboard the boat, but somehow he'd ended up back in the water. That's when he saw the mermaid. Much later, he'd found himself back on board the boat with her, and he'd heard her ordering someone or something to take them home. The mermaids, or maybe even the ocean itself. And he'd arrived safely on the shore, but alone.

She couldn't have perished. It just wasn't possible. He'd return to Beacon Isle and find her and...

"Arise, Sir Erik. As crown prince, you are now heir to the throne in your brother's place," Father said, before the courtiers erupted in applause.

Crown prince? No, he had to return and find her. He'd dreamed of her every night, and every morning felt lost to find her gone.

"You will report back to me here on the morrow. Before you can become king, you have a lot to learn," Father continued.

Erik's heart sank. He resolved to learn all he could about kingship as fast as possible, the sooner to return to the mysterious girl. And he would find her. Some day, some how, he vowed, he would hold her in his arms again.

Seven

Unbeknownst to Margareta or Penelope, the nuns had commissioned a stone plaque to mark Sir Godfrey's grave. The stonemason brought it on his pony cart and the nuns decided to make it into a solemn celebration of the knight's deeds. Penelope and Melitta walked at the head of the procession, followed by most of the priory's residents, who had traded their white robes for mourning black. The pony cart brought up the rear, kicking up a great deal of dust that spurred Margareta to hurry to the front, where she could walk at Penelope's side, ostensibly to offer the widow support.

Penelope walked with her spine straight and her head held high. Her eyes were dry, and though her gown was as black as those worn by the nuns, her face was unshadowed.

Either there was little love between Sir Godfrey and Penelope, or her sorrow ran so deep she could not bear to show it on the surface, Margareta mused. She watched Penelope through the drawn-out erection ceremony, as the knight's monument was carried from the cart to its final resting place over his grave and a great number of prayers were uttered for his soul, but Margareta could not decide the truth of her friend's heart.

She had no chance to ask her during the sombre funeral feast in the priory's great hall, where the silence was broken by Melitta's insistent wail that it was time for her meal, too.

Penelope excused herself and Margareta followed her back to her chambers. The widow and her daughter slept in one of the priory's guest apartments, large, airy rooms with windows facing the sea. Penelope had set up her loom before one of the windows, where the light was brightest, though she had not yet started to make cloth.

Penelope took her accustomed position on the bed, propped up by pillows, as she fed Melitta. Margareta had seen the other woman feed the infant many times, but it still made her hungry for something she could not yet have. Not the milk – there were goats and cows aplenty on the island, and she could send down to the kitchens for fresh milk any time she wanted. No, she wanted a child like Melitta. To beget a child, she would need a husband, though, and would the child be enough to keep her from mourning if she lost her husband?

"You think me heartless, don't you?" Penelope said suddenly. She laughed softly. "No, I am not using magic to read your thoughts. I can see it in your eyes. You think because I do not cry for Godfrey, that I am not prostrate with grief at his passing, that I could not have loved him."

Margareta shook her head, but Penelope had turned her gaze on the baby at her breast.

"You're wrong, you know. He was a good, kind man, and I did love him. Perhaps not as much as he loved me, but then he was passionate in ways that I am not. And it killed him. He believed we were in danger, and he acted recklessly. Without thought. Anyone who'd paused for even a moment's reflection would have seen that the brigands were not interested in me. What was one waddling pregnant woman, when what they really wanted were the novices. Young maidens who were already prepared to serve. I've seen so many such women in the slave markets at home. Maidens fetch a higher price, though they do not remain maidens for long. Too many men believe dipping their wick in one can work miracles, and it's too late for the girls when the men discover what they were told is wrong. The brigands and slave sellers probably spread such rumours themselves, so that they can command a higher price for the girls they capture."

But there were no brigands on Beacon Isle, Margareta knew. Her father would have driven such ruffians off the island in a heartbeat, if he did not choose to hang them. She willed Penelope to read her mind and finally tell her what had happened the night her husband died.

Penelope looked up and her gaze met Margareta's. "I will tell you," she said slowly. "I know you think your rank protects you from the fate awaiting any common-born maiden the slavers capture, but you are wrong in that, too. Without a strong male protector or a powerful enchantress at your side, you are merely property in their eyes – and you can be bought and sold."

And on that chilling note, Penelope began her tale.

Eight

A rare summer storm had closed White Harbour to ships, for the normally calm stretch of water was battered by waves that would break stronger ships than the cog they rode in. The captain dropped anchor on the eastern side of the island, in what he called calm water, and sent them ashore in the boats.

Penelope and the other girls had clung to the sides of the boats as waves rocked them, threatening to capsize them. They were all soaked by the time they reached shore, where the novices huddled in a miserable little flock while one of the sailors headed for the nearest village to ask for a cart to carry the women.

Penelope settled on the sand to wait, for she felt the pains begin again. She didn't think they were birthing pains yet, but Godfrey worried so about her. The cart had been his idea, of course.

Then Kun, the enchantress, came ashore. She was as wet as the rest, for her strength lay in earth and not water magic, but she insisted she knew the island well, and the nearest village was further away than White Harbour, so they might as well walk.

Godfrey had the temerity to protest that Penelope could not walk so far in her condition, but something in her had rebelled at his coddling. She'd heaved herself to her feet, feeling an urge to move.

"But what if the cart comes and finds us gone?" Godfrey asked.

"Then it can come and get us," Kun said with a shrug. The afternoon sun shone, but her dark hair seemed to drink the light instead of reflecting it. Even Godfrey would not look at her for long before turning away.

Kun beckoned for the novices to follow her, and they made a strange procession. Penelope leaned on Godfrey's arm, for the knight's horse had remained aboard the ship and he walked with the rest of them.

They walked through the fields in the afternoon light, so the setting sun was in their eyes when they entered the wood. Penelope welcomed the cool darkness, but there were more than trees waiting for them. She heard the shouts, but couldn't see past the novices in front of her. She and Godfrey had fallen to the rear, so when one of the brigands circled around to attack them from behind, Godfrey wrenched his sword from its scabbard and charged the man.

More men stepped out of the trees to assist Godfrey's man, and for a moment, he was surrounded before they cut him down. It was done so quickly, so silently that he was dead before she was aware of what had happened.

Penelope felt magic billowing out from the enchantress, and she bit her lip to offer what little help she could. Then she saw into the men's minds. They wanted the girls, but more than that, they wanted to chase them as they ran, their desire building as they hunted. Penelope herself was dismissed as poor sport, but when one of the novices bolted, their fierce joy was almost unbearable as they leaped as one to follow her. Penelope fell to her knees.

Kun's magic engulfed them all, shaking the earth so hard no one remained standing but the enchantress herself.

One of the men fell near Penelope, and she was surprised to see he wore fine clothes. They all did. Brigandry evidently paid well on Beacon Isle.

Kun shouted something and the man before her began to shimmer, then shrink. He gave a horrible cry, but he grew smaller and smaller until Penelope could have cupped him in her hands. Then he shivered, throwing his cloak out wide and it caught the wind, buoying him up like wings. No, they were wings.

Penelope watched in amazement as the brigands turned into birds, which flew away.

Then pain engulfed her once more, and she knew that this pain was not the same as before. Her baby was coming, and she was helpless to stop her birthing blood from mingling with her husband's lifeblood on the road.

Nine

"I will not do this!" Margareta burst out. After being silent so long, her voice sounded strange in her ears. "I will not save them from a fate they so richly deserve. She should have killed them, not let them fly away. How dare they…"

Penelope's mouth dropped open in shock. "But an enchantress cannot use her power to kill. It is against the laws of their kind. If she does, she will be enslaved like the other djinn, who were once free to practice magic until they turned to evil."

Margareta would not be silenced. "So an enchantress who puts down a pack of rabid dogs who prey on women is punished, while the men get off lightly, with the gift of flight?"

"That was the enchantress's choice of punishment. I am sure Mistress Kun had her reasons. A lesser witch does not question an enchantress, for she understands far more than I ever will," Penelope faltered.

"Where is this enchantress now?" Margareta demanded.

"I do not know. I was busy with childbirth when she left and I did not see her again," Penelope replied.

So she could not question the enchantress, Margareta mused. But there was one person she could speak to, who would not be allowed to hold back information this time.

She stormed through the house to her father's solar. He had aged since she'd seen him last, though it had only been a few weeks. Right now, though, she didn't care if he looked twice his age.

"I won't do it. I won't stay silent. They deserve their fate," she said through gritted teeth.

"They're boys. Your brothers. Boys shouldn't be punished for pulling a prank. They weren't hurting anybody. Those novices were too easily frightened." Father dismissed her concerns with a wave of his hand.

"And what of the witch? Or Lady Penelope? Or Sir Godfrey, the knight they murdered?" Margareta demanded. "A man is dead. His wife a widow, his child fatherless. They demand justice."

Her father surveyed the study. "Yet I don't see them here. Just you."

Margareta slammed her fist into the table. "Yes, me. The daughter you duped into helping you free my dastardly brothers from a curse they deserve."

"They killed a man who attacked them, Meg. There is no crime in that. They are my sons, and one day Beacon Isle will belong to them. In the meantime, they carry my justice from one end of the island to the other. Perhaps they might have overpowered the man, and brought him here to face justice instead of killing him outright, but there were a lot of women present who might have been in danger from the madman. If they were here, I could ask them, but they are not, and they will not return until the curse is broken. A curse you swore you would break."

"That was before I knew how much they deserved it!" Margareta cried. "If I break this curse, one day they will be masters of Beacon Isle, and heaven help the islanders when you are gone. There will be no justice, for they will be lords who take whatever they will, and no woman will be safe. I will not be a part of this, Father."

"So you will let your brothers remain birds forever, because you, a girl who has not been taught to rule like her brothers have from their infancy, think you know better?"

Margareta folded her arms across her chest. "Any village idiot knows better that to torment innocent women for their own amusement. I would do a far better job at ruling this island than any of my brothers."

"No woman can rule," Father scoffed. "That is why girls must marry. So their husband can rule their lands with the strength required to hold them, or they would soon lose them to conquest."

In the human world, Margareta knew this to be true, but beneath the waves, it was a different story. "Not my kind. Under the surface, women rule the oceans. And the men who think they are strong enough to challenge us for our domain die," she said fiercely.

The Master of Beacon Isle leaned back in his chair, considering her. "Very well. If you lift the curse on my sons, I will give you Beacon Isle as your dowry when you marry."

Margareta held his gaze, knowing the lie that lurked beneath his promise. Her kind did not marry, and no human male would survive long in her bed. But he would only need to survive long enough to claim her dowry, and Beacon

Isle would be safe. Her brothers could never inherit.

"We have an accord," she said.

The Master was quick to follow up on what he thought was his advantage. "Indeed we do. See that you keep your promise and save my sons."

Mutely, Margareta nodded. If by breaking the curse, she could free Beacon Isle from the curse of her brothers, her silence was a small price to pay. One which would yield lands, a husband and maybe even the one thing she wanted most – a child like Melitta.

Ten

Later that evening, in the solitude of her chambers, Margareta took a knife and sliced the skin of her arm, letting the blood flow. She was a weak spellcaster with anything that wasn't water, and she wanted this spell to work. What might take another enchantress merely a drop of blood took much more from Margareta.

She wove her magic carefully, making sure the spell affected only herself. When she was done, silence settled over her tongue. There would be no mistakes or changes of heart this time. She would not, nay, could not speak until her brothers' curse broke and they returned to Beacon Isle. Until then, her voice would not be heard.

Not a word or a laugh or a single sound would pass her lips for more than six years, when fate intervened.

For a siren whose voice is never heard is hardly a siren at all. Maybe enough to make a man wonder whether she might make a suitable wife.

Had Beacon Isle been this green the last time he was here? Erik wondered as the island came into view. He couldn't remember. Last time, he'd been too caught up in the sheer adventure of it all, his first sea voyage, his first journey at all. He'd had responsibilities then, too, which had taken much of his time. Armour did not polish itself and salt from the sea voyage had conspired to make his duties tenfold more difficult.

He'd learned a lot about the sea since then,

and those who made their living on it. Enough to know how to keep his sword from rusting, and to wear leather armour, when he wore any at all. He was on a mission of peace, not war, and he was under strict instructions not to risk his life unnecessarily.

Just as his brother, Philip, had not risked his own in anything more ordinary than a sea voyage. A voyage that had both blessed and cursed Erik, for he alone had survived. He and a girl he swore he'd find.

Six years it had taken to convince his father to allow him to go to sea. Anything could have happened to her in that time. She might have died, or married, or run far away from Beacon Isle, but that was the last place he'd seen her, so that was where he would start his search.

That Beacon Isle was at the heart of other, stranger stories than his intrigued him. His father dismissed the tales as the fantasies of sailors embellished by nurses who wished to frighten children. Yet Erik knew something his father did not – he had his own dreams and memories to go on, the proof of his own eyes. A moment of foggy memory that would not leave him alone gave credence to all the tales the way nothing else could.

And yet…

Erik sighed. The tales told so many conflicting things, it was hard to make any sense of them. That was why we sought the source of such tales – and the library on Beacon Isle was famed far and wide. Why, it was said that some of the books from the library of the ancients, which burned a thousand years ago, had been salvaged and were kept even now in the priory at Beacon Isle. Not that he wanted scrolls from so far afield. He wanted the history of Beacon Isle itself and the waters surrounding it. Especially the waters…

Water he would have to cross if he was to find what he sought, Erik told himself, forcing himself to step across the gangplank to shore. There, that was not so difficult, he chided himself as his boots touched the cobbled surface of the dock.

He'd surprised himself with how easy it was. Weren't all seas the same water, after all? He'd sailed many of them in his thankless quest, but still he had no more answers than when he'd started. That's why Beacon Isle must hold the answers. Here his quest had begun, and here it would end, one way or the other. Either he would find the answers he sought, or he would be forced to agree with his father that whatever he'd seen in the water was nothing but an illusion invented by his own fevered brain.

Erik took a coin, tossed it into the air and caught it on the back of his hand. Heads and he was delusional; tails and he would find what he sought here. Erik lifted his hand, and cheered aloud when he did not see his father's engraved profile on the uppermost side of the coin. He would find something here, he was certain of it. If not her, then perhaps the book he wanted waited in the library.

Erik itched to begin his search, but he knew

better. Politics demanded he present himself to the Master of Beacon Isle first, for he was his father's son, and his father had his own reasons for keeping the Master happy.

Aside from its value to Erik, Beacon Isle was one of the richest trading ports in the region, accepting goods from all corners of the globe and trading them far and wide. It was strategic to the defence of half a dozen countries that surrounded it, and it had its own navy that served Beacon Isle and acknowledged no king as its sovereign except the Master of Beacon Isle.

A Master, yet not a king. It even piqued Erik's curiosity how a man could hold such power without a crown. Almost as though there was more to Beacon Isle than anyone thought.

Calling his thanks to the captain for the ride, Erik set out across Harbour Town to reach the Master's house, and the priory beyond.

The town quickly dropped behind him as he ascended the hill where legend said one of the saints had founded the first priory on the site. The rude wooden huts that had once stood there were long gone, replaced by the edifice of white and grey stone that occupied the crown of the hill overlooking White Harbour. On a beautiful day such as this, it was a view fit for a king.

Erik stepped through the gate into the bailey, his rich clothing announcing his arrival before he could open his mouth.

Men set off for the port to bring his belongings while another asked for his name and ushered him into the great hall, where he was offered food and wine while he waited for the Master.

Bemused, Erik accepted the offer of wine, wondering how far afield the vintage had come from, for it was surely too cold for grapes on Beacon Isle. A cautious sip told him all he needed to know – the wine was not from grapes at all, but made with berries in the style made famous by a kingdom to the south of his father's that backed onto the mountains, and a particular favourite at his father's court. His father had hinted that a marriage between Erik and the king's only daughter would be advantageous for both kingdoms, but Erik had no intention of marrying a woman he'd never met. Life would include enough unhappiness without sharing it with a woman he didn't love.

"Prince Erik. It is an honour," a deep voice said. The man who entered the hall looked ancient, instead of the same age as Erik's own father. But no one else would walk into the great hall of Beacon Isle like a king granting a great favour to one of his subjects. This ageing nobleman was stronger than he appeared, for no weakling could hold the rich lands of Beacon Isle without even a crown to legitimise his claim to the neighbouring kingdoms.

Erik set his goblet on the table, turned and bowed. "Master Nicholas. I thought you would send one of your sons to greet me. I had no idea that you would take the time to meet me yourself. The honour is mine."

Master Nicholas's eyes clouded with

something like grief. "My sons, like so many others, have gone on a long journey to seek redemption for their sins. I hope to see them home soon, but I fear I shall find them changed men, after such a long absence. Many years."

Erik murmured something appropriate about how proud he must be of his sons. While Master Nicholas waxed lyrical about his numerous sons and their even more numerous talents, Erik wondered what it would be like to undertake a crusade to free the Holy Land like Nicholas' sons evidently had. It seemed such a pointless business that one would surely have had to commit some truly grievous sins in order to require such lengthy reparation.

He debated whether Master Nicholas's boys had done something particularly bad, or whether the fervour of others had caught them up like so many other young noblemen. Surely the latter.

"And what brings you here to my humble isle?" Master Nicholas asked.

Erik managed a smile. "Why, a quest of my own. I have developed a singular interest in the history of the region, and I've found a large gap in the history of Beacon Isle. Considering the fame of your library, I naturally assumed the information I sought would be here."

Master Nicholas laughed, though it sounded hollow. He knew as well as Erik that the one thing Erik's father, and in fact all the neighbouring kings, wanted to know, was which king had last held sovereignty over Beacon Isle…and how, if at all, he had lost it. Such a secret would surely be within the archives here on Beacon Isle.

"I will see to it that you have a research assistant who is an expert in all of our library collections, the day after tomorrow. First, you must rest from your journey, and tomorrow is our harvest feast, so you must join us. I will introduce you to my daughter at the feast, too."

Erik suppressed a sigh. What was it with men once they had a daughter? The moment she was old enough, they all wanted to marry the poor girl off, and they all looked eagerly at him as the prospective husband. As if a good marriage began with a desire to please the girl's father, and not the girl herself. When he found the girl he wanted, he would do everything within his power to please the girl. She was the one he intended to share his life with, after all.

He made noises that he hoped sounded eager, then escaped the Master as quickly as he could without being rude.

Twelve

Penelope finished tying the laces of Margareta's gown. "There," she breathed, standing back to admire her handiwork.

"She looks beautiful, Mama. Like a princess," six-year-old Melitta squealed, clapping her hands. "Can I be Harvest Queen, too, when I'm all grown up?"

"She's not the Harvest Queen, sweetheart," Penelope said. "The Harvest Queen wears gold, not blue. Lady Margareta is the Lady of Beacon Isle, and one day she'll be the Mistress of the whole island."

"What about me?" the child demanded.

Margareta couldn't hide her smile. When she was that age, she'd admired the village girls chosen to be Harvest Queens, and wished that some day she might be one of them. Now, she knew better. The girl chosen to lord it over her fellows at each Harvest Festival never lacked for partners when the dancing started, and she never failed to find a husband before the first winter snows. From the moment the blessed crown of flowers touched the Queen's head, she became the sole focus of every man present. For the blessing was one of fertility…and any man who could win the Queen's affections that night was certain to sire a child on her, hence the rapid weddings.

She remembered her brothers being among previous queens' suitors. As a child, she'd seen the uncrowned queens marrying other men, and she'd pitied her brothers for being rejected. Now, she realised that wasn't the case – the girls had been hurriedly married off to save what honour they had left after her brothers had finished with them.

That wouldn't be the fate of tonight's Queen, however – Margareta was certain of that. Queen Gerda was safe from her cursed brothers, and well known to be walking out with young Kay, a boy orphaned by the very same shipwreck that Prince Philip and his entourage had died in. Margareta hoped she'd see Gerda and Kay reach a marriage accord tonight, and that the competition of other men wanting her hand would spur the boy into action before he lost the girl.

"Perhaps when you are older, you will be Harvest Queen, and I shall make you a beautiful dress in gold," Penelope said to her daughter.

"No! Blue like Lady Margareta!" the child shrieked.

Penelope shook her head. "Your spirit is all spit and fire, child. If you are ever Harvest Queen, the boys will burn the city for you, thinking it is Midsummer and not harvest at all." She dropped her voice lower so only Margareta could hear. "I already told you, the competition will frighten the boy off. I'll wager you the first piece of velvet off my loom that he is too cowardly to ask the girl. He doesn't think he's worthy of her."

Margareta had to admit Penelope had an edge on her, being able to read the boy's thoughts and all, but Margareta wanted to believe some happiness would come of tonight's feast. Besides, watching the Harvest Queen while she was stuck at the high table, where no man would dare ask her to dance, would provide some amusement in an otherwise tedious evening.

"Let us go," Penelope said, straightening the veil she wore over her hair. To the two veiled novices who'd appeared in the doorway, she added, "Make sure she's in bed as soon as she's finished her supper. I don't want her sneaking downstairs to the feast again."

The novices murmured their agreement.

To the sound of Melitta screaming about

wanting to come to the ball, too, Penelope and Margareta made their way down to the great hall. Penelope's dove grey gown and matching veil marked her as a widow, though she was long since finished with her mourning period. Margareta's blue gown glowed like the sky above, setting off her curved figure to perfection. When she arrived at the door to the great hall, silence fell without anyone needing to announce her name. The breath caught in every male throat as each and every man present desired to possess her, and every feminine gasp spoke volumes about how much they wished they could be her.

Margareta did not need the Harvest Queen's crown or Penelope's mind-reading magic to know these things – it was plain in the expression on every face. Even when her tongue was silent, a siren's body sang a song so enticing no human could resist.

Ignoring all the eyes on her, Margareta led the way to the high table. She paid little heed to the men already seated at her father's right and left hands as she headed for her accustomed seat at the far end of the table. She shared her small bench with Penelope, because after her, Penelope was the second highest ranking woman in the room.

The feast itself passed much like any other – everyone ate too much and drank more, until the volume of their collective voices rose to a roar that echoed around the room. When the roar approached what Margareta thought was its crescendo, her father rose to announce the Harvest Queen, who would open the dancing.

Clad in the traditional saffron-coloured gown worn by Harvest Queens for as long as Margareta could remember, Gerda approached the dais and dropped a deep curtsey, letting her skirt puddle around her as she'd no doubt practised. Father, as Master of Beacon Isle, laid the blessed crown of flowers on the girl's head and bade her to rise as royalty.

The moment the crown touched her hair, the atmosphere in the room changed from the sated merriment after a feast to charged anticipation.

"We're not the only ones betting on who the little queen chooses to be her king," Penelope whispered.

If it weren't for her spell of silence, Margareta would have had to smother a laugh. A lot of young men had turned their eyes on Gerda, as though seeing the girl for the first time. Poor Kay, who'd sat beside her at the feast, now stared into his mug of ale as though he couldn't bear to see how beautiful Gerda looked tonight.

The Master gave the order and the tables and benches were swept aside to make space for the highlight of the evening – the Harvest Ball.

Gerda and her golden gown were soon hidden among a crowd of eager young men, while other couples lined up for a country dance. Margareta longed to be among them, but her father would never allow her to dance, because there was no knowing when her siren side might take over and decide the poor boy needed to die instead of dance with her.

So Margareta watched and kept Penelope company, for no man would think of asking the widow of a saint to do something as frivolous as dancing, or so Penelope said.

"How fares young Kay?" Penelope asked.

Margareta pointed at the boy, who sat moodily in the corner with his ale.

Penelope clapped her hands. "You'll be taking me out on the boat for sure. I hope we'll have fine weather tomorrow, because I fancy a trip out on the ocean!"

So would Margareta, she admitted to herself. To be out on the waves, breathing in the salt spray and listening to the swish of the hull cutting smoothly through the sea, instead of the smoky air in the hall full of music and shouting and the stomp of booted feet.

"Lady, would you do me the honour of joining me in this dance?" the man to Margareta's right asked, extending his hand.

Margareta shook her head and Penelope piped up, "The Lady Margareta is under a vow of silence until her brothers return."

"But that won't stop you dancing, will it, my lady?" the man persisted. "Your father said –"

"Her father wants his sons to return just as much as Lady Margareta," Penelope said smoothly, cutting the man off.

Margareta dared to look into his eyes. They lit up with his eager grin, as if he truly didn't believe she could refuse him. She lowered her gaze, frowned, then shook her head emphatically.

"Meg, be a good girl. Go dance with the king's envoy," the Master ordered, stabbing a finger at the dance floor.

She shot her father a look of surprise. Didn't he care what happened to the ambassador? What if something happened and her true nature took over and…

"Dance, girl!" the Master commanded.

Unable to refuse, Margareta laid her hand on the envoy's proffered arm, and allowed herself to be led onto the dance floor. She shot Penelope an imploring look, begging her friend to keep an eye on her thoughts and that of the ambassador.

Margareta glimpsed Penelope's grave nod before she and the ambassador were whirled away into the organised chaos that was a country dance.

Thirteen

The moment she stepped into the great hall, Erik knew his search was over before it had even started. She was here – the girl in his dreams. Or at least he thought she was.

He didn't remember her having curves like that, or perhaps he'd been too young to notice. Her dark hair was hidden mostly under a veil, but a rebellious tendril had escaped. She moved like a stately lady, which indeed she was, if she was the Master's daughter. The grey-clad widow at her side looked like her companion or her chaperone, Erik wasn't sure.

The girl sat beside him, close enough to reach out and touch, though he didn't dare. She shared a bench with her chaperone, he judged, when the widow shot him a shrewd glance that seemed to size up his very soul.

He met the widow's gaze, willing her to believe that his intentions toward the girl were honourable. How could they not be? He'd come here to find her, and here she was, not a foot from him!

Erik scarcely tasted a bite of his meal as he struggled to keep his breathing even. He wanted to blurt out everything to her, everything that had kept him away for the last six years and what brought him here now, but every time he tried to say something to her, his voice died in his throat. What did a man say to the woman of his dreams, when he saw her for the first time in six years?

And so he waited for her to break the silence. A silence he should not have noticed, amid the noise of a hall full of people making merry to celebrate the harvest, and yet the silence stretched in his mind until it lay like a great gulf between them.

The tables were cleared away to make space for dancing, and Erik's heart leaped. A ball! At home in his father's court, the ladies would form up and dance, spinning around one another like flower petals blown by the wind, before coming together as the complex pattern drew them in at the end of the dance.

Erik held his breath for a moment in eager anticipation as the first girls stepped out into the cleared space. But they were followed soon after by men, forming up in couples like no ball Erik had ever been to. Only then did it strike him that none of those present were nobles – the hall was full of common people, dressed in such bright colours that it hadn't occurred to him to look more closely at their clothes. This was a prosperous place indeed if even the peasants' clothes were as coloured as those of his father's courtiers.

He waited for the girl beside him to join the

dance, but she remained resolutely in her seat. No partner, perhaps?

Before he'd truly thought the words through, he blurted out a clumsy invitation for her to dance with him.

Her eyes met his — two blue jewels that seemed to hold the depths of the ocean inside them. But the one thing that they didn't hold was any spark of recognition. She shook her head, which made the grey widow pipe up in the girl's support.

Erik's heart ached at the thought that this wasn't the girl he was looking for — how could she not recognise him, when he knew her instantly? — but his ever-optimistic imagination ventured that if she had changed in the intervening time, so had he, and it would take time for her to remember him. Just because he hadn't been able to forget the shipwreck and how she'd saved him from it, didn't mean she had been similarly affected. Perhaps she had endured many shipwrecks, and rescued many helpless boys, and there was nothing special about him at all.

No, he'd felt it then and he knew it now. There was something between them, a connection that once made could not be broken. He felt it in his bones.

The grey widow would not stop him from dancing with her.

Erik countered her arguments as to why the girl shouldn't dance, and just as he felt he had the upper hand, a male voice cut in.

Master Nicholas ordered the girl to dance with him.

The girl's eyes widened, and she looked affronted at her father. She was no dutiful daughter, this one. If not for her vow of silence, the girl would have given her father a piece of her undoubtedly strong mind.

The Master either ignored or dismissed her rebellious glance, and repeated his command.

With an expression that said her father would rue this later, the girl rose gracefully, every inch a veritable queen as she took Erik's hastily proffered arm.

The dancers parted and bowed to allow them to take their place at the head of the formation. The musicians faltered, then began anew, hesitantly at first, then more boldly as the girl stepped across the divide to place her palm against Erik's.

Heat flared between his hand and hers, surprising him. She should have been cold, icy, not warm to the touch. Perhaps he was wrong, and she wasn't…

Deep blue eyes sucked at his soul as they whirled among the other dancers, assessing him as frankly as though she were the Master himself.

Erik stumbled, forgetting the steps, nearly sending them crashing into another couple.

Her arms grew rigid around him, steering him bodily away from the others for all the world as though she had the strength to lift him off his feet. Or pluck him from the ocean into a boat.

Now it was Erik's turn to stare at her. Either she was, or she wasn't.

They moved apart, as required by the steps of the dance, and Erik was forced to partner three other girls before he could approach her again.

"Do you remember me?" he asked urgently. "That day in the water?"

She grimaced as he trod on her foot.

Erik opened his mouth to apologise, but she brought her slippered heel down so hard on his instep all that came out was a pained yelp.

She broke free of his hold, weaving expertly through the dancers until she reached the edge of the room. An imperious wave of her hand brought a servant with a goblet. The girl took the goblet, turned on her bone-breaking heel, and strode out of the great hall, with the grey widow hard on her heels.

Disappointment welled up in Erik's throat. If he hadn't been so clumsy, she might have answered his question. Then he'd know if she truly was the right one.

With considerably less grace than the girl, Erik made his way through the dancers and back to the dais, where he slumped to the bench beside Master Nicholas's chair.

Gesturing for a servant to fill his cup with wine, Erik said to Master Nicholas, "Your daughter is certainly a very spirited girl."

Master Nicholas drained his cup. "That she is. Break her, and she's yours. Consider her a gift."

Erik's mouth dropped open, and he hastened to close it. Break her? She would outlast the strongest granite, Erik was certain. For a wave might break against a rock, but no man could master the ocean. Least of all him.

"My father would welcome a marriage alliance between his kingdom and yours," Erik managed to say. He bowed to the Master and bade him a good night before heading up to his chambers.

It wasn't until he was alone in bed that Erik realised he hadn't even asked for her name.

Fourteen

The moment the door to the great hall closed behind Penelope, Margareta slowed her steps. Her feet hurt after being stomped on by that boor. What had possessed him to ask her to dance when he was so abysmal at dancing, and he didn't even know the steps?

The water in the ewer splashed over the side with the force of the waves Margareta's fury had created. She forced herself to calm down, at least a little.

"From the moment he entered the room, he

fell under your spell," Penelope said softly. "He could think of no one and nothing else but you."

That made him no different to any other man present tonight, Margareta knew. The lure of a siren was almost impossible to resist, which was why she'd refused to dance with him. What had her father been thinking, telling her to dance with him? If she killed some king's ambassador, there could be war. Already she seethed at his touch.

"I didn't read your father's thoughts, so I don't know the answer to that," Penelope replied. "I was too busy keeping an eye on you and your lover boy."

She would never take that boor as her lover, Margareta fumed. His thoughts had undoubtedly been filled with all the things he dreamed of doing to her if he could get her alone and naked. Margareta's money was on him being the forceful sort, who dreamed of pinning her to a bed beneath his weight and forcing himself between her legs. Marginally better than the ones who delighted in the dream of forcing her to her knees to pleasure him with her mouth.

"Neither of those," Penelope said cheerfully. "His thoughts were quite refreshing, really. Yes, they were of you, but mostly he focussed on your face. And the light was sort of blue, like you were under water. There's something different about him. Not that it really matters. You probably won't see him again. He's here on some sort of quest, but he keeps those thoughts hidden. At least, he did last night, when you were there to distract him." Penelope dropped her voice to a conspiratorial whisper. "Judging by the tone of his thoughts, he'd make a more attentive lover than most men. He was genuinely sorry when he stepped on your feet."

Not as sorry as Margareta intended to make him if he ever touched her feet again, she resolved grimly.

Penelope laughed. "I'm sure you'll think of some truly diabolical torture for the man. You can tell me what you've decided in the morning. I am going to return to my chambers, where I hope the sisters have managed to get Melitta to sleep, and where I intend to do the same."

Margareta wished her friend a silent good night. When she was certain Penelope was far enough away, Margareta left her room and headed for the beach. A swim in the cool water would do her good. She could dive down deep and change the currents to her heart's content until she felt better. Damn her father for putting her too close to that man. It was almost as though he wanted her to kill the ambassador.

No, surely not.

Fifteen

By the following morning, Margareta was back to her usual sunny self as she sat in the brightly lit bower with Penelope. As had become their custom, Penelope worked on her weaving, while Margareta busied herself copying some of the older, crumbling manuscripts from the library before they became entirely unreadable.

Father often commented that writing was a man's job, and not suitable for a lady. The priory had a group of monks whose sole occupation was to illuminate the manuscripts they found in the library, as Margareta knew well, but she'd watched the monks at their work, and it left a lot to be desired. Oh, their books were beautiful enough, written in lovely letters and illustrated with the most exquisite pictures, but for every manuscript they copied, another dozen crumbled to dust, they were so slow. Completing a single page could take days, the way the monks did it, and on her father's death, this library, like all of Beacon Isle, would be hers. And she did not want to lose any of the texts it contained.

So, while the monks made beautiful books, she collected the scrolls they left behind, and transcribed what she could decipher. Her pages were plain but readable, which was more than she could say about the originals, and if the monks wanted to turn her work into beautiful books, at least they'd still have the text from the source to go by, instead of it being lost altogether.

One winter, when the harbour had completely iced over and kept all the ships away for weeks, Margareta had run out of ink. Bored beyond belief, she'd undertaken to reorganise the library. Through the centuries, the books and scrolls had been placed on shelves based on the date they were bought or last read. That meant the earliest scrolls had crumbled together into indecipherable fragments that Margareta lacked the patience to piece together, but it also appeared that some of the older scrolls had been removed from their original shelves and shoved back into pigeonholes which were already occupied by more recent manuscripts, making a mess that had only worsened through the centuries.

Two days after she'd finished her Herculean task, the harbour ice had finally cracked and more ink had arrived.

Margareta had intended to write a document, summarising her filing system so that anyone could easily find what they sought, but in the course of her cleaning, she'd found so many scrolls in need of copying before their contents disappeared altogether that she'd had other priorities for her time. Even now, she fought against time to preserve all of them.

Most days, she was fascinated by what she read. Stories about wars fought in lands she'd never heard of, with exotic names and all sorts of strange animals, or accounts of men and events she couldn't even begin to understand. Senates and votes and pharaohs and all manner of strange words came up in these manuscripts.

Today's scroll tried her patience. Not only had the writer failed to put spaces between the Latin words so that the reader might know where one word ended and the next began, but the words themselves left a foul taste in her mouth. The unknown writer who had first penned the words believed that all the ills of the world could be cured if only husbands controlled their wives, who were apparently all violent, uncontrollable creatures. So either they could be controlled, or they couldn't, Margareta fumed. She was tempted to drop this scroll in the fire and be done with it. A violent, uncontrollable creature…why, she hadn't attacked anyone yet!

The servant who entered the room was a welcome interruption.

"Mistress, the Master asks for some scrolls from the library, which he says only you can find."

Margareta glanced at Penelope.

Penelope waved her away. "Go, help your father. I'm poor company anyway. One moment, I am so close to getting this cloth right, and the next…it falls apart and I must try again. If I hadn't seen that finished piece of velvet with my own eyes, I'd swear it wasn't possible. Perhaps I should stick to silk."

Margareta smiled. She knew Penelope would never give up. The woman was as gifted with a needle as she was with a loom, and if anyone could create a new cloth by herself, it was Penelope.

"Bring back something interesting this time, instead of that dry old history scroll. Knights and dragons and…violent, uncontrollable creatures," Penelope called after Margareta.

Margareta chuckled silently to herself. These six years of silence would have been impossible but for Penelope's mind-reading talents. As she marched purposefully through the corridors of her father's house and into the priory, Margareta resolved to deal with this errand as quickly as possible, because she knew exactly which book to bring back to share with Penelope.

Sixteen

A servant brought Erik breakfast, along with the welcome message that Master Nicholas had not only granted his request to use the library today, but he'd given him an assistant to help him navigate their collection of books. Erik was under no illusions that the assistant wouldn't report his every move back to the Master, but it was of little concern. He could easily hide his father's mission under the cover of his own project. Master Nicholas would think him crazy, which he undoubtedly was, and leave him to his own devices.

Erik wolfed down his breakfast, dressed and demanded to be shown the way to the famous library. The maidservant lost no time in leading the way – Erik had trouble keeping up with the girl as she trotted through the richly decorated passageways. It wasn't until they reached the bare corridor that marked the start of the priory that she slowed down. Erik thought he heard her breathe a sigh of relief as she weaved through the monks. Almost as though she feared walking through the corridors of the house proper. Or was he the one who scared her?

The girl abruptly stopped, then spun on her heel to stand beside the doorway instead of passing through it. She dropped a deep curtsey. "The library, sir." She dashed off before he could thank her.

Erik stared after her for a moment before giving himself a shake. He had his own mystery to solve – he didn't need to know what frightened the maids of Beacon Isle.

He stepped through the doorway and had to stop. He'd entered what might have been just another passage, if it weren't lined from floor to ceiling with shelves full of books. Erik couldn't suppress a grin. This was what he was here for.

Selecting a leather spine at random, he pulled a book from the shelf. The pages were filled with strange symbols, interspersed with letters he recognised. Erik laughed. Trust Beacon Isle to keep their books in some sort of code, indecipherable to all but those who lived here. Maybe an assistant would be useful after all.

An assistant who didn't appear to be anywhere in the library. Erik strolled between the shelves, not sure where to start. When he reached the end of the corridor, he realised he'd been mistaken – the biggest library he'd ever seen was merely the antechamber to the real, much more massive collection that filled a chamber easily as big as the great hall itself. Some shelves were divided into pigeonholes occupied by scrolls instead of birds, while others were nigh as tall as him to accommodate huge books that would take two men to lift.

A table sat in the middle of the room, as large as one of the feasting tables in the hall below, dwarfing the stack of books that lay at its head.

"Uh, hello?" Erik called.

From behind the stack of books, which were taller than he'd thought, a figure rose to her feet.

Erik's heart leaped as he recognised the lady he'd danced with last night. The Master's daughter, whose name he still did not know.

"Beg pardon, my lady, but your father told me to meet my assistant here, as I'll be doing some research about the island's history in your remarkable library. Can you tell me where he might be?" Erik ventured.

The girl's eyes grew flinty. She picked up the hefty stack of books, thrust them at his chest so hard she nearly knocked him over, then stalked out of the library without a word.

Erik set the books down on the table, wondering how such a slight girl had had the strength lift such a heavy load.

There was still no sign of the promised assistant, so he sat down and flicked open the first book.

He found a list of ships, along with their date of arrival, cargo, and duty paid on that cargo. They dated from the previous century.

A quick examination of the other books in the pile revealed they all contained information about the history of the isle.

Had the Master given him his own daughter to be a research assistant? No wonder the lady was angry at being assigned a task that surely should have been given to a servant.

"Thank you," Erik called after her, but he doubted she heard. Even if she did, she certainly didn't return, so Erik set to work.

Seventeen

This could only end badly. A polite ambassador who did his best to charm her spelled trouble for her and for himself, Margareta knew. Her father couldn't possibly have meant for her to work closely with him as his assistant. Why, the ambassador wouldn't last the week. She'd already seen that look in his eyes that told her he was under her spell, and not only was he less boorish away from the dance floor, but she could feel her heart softening toward him. If she hardened her heart to him like any other man, he might stand a chance. But if she let him win her over, maybe even try to seduce her a little, the ambassador was a dead man, and whatever king he served would want to know why.

And whatever he thought about the matter, Margareta knew that her father was no longer capable of leading the island to war, let alone victory.

Margareta didn't often question her father any more, and not just because she maintained her vow of silence. She'd seen him deteriorate from the strong man she remembered, revered and feared as a child, to a shadow of himself. Oh, some days, like at the Harvest Festival, he covered his thinning hair with a horsehair wig and dressed to outshine even the richest merchants. But others…Margareta sighed.

Her father had taken to his bed today, much the worse for last night's wine, and he refused to see anyone. Margareta was the exception, for no one could keep her out. Not even her father on days like this.

The moment he saw her, he sat up, leaving his bedcap on the pillow. "Have they returned? Do you bring word?" he asked eagerly.

Margareta shook her head. No, her brothers had not returned. She hadn't yet broken the curse.

His face crumpled. Some days he dissolved into tears, but today wasn't one of them. Instead, his face twisted into a snarl. "Bring them back. You must bring them back. Without my sons, the isle will be defenceless against all those kings who fancy my island. Not least of all that sneaky ambassador who's rooting around for his king. He'll never get what he's looking for. See that you help him with the books, for the sooner he's off the island, the better. You'll take care of him, won't you?"

Margareta's heart sank. When her father was having a bad day like this one, she could refuse him nothing. So she nodded dutifully, praying that the ambassador would leave before he came to harm.

Eighteen

Every day for a week, Margareta set a stack of books on the table for the ambassador, then left him to his reading. After the way he'd looked and spoken to her that first day, she didn't dare to spend more than a few minutes in his company. If she lingered, he would give in to the desires she could read clearly through his eyes, and when he did, he would die.

Much safer to let him read the port logs than to meet his gaze and wonder what it would feel like to surrender to her siren desires. Her father made them sound like such terrible things, but anything you didn't want to stop doing surely resulted in a great deal of pleasure. How could that be so terrible?

Yet every time the ambassador bade her good morning, thanking her for the books and wishing her a pleasant day, she longed to linger. The only thing that stopped her was the stack of ledgers she'd handed to him, and the sheer boredom she'd experienced on the rare occasions she'd copied one out.

Why anyone wanted to know which ships had touched at the island a hundred years ago, she wasn't sure, but she had no intention of keeping him company while he read books that would put any normal man to sleep.

Yet he certainly didn't sleep, as evident by the pages of notes he scrawled each day. Margareta had glanced at them, but his writing was harder to read than the books she copied. What she could decipher appeared to be records of ships lost near the island. The list looked long after three days, and grew with each new day.

It seemed to Margareta that merchants would avoid what appeared to be such a dangerous trading port, but a quick peek at the harbour outside told her otherwise. Only on the rare winters when the ocean froze over entirely was White Harbour ever empty. It was almost full today.

The ambassador didn't seem to notice, though. He was too intent on reading the books she'd given him yesterday.

Margareta thumped a new stack onto the table beside him and turned to leave.

To linger was to lose control, which she couldn't do, Margareta reminded herself.

He caught her arm, and though she tried to pull away, his grip on her wrist tightened.

"Please, my lady, stay. Shipping logs are all very good and well, but they're also boring. They say this ship carried this cargo, or was lost on this date, but none say how the ship was lost."

Margareta shrugged. Ships were lost. Such

was the fate of men who thought to control the ocean. She yanked out of his grip and glared at him.

To her surprise, he looked suitably contrite. "I'm sorry if I hurt you, my lady. It's just that I don't know your name and if I didn't catch you, I would lose my chance for another day. You see, your father promised me an assistant, but all he seems to want to give me is you." He caught the anger in his eyes. "Not that the books you've found for me haven't been a great help – they have, I swear. It's just that I want to know more, and you are the only other person who comes here. As the lady of the house, I'm sure you know who I should ask for help instead?"

Margareta considered sweeping out of the room, but the pleading look in his eyes plucked at her heart in such a way that she relented. She perched on a bench, placed her hands on her lap, and lifted her eyebrows in mute query. What exactly did he want to know?

He leaned forward. "You see, I want to know why the ships were lost. Was it storms? Pirates? A battle with enemy ships? Sea monsters?"

Margareta bit her lip, wishing she could laugh. What would the ambassador say if he knew that she was the only kind of monster that lived in the sea? She shrugged again.

"Have you ever seen a sea monster?" he asked eagerly. "I've heard some of them can take the form of a beautiful woman who entices sailors to their deaths."

Margareta gasped – could he read her thoughts? Quickly, she schooled her expression into one of bewilderment, but it was too late. He'd seen her surprise.

"You have, haven't you?" he guessed. "I knew it! It is you. You're the same girl who was aboard the *Golden Eagle* when she sank. You're the girl who survived."

Margareta wished she could tell him what a fool he sounded, saying such things. She was the sea monster who had survived, not some weak-as-water maiden who needed to be rescued from the ocean, of all things. Her eyes narrowed. And how did he know such a thing, after all this time?

"I was the boy who was aboard the *Golden Eagle*, too," he continued. "We were in one of the ship's boats that made it to shore, except when I woke up, you were gone. I'm Erik." He held out his hand to her, palm up.

This ambassador was the squire? Margareta squinted at him, trying to see the boy in the well-built man before her. Maybe around the eyes and the mouth she could see a faint resemblance, but…

Her father had told her he'd searched for the boy, but found no trace of him anywhere on the island. It was as though he'd leaped back in the water to drown with the prince he'd served. Her father had suggested that the boy had never existed at all, until Margareta almost believed it. Sirens didn't suffer from the same maladies as sailors at sea for too long, though, so Margareta knew the boy had been real. So if he'd survived and this was him…that put him in a different light. He wasn't just some neighbouring king's ambassador. He was…a friend, of sorts. One she'd mourned who wasn't dead. Who wouldn't die here, no matter what she had to do to ensure it, Margareta swore.

She realised he'd continued speaking, and she shook her head, focussing on his words. Only her father knew she'd saved the squire, and he would never have told a soul, for it would mean telling people he had a siren for a daughter. So the only other people who knew were herself and the squire. He had to be the same boy.

"I had to go home to report Philip's death. My father was devastated at first, and then…well, there was so much to do. Learning to be a squire and one day a knight is one thing, but learning to be a prince, and politics, and how to rule a country…" Erik shook his head. "It's taken me this long to find my way back here, but I have to know. Do you have any books about sea monsters in these waters?"

All her parents' warnings about secrecy screamed at her to stop, and show the man nothing. And yet…something about him whispered to her that he was different – just as she'd known he was the day she saved him from the sea.

Perhaps it was time to find out what humans did know about her kind, so she could make sure they didn't learn more. Maybe they knew more than she gave them credit for. Her father certainly seemed to know plenty. Maybe he'd learned it all from a book in this very library. A book she could also learn from, so that one day she might manage to control her monstrous nature and not worry about how she might kill someone without meaning to. Maybe she could work out how not to kill Erik.

She regarded Erik for a long moment. He already owed her his life, if he truly was the squire she'd saved. Perhaps he could help her, and in some small way repay his debt.

Margareta winked at him, then set off for the section on myths and legends for the first time in what felt like forever.

Nineteen

Had she actually winked at him? The frosty maiden who hated him? Oh, not that she didn't have good reason to do so – she surely did, being forced to spend her time in the library with him instead of doing…whatever it was ladies did all day. Knit? Sew? Spin? He had no sisters and he could scarcely remember his mother, so Erik had never seen what highborn ladies did when no men were around. Surrounded by servants, they didn't need to do anything, but he couldn't imagine this girl sitting still and doing nothing for very long. She was as restless as the ocean. Erik had half expected her to open her mouth and shout at him a few times during their conversation, but she evidently took her vow of silence very seriously. In his memories, she was certainly no mute, and she understood him just fine, so her brothers must be very important to her.

And why not? They were family. Surely the girl loved her brothers, as all good girls did, and it would be a great loss to her whole family if they never returned from their holy crusade. Many others had perished, or disappeared, never to be heard from again, but he didn't dare say such things to her. The intelligence that shone through her eyes meant she probably already knew, and if she did not, he would not be cruel enough to tell her. Besides, she'd already worked one miracle when she saved him — another might not be as impossible for her as it would for ordinary people.

She returned with two leather buckets of

scrolls, that Erik helped her to set on the table. She unrolled the first one on the table, and Erik was mesmerised by the detailed drawing of a sea serpent, wrapping its massive coils around a sailing ship amid fierce waves. It was a monster, all right.

A fleeting image of blue scales on a creature easy as wide around as he himself, racing through the water beside him, passed through his mind, as if it was only yesterday he'd seen it. Had he seen a sea serpent? Is that what had brought him to the surface when he'd drowned? Or had the creature been a mermaid, like he'd dreamed? Whatever it had been, the creature had been doing the girl's bidding. That he knew for certain, for he'd heard her commanding the ocean itself. And a woman who could command the ocean in a world that relied on ships for trade was worth more than gold, jewels and the highest pedigree.

"Do you get many of these here?" he asked, trying to sound casual.

Her expression was impassive. Then she sighed.

She pulled a blank sheet of parchment toward her, picking up his quill with the ease of one who was familiar with writing, dipped it expertly in the ink, before scratching out the words:

Too cold. Serpents prefer warmer waters.

"Like most snakes," Erik mused. "But the ocean here is full of fish, and seals and maybe other creatures, too."

She nodded slowly. He got the impression she was waiting for him to continue.

Emboldened, he asked, "My lady, are there mermaids in these waters?"

The quill appeared in her fingers once more, flying across the parchment:

Don't be a fool. Mermaids don't exist outside of stories.

Her dark eyes held his. Mesmerising, that's what she was.

Would her gaze be equally cold if he kissed her?

Erik shook the idea from his head. If she was truly as powerful as he remembered, to kiss her would be to take his very life in his hands. But, by God, how much he wanted to. Even if it was the last thing he did, he would die a happy man.

She broke his gaze, turned on her heel, and marched out of the library.

Erik sighed. He'd been going so well, and then, like the bumbling fool he was, he'd made a mistake that sent her away again. But at least he'd managed to persuade her to show him some new scrolls that didn't mention a word of how many measures of wheat were aboard a ship when it sank.

Erik returned to the scrolls, which were filled with drawings that his eyes didn't see. Instead, his mind was fixed on her ocean-coloured eyes, and how they might light up if he kissed her.

Twenty

For the first time in his life, female voices arguing woke Erik. As his last dream faded, he realised he only heard one voice, but it was arguing loudly enough for two.

"I still don't see what you need me for. I am so close to getting the cloth right, I might have it finished this week. Instead, you want me to wake some man when you could easily do it yourself. You don't even need to touch him. Just throw a bucket of water over him, or whack him with a book, or…"

Erik jumped to his feet and met the annoyed gaze of the grey widow, who folded her arms across her chest.

"See?" the woman said. "He's awake. You don't need me. I'll go find someone to fetch food for him to break his fast."

A hand grasped the widow's sleeve, and Erik realised the girl stood behind her, using the widow for a shield. From him.

Pain smote his heart. "I'm sorry if I frightened you, my lady. The books you gave me yesterday were so interesting I stayed here late into the night to finish reading them. I must have fallen asleep on the table. My apologies if my snoring made you fear there was a monster in your library. I swear to you I mean you no harm. I am just a man."

The widow snorted. "Lady Margareta isn't frightened by much, sir. But a man who swears to do no harm had best keep his word, or evil will befall him. That I promise you."

Don't harm my charge or you will answer to me, Erik translated in his head.

"I spoke the truth. I mean her no harm. Both yourself and Lady Margareta are safe with me, Mistress…?"

"Lady Penelope," the widow supplied. She offered her hand, and Erik kissed it lightly. She lowered her voice so that only he could hear. "You should probably shave before you kiss her. She's not used to stubble."

Erik's hand flew to his face. Sure enough, he did need to shave. Muttering something about needing to wash, he hurried back to his chamber.

Penelope's disapproval weighted heavily on Margareta. Penelope simply didn't understand the risks inherent in what Margareta was. If she touched the man, she could harm him.

"You danced with him just fine at the Harvest Ball,"," Penelope said. "Touched his hand and everything, so don't tell me there wasn't skin contact. And if he really is the boy you knew all those years ago, you definitely didn't hurt him then."

Margareta shook her head. Penelope could

never understand. She was human, and –

"So are you!" Penelope exploded. "As human as I am! All right, you swim more often than most, but what's a little magic, when it's in your blood? There is no law that says you're not allowed to love, or touch people or…do any of the things normal people do! How many people have you killed?"

Margareta knew as well as Penelope did that the answer was none.

"You've saved one man's life, and killed no one. That makes you pretty safe to be around, in my opinion. Why don't you just let things happen the way they should, and worry about the consequences later?" Penelope asked.

If one of the consequences was Erik's death, Margareta didn't want to just let things happen. She wanted to protect him, not kill him.

"Well, he wants to protect you almost as much as he wants to kiss you, so that's a good start," Penelope said.

Kiss her? He wanted more than that. He

wanted what every man wanted, Margareta was certain.

"Perhaps," Penelope said, "but that's not what he keeps thinking about. Not even what he dreams about. The only thing I've seen in his thoughts is visions of him kissing you. His eyes are fixed on your face. Except for the moment he first saw you, when he looked at your whole body, his focus is your eyes. Apparently, that's how you'll tell him whether his kiss is as perfect as he plans it to be."

A perfect kiss? Was there such a thing? The very idea intrigued Margareta. What would it be like to press her lips against Erik's and…

NO!

Margareta forced the thought from her mind. A kiss could lead to more and it was immodest to have such desires. If her father knew, he would only say it was her siren nature coming to the fore. No human girl would have such desires.

"Your father is a prude. Most girls dream about their first kiss, the same way he does about you. You could do worse, you know," Penelope said.

Of course she could. She could kill him.

"Just as long as you get the kind of kiss other girls only dream about first," Penelope said. "He'd die happy, you know. He's afraid of you, and that's one of the things he tells himself to bolster his courage. That if he died after kissing you, he would die happy."

No he wouldn't, Margareta thought angrily. He would die screaming, because sirens enjoyed the pain of their victims. She would –

"Now I'll go see that some breakfast is sent up, and leave you two alone," Penelope said, striding out of the library as Erik entered it. "And if she doesn't let you kiss her before I return, I'll see that the whole island knows she's an ill-mannered sea-cow!" she threw over her shoulder before vanishing from sight.

Margareta's face grew beet red.

Erik took pity on her embarrassment. "My apologies, my lady. Despite our history together, we have not been properly introduced. Allow me to correct this terrible oversight. I am Prince Erik, and I am honoured to meet you, Lady Margareta. Never have I met such a fair lady, who is also a graceful dancer and a learned scholar. I am quite entranced." He held out his hand.

A hand Margareta knew she should cover with her own. Custom demanded it. So did Penelope, who would know if she did not. She'd touched him before, as both a human and a siren, and he was still alive. If she could control herself for a few brief seconds, he would live to see tomorrow, too.

Margareta stretched out her arm, biting her lip as she saw her fingers shaking. If only she didn't have to touch him. She didn't want to hurt him. She wanted…

Erik captured her trembling fingers and brought them to his lips. Warm and soft, his lips made her fingers tingle as he kissed each one. Her mind screamed at her to pull away, but Margareta could not. Her own lips parted as she stared at him, eager to know what he would do next.

"Lady Penelope was right to berate me for being so unkempt. I was so caught up in my research, I forgot myself. Now, perhaps, I am in a fit state to greet you as I should have on the day we met. If I meet with your approval, then perhaps…" Erik swallowed, then lifted her hand to his now smooth cheek. "If my lady would permit, I would like to offer you a kiss of peace."

As her father's vassals offered to him, Margareta knew, and the captains who sought his favour. It was a religious thing, a chaste thing, a ceremony of power. It shouldn't send her heart racing like hers did now.

And yet…to refuse would be churlish. He honoured her, for such gestures were for leaders like her father. Not his youngest daughter.

Shakily, Margareta gave a nod.

Erik lifted his hands to touch her shoulders.

A fountain of butterflies erupted in her belly. This was dangerous, she shouldn't…

Margareta brought her other hand to his cheek so that she could cup his face. She took a deep, steadying breath, then stretched up to lay her lips against his.

For one brief moment, their kiss was a chaste thing. Then Margareta forgot everything but the feel of Erik against her, the taste of his mouth and the hardness of him between her thighs as he pulled her closer, closer, still kissing her as if she was the very air he needed to breathe. She needed more than air from him, more than the deep, gasping breaths she drew in as she tugged at his tunic, sliding her hands inside to feel soft skin over firm muscles, stroking every bit of him she could reach until she wrapped her fingers around the hardest part between them and –

Her eyes on fire with desire, Margareta met Erik's gaze. God, he wanted her as much as she wanted him. She wanted, oh how much she wanted…

"Oh God, Margareta, I love you," he groaned.

Love? What she would do to him wasn't love. Hers wasn't a kiss of peace. It was a kiss of death.

Margareta tore herself away from him and ran.

Twenty-Two

Erik buried his head in his hands. He shouldn't have said it. Shouldn't have admitted that he'd loved her for years, since they first met in the boat, because no girl could ever compare to her. And turning a kiss of peace into one of raging lust with a woman who was already frightened of him…he deserved to be scourged for such blasphemy. No wonder the girl had run.

But the feel of her hands on him, stroking him in exactly the right way, as if she was as overcome by her own feelings as he was by his…

No. He'd imagined it, surely. No woman in creation would be so bold. A woman who could control the ocean could certainly control herself.

Whereas he was…an uncontrolled mess.

Cursing himself, Erik set off to find some cold water to douse his desire.

Twenty-Three

Margareta slammed the door behind her, then put her back to it, breathing hard. She wasn't sure if it was because she'd sprinted from the library to Penelope's chambers or whether it was the strange siren heat that still coursed through her that made her heart beat so fast within her chest that she could scarcely catch her breath.

"That good, was he?" Penelope asked calmly, wetting the end of her thread before inserting it through the eye of her needle. "I would have thought you'd have taken your time, but it's hard to savour your first."

Margareta tried to calm the jumble of images in her head so that Penelope would understand, for no one could be so calm in the face of what she had just experienced.

"I remember the day I first kissed Godfrey," Penelope said dreamily, as if she wasn't paying attention to Margareta at all. "We'd met at some of my father's feasts, but I'd never been able to exchange more than a few words with him. He'd told all sorts of stories about war and what he'd seen, stories I could listen to for hours, but my father never allowed me near enough to tell him so. But our eyes met across the hall enough times for him to start seeking me out, or find excuses to visit my father at home. One day, he brought an urgent message for my father when he was out, and only I was home. As was proper, I offered him refreshments, and suggested he wait for my father. He paid me some pretty compliment about how he'd wait forever for me, or some such thing, and he stumbled over the words as he never had in his stories. That's when he first kissed me. Well, I pushed him against the wall and kissed him, actually. Didn't take more than a moment before he was kissing me back just as eagerly. We kissed for quite a while, long enough for him to get good and excited so I could assess the goods, so to speak, which I admit were quite impressive, before my father's arrival interrupted us. The bustle at the door was enough for us to straighten our clothing and for me to whisper an invitation to meet me in the garden later that night, and the rest, well..." Penelope laughed. "By morning, I wanted no other man for my husband. Though from the way that man looks at you, he might be cut from the same cloth. My advice is to make sure he's as good with his hands as he is with his mouth before you agree to more. A good lover should give more pleasure than he receives."

Margareta's mouth hung open. Penelope had to be jesting, surely. No woman…

"No woman wants a bad lover," Penelope finished for her. "I'd rather join the nunnery permanently than share a bed with a man who doesn't absolutely adore me, or at least love me."

A fleeting memory of her mother's people, and what they did to men who didn't please them, fluttered through Margareta's mind. She didn't want to see sharks devour Erik. She liked him. At least a little. He spoke to her face instead of her chest, and seemed to care what she thought. No one else except Penelope did that – not even her father. All he cared about was getting his sons back, her bawdy brothers who would go back to their violent ways the moment they regained human form, she was certain of it. At least she could save the people of Beacon Isle from them, if the island belonged to her. Or her husband, which was almost the same thing.

"Your brothers don't deserve the sacrifice you're making for them," Penelope said sadly. "But the prince you left in the library? Why don't you give him a chance to show you what kind of husband he'd make?"

Margareta regarded Penelope for a long moment. She might not want to admit it, but her friend was right. Her brothers didn't deserve what she was doing for them, but that didn't matter. She had given her word, and the people of Beacon Isle would suffer if she broke it.

But if she hadn't given her word…then she could speak to Erik, and tell him why he couldn't possibly be in love with a sea monster, for that's what she was to him. A creature in a book that sank ships and killed the prince she now knew was his brother. Who could kill him just as easily if she lost control and gave in to her siren nature.

One thing was certain: she didn't want Erik to suffer his brother's fate. She didn't want to watch a man she knew and perhaps even liked be ripped apart by sharks.

Never mind that she'd wanted to rip his clothes off earlier. It was a small miracle she hadn't ripped off his head, or any other part of him.

Margareta turned on her heel and left the room. She knew what she had to do.

There was only one thing that would stop her from turning into the most lascivious siren ever to step out of the sea: immersing herself in the ocean for a swim. Surely that would cool her desire.

She hurried down the stone steps to the now deserted great hall, making her way out the gate with her head held high to forestall any questions. None of the guards would dare stop her – they knew who she was.

A flock of ravens flapped over the high walls of her father's house as she left its shelter, but Margareta paid them no heed. The only ravens she cared about were her brothers, and as long as she maintained her silence, she was doing all she could for them.

Her private cove was empty, as it should be. Margareta lost no time in removing her clothing – all of it, this time.

The waves kissed her skin as she trudged through the sand, until the water reached her waist. Then she lost all pretence of humanity and shifted into her true form, extending her fins past what had been her toes as cool skin enveloped her legs, turning them into a powerful tail as blue as the deep ocean waters where she was headed.

Twenty-Four

Erik splashed himself with cold water until the ewer was empty, before he dressed and headed to the highest part of the house, the passage that looked out over White Harbour to the sea. The waves were as turbulent as his own thoughts today. Though he hated to admit it, he had the answer his father sought: Beacon Isle paid tribute to no one, for it had no lord or monarch aside from its Master, who was a rich man indeed. The contents of his father's treasury were nothing to the port duties Master

Nicholas collected in a single year.

Beacon Isle would be a rich prize to anyone who could conquer it, but the very nature of the island made it near impregnable. Master Nicholas had a neat navy of merchant ships that could turn to war as easily as they did to trade. Erik's father would never win the island by force.

And so he lingered here, pursuing his real quest – twin quests, truly. His pursuit of the mythical creatures who had saved him, and the girl who commanded them. A girl who drove him to insanity, so that he kissed her and professed his love in the most awkward way.

No wonder she'd left, undoubtedly disgusted that he would do such a thing.

He must have imagined her hands on him.

Even just the thought of it heated his blood to boiling again. Erik cursed and headed back to his chamber for more water. No, he'd go to the sea for a swim. Immersing his whole body in cold water would be a much better idea.

He reached the stairs, then stopped when he

heard voices. Male voices this time.

"Did you see her again last night?"

"I see her most every night. She swims into the shallows in that cove just past the breakwater, lays herself down on the sand, and sleeps."

"Why haven't you taken her for your own if she's so pretty, then?"

"Oh, she's pretty enough, but she's a mermaid, man. What use is a woman who has a tail where her legs should be? Waste of a pair of tits if she has no legs to dive between."

"I heard of a brave man who tamed a mermaid once. They say she was the sweetest lay who ever lived, and she was his, because he tamed her. See, the trick is to stop her going back to the ocean – she's powerless on land. What he did was cut off her tail, I heard. Not like you would with a fish. No, she's got legs beneath those fins, and if you want to get between them, you have to cut her legs free. Do that, and she'll be your slave for life."

"A man took a sword to a mermaid and

lived to tell the tale?"

"On my honour, though I heard it was just a knife. And the man was no ordinary man, but the Master of Beacon Isle himself."

"The Master? Master Nicholas?"

"Maybe. Might explain that daughter of his. Proud and beautiful as the day is long, not like normal girls. Wouldn't surprise me if she was half mermaid."

The other man laughed. "But which half? Now we know why the Master hasn't married her off yet."

"Maybe. Hey, when does she come ashore? Maybe I should try my luck, if mermaids are such sweet wives."

"Just after sunset."

At sunset he could see a mermaid? Without hesitation, Erik took the stairs three at a time, but he saw no sign of the men who had spoken. Only a pair of ravens perched on the window ledge, which flew off as he approached. Never mind, he told himself. If he could see a real mermaid with his own eyes, he could show the creature to Margareta. Then she might trust him with her secrets, or at least stop thinking he was a fool.

He felt for his knife, closing his fingers reassuringly around the hilt. A mermaid was a wild creature at best, and all the stories agreed on one thing: she would kill him without hesitation if she felt threatened. The knife was for his protection.

Twenty-Five

Erik reached the breakwater, and only when he stood on it could he see the small cove he'd heard the men speak about. Small, private, and empty. On a hot summer's day, he'd love to take a dip in the water himself. Now, though, he had no intention of entering the sea. Not if a mermaid lurked close by.

Feeling like a coward, he climbed a tree, hoping its branches would hide him from sight. None of his research suggested that mermaids could climb trees, but Erik didn't let himself feel too secure on his perch. Research and myths were one thing, but facing a mermaid in the flesh was something different entirely.

For what felt like forever, Erik clung to his branch, watching and waiting. He'd spot a shadow in the waves, only to realise it was a piece of seaweed or flotsam. His eyes began to grow heavy as he squinted into the sun, straining for even a glimpse of the mythical mermaid.

When she did appear, he almost missed it. A wave washed further up the beach than its fellows and when it retreated, it left behind what Erik at first thought was the decoration from the bow of a ship. A stylised fish-woman, stretching her arms and her breasts before her while her tail fanned out behind.

And then….she moved, flicking a piece of seaweed off her tail, before she combed her fingers through her dark hair.

Erik almost fell out of his tree. A mermaid. A real mermaid, not fifty feet from him!

With care to make as little sound as possible, he climbed down, creeping through the shrubbery to get a better look at the mythical creature he'd sought for so long.

Slowly, slowly, he raised his head above a bush. He saw her dark hair, then the pale skin of her back, and his breath caught in his throat. Legs. She stood on two legs, just like him, though hers were bare.

In one moment, she'd shredded half the tales he'd read about her kind. Erik grinned. He'd write his own book, perhaps, and give Master Nicholas' library a copy. Or give it to Lady Margareta as a gift. Now that was an idea.

He should have asked Margareta to come with him to see the mermaid. Tomorrow he'd bring her to the cove and watch her reaction.

He must have made some sound, because the mermaid suddenly stiffened. She scanned the cove, then turned around and directed her piercing gaze at the bushes where Erik hid. His instincts screamed at him to duck, to get out of sight, but he was mesmerised by the woman before him. And she was a woman. Mermaid or not, the goddess who stood on the sand had two shapely legs, a flat belly and a pair of breasts he ached to touch.

The siren had him under her spell, his fuzzy mind told him, but Erik waved the thought away. Who cared? She was beautiful and alluring and everything a man could want. Everything he could ever want.

Erik rose to his feet and stepped out of hiding. He narrowed the distance between them and held out his arms. When she pressed her cold body against his, he closed his arms around her, and knew nothing but the bliss of holding his heart's desire.

Twenty-Six

Margareta let the wave carry her up the beach, then stretched out on the sand as the water retreated. Perhaps she'd swum a little too far today, after so long on land. She should swim more regularly, instead of spending so much time with Penelope and Melitta, or in the library. That would keep her away from Erik, too, which could only be a good thing for both of them.

Slowly, she let her body transform from tail to legs once more. Life was so much simpler under the sea. But without her tail, she most certainly felt the chill in the evening air, so she couldn't stay here for long. She'd need to dress and head back up to her father's house before dark, or her father's guards would shut the gate. They'd open it for her if she commanded it with an imperious wave in the absence of words, but her father would hear of it, and no good would come of that. At the least, she'd receive a long lecture about how she shouldn't give in to her siren and swim. More like he didn't want her messing with the ships approaching the harbour before they'd paid their duties. He never mentioned ships that had recently left the harbour, though. Maybe he didn't care about those.

Margareta flicked her hair, running her fingers through it to free it from some of the tangles.

A gasp from behind her made her whirl on the spot, looking for the hidden watcher. Had he seen her tail? Had he seen her transform? If anyone told her father…

No one would tell her father, for none would live to tell tales, Margareta resolved. She sent out a silent call, whispering through the trees where she was certain someone hid. No man was immune to a siren's call.

A man stepped out of the shadows, stumbling across the sand to obey her call. One man, no more.

He held out his arms, eyes begging for an embrace. For death's embrace.

Margareta stepped into the circle of Erik's arms and looked into his eyes. Though she might look like a human, all her siren senses were awakened. If you love me, show me, she silently commanded him.

He nodded, and brought his lips to hers for a kiss. Her lips warmed at his touch, wanting more. If she could have spoken, she would have said so. As it was, she let her eyes speak for her.

Erik's hand stroked her leg, trailing his fingers higher until he reached the junction of her thighs. Margareta gasped as his fingers slid inside, stroking her even more intimately than before.

"I love you," he whispered, tightening his grip around her with one arm as her knees weakened from the caresses from his other hand. His gaze held hers as he did something with his fingers that sent waves of pleasure washing over her.

Margareta opened her mouth in a silent scream of joy, while Erik's fingers moved within her again.

When the next tide of pleasure swept through her, Margareta forgot caution and secrecy and all the things that might make her stop. She tore at Erik's clothes, pushing him to the sand. She would have him, and silly human social conventions meant nothing.

For the first time in her life, Margareta lost control as she surrendered to her siren.

Twenty-Seven

Margareta woke slowly, revelling in the unaccustomed warmth of her bed. She must have fallen asleep on the sand in her tail again. She'd best turn back to human and get some clothing on before some fisherman stumbled across her.

She blinked away the sleep from her eyes, stretching. Her legs touched warm flesh and cloth. Margareta tried to jerk away from the other body, but a heavy arm lay across her, holding her close.

By all the saints, who had she killed?

She squirmed out from under the man and flipped him over. She almost cried with relief when she saw his chest rise as he drew breath. She hadn't killed him. Hesitantly, she reached for the cloak that shrouded him and pulled the fabric away from his face.

Margareta staggered back, falling to the sand.

Erik. She'd surrendered to her siren nature and seduced Erik.

Now, more than ever, she wished she could speak to him. Damn her stupid brothers for getting cursed, and twice damn her father for persuading her to break their curse. It was almost as bad as being cursed herself, and what had she done to deserve it?

She stared down at Erik. If what her father told her was true, she might have permanently damaged Erik. She wouldn't know until he woke whether he'd been driven mad by whatever she'd done to him.

Seven hells…what had she done to him?

She'd never allowed a man close enough to her for something like this to happen before. A small part of her whispered that now she'd tried intimacy with a man, she would want plenty more, but Margareta hushed it. If her pleasure came at the cost of Erik's sanity, it was too high a price to pay. Ever.

Margareta shook Erik, but he didn't wake. Her heart sank. If he'd lost his senses, he might never wake. Killing him would be a mercy, and it would be her responsibility to end the suffering she had inflicted on him.

She was a true siren. She'd destroyed a man, and nothing could fix this.

"Whore!" screamed a voice, as something sharp hit her shoulder.

Margareta whirled, and something hit her back.

"Could have saved us, but a whore like you couldn't stay a maiden for long enough!" shrieked another voice.

"Whore!" hissed a third as dark projectiles hit her on both sides.

This time, Margareta saw one of them. It wasn't a projectile at all, but a dark bird that darted down to peck at Erik. Margareta flapped a hand at the bird to shoo it away from her unconscious lover, but she was too late – its beak was already red with blood.

For the second time in two days, Margareta lost control of her human nature. But this time, the siren reigned supreme.

The ocean surged up the beach at her command, circling her and Erik with an army of waves while the sand beneath him remained untouched.

Suddenly the air was filled with dark feathers as half a dozen ravens flew in to attack Margareta from all sides. She directed the water to fight them, but it wasn't enough – some of them reached her, clawing and pecking at her face before she managed to stun one with her fist. She only had a moment's reprieve, though, before the stunned bird was replaced with two more, angrier and more intent on drinking her blood than their disoriented brother.

All the while, their caws sounded more like cries of "Whore!" than the calls of ordinary birds.

One of them fastened onto a chunk of her hair, beating its wings furiously as it tried to rip the hair from her head. If she could have made a sound, Margareta would have screamed, it hurt so much when the lock of hair parted from her scalp. She felt something warm against her back and spun around, terrified that it was a cascade of her own blood. Instead, she found Erik, risen to his feet with murder in his eyes.

"I won't let them hurt you," he vowed, brandishing a knife. A bird darted toward Margareta, then changed direction, aiming for Erik's eyes. His arm whipped out, swifter than a bird in flight. Light flashed on his blade as he separated the bird from its head, and both fell at Margareta's feet. "I count ten more. Keep doing whatever you're doing, and leave killing them to me."

Margareta nodded, not sure what to think. The only clear thought in her head was that Erik had most certainly not lost his wits, and whatever she and Erik had done last night, he hadn't paid the price for it.

She punched another bird as it dived for her, sending it into the crest of a wave, which quickly sucked it under. Concentrating on the water, she built up a particularly big wave and used it to engulf three more birds. Panting, she lifted her arm to clout another, only to see Erik cut it down before it could reach her.

"That's all of them, my lady," Erik said, sounding just as breathless as she.

Margareta turned to face him. Erik was as naked as she was, except for the cloak he'd wrapped around them both while they lay on the beach.

Memories trickled back of their night together, two bodies so entwined even she hadn't known which limbs belonged to who. Nor had she cared. He might be her first, but no other man could compare. And not only had she not killed him, but she'd chosen to protect him even in the throes of unbridled passion. Somehow, Erik had succumbed to her siren call and lived. That made him a very special man indeed. Perhaps Penelope was right about him.

Staring into Erik's eyes, she felt lost.

Margareta dismissed the ocean, so that she stood alone with Erik on the damp sand.

He chuckled. "My lady, you should probably cover yourself. Looking like that, you could charm the birds from the sky as well as the fish from the sea." As he wrapped his cloak around her, he winked.

It took Margareta a moment to realise what he'd seen. Not just her naked body, but her power over the ocean. Her blood ran cold, colder even than when she swam the depths as a mermaid. Had he seen…?

"I heard rumours of a mermaid, and I came to spy the truth of it for myself before bringing you to the cove so that you might see the creature. Only to find…you know far more of such things than I ever will." Erik pulled her close, laying his cheek beside hers so that his lips brushed her ear. "Marry me, my lady of the seas. I will love you and keep your secrets as long as I live, and all I ask in return is your love, if you are willing."

Margareta wanted to shout her answer at the top of her lungs, but her silence stole her voice, even as her lips formed a YES.

"Whore!" screeched a voice. "Faithless woman! How dare you take this man into your bed while we suffer. The man who killed your own brothers. Neither of you deserve to live!"

To Margareta's stunned horror, a raven with an injured wing hopped across the sand to attack her feet, screaming obscenities and accusations.

A firm hand grasped the bird by the neck and held it up in the air. "You're a fool, Corbin. I gave you and your brothers a chance to live, to atone for your crimes. I even told you how to break the curse. You couldn't get girls to fall in love with you, but your sister, whose loyalty to her family made her vow to save you, still might have freed you. If you'd waited a few more hours, she would have broken the spell with seven years of silence, virgin or no. But now…you have forfeited your right to even a sister's love." The woman who'd spoken wrung the neck of the bird and tossed it on the sand beside the other piles of damp feathers that Margareta now realised were the corpses of the rest of the ravens.

Her brothers.

The woman bit down hard on her lip, raising her hands high. The birds moved, floating until their bodies formed a line on the sand. Only then did they begin to lose their feathers, growing until they became not birds but young men. Young men she remembered, though they were older now. Raban had been a boy of her own age when she last saw him, the youngest of her brothers, and now he was a man grown. A man decapitated, too, for his head lay a foot from his body.

Margareta let out a sob, and another. The

sound of her voice seemed to echo in the cove, for it had been so long since she had heard it. "I didn't want them to die!" she cried, falling to her knees.

The same strong hand that had wrung Corbin's neck landed on her shoulder. "Then you are a better person than any of your brothers. They would have killed you, and your boy here." The woman nodded at Erik. "He'll make a better Master of the island than any of your kin."

"But Father," Margareta began, horrified anew at the thought of what her father would say when he saw his precious sons laid low like this. They had died, while she yet lived. "Father is Master here. He will never forgive me for this, and Erik…"

"I summoned him to the cove when I arrived. He is already on his way," the woman said.

Sure enough, Father limped onto the sand, leaning heavily on his stick. He looked so frail now, as though the seven years which had passed were seventy instead. "What do you want, witch?" he demanded. "First you take my sons from me, sending them far away, and now you think to take my daughter, too?"

"I am Mistress Kun, no mere witch, and you would do well to address me so, Nicholas," the woman said. "Your sons sealed their own fate seven years ago, and today, they demonstrated that they have no right to live among decent people. They died at the hands of a woman. I call it justice."

"My sons?" Father faltered.

Mistress Kun pointed at the bodies, hidden from Father's sight by a sandbank.

It seemed to take him forever to reach the top, and when he did, his expression changed from bewilderment to something Margareta didn't think looked entirely human. His lips peeled away from his teeth and his eyes grew wild.

"What have you done to my sons?" he howled. His gaze fixed on Margareta. "It was you! A whore like your mother, opening your legs to every pretty man you can find. I might not have managed to kill your slut of a mother, but I will deal with you!" He advanced on Margareta, who cried out in fear, unable to move. He managed to take three steps before he keeled over face first on the sand.

Margareta wanted to dash forward to help him to his feet, but she remained rooted to the spot. Had her father really threatened to kill her? Or tried to kill her mother?

Mistress Kun knelt down to examine Father. "Dead," she grunted as she rose from her crouch. "Good riddance, too. You two will make a better job of ruling this place."

Two? Margareta stared at Erik, who looked as bewildered as she felt.

"My father sent me here to find a way to bring Beacon Isle into his kingdom. I was to discover which king the Master owed fealty to, and persuade him to become a part of my father's kingdom instead. Master Nicholas would not agree, but perhaps his heir..." Erik cleared his throat. "Lady Margareta, when your father's heir becomes Master of this island, perhaps you would be willing to put in a good word for me, and arrange a meeting?"

Heir? With her brothers dead and their curse broken, her father's heir would be…her.

"Marry me," she said.

Erik laughed. "I intend to, if you'll let me."

Margareta shook her head. "No, marry me. Beacon Isle belongs to me, and to my husband. Marry me and you may have the island." She gazed at Erik. "I ask only one thing."

"Name it," Erik urged.

Margareta wet her lips. "That you love me every night of your life as you did last night."

"I will," Erik vowed.

Mistress Kun cackled. "Sounds like happily ever after to me." She waved at the bodies lined up along the beach. "I will see that everyone knows the boys died far from home and when your father found out, he died of grief. You will inherit, no matter what his wishes were. You are the last of his line now."

She gave a little bow to Margareta.

Enchantresses did nothing without a price. "I thank you, Mistress Kun," she said steadily. "How may I repay you for all that you have done for me?"

"For us," Erik corrected.

Kun grinned. "He's right, and I'll ask a favour of you both. Take Melitta and her mother with you when you leave the island. And when you are dowager queen, return to the isle and rule until your grandson comes of age to inherit the position of Master."

"It will be done," Erik vowed, and Margareta nodded, forgetting that she now had the use of her voice.

"A blessing on you both," Kun said gravely, waving her hand in their direction. "May you have your happily ever after as long as you both shall live." And with that, she disappeared.

Erik turned to Margareta. "Is this truly what you want? Will you be happy?"

For the first time in seven years, Margareta

laughed aloud. "You already owe me your life, squire. I know you'll make me happy. I only hope I can return the favour."

"You already do," Erik said fervently. "And you always will."

Awaken: Sleeping Beauty Retold

DEMELZA CARLTON

Book 6 in the Romance a Medieval Fairy Tale series

One

In King Erik's crowded cathedral, where countless courtiers jostled each other for a glimpse of their radiant new queen, Lady Margareta of Beacon Isle, Princess Rosamond stood alone.

Or as alone as a girl could be with some lady's elbow in her midsection and yet another baron's cape trying to sweep her veil from her head for the dozenth time that day. Rosamond wished she could have worn her hair uncovered, like Queen Margareta did, restrained only by a crown of roses.

Rosamond longed to be back outside in her own garden at home, far from this foreign kingdom, but her father, King Almos, insisted that a girl her age was old enough to be betrothed, so here she was, an unwilling guest at someone else's wedding, while she wore the gowns and veils her mother had insisted upon in order to tempt some royal younger son to ask for Rosamond's hand in marriage.

Contrary to her father's wishes, Rosamond intended to keep her hands to herself for some time yet. If she could only…

The herald bellowed something about presenting their respects to the new king and queen. Rosamond found herself swept along in a wave of silk-clad humanity as the courtiers hurried to kiss the king's arse. Well, officially his hand, but if he'd turned around and presented his backside, they wouldn't have hesitated.

After what felt like forever, finally the herald announced, "Her Royal Highness, Crown Princess Rosamond, daughter and heir of King Almos…"

Rosamond didn't wait for him to finish listing her father's various titles. Instead, she strode forward and bobbed a curtsey to the king and queen as two guardsmen brought forward her coronation gift for the couple – a pair of pink rosebushes that matched the shade of Rosamond's dress perfectly.

Behind her, she heard the hiss of malicious whispers from men who'd bowed so low their hats fell off and ladies who might as well have dropped to their knees when they'd curtsied. Rosamond lifted her head high, trying to ignore them.

To her surprise, both King Erik and Queen Margareta rose to offer Rosamond similar courtesies. As the queen straightened, she held out her hand to Rosamond, asking the girl to sit beside her.

Anything to get her out of the crush of

bodies. Rosamond took the chair beside the queen happily.

"Where did you manage to grow such a delicate shade of pink?" Queen Margareta asked her. "I had an extensive rose garden in the house where I grew up, but all our roses were white." She paused to nod in acknowledgement to some courtier and his family who prostrated themselves face-down before the throne.

Rosamond tried not to laugh. "I am gifted with plants," she replied with no small amount of pride. "When I was born, my fairy godmothers blessed me with two talents – that of healing, and an affinity with plants. When my father heard of your wedding and coronation, he insisted that I bring you two of my finest roses as gifts. So here I am, and so are they."

"But how do you make them that colour pink?" Margareta asked.

"I asked them to make flowers the colour of my newest gown, so that I might wear them in my hair," Rosamond admitted. Her father's kingdom was not as rich as that of King Erik, which was richer still with the addition of Margareta's dowry of Beacon Isle, so Rosamond had fewer jewels than most of the courtiers present that day.

"So you are saying it is magic? That you can speak to plants, and they do your bidding?" Margareta said, looking intrigued. She removed her flower crown. "Here. Can you make these pink to match your gown, too?"

Rosamond took the wreath in her hands. The roses were wilting in the hot hall, poor things.

She had never tried to change the colour of cut roses, only those still attached to the bush, but she could not refuse the queen's request without at least attempting to fulfil it. Rosamond concentrated on the flowers, feeling the drying sap flow sluggishly through the stems as they valiantly tried to survive just a little longer.

There was no plant to talk to in the dying

circlet. Sighing, Rosamond pricked her thumb on a thorn and sent a wave of healing into the twined flowers. The limp stems she touched stiffened once more, as waterfalls of wilting petals turned into perfect double crowns. Within moments, the queen's coronet looked as fresh as if had just been picked from the bush, ready formed, but they were no pinker than before. These were as white as the moon.

"Oh, you have made them so beautiful!" Queen Margareta exclaimed in delight. "But I would so love them to be pink."

Swaying in her seat, Rosamond concentrated harder on the flowers. Now they were healed, they should do her bidding. They should...blush, just as the queen commanded. Blush as prettily as a maid surprised as she bathed. So they would be pink as...as...

Rosamond fainted before she could finish that thought.

Two

"Mistress, you must wake and eat something," Rosamond's maid urged.

Rosamond's head hurt, as it always did after she'd tried to perform magic. What sort of witch swooned whenever she cast a spell? One who shouldn't perform magic at all, her mother's voice echoed in her head. A princess, and a future queen, should be practicing protocol and learning all the arts of a highborn lady so that she could be an example to her subjects.

As this apparently didn't include spending long hours in the castle gardens, Rosamond had ignored her mother as much as possible. What was the point of being a queen if you couldn't do what you liked once in a while? After all, it was the king who ruled. Queens were just…for decoration, and doing whatever it was women did to get children. Oh, she knew it involved men and clothing was not required, but no one had been willing to tell her all the details. Her mother had promised to tell her everything on the night before her wedding.

Wedding. Ugh. Rosamond didn't fancy a single one of the noblemen she'd met at King Erik's court, and she fervently hoped the feeling was mutual. She'd be happy in her ignorance until the right man came to his senses and asked for her hand.

Just thinking about men made her head hurt all the more.

"Bring me willow bark tea first," Rosamond ordered.

"I have it here already, mistress," the maid said, sounding aggrieved.

"Give it to me, then."

A cup touched Rosamond's lips and she gulped down the contents, barely tasting the tepid tea.

"Now you must eat something," the maid insisted.

Rosamond gritted her teeth. Monika had been her maid for as long as she could remember, and she swore the girl liked to boss her around as much as Rosamond's mother did. More, perhaps, because Monika was not much older than her mistress and Rosamond was certain she reported everything she said to Queen Maria, Rosamond's mother. Hence why Rosamond was stuck wearing the gowns and veils her mother had insisted upon for every royal event at court.

So Rosamond took the small loaf of bread Monika held out, broke off a piece and popped it into her mouth. Food helped combat the weakness she felt after casting a spell. More helpful was a visit to the palace gardens, where the plants would restore her far faster, but the memory of yesterday's whispering courtiers was enough to make her wish to keep to her chambers until she was well enough to return home. Under no circumstances did she want even one of them to see her in the palace gardens, talking to the plants. It only took one to spread vicious rumours.

But one vicious rumour might mean no marriage proposals, too, which would be a godsend in Rosamond's eyes. And she would so love to see the roses which had provided the queen's crown.

Rosamond stuffed the rest of the bread into her mouth, forgetting all propriety in her haste. With an effort, she swallowed. "Help me dress," she commanded.

Monika set her hands on her hips. "Are you sure you're well enough? You've been abed, senseless, for a day and two nights, mistress."

The way Monika said it, she made "mistress" sound like "helpless child". This wasn't new.

Rosamond smiled sweetly. "I've rested plenty. Time to be up and about. Doesn't Mother want me to bring a husband home?"

Monika gave her a dark look, but all she said was, "If you hurry, we might make it to the tournament before it starts."

A tournament? Rosamond had heard of such things, but never attended one before.

"With knights? And jousting?" Rosamond asked eagerly.

"That was yesterday," Monika said, helping Rosamond change into a fresh shift. She selected a gown the colour of ripe strawberries and held it out for Rosamond to put on. "Today is the melee."

Rosamond slipped her arms through the sleeves and forced herself to stand still so Monika could thread and tie the laces of her gown. "What is a melee?"

"I am not sure," Monika admitted, giving

the laces a sharp tug so that Rosamond was left breathless. "But Sir Warin has entered."

"Sir Warin? But who will guard me?" Rosamond demanded.

"You have a place beside the queen, if you are well enough," said Monika. "I'm sure her royal guard won't mind taking care of one more."

That sounded all right to Rosamond, so she submitted to Monika's toilette with good grace as the maid dressed her hair and tucked it under a white veil.

They made their way out to a field Rosamond barely recognised. Gone were the sheep that had grazed there when they'd arrived. Now it was crowded with brightly coloured pavilions crowned with flags that snapped in the breeze. At one end, there was tiered seating that held a crowd of courtiers. Rosamond suppressed a groan as she felt their eyes turn on her.

"This way, mistress," Monika said, touching Rosamond's elbow. She pointed at a stand shrouded in a purple canopy. In the shadows beneath it, Rosamond could just make out the king and queen.

Rosamond took her seat beside Queen Margareta and tried to hide her surprise as Monika placed herself on the boards at Rosamond's feet.

Margareta turned to Rosamond. "It is good to see you better, Princess."

Before Rosamond could reply, the king added, "She looks like a strawberry with cream on top. She'll distract the knights from combat in those colours. Ha, they'll all want to eat her up!" He laughed at his own joke, as did most of the courtiers within earshot.

Rosamond blushed as red as her dress.

"Do shut up, Erik, or the girl will return home convinced there's an ass on the throne here and her father's army will be at our gates within the week," Margareta said in a low voice, so that only Rosamond and the king heard. The queen's serene smile never faltered. "Now, Princess, let me look at you. He is right about one thing. That colour does suit you. I hope you brought a lot of favours, for all the knights will be asking for yours today."

"Favours?" Rosamond faltered.

Monika pushed a bundle of cloth into her lap with a pointed look.

"Is this your first tournament, Princess?" the queen asked. When Rosamond nodded, Margareta continued, "It is mine, too, but I have had both my husband and many of his knights explaining the intricacies of tournaments to me for weeks until I agreed that all of the men would be allowed to show off in my honour. Apparently, beating each other senseless is a sign of respect to their new queen. Quite barbaric."

While they waited for the day's combat to begin, Margareta regaled Rosamond with tales of yesterday's jousting. Two horses had been killed, several knights had broken arms and legs, and one was sporting two black eyes so dark he'd refused to remove his helmet.

Rosamond couldn't hide her shock. "You

mean men were hurt? All I have heard of tournaments is that they are heroic. Romantic, for knights fight for their lady-loves. I had not heard that men were injured."

The king heard this and laughed. "Silly girl, of course men are hurt. This is good practice for battle. And just like in battle, we have physicians on hand to help set bones and the like."

Rosamond felt ill, as though she would bring her breakfast back up again at the king's feet.

"Erik," the queen said warningly.

The king opened his mouth as if to protest, then closed it again without a word and turned to face the empty field.

"I would like to hear more about how you choose your gowns, Princess," Margareta said. "First the pale pink at the coronation, and now this deeper rose for today. What will you choose tomorrow? Purple? So that on the day of your departure, you wear black?"

Embarrassed again, Rosamond mumbled

something about how her mother had chosen her gowns for this trip.

"Then you are very lucky. My mother would be perfectly happy to send me out naked, as long as I wore a string of pearls," Margareta declared.

Rosamond couldn't help herself. She burst out laughing. "Your mother would let you go out naked? Not even wearing a shift?"

Margareta nodded. "Naked. Clothing is just a distraction, she said, when the way to catch a husband is to show him what you will bring to the marriage. If you truly wish to enchant a man, let him see you naked. I assure you, it will torment him until he finds the courage to ask for your hand so that he can see such beauty again."

Rosamond doubted she would ever have the courage to do something so brazen. Not to mention that there was little chance she would ever want to enchant a man. King Erik seemed like a nice enough husband to Margareta, yet she'd called him an ass. If even the best men were donkeys, where did that leave her?

Thinking to change the subject, Rosamond ventured, "I can't imagine it. You look so lovely in your gown, Your Majesty. What manner of creature grows fur in such a rich red colour?"

The queen laughed. "This is not fur. It is velvet — made on a loom by a weaver who brought her knowledge of its craft from distant foreign lands. I shall make you a gift of some, if you wish it."

"I do," Rosamond said fervently.

Conversation ended for a little while, as a cacophony of trumpets signalled the beginning of the tournament. Two teams of knights lined up on opposite ends of a field, while a page in the king's colours set what looked like a blown-up pig's bladder in the middle of the field.

Rosamond turned to the queen to ask about the bladder, but someone blew a short blast on a trumpet and the thunderous clatter of two dozen men charging across a field toward one another drowned out any sound she made.

She lost sight of the bladder amid the madmen trying to kill each other, though only armed with wooden staves.

It was nothing short of brutal. She went from gasping at every blow to leaving her mouth permanently open. Rosamond tried to close her eyes but a fresh shout or crack of bone only made her snap her eyes open again until finally she clapped her hands over her eyes so she could only peek through her fingers. Even that limited field of vision made her sick to her stomach.

All around her, people cheered and groaned as their favourite knights gained or lost some sort of victory, but Rosamond couldn't tell one mud-spattered man from another, especially with them clad head to toe in boiled leather.

Finally, when she was certain she could endure no more of this violence, the king called a halt to the match. Servants stood beside the field with flagons and the squires raced to get their knights a drink. Only then did helmets come off, and Rosamond realised she recognised one of the half-dozen men left standing as the captain of her guard, Sir Warin.

The king saw him at the same time Rosamond did. "You man fights well," he said. "You should make sure he carries your favour into battle, for if he fights for one of the ladies in my court, I will do everything in my power to persuade him to stay in my service instead of your father's."

Her man. Rosamond hadn't thought of the knight that way before, but now that she looked at him, she had to admit he was quite handsome. He was no simpering courtier but a brave knight who fought well. Who would fight for the woman he loved, and her honour. She sighed. So romantic.

Rosamond flapped her hand to get Monika's attention. "Go to Sir Warin and give him this," she instructed, thrusting a piece of pink fabric at her maid. "Tell him he fights for his princess's honour."

Monika didn't say anything. She simply took

the handkerchief and made her way from the royal stand to where Sir Warin stood, drinking his cup of ale.

The queen, noticing Rosamond's preoccupation, followed her gaze. "So that's why you aren't flirting with the courtiers here. You have better men at home."

Rosamond reddened. "I don't know how to flirt, Your Majesty. And even if I did…"

Margareta patted her hand. "Most men won't notice anyway. They're simple creatures, really. Let him kiss you, find a way for him to glimpse you naked, and then refuse all else until you are married. Everything else is just so you can make sure he's not a complete ass, right, Erik?"

"Mm?" the king said. His attention was on the remaining six men forming up on the field once more. "Yes, of course. They're about to fight again."

Margareta's serene smile surfaced as she added softly to Rosamond, "And never agree to host a tourney. I swear, this will be our last."

The horn blasted its command for the fight to begin, and Rosamond hid behind her hands. But if she peeped between her fingers, she could still see the pink handkerchief tied to the shoulder of Sir Warin's cuirass as six men became four, then three, then two, until he faced a single foe who was much larger than him.

Their staves clacked together like practice swords, but both men wielded them like steel blades they intended to kill one another with. They circled, crossed, thrust…it looked like an elegant dance, until Warin stumbled on an uneven patch of ground and his thrust went wide. His opponent saw his chance and brought his stave down hard against Warin's sword arm.

Rosamond heard the crack as Warin's arm broke, but the shouts and cheers from the stands drowned out her frantic cry.

The other man lifted his wooden sword in salute to the king, turning his back on Warin. Warin still held his stave in his injured arm, but he transferred it to his other hand and assumed a fighting stance.

"This is not over – I do not yield!" Sir Warin roared, loud enough for even Rosamond to hear.

Her heart beat rapidly in her breast. How could he be so brave, when he was injured?

The bigger man turned, and brought his stave up slowly. He, too, was tired, but he wasn't as badly hurt as Warin. The dance resumed. Warin's opponent dragged one foot, as though his knee had been damaged. Warin kept his broken arm close to his body, but as far away from the other man as possible. Each time the staves knocked together, it seemed softer, as though both men lacked the strength to continue.

Time ticked by. A second. An hour. An eternity. Or so it seemed to Rosamond, who longed to run out onto the field and heal her hero, but she could not until this duel was over.

A collective gasp rose from the stands as the

big man overbalanced and fell to his knees. Warin, in an almost leisurely movement, set the point of his stave to the man's throat.

Rosamond heard wild cheering, and it took her a moment to realise the sound came from her own throat.

"Do we have a winner?" King Erik boomed.

Warin pulled the pink handkerchief from his cuirass and waved it above his head like a flag as he staggered to the royal box. When he reached it, he fell to his knees. "I am the victor, Your Majesties," he said.

"To the joy of your countrywomen. I'm sure they are glad they will be protected by an able knight like yourself for their journey home," the king replied.

Countrywomen? Oh, of course. Monika. Rosamond dismissed the maid from her mind easily. Sir Warin was the captain of the princess's guard. He would defend her with his life, before he even glanced at Monika.

That was why she needed to heal him. She might be a poor witch, but he had fought for her honour and won. Rosamond rose and descended to the grass, or what had been grass before the fighting had churned it into dust. Heedless of her gown or who saw, she knelt beside her valiant knight and reached for his broken arm.

Blood. She needed blood to cast a spell. There were no thorns today, so she scraped her hand along the edge of his stave until she felt the prick of a splinter. With her fingers bleeding, she touched her wounded knight, closed her eyes and concentrated on healing him.

She concentrated so hard she barely noticed when the spell sent her into yet another deep swoon.

Three

When Rosamond opened her eyes, she met the frightened gaze of a maidservant she did not know. The girl bobbed a curtsey, said, "I shall fetch the queen," and hurried off, leaving Rosamond alone.

Alone with a tray of food, at least, Rosamond noted, reaching for one of the strange orange berries. It burst like a bubble of white wine on her tongue. Eagerly, she reached for another.

"So you like cloudberries, too, Princess?" Margareta asked as she swept into the room. "Erik says they aren't sweet enough for his liking." She reached for one and popped it into her mouth. "More for me."

Suddenly awkward, Rosamond didn't know what to do. Surely she should curtsey, or offer the queen a chair. What did one do when a queen visited your bedchamber?

Margareta dragged a bench from the corner to the side of Rosamond's bed and enthroned herself on it. "Your maid tells me you are unwell, and must return home. The royal physician says you should not be moved, you are so gravely ill. What say you?"

Rosamond wet her lips. "I am fine, Your Majesty."

"Are you with child?" the queen demanded. "If he refuses to marry you, I can make the man change his mind." Her smile was fierce.

Rosamond shivered. "No, Your Majesty. I have not chosen a husband yet, and my father has not chosen one for me."

"Not with child, and not ill," the queen said, ticking them off on her long fingers. "Then whatever is the matter?"

"My...gift. The magic I was born with. It is not strong. When I try to use it, I...am not strong enough, either." Rosamond swallowed. "At home, I only used my powers on living plants, and it was not so bad. Here...on cut flowers, and on men, I am not strong enough."

Margareta laughed. "So, what you are saying is that men are hard work while plants are not? I will agree with you there!"

Rosamond wasn't sure what to say to that. Queen Margareta was nothing like she'd expected. Fortunately, she was saved from finding a response by the entry of a maidservant carrying a wooden box.

"I have a gift for you," the queen announced, taking the box. "It has been a week since my coronation and...look!" She flipped open the lid and revealed the crown of roses she'd worn on her coronation day.

Yet…this could not be the same crown. The roses were as fresh as if they had just been picked, instead of dried out in the summer heat as they surely should have been.

"Whatever spell you cast on them, these roses will not die. They remain perfect. You are gifted with powerful magic, Princess. I have little magic, but I have placed a blessing on the crown. When you take a husband, he will be loyal to you from the day you first wear this crown until the day he dies. I would advise wearing it on your wedding day." Margareta set the crown back in its box, and closed the lid.

"Thank you," Rosamond said. She didn't have the heart to tell the queen that she didn't want any husband, loyal or otherwise. "I thought you said you would give me some of that new cloth to take home, not a crown."

"So I did!" the queen exclaimed. "I forgot to ask Penelope if she has enough, or whether she must make more for you. I will send someone directly."

The maidservant who'd brought the box

was quickly despatched, but the queen stayed to tell Rosamond all about the remainder of the tournament, which she'd missed. From the sound of it, that was a good thing. The melee on foot had been followed by one where the combatants rode on horseback, and Margareta sounded almost gleeful at the number of broken limbs she described in vivid detail.

Rosamond's stomach roiled, making her regret breaking her fast at all.

Four

Three days Rosamond waited for the queen's gift, while watching the crowds at court dwindle as other guests returned to their homes. When Rosamond hinted at her plans to depart, too, Queen Margareta insisted that the princess's gift would be ready within the hour, but hours came and went with no sign of any cloth.

Finally, Rosamond lost patience and sent

Monika to find the weaver. The maid returned with a puzzled look on her face.

"Did you say the weaver was a woman named Penelope?" Monika asked.

Rosamond nodded. "That's what the queen called her. Yes."

"I found a Penelope. She is the queen's own dressmaker, not just a weaver, and a noblewoman in her own right. Lady Penelope is a knight's widow and the queen's companion. She has not been at court because her daughter is ill." Monika frowned. "She says that if you are willing to come to her chambers, she will measure you for a new gown directly."

"I do not understand. The queen said…" Rosamond stopped. She had been the queen's companion in place of Lady Penelope. Queen Margareta evidently did not wish to give her up until her original companion was at her side again. "No matter. I shall go now."

Monika led the way back to Lady Penelope's chambers, an airy apartment that was bigger than the one Rosamond had been given. Evidently the queen's companion was held in high regard.

"Her Royal Highness, Princess Rosamond," Monika announced.

Movement in the window alcove drew Rosamond's attention as a petite, dark-haired woman climbed down from the window seat, setting down her sewing. She bobbed a curtsey. "Your Highness. I'm Penelope. Queen Margareta told me you wanted a gown like her red velvet one, but when my daughter took ill, I could not leave her side." Penelope tilted her head to the side, like a curious bird. "I don't think the red would suit you. Too dark. Perhaps pink or sage…" She crossed the room and knelt by a chest beside a small couch that Rosamond realised was occupied.

The pale girl on the couch looked perhaps ten years old, but her skin had a waxen sheen like she was not long for this life. Rosamond's heart went out to the girl, and to her poor mother.

"Melitta fell ill so suddenly. For three days, she unpacked the chests of cloth that arrived in port last week, exclaiming over all the new colours. And on the fourth…she could not rise from her bed." Penelope's tears spilled over and she wept into her hands.

Melitta looked like she would never rise again, in Rosamond's opinion. Unless she could heal the girl. Rosamond glanced around the room, looking for something sharp. She spotted a strange contraption with a wheel mounted on a low table, and a short staff with a spindle sticking up from the table. Rosamond swiped her finger across the spindle, wincing at the sting as the sharp point drew blood, then knelt beside the girl.

Laying her hand on Melitta's forehead, Rosamond closed her eyes. She focussed first on cooling the girl's fever, then on ridding the girl's blood of the disease. As Rosamond felt her own head grow fuzzy, she released the girl and rose unsteadily to her feet. She fumbled blindly for the windowsill, then cried out as something sharp pierced her hand. Yet something about the pain cleared her vision almost instantly.

Rosamond glanced down. She had grasped a briar rose growing through the window, and the thorns had bitten deep into her palm. In the back of her mind, somewhere in the memories of how her magical gifts were supposed to work, Rosamond remembered that her healing ability was linked to plants. Suppressing a second cry of pain, she wrapped her hand firmly around the flower stem, burying the thorns even more deeply, and reached for the girl with her free hand.

Within moments, the girl's eyes fluttered open. She coughed wetly before she murmured something that sounded like, "Mitera?" and coughed again.

"I am here," Lady Penelope said.

The disease had settled in Melitta's lungs. Rosamond felt blood trickle down her wrist, but she closed her eyes once more to focus on the girl's lungs, where fluid was making it hard for her to breathe. Rosamond concentrated, and the fluid seemed to lessen a little. Slowly at first, then more strongly, she poured what magic she had into the girl. Melitta coughed again, not so thickly this time, and Rosamond took hope as she rid the girl of the disease that had plagued her.

In triumph, Rosamond pushed away from the girl, panting, as black spots danced before her eyes. She would not swoon today, she swore. Today, weak as she was, she was mistress of her own magic.

Five

Rosamond surveyed the horses. They all looked well rested and well fed — perfect for the journey home. If anything, their loads were lighter, now that the king and queen had their coronation gifts.

"What is all this?" Warin demanded.

Half a dozen servants came into view, each pair bearing between them an enormous chest.

"From Queen Margareta and Lady

Penelope." They set the chests down and took off back into the palace.

Lady Penelope? Oh, then this must be the cloth the queen promised her, Rosamond decided. She had not expected this much. Perhaps this was Lady Penelope's doing. After all, if it weren't for Rosamond, her daughter Melitta would be dead. Rosamond shivered. They were all but a breath away from death, though she hoped her life would hold a great many more breaths than just one.

"We are not taking those chests with us," Sir Warin said. His deep voice held a command that any of his guardsmen would hurry to obey.

Rosamond was no guardsman, though. The princess gave orders. She did not obey them. She smiled. "And refuse the queen's gift? I think not. That would be rude. Some might see it as a declaration of war."

Sir Warin snorted, but he did not say a word.

Monika stepped forward. "Mistress, the

chests are too heavy for the horses to carry. But I could pack the cloth into the saddlebags on the packhorses. Then we need not refuse the queen's gift."

So Warin nodded curtly. "Do it, then." He strode away, muttering under his breath.

Rosamond admired each folded length of fabric as her maid packed them into the saddlebags. There was pink, as Penelope had promised, but also sage, gold, cream, and a deep red that her mother might fancy. The only colour missing was blue. As the queen seemed to favour blue gowns for her wardrobe, Rosamond supposed that the queen had used all the blue fabric already and Lady Penelope had not had time to weave more. No matter. There was enough rich fabric here to keep her mother's dressmaker sewing into winter. Rosamond liked that idea. She could have new gowns for Yule.

Finally, they were finished. Sir Warin returned, with a squad of guards in tow. Princess Rosamond mounted her horse, and

Monika did the same. They had said their farewells to the king and queen the previous evening, before retiring, so now they formed up and rode out the gate, with far less fanfare than when they had arrived.

Nevertheless, when Rosamond glanced back at the palace she saw the queen standing at the battlements, dressed in blue and waving a blue handkerchief in farewell.

Six

Rosamond tired easily on the first day, and the second, and the third. When the guards pitched her pavilion by the setting rays of the sun, she had been quite ready to retire early for the first week of their journey home. Perhaps travelling did not agree with her, or the magic she had expended in healing Lady Penelope's daughter Melitta had taken its toll on her strength. She might not have swooned, but she was certain if she tried to use her magic again, she would most certainly faint.

So she stumbled to bed with the sun, falling asleep to the low hum of conversation between the guards, Monika and Sir Warin. Aside from Monika and Warin, the others maintained a respectful silence in her presence, but once she was inside the pavilion, they thought nothing of making bawdy jokes that still made her blush. So much for not knowing what a couple did on their wedding night, though that seemed tame compared to their stories about the goings-on in the brothels they'd visited while staying in King Erik's capital.

Usually, Monika rode at her side. No matter how many times she asked Sir Warin to ride with her, he insisted that he was better at protecting her than making conversation that would amuse her.

Rosamond privately disagreed. Monika said little, and what she did say usually involved minding the skirt of her gown, or not overexerting herself. It was like travelling with her mother.

At the end of the sixth day, Rosamond was delighted to find Sir Warin riding beside her. "Welcome home, Princess."

Rosamond glanced around, but she saw nothing new except the edge of a wood they were about to enter. "Are we home already?" she asked, wrinkling her nose in puzzlement.

"You are, for those bramble hedges mark the boundary of your kingdom, Princess. One of your ancestors decreed that his borders must be marked with berry bushes, and no one disobeyed the king, so it was done. Now the thickets are so dense the farmers at the borders regard them as another crop. If we didn't export our berry wine, every man in the kingdom would be drunk as a lord, every day of the year!" Sir Warin laughed.

Rosamond shuddered. She'd seen far too many drunk lords at King Erik's court. There were so many reasons she didn't want a husband.

Sir Warin had not been drunk, though. She had never seen him anything but sober and alert, as befit a knight and a captain of the guard.

Could a princess marry a knight? Her mother had told her to look for a prince or a lord at least, but they were all foreigners. A knight who was her own countryman was surely more acceptable than some foreign barbarian, no matter what title he held. Sure, foreigners might bring extra lands to the kingdom, but what need had they for more land? Her kingdom's borders were already marked by berry bushes. If they expanded their territory, her people would have to plant more bushes just to know where the boundaries lay.

Rosamond trailed her fingers through a bush that grew beside the road, and felt an overwhelming sense of welcome, as if the plants were as delighted as she was that she would soon be home again.

Rosamond almost laughed. Such sentimental nonsense. Plants didn't have feelings. She stripped off a handful of berries and nibbled on them as she rode.

Sir Warin called a halt, setting up camp in a clearing amid a collection of particularly bountiful berry bushes. Some of the guards had picked handfuls already, but Sir Warin called them to set up camp first. They set to work as Rosamond slid from her mount, intent on picking her own share of the red berries before her greedy guards could choose the best ones.

For when it came to picking wild berries, a princess had as much right to them as the lowliest peasant. Her several times great-grandfather, the first King Almos from whom her father got his name, had decreed as much when he ordered the berry bushes to be planted, and no one had dared to rescind his law. Why would they? There were berries aplenty. Far more than the royal household could ever need.

But the more she picked, the stronger the feeling of welcome became. Rosamond thrust both hands deep into a berry bush, heedless of the thorns, and grasped a branch thicker than her arm. Power surged into her – like magic, but more, somehow. It coursed through her, singing of leaves and buds and berries, sap flowing and new growth stretching toward the sky, with the thunderous percussion of the deep draught of sustenance roots drew from the rich soil. The bush lived, with as much passion as she did, and it bade her welcome home.

"Are you all right, mistress?" Monika called, making her way over.

Rosamond released the bush, and wiped the tears from her cheeks. Never would she have thought plants could have such powerful emotions, let alone share them with her. "I'm fine," she said.

"No, you're not. Look at your poor hands!"

Rosamond glanced at the slight scratches on her hands, which faded even as she watched. The blood that had trickled from the cuts still looked ominous, though. "I am fine,"

Rosamond repeated, lifting her chin as she looked Monika in the eye. Her maid did not look fine at all. In fact, she looked unusually pale, with a thin sheen of sweat on her face. "Are you well?"

"Of course, mistress," Monika said. "It is hot, is all. Perhaps I have been too close to the fire. Surely you are thirsty. Shall I fetch you a drink?"

Monika needed refreshment more than Rosamond, but the princess followed her maid back to the pavilion where there was a jug of cider waiting for her. For them both, Rosamond corrected, making sure the maid poured two cups instead of one.

She vowed to watch Monika carefully tonight. The woman was certainly behaving very oddly.

Seven

Rosamond lay in the darkness of her pavilion, listening to Monika's even breathing. Low voices outside told her that the guardsmen were still awake, sitting around the fire, she presumed. After falling asleep almost instantly for a week, she was restless.

Perhaps it was the magic of communicating with the berry bush today, or maybe it was simply because she knew she was home.

Rosamond was not sure, but she certainly did not feel like sleeping.

The sound of Sir Warin's deep voice decided her. Her maid might sleep, but Rosamond was not ready to retire yet. She neatened her gown as best she could in the darkness, then pushed aside the tent flap to emerge into the firelight.

Silence greeted her.

Only Sir Warin dared to break it. "Good evening, Princess," he said. "Are we making too much noise, so that you cannot get your beauty sleep? Though a princess such as yourself has no need to be any more beautiful than she is already."

Rosamond felt a blush colour her cheeks. She prayed it was too dark for Sir Warin to see the effect of his compliment. "I could not sleep," she confessed. "I thought perhaps a cup of wine…"

"Ludd, fetch the princess some wine," Sir Warin said. One of the guardsmen rose to do his bidding.

By the time the guardsman returned, the rest of the men had melted into the darkness. Once Rosamond had accepted the cup Ludd offered, he disappeared, too.

"Where did they go?" she asked Sir Warin, who alone had remained.

He stirred the fire. "Not far," he said. "Like every other night on this journey, they form a perimeter to protect you, Princess. Some will sleep, while others stand watch. We may be home, but it does not do to relax one's guard. There are still dangers on the road."

"Dangers?" Rosamond swallowed. "Who would dare attack a royal travelling party in our own kingdom?"

"Not who, but what. There are bears and wolves in these woods, and there are tales of evil witches in the world who respect no borders. It is my duty and theirs to protect you from all dangers until I return you home to the king and queen." Sir Warin bowed his head. "I will not let any harm come to you, Princess."

His words made her feel oddly warm inside,

which had nothing to do with the wine or the fire, she was certain. As though he took his responsibility for her safety personally. She liked that. Rosamond drank deeply from her cup. "Would you lay down your life me?" she asked. She licked the wine from her lips.

"As the captain of your guard, it is my duty to do so. But it will not come to that." He laughed. "No one has seen a wicked witch in these parts for many a long year, and any one of my men is easily a match for a wolf or a bear."

"I have never seen a wolf, or a bear," she mused.

Sir Warin laughed again. "And I hope you never do, Princess. One day you will be queen, and you will live in your castle, ruling over all of us, and in return we will keep the castle safe from bears and wolves and even witches."

"How do you defeat a witch?" Rosamond asked. "I thought only a more powerful witch could defeat another. There are tales of enchantresses who…" She tried to dig out the memory, but her head was too fuzzy.

"I am but a common soldier," Warin said ruefully, touching his arm. "Good with a sword, and little else. That is why you healed my arm, was it not? So that I might wield a sword in your defence, as you practice your benevolent witchcraft for the benefit of the kingdom. You will be a powerful queen one day, Princess. It would be an honour to lay down my life for you."

Rosamond laughed softly. "You are so sweet to say that," she said. "No man has ever…"

He was so close. So close and warm and tempting and…

Rosamond kissed him. For a moment, everything was perfect as her lips connected with his. Then, the moment shattered as he stiffened and pulled away.

"Your pardon, Princess," he said. "I fear you have mistaken me for someone else."

Rosamond licked her lips. He tasted of wine and salt, and she rather liked it. "No, Sir Warin.

I gave a brave knight a kiss, as I should have when you won the melee at the tournament."

He stared at her for a long moment, before muttering something about checking the perimeter. He disappeared into the darkness.

For a long time, Rosamond waited for him to return. When he did not, and her eyelids began to droop, she returned to her pavilion. There were seven more nights before they arrived home, and a week was more than she would need to convince the knight that she was the woman for him.

After all, her mother had ordered her to find a husband while she was away, and no one disobeyed the queen.

Smiling to herself, Rosamond drifted off into sleep.

Eight

When Rosamond awoke the next morning, she couldn't smell breakfast.

"Monika?" she murmured, but received no answer. Perhaps it was too early and the maid was still preparing it. Rising, Rosamond decided to begin making herself presentable for the day. There was still a jug of water half full from last night, so she used that to wash before hunting for a comb to untangle her night-mussed hair.

A terribly unladylike snore made her stop, for it came from Monika's pallet. Surely the maid had not allowed a guardsman to sleep in her mistress's pavilion? She would soon feel the rough edge of Rosamond's tongue if she had. Wait until the queen heard about it.

Rosamond marched over to Monika's bed and wrenched the coverlet aside. Monika herself lay there alone, breathing so laboriously that it sounded like snoring.

"Monika, wake up. I need breakfast," Rosamond ordered.

The maid slept on.

Angrily, Rosamond shook the woman, but Monika simply fell back to her pallet, as limp as one of the rag dolls Rosamond had once played with as a child. She seemed unusually warm to the touch, too.

Feeling fear for the first time, Rosamond cupped Monika's cheek so she could gaze upon her face. The maid's eyes were closed, but her skin had the same waxy sheen as

Melitta.

Rosamond tore her hands away from Monika and stumbled out of the tent as fast as she could. "It's Monika! She won't wake. She won't wake!" she shouted.

Strong hands fastened around her shoulders, spinning her around to face Sir Warin. "What's this about Monika?" he asked, his eyes filled with concern.

"She didn't wake. She usually wakes before me. I called her. I even shook her, but she won't wake!" Rosamond babbled, shaking her head. "She is ill. The same ailment as the weaver's daughter, I know it!"

Sir Warin gestured to the nearest guard. "Is anyone else ill?"

The man shook his head. "I don't think so, sir. I'll go check the other men." He returned a few minutes later, still shaking his head. "No, sir. Not a single man still abed, seeing as the sun is so high in the sky and all. If the princess had risen earlier, as is her usual habit, maybe one or two might have been but..." He coughed. "I'll go help saddle the horses, sir."

"Monika usually wakes me," Rosamond said. "I don't understand. If she is so ill, why am I not ailing? She rarely leaves my side."

Sir Warin's eyes narrowed. "What has she done that you have not since we left the city?"

Rosamond spread her arms wide. "Everything." Princesses did not do things for themselves, Monika and her mother had told her so many times it had become a habit. "She cooks for me, packs my things, brings water to wash with, sets out my clothes and helps me dress, even mends my clothes when I tear them. When we get home, she says I must have new gowns made with the queen's gifts, because my travel-stained dresses will not be fit for anything more than rags. Those new velvets will be perfect for court…" She might have prattled on for longer, but Sir Warin held up a hand to silence her.

"You said the weaver's daughter was ill, and Monika has the same ailment?" he asked.

Rosamond nodded.

"Did you touch the cloth the queen gave you?"

Rosamond's mouth seemed suddenly too dry. "I…no. It came in so many chests, and you were angry, so Monika said…she said she would load them onto the packhorses. The weaver's daughter unpacked those chests when they arrived, at about the same time we did, but no one else had touched them…" She stopped dead, clapping her hand to her horrified mouth. "You don't think Queen Margareta gave us cursed cloth?"

"Mayhap the queen herself did not know. Whether she did or no, the curse is undoubtedly real. We cannot take it home." Warin pointed at four guardsmen. "You! Fetch more wood. We must have a bonfire before we leave this spot."

The men obeyed, piling wood beside the small morning cookfire. They coaxed the cheerful flames into a roaring blaze under Warin's watchful eye, until he nodded and strode off.

"Where are you going?" Rosamond demanded, following him.

"To the picket lines, where the packhorses' burdens are piled, to fetch the cursed cloth. I will do what I must to protect you and the kingdom." He marched grimly to the pile of bags, seizing several before heading back to camp. When he reached the fire, he unfastened one of the sacks, reached inside, and tossed the bundle of cloth onto the flames.

"No!" Rosamond shouted. "You can't burn the queen's gifts. They are gifts. To do so would start a war." She seized the next bundle of cloth before Sir Warin could throw it into the fire. "You can't!"

Warin wrenched it out of her grip. "Do not touch the cursed stuff, Princess. What the queen does not see, she will never know. Unless you know how to remove curses, we must destroy it with fire. Can you break curses, Princess?"

Rosamond wrapped her arms around herself as tears sprang to her eyes. No one had ever spoken so roughly to her before. "No. I am a healer, and I help plants. Only a powerful enchantress – "

"Then let me do my job, Princess, which is protecting you." Another bundle of bright-coloured cloth landed in the fire, sending up a shower of sparks, followed by two more.

Realisation dawned. "If she was cursed by merely touching the cloth, then so are you." Rosamond gulped. "So am I."

"I pray that you are not, Princess." Warin would not meet her eyes. He turned and cupped his hands to his mouth, shouting for the attention of his men. "Ride for the capital. Tell the king we were taken ill on the road. God willing, we will be but a day behind you." He gave Rosamond a hard look. "You should go with them, Princess. Monika and I are cursed, but you are surely free of such evil spells."

Rosamond's fingers itched where she'd touched the velvet. "No, I cannot. What if you are wrong, and it is not a curse, but some plague that others can catch from me? I dare not bring it home."

"Go with them, Princess," Warin said through gritted teeth. "They will keep you safe. When this illness takes hold, I know that I cannot."

She lifted her chin as she glared at him. "Who will keep them safe from me if you are wrong? I am a Princess and a healer, and they will be no help to me when they are dead." She swallowed. "Or if I am dead, for surely the disease will take me first." She closed her eyes in horror. She didn't want to die. She didn't want him to die. Or Monika. Or anyone.

"Can you heal it?" Warin demanded.

Rosamond thought of Melitta. "Yes, perhaps. But it may take some time. We can't stay here beside the road, where any traveller might happen upon us, lest they be afflicted, too. We will need shelter while I try to heal you."

"Heal all three of us," Warin corrected, surrendering the last piece of cloth to the flames. "First Monika, then yourself, and if you have the energy and I still live, you can heal me."

Rosamond did not know how to heal herself, but she didn't tell Sir Warin that. She drew herself up. "Find us shelter, and I shall."

He nodded. "There is an old convent near here that I know of. It is one of the best spots in the kingdom for hawking, but as the king and queen are not fond of falcons, we should be safe."

"What about the nuns?" Rosamond demanded, horrified. "Their faith will not save them from whatever disease we are carrying, or a curse."

Warin flashed a bleak smile. "The convent has stood empty for my lifetime, Princess, and that of my father. The order who built it left, and did not come back. At least if we die there, it will be on hallowed ground."

Rosamond did not want to die, but she saw no other choice. "Help me with Monika. We must get her to this convent you speak of so that I may heal her." Before it was too late, she thought but didn't say.

Nine

After travelling for most of the afternoon, Rosamond wanted to scream at Sir Warin for his mistaken idea of what nearby meant. Even when they stopped, she saw no sign of any building at all. Perhaps the knight had only imagined this convent.

"In here," he said, taking Monika in his arms. He carried the unconscious maid toward a rock covered in thick briars.

No, not a rock. A stone wall, Rosamond realised. The briars bore so many flowers that they hid the joins in the stonework. "How do we get in?" she blurted out.

"When I was a boy, there was an entrance here. Under the briars, it will be here still." Sir Warin glanced down at Monika. "I will set her down. Keep watch over her while I work." He placed Monika carefully on the grass, then unsheathed his sword.

"No!" Rosamond cried out. "You don't need to cut them. I will ask the plants to move." The instant the words left her lips, she regretted them. Yes, plants usually did her bidding, but these were not the small rose trees in her garden at home. No, these were mighty monsters, wild and free. Yet she swallowed and stepped up to the tangled briar. Cupping her hands around a full-blown pink rose, she felt the sting as the tiny, needle-sharp thorns at the base of the bloom pierced her skin. "Permit us to pass," she whispered, closing her eyes.

She felt an answering whisper of greeting as she heard the rustle of leaves, moving in the breeze and scraping against stone. Except…there was no breeze in this still hollow.

Rosamond's eyes flew open. Before her, the briars had parted to reveal an arched portal into the building. She expected it to lead into darkness, but the ruined roof was open to the sky, letting in dappled sunlight.

Sir Warin stared at her with an intensity that made her feel uncomfortable. "I am glad to be on your side, Princess. I would hate to be your enemy," he said. He lifted Monika's limp form and strode into what remained of the convent.

Rosamond hesitated for a moment, before following him inside what turned out to be a chapel. Little remained except the stone altar, which was now wreathed in roses. She stepped up to the altar, brushing aside the leaf litter that had collected on its surface. "Put her here," she commanded.

Now it was Sir Warin's turn to hesitate.

"Witchcraft in a holy chapel? Won't we be struck down?"

Rosamond made an impatient sound in her throat. "We are already struck down with a curse, remember? Perhaps the holiness will help. We will need all the help we can get, for I am but a novice at this."

Reluctantly, he set Monika on the altar. Then he backed away, staring at the maid in horror. "She looks like one already dead, laid out for burial," he whispered. "Save her, Princess. Please, I beg you. Save us all." He dropped to his knees.

Save them all. If only she could.

Rosamond wrapped her hand around a tangle of briar, feeling warm blood slick her palm, before she set her other hand on Monika's breast and sent her healing magic flowing through the dying maid.

Ten

Three days it took her to heal Monika of the disease, for Rosamond's waning strength took its toll on how much magic she could use before she swooned. Even calling on the roses for assistance did not help as much as she had hoped…for Rosamond knew the disease coursed through her blood, too, threatening to steal her life, even as Monika recovered.

Sir Warin had caught a plump bird, which

now roasted over the fire he'd built in the old convent courtyard. "Good evening, Princess," he greeted her, wiping at the thin sheen of sweat that seemed to permanently coat his brow. He had caught the plague, too, Rosamond realised, but he would not allow her to heal him until Monika was well.

Which was now.

"It is a good evening," she replied. "The last of the disease is gone from her body. She sleeps now, but soon she will wake. Monika is healed."

He flashed a tired smile. "Then you are truly a good witch and a worker of miracles, Princess. I am grateful for your care, and I am certain that when she wakes, Monika will be, too."

"I must heal you," Rosamond insisted. "Monika will be weak for a while yet. She will need your help, and you cannot return to the city if you carry the sickness."

"She will have you, Princess. You have enough strength for a whole kingdom."

Rosamond wanted to laugh at the irony of his statement. She barely had the strength to stand. She knew what the knight did not – that she had contracted the disease when she healed Melitta, and soon she would no longer be able to hide it from him. She suspected she had only lasted so long because the healing energy coursing through her into Monika had kept the disease at bay somewhat. Not enough, though. It was only a matter of time before the disease won. Rosamond could not heal herself – magic didn't work that way.

If Sir Warin would not allow her to heal him, then she would wait until he was asleep tonight and take care of him then, Rosamond decided. She had so little time left.

Fortunately, she didn't have long to wait. Sir Warin had scarcely finished his dinner before he stretched out before the fire, mumbling something about the lateness of the hour.

Rosamond's eyes darted to the sky, where the sun had not yet set. Sir Warin was sicker than he was willing to admit, too.

He had chosen a patch of grass to lie on, so Rosamond lay beside him. One of the briars on the wall had sent runners snaking through the grass, which was all she needed to help her heal him. At least, she hoped it would be enough.

Grasping a handful of thorny runners, she sent a wave of healing through Sir Warin's sleeping body. She would not have days for this; if she did not heal him completely in one go, she might not manage to heal him at all. So even as her head ached and her body grew numb, still Rosamond worked her magic. The brave knight must survive, even if she did not.

The full moon had risen high in the sky by the time she had rid Sir Warin of his ailment. He would sleep for some time yet, as his body still had healing of its own to do. If she were stronger, she would help him, but as it was…

She climbed laboriously to her feet. Rosamond wanted to check Monika one more time before she lay down to await her fate. There would be no healer to save the princess, but Rosamond knew this was the only way to save the kingdom. She could not carry this curse home.

Rosamond had already chosen her resting place. She believed it had once been a kind of courtyard, open to the sun and rain, because very little of the roof had fallen onto the mosaic tiles still visible beneath the leaf litter. In the middle of it stood a fountain, though it held no water now. Instead, the basin had filled up with roses, so that it resembled a bed of flowers. This would be her deathbed. Far more befitting of a princess than the cold vaults beneath her parents' castle. A castle she would never see again.

Would her last sight on this earth be of sunny blue skies or sparkling stars? Rosamond wondered. It mattered little. She would be surrounded by the scent of roses, which would be enough.

With considerable effort, she made her way to the chapel where Monika lay resting.

Rosamond laid a hand on the maid's

forehead, searching for signs of the disease, but finding none.

"Mistress?" Monika croaked.

"Rest. You were ill, but you are better now," Rosamond soothed her, struggling to keep her voice from shaking. No one would reassure her when the time came. "Sir Warin sleeps in the courtyard, but he will wake when he is well, too."

"What of you, mistress? Who cares for you?" Monika asked.

No one. Rosamond didn't dare speak the words aloud. "I am well cared for, I assure you. My sleeping chamber is over there. The roses guard me while I sleep. They will allow no harm to come to me." For she would soon be beyond harm, and the kingdom would be safe.

"Mistress…"

"It is time for me to retire. I only came to check on you. If Sir Warin survives until morning, you must return with him."

"What of you, mistress?" Monika said again, more urgently this time.

Rosamond smiled sadly. "If I do not succumb before morning, then I will return with you. If my body lacks the strength to fight this plague…you must leave me here. Do not bring my remains home. Tell my parents I died on the road, of an illness that I would not wish to visit upon my people. Promise me, Monika."

"No, mistress!" Monika tried to rise, but she was too weak.

"Thank you for your service to me. Please thank Sir Warin, too, when he wakes."

And with that, Rosamond bent her final steps toward the rose-shrouded fountain. Perhaps it was selfish to use the last of her strength to reach the pretty courtyard, but she did not care. She had used so much of what she had left to heal others. If she did not put enough distance between herself and her travelling companions, they might contract the disease again from her remains, and she would not be around to heal them a second time.

When she reached the stone basin, she

nearly tumbled in, she was so tired. The briars would not let her, though, snaking beneath her to hold her weight until they formed a proper bed. Thorns shredded her clothes and some pierced her skin, but she felt little any more.

The world was no more than a dream to her now.

Rosamond lay on her bed of roses, weaving her fingers between the blossoms. She could feel the disease running riot through her blood, though it had not invaded her lungs as it had Melitta, Monika and Sir Warin. As her energy waned, she fancied she felt the tiny disease motes slowed their dance, almost as if they would die with her. That was a good thing.

The briars she touched – a dozen bushes, at least, all sending their runners toward her – offered her welcome, wishing her health in ways that felt like sap running through her veins instead of blood.

Protect me, she told them, envisioning vines closing off the courtyard to all but the sky, so that no one could reach her while the disease still survived in her body. Protect the kingdom. In her mind's eye, this involved all the plants in the kingdom forming up like armies for battle, keeping anyone at bay who might threaten her people with a plague like hers.

She lay facing the sky, but Rosamond saw neither stars nor moon as her eyes closed and her consciousness sank into oblivion, surrounded by the plants she loved, promising to obey her wishes.

While she lay alone in the moonlight, briars wove themselves into an impenetrable wall, blocking off the courtyard. Leaves whispered in the night breeze, telling trees and bushes of the princess's desire, until every bush along the borders had heard her final command.

Roses cradled her body, while berry bushes built a wall of their own around her lands. They would keep the kingdom safe for her, they promised, as only plants can.

Eleven

"You should be here, planning a coronation ceremony and ruling the kingdom. Not riding about, chasing birds in the woods!" Lady Schutz hissed.

Lord Siward sighed. "Grandmother, this kingdom is so small, it almost rules itself. And it has been scarcely three weeks since the king died. The earth has not even had time to settle over his grave. It would be an insult to his memory to attempt to steal his throne before we know whether an heir can be found."

"Normal kingdoms name a new king on the same day the old one dies. A kingdom should not be without a ruler for even a day!" she insisted.

"If only our kingdom could be normal, but it is not. Neither is it without a ruler. I am not leaving the kingdom. I am simply riding out of the city for a little while. I shall visit the borders and the outlying villages, make sure all is well, and if I choose to spend a day or two hawking, what of it? It is the sport of kings, after all, and you are so set on me becoming one. It seems to me I should enjoy some of the privileges, seeing as I already shoulder the burdens of a position which are not mine to bear."

She threw her wrinkled hands up into the air. "Be it on your own head, then, if some other noble tries to claim the throne while you are playing with birds!"

"If some madman attempts it, then he is

welcome to the throne," Lord Siward snapped. If only another man would lay claim to that much-vaunted chair, then he could do the job his father had done, instead of trying to rule in the king's stead. If they could find an heir…

But there was no heir. The king and queen had managed to have one child, and she had died young. A normal kingdom could ask for a near relation who had married into one of the royal families of a neighbouring kingdom, but this was no normal kingdom.

So that left him. Siward sighed, knowing he would have to ascend the throne on his return. No other man in court was capable of ruling, though others had blood far more noble than his. Yet the king on his deathbed had appointed him Regent, for his sins.

All the more reason to take this trip now, for it might be his last chance at freedom before the heavy yoke of kingship settled on his shoulders.

His head started to clear as he left the city. Perhaps it was the lack of courtly arse-kissing, or maybe it was the clean scent from the woods instead of the smoke from cookfires, but he took heart when the city walls vanished from sight.

It was easily a week's ride to the border by way of the main road, but checking the borders was his first task. Every year, like his father and grandfather before him, Siward rode the borders, checking for signs of weakness. He hadn't found one yet, but if ever there was a time he needed one…it was now.

When he arrived at the end of the road, Siward sighed. He hadn't expected any change, though he had hoped for one.

Bramble hedges soared into the sky, forming a wall more formidable than simple stone. This wall ringed the kingdom, allowing no one in or out, and it had stood since his grandfather's time. His grandfather, Lord Schutz, had said the Wall had been a simple hedge once, but when the princess passed, the plants had risen up in protest to protect the kingdom. Siward never understood what they protected the kingdom from, for his grandfather had rambled considerably in his old age. Sometimes, he'd said it was to prevent a plague. At other times, he'd insisted it was to prevent war with a neighbouring kingdom, who had apparently killed the princess.

The truth of the tale was lost in time – and with his grandfather, who had lain in his grave for many years now.

Yet the Wall still stood, testament to some mysterious truth. Perhaps someone had cursed the kingdom, Siward decided. It seemed as good an explanation as any. If it weren't for the Wall, he could send messengers to neighbouring kingdoms to search for an heir. With it…he would be king.

The first time he'd seen the Wall, Siward had slashed at it with his sword, determined like a hundred other men before him that he could cut his way through. The brambles would have none of it, wrapping tendrils around his sword until they dragged it from his hand as they repaired the damage to the Wall as though he had never sliced a single stroke. The Wall was magic, most certainly. Which made it all the harder for a soldier like himself to understand. There were no witches in the kingdom, so whoever had cast it must be on the other side of the Wall, and out of his reach.

Astor, his hunting hawk, ruffled her feathers as if impatient to do something more than sit on her perch.

"You have the right of it, my friend," Siward told the bird, pulling off the creature's hood. "Let us hunt, and forget politics for a time. Worrying about it will not bring down the Wall."

He headed off the road, toward a spot known only to his family. It had the best hawking in the kingdom, and so it would continue as long as its location remained a closely-kept secret. Not even his grandmother knew this spot, he'd wager, for she had no desire to hunt.

He unhooded Astor, held his fist high in the air, and watched the bird fly off with powerful wingbeats. Siward wished for a moment that he could fly with her, high above the Wall, to see the world outside. Was it so different to their kingdom? As long as the Wall stood, he would never know.

With his eyes on Astor, Siward urged his horse to follow the bird. The forest was not so dense here, though there was no village nearby. Perhaps there once had been one, but it had been too close to the border that before the Wall it had been attacked too many times until it had been abandoned. Surely there would have been some ruins left, then, to mark where the town had stood. Yet Siward had never seen them. Perhaps the brambles and briars had consumed those, too.

Astor hovered, and Siward held his breath for a moment before the hawk dived, gracefully seizing a bird on the wing before her prey had even been aware of her presence. Astor swooped down with her catch still in her talons, toward a briar-shrouded rock.

Siward thought she would perch on the

rock, but Astor dipped down behind it and disappeared. Swearing, he rode around, trying to find the bird, but the rock seemed solid on all sides, and the bird was nowhere in sight. He called her and heard an answering cry, but she did not reappear.

He swore again. The rock must be hollow, and his bloody bird was in the middle of it. If he didn't catch her before she devoured her prey, he'd lose her as a hunting hawk. Bird be damned, but she was his best, and he was loath to lose her. If there was no other way in, he would have to climb.

Siward had not climbed rocks or trees since he was a boy, but he was not so old that he did not enjoy doing it again. Just as long as his grandmother or his future subjects didn't catch him behaving like a youth.

The rock had a surprising number of easy toeholds for him, so it wasn't long until Siward had reached the top. The view he saw from his vantage point, though, made his mouth fall open in surprise. What he had taken for a rock was in fact a sprawling building – he'd been climbing the walls. Astor, bright bird that she was, had perched on a wall that had partially fallen down, hiding her from his sight until now. He called her again, but the stubborn bird did not move.

Siward swore again. He would have to fetch her. At least it would be a simple matter of walking along the walls to her current spot, scooping her up and hooding her once more.

He could not keep his eyes on the bird and his footing, though, and by the time he looked up, the blasted bird had moved to a wall in the middle of the building. She teetered there for a moment, before diving into the room below.

Siward made his way to the spot where he'd last seen Astor, and stopped. Below him was a courtyard, free of the collapsed roof fragments most of the other rooms had sported. Yet it was not the courtyard that drew his eye, but the incredibly lifelike statue of a woman in the middle of it, surrounded by roses.

Made of alabaster or white marble, she

looked as though she would open her eyes and rise at any moment. Some virgin goddess or the Queen of Heaven, Siward guessed, depending on how old the statue was. Yet it looked newly carved, not as though it had been lying in this ruin for centuries, as surely it had been. A wondrous work of art indeed.

If he had to take the throne, he would place this statue in the throne room, so that every time he was bored, he could stare at her and wonder what her story was, and remember how he'd found her on his last days of freedom.

Siward jumped down from the wall, bending his knees to cushion the impact of his landing. Good thing, too, for the ground beneath his feet was harder than he expected. Swiping his booted foot through the leaf litter, he pushed aside the thin layer to reveal a mosaic floor of remarkable craftsmanship, though it paled into insignificance when compared to the magnificent statue.

Now he was closer, she looked even more

divine. Like his every desire made flesh – or stone, at least. Siward laughed at himself. A statue so real it stirred his loins. Perhaps becoming king would not be such a bad thing. He would be expected to take a queen, and ensure a clear succession. That would stop him from lusting after statues.

No, he decided, inspecting the goddess, for no real woman could look so perfect. He must have this statue in his throne room.

He reached out to touch the stone, to see what fastened her to the plinth below. Perhaps he could move her out of here and send someone to collect the statue, so that it would be in place when he returned. If she had been fastened by her feet and fallen over at some point, he might be able to…

A briar shot out, twining around his wrist so fast he could not move it. "What in blazes – " he began, only now realising that the plants had sent tendrils around both of his legs and his other arm, too. A thicker branch snaked around his middle, yanking him away from the statue.

Siward shouted for help, but he was alone in the ruin, as he well knew.

No, not quite alone.

Astor, his traitorous bird, landed on the plinth beside the statue's shoulder and peered at the goddess' face, as though working out what her lips would taste like. That beak could chip stone, and ruin the statue. The bird had caused enough trouble today.

"No!" Siward commanded. "Leave the girl alone. She is not to be harmed."

Finally deciding to be obedient, the bird flew off, perching on the wall once more.

Siward breathed a sigh of relief. She was safe.

He thought he heard something rustling through the leaves, and turned his attention back to the statue. What he saw stole his breath and his voice.

For the statue's closed eyes now stood open, green as emeralds, as she stared back at him.

Twelve

Rosamond's mind drifted as she slumbered, dreaming of the endless cycle of the seasons as the plants around her grew, flourished or lay dormant, all the while whispering that they kept her safe. If such was her afterlife, she would not complain. Sometimes in her dreams she was a tree or bush herself, fighting the bite of an axe or blade as she defended her kingdom. Even if it was no longer hers in death.

Today, the dream was different. For a moment, she was a briar, defending herself from a fool who would bring plague to the kingdom, and the next, she had the limbs of a woman again, and eyes with which to see that he was no fool, but Sir Warin, brave knight that he was, trying to save her.

While she held him fast to the wall, out of reach, she directed her thoughts inward. If a single mote of the insidious plague lived inside her, she could not allow him to touch her and infect himself and others. But if the plague was gone and she yet lived…

Deep joy warmed her heart as she felt no trace of the disease within her.

Of course she would not. For she was dead, and this was merely a dream, like all the other times she had seen Sir Warin.

A dream where she could finally indulge her feelings for the knight whose life she'd saved.

With a thought, she released him from his bonds, healing the cuts the briars had inflicted, for she could reach through plants now without needing to touch him herself. She could do little with his shredded clothing, and she rather admired his well-muscled flesh she glimpsed through what remained of his tunic and hose.

What was it Queen Margareta had said? Let a man glimpse you naked, for he would do anything to see such beauty again. Rosamond had not realised the desire would run both ways – that she herself would want to see more of the man.

There was only one course of action, then.

"Come, my love," Rosamond said. "I have been waiting for you, for this moment. Take me as a bride on her wedding night, for soon we will be wed, and we have waited far too long already. The responsibility of the throne awaits, but for now, we should take pleasure in each other's arms. We must become one before others try to tear us apart."

He stumbled toward where she lay on her bed of roses, then took her hand and kissed it.

Rosamond tingled delightfully at his touch. Much better than their first awkward kiss by the campfire. But she burned for more. "Come to my bed, and love me," she said.

Warin climbed into the fountain beside her, then took her face in his hands and kissed her. This was no awkward peck like the first time. No, his lips moved with hers, parting so that they might share a breath before their tongues danced like the lovers they would soon be.

Warin paid no attention to the briars tearing the rags of his clothes from his body, until they both lay naked, and the desire burning between them was too much for either of them to resist. In her dreams, she had seen many things, including how a husband made love to his wife, and she wanted all this and more from her valiant knight.

"Love me," she commanded, parting her legs as she invited him inside.

Rosamond felt a sharp sting as he entered her, but it was no more than the prick of a thorn amid the overwhelming pleasure he gave her. Kisses and caresses were nothing…nothing, compared to this.

He made love to her as the sun set, and twilight settled over the land, so that when the first star sparkled in the sky and she cried out for joy once again, she could truly say she flew among the stars.

If only every awakening could be so joyful, but in her heart, Rosamond knew this could only be a dream.

Thirteen

Siward woke from a fevered dream. What kind of man dreamed he made love to a statue come to life? Or plants that moved like snakes, snaring and trapping him before the statue commanded them to stop?

He must have taken a stronger jug of wine than he'd thought. For only in his cups could he possibly place himself in such a silly fairy tale.

He stared up at the sky for a moment, reaching for the jug he knew should be beside him. All he touched were leaves, before pricking himself on a thorn. He had slept in a rosebush, then, instead of rolled in his cloak on the ground. He must do this again, for it felt far softer than the unforgiving ground. In fact, he could almost imagine the woman of his dreams beside him, pressing her breasts along his side as she reached for him once more.

"I see you are ready for me again, beloved," a distinctly female voice said, sounding amused as a warm, soft hand wrapped around his shaft. "Good. I wish you to love me again, just as you did last night."

Siward swallowed, then turned his head to meet her green eyes. The green eyes of a goddess, a divine statue come to life.

He bolted out of the bed, which he now saw was a fountain full of roses. He should have been covered in scratches from the thorns, but he was unscathed. A minor miracle, seeing as his clothes were little more than rags as he stood naked before a woman…nay, little more than a girl, who he had deflowered scant hours before.

Oh, he had done so at her command, which he could not refuse at the time, but now…honour demanded he make this right by her. That meant making her his wife.

He didn't even know her name.

"Are you real?" he asked.

The girl laughed. "I am no more or less real than you. Are you real?"

"Of course," he said firmly, trying not to be distracted by his body's response to her nakedness.

She was not so restrained. "Prove it. Come back to bed and love me again in daylight, or I shall fear last night was but a dream."

Siward shook his head. "I cannot. I should not have…I dishonoured you. I will make this right. I will take you as my wife, if you wish it."

"I do wish it, but I also wish for you to take me as you would your wife, here, now," the girl commanded imperiously.

No one in the kingdom commanded Lord Siward. Who was this slip of a girl who thought she could?

"Who are you?" Siward said.

The girl tossed her hair. "As if you do not know. I am Rosamond."

Named for the lost princess, like so many other girls in the kingdom, Siward thought. Every third woman under the age of fifty answered to the name Rose, for the princess had become legend.

He gave a wry smile. "Lying there like that, you look more like a goddess of love than a princess. You should be Freyja or Venus, not a mere princess."

Rosamond blushed redder than the roses around her. "You give pretty compliments. It is one of the many things I like about you. Of course, there is also your strength, your sense of honour and duty, your prowess in battle, and now your prowess in bed. I shall list your virtues when we see my mother and father, so that they will consent to our marriage."

Siward almost smiled at her naiveté. No parent in the kingdom would refuse his offer of marriage for their daughter, especially once he claimed the throne for his own. Even if he hadn't deflowered their virgin daughter. He sighed. When he'd thought of taking a queen yesterday, he had not thought to make a decision already.

"Where are your clothes?" he asked.

She laughed softly. "You can probably answer that better than I can. I never took care of the horses."

Puzzled, he opened his mouth to ask for an explanation, but he closed it again when he realised his spare clothes were with his horse, too. Climbing out of here naked, with the walls full of briars, would not be without pain. He could save her a little of that, though, if he lifted her to the top of the wall. "Come here," he said. "I will help you get out of here, and then we can find you some clothes to wear."

Reluctantly, she sat up, wincing a little as

though not accustomed to being upright. She shook her head slightly and slid her legs over the side of the fountain, so they dangled above the mosaic floor. Rosamond took a deep breath before she stood up. She remained on her feet for a moment, before her knees buckled and she would have crashed to the tiles if Siward had not leaped forward to catch her.

"I am sorry," she murmured, closing her eyes. "I must still be weak from lying so long abed. Forgive me."

Realisation dawned on Siward, and it was not a pleasant feeling. Her weakness was his fault, for last night had been her first time and he had not held back. No wonder the girl was weak. He'd been a brute. He lifted her in his arms, like the bride she would soon be, he swore. "If I lift you to the top of the wall, do you think you have the strength to stay there until I climb up to you?" he asked.

Rosamond rested her head against his chest. "Why are we climbing walls? The way out is that way." She pointed at a gap in the briars Siward had not seen before. Not that he'd been looking, he admitted, for his eyes had been too busy feasting on her beauty to notice anything else. She directed him through the ruin, following a path that was miraculously free of the briars that covered everything else. Almost as though someone had cleared it deliberately.

Surely delicate Rosamond had not done it. "Do you come here often?" he asked her.

She stared at him, as if he had made a joke. "No, this was my first visit."

"Do you live nearby?" he persisted. If she did, he could ride by her parents' cottage to ask for her hand today. It would ease his conscience immeasurably.

"Of course not. I lived with my parents in the castle."

In a bigger kingdom, there might be more than one castle, but in a place this small, she could only mean the late king's castle. The one Siward's grandmother insisted should be his.

"Why have I not seen you there?" he asked.

"Perhaps because your duties keep you busy, and I prefer to spend as much time as possible in the gardens."

Siward could not recall ever seeing the castle gardens. She evidently knew him better than he knew her. If he had ever seen her before, he would have been just as transfixed as he'd been yesterday. More, perhaps, for a living woman was infinitely better than a cold stone statue.

"You must be right," he allowed.

Rosamond laughed. "I usually am."

She had the prideful manner of royalty already. Not a bad thing in a future queen. Perhaps destiny had led him to her yesterday, and played a hand in kindling their lust. Nothing else could explain his complete loss of control, Siward was certain of it. The only other explanation was…magic. And how could a girl so young be a witch? Siward wanted to laugh at the thought.

Destiny it must be, then. At least destiny favoured him.

"Where is my horse?" she demanded.

Siward had the distinct feeling that destiny was laughing at him, too.

Fourteen

Rosamond didn't want to admit it, but her illness had left her so weak she could scarcely walk. Delightful though it was to be carried in Sir Warin's arms, she had no desire to be known as the princess who swooned at the slightest excuse. As she'd slept, she'd mastered her gifts, so that she'd healed Warin's scratches even as he made love to her.

If only he'd taken the time to do it again this

morning, once she realised this was no longer a dream. She lived, and she had successfully persuaded him to make her his wife. A wife who intended to take great delight in her marriage bed, for her husband knew how to please her.

Her return home should be proud and triumphant, as befitted a betrothed princess, but between her own frailty and the absence of her horse, she wasn't sure how she would achieve such a spectacle. Least of all in the hose and tunic Sir Warin tossed to her.

Of course she could hardly ride naked, but she'd had countless new gowns made for Queen Margareta's coronation. Surely Sir Warin could not have burned them all.

Yet…it seemed he had. Not only was all the cloth gone, but all her clothing, too. She toyed with the idea of sending him to the nearest town to procure something proper for a princess to wear, but that meant he would have to leave her alone here, for who knew how long?

No.

It was a set of his own ill-fitting garments or nothing. When they reached a town, then she would insist he find something to replace what he had burned.

He helped her dress, then lifted her onto the back of his palfrey. For a while, he walked beside the horse, with the reins wrapped around his hand, but when Rosamond came close to fainting in the summer heat, he mounted up behind her, and only his strong arms kept her from slipping out of the saddle.

"Rest, Rosamond. I shall keep you safe," he promised.

Sleepily, she nodded, and the rest of the journey passed in what she described as a blurry doze. Sometimes she opened her eyes to bright sunlight, and at others to starry darkness. The one constant was Sir Warin's reassuring presence, for even at night, he held her in his arms. Though his hands did not slide under her tunic even once, to her disappointment. She was too weak to properly enjoy the attention, she told herself. Once they were home in the castle, and she had recovered properly, then she would tell him to take her again and again until she was sated.

She drifted from dream to dream, waking only to dream again, until one morning she opened her eyes and saw the wooden beams of a ceiling instead of the sky above. Now she woke fully, aware of being alone in a bed, with no idea of how long she had been there.

"Hello?" she called, annoyed. "Monika? Sir Warin? Anyone?"

The door to the room opened and a maidservant entered, bowing her head. She was too young to be Monika. "They are not here, my lady," the girl said. "I have orders to serve you and see that you are well when the master returns. Is there anything I can bring you, my lady? Some wine, something to eat, or a physician? The master thought you might be ill."

"I am not ill," Rosamond snapped. As a healer, she was far more knowledgeable about such things than some stupid physician. "Bring me fruit, and meat, and yes, some wine. Then fetch me my clothes."

The girl dropped a deep curtsey. "Yes, my lady."

She returned some time later with a tray of food and drink. Rosamond did her best, but she could barely eat more than a few mouthfuls. The wine was much too strong, threatening to turn her stomach. She had eaten little on the journey, and she estimated that she had stayed in the ruined convent for perhaps a week, so perhaps her stomach had shrunk from eating so little. No matter. She would be back to normal in no time.

When she was certain she could not eat another bite, Rosamond said, "Where are my clothes? I must dress. I wish to sit in the garden."

"I will ask the housekeeper, my lady. She was still searching for your clothes when I brought your breakfast." The girl took the barely touched tray and hurried out.

When the girl returned, Rosamond had fallen into a doze, but she roused herself quickly. "Well?" Rosamond demanded.

"Draga says you had no things with you when you arrived, but she is looking through some of the chests of old clothes, to see if we have anything that will fit you, my lady."

Old clothes. Rosamond sniffed. When she was well once more, she would summon a dressmaker to make anew all the garments Sir Warin had burned. In the meantime…she would accept the housekeeper's charity, for it was surely the best the woman had. When she saw Sir Warin again, she would instruct him on how to treat a princess when she was a guest in his home, for she guessed she was in his house. She was certainly not in her parents' castle, for there was no stonework to be seen.

Two menservants entered the room, bearing an enormous chest between them. An older woman, who Rosamond assumed was Draga, the housekeeper, followed them.

Draga stood with her hands on her hips,

eyeing Rosamond as though she was a piece of meat. "Skinny, with no hips to speak of. A poor choice in a wife, and I shall tell the master so."

Rosamond's temper flared. "Your master has better judgement than you. There is nothing wrong with my hips, as your master knows well." In fact, his hands had held her hips fast as he thrust deep into her, and she longed for him to do it again. "I hope you brought clothes befitting someone of my rank. I will not dress like a peasant, nor a man."

Draga's eyes flashed. "The clothes in that chest belonged to the Lady Schutz when she was a girl. Nothing else in the house will fit. If they are not good enough for you, then I suggest you return from whence you came and leave the master to find a proper wife, not one so full of airs and graces." Her eyes narrowed. "With no hips." She waved at the young maidservant. "Agnna, you take care of her highness. I have more important things to do." The housekeeper strode out of the room before Rosamond could form a reply to such breathtakingly bad manners.

At least the housekeeper had recognised her as a princess, Rosamond consoled herself, though the honorific had sounded more like an insult on Draga's lips. No matter. As the lady of the house, Rosamond could dismiss the woman and engage someone more appropriate, if she wished.

Agnna didn't seem to have noticed the housekeeper's rudeness. Perhaps the girl was used to it. She fell to her knees beside the chest and lifted the lid. "Lady Schutz always looks so lovely. I'm sure these gowns will be everything you could want, my lady," she breathed, drawing out the first one, a simple dress of black linen. Or was it dark grey? Rosamond could not be sure. The second gown the girl lifted out was a much more becoming shade of pink, though it, too, looked like it might have faded. "This is beautiful. I have never touched cloth so smooth."

That got Rosamond's attention. "Is it silk?

Bring it here." She reached for the dress and was relieved to find that it was indeed silk. As were most of the dresses in the chest. Rosamond selected the gowns in shades of pink and green, before dismissing the rest as unsuitable. She breathed a sigh of relief. At least she would have something to wear until the castle dressmaker could create a new wardrobe befitting both a princess and Sir Warin's new bride.

For a bride she would be. He had asked, and she had accepted, and they had already consummated their union beneath the moonlight.

Her father would not refuse this match, she was certain of it. Especially not if she announced it to him herself before Sir Warin asked for her hand.

"Does my father know I am here?" Rosamond asked.

"I do not know, my lady. I can send word to him, if you wish. But surely he must know, for if you are to marry the master, he would have your father's blessing. He is very strict about matters of honour, is the master. There are tales of maids in other households being…dishonoured, but you will never hear of such a thing here." Agnna sounded quite proud of this.

"Is that because the dragon of a housekeeper does not allow the servants to spread such vicious rumours?" Rosamond asked.

Agnna clapped a hand to her mouth to smother a giggle. "No, my lady, and her name is Draga, not dragon, though when she is angry, sometimes I think she might breathe fire, she is so fearsome. They are more than rumours. Why, Lord Vamos has sent away four kitchen maids this year alone. All pregnant, and all unwed. Some say it is the lord himself who does the deed, but others whisper that it is his son, Fodor."

"A lord and his son who seduce the women of their household, pledging their love with no intention of marrying the girls? Who would do such a thing? Surely, honour cannot be so dead!" Rosamond exclaimed.

"My lady, there is little of love when a man desires a woman. It is different with the master, for what woman would not want him? High and honourable as he is, I do not believe he would seduce a woman without marriage on his mind. But any other nobleman…if he wishes to bed one of his servants, the girl has no choice but to obey. I heard that Moxa, Lady Vamos' maid, tried to refuse, but they beat her so badly that in the end she begged Fodor to take her so the beatings would stop. She still lost her position, and none will employ a fallen woman."

"Fallen? Or forced?" Rosamond asked sharply.

Agnna shrugged. "There is little difference in the law of the land. It protects noblemen, not us."

"When I am queen, I will change that," Rosamond vowed. "No woman should be forced to lie with a man against her will. It is barbaric."

"I wish you every blessing in your endeavour, my lady," Agnna said. "But…better not to speak of such things to the master for a while yet. He has so many other, more important cares on his shoulders nowadays, what with being Lord Protector and all. Best to pay attention to making him happy and saving your strength for the wedding." She looked up at Rosamond. "Will you need my help dressing, my lady?"

"No," Rosamond replied. "I think I still need to rest a little longer. Perhaps tomorrow. You may go."

The girl left the room, but Rosamond was so deep in thought she barely noticed. Before, Rosamond had believed that being queen was an irritating obligation, and marrying well would allow her to leave ruling up to her husband. No more. Not if women were being raped by the very noblemen the kingdom depended on to protect the people.

Lord Vamos, his son and any other man

who thought women were chattels to be used and thrown away were in for a rude shock when she ascended the throne. For the first time in her life, she looked forward to her coronation.

Fifteen

Rosamond waited for Warin to visit her, but there was no sign of him, and when she asked Agnna about her master's whereabouts, the girl simply said she did not know.

Patience had never been Rosamond's strong point, so after two days abed, she decided to try walking again. Slowly at first, holding onto the bed for a few steps before she needed to sit down again, then a little longer each time until she could walk about the room without needing a rest. She needed to speak to her father before Warin did, for even if he had been named Lord Protector – a prestigious promotion for a captain of the guard – her parents had wanted her to marry some foreign prince.

She simply had to convince them that Warin was the better choice. But first, she had to regain her strength, and the fastest way to do that involved spending time in Warin's garden, if she could find it. If not, she could always cuddle up to the nearest tree. A mighty oak did not have the ebullience of something faster growing like a rose or berry bush, but she did not need to borrow much energy for what was more a tonic than proper healing.

Cautiously, Rosamond made her way downstairs. The bedchambers were on the highest floor of the house, above the great hall, with the kitchens and servants' quarters in the partially subterranean lowest level, she discovered as she descended.

A mob of wide eyes greeted her as she reached what must have been the servants' dining hall.

"What are you doing here, my lady?" Agnna asked, no less surprised than the rest.

A princess did not apologise to those lower than her, Rosamond remembered, as if her mother was even now hissing the words into her ear. Rosamond lifted her chin. "Looking for a garden to sit in."

"The master does not have a garden to speak of, my lady, unless you count the kitchen garden, with the herbs and vegetables…"

"Or the orchard," a young boy piped up. "I'm supposed to pick the ripe ones from the berry patch this afternoon, but there's still plenty for you, my lady."

Berry bushes, the next closest thing to roses. "That sounds wonderful. Will you show me?"

The boy nodded happily before bounding up the steps too fast for Rosamond to follow.

"I will take you, my lady," Agnna said, proceeding at a much slower pace up the stairs.

"If you will follow me? Someone will bring you refreshment, for you will need it outside in the summer heat."

The servants' quarters of Warin's house were far more confining than those in the castle, but then his house was so much smaller. Not as tiny as one of the peasant cottages she'd passed on the road, but still…much smaller than she was accustomed to. The walled garden Agnna led her to did not disappoint, though, for the orchard surpassed the small copse of trees in the castle garden by a considerable quantity.

Not to mention Rosamond spotted…

"Cloudberries!" she exclaimed. "I did not know there were any in the kingdom."

"I believe these are the only ones," Agnna said. "The master's grandfather brought the seeds back from foreign lands in his youth and planted them here. While the other, more common berries may be eaten by all, those yellow ones are reserved for the lord's table alone."

"I look forward to tasting them again," Rosamond said. She dropped to her knees and reached for the nearest plant, whose flowers were just beginning to open. The leaves curled up to touch her fingers, like a cat begging to be stroked. "I predict a bountiful crop of cloudberries this year." As she caressed the leaves, she felt the plants' delighted acquiescence to her desire for more berries.

"They are called princess berries here, my lady, on account of the lost princess. The master's grandfather travelled with her until she was lost. The berry seeds were a gift to her from some foreign queen, but when m'lord's grandfather brought her things to the king and told him of her loss, the king refused to allow the queen's gifts in the castle, swearing they were cursed, like the other gifts the evil queen gave the princess before she died. So he planted them here instead, in her memory."

This was a story Rosamond had not heard before. Perhaps her nursemaids had not thought it fit for a young princess's ears, to hear the grisly fate of one of her ancestors. Curses could be as cruel as their casters. Yet Agnna knew the story. "How did she die?" Rosamond asked.

Agnna shrugged. "No one knows. The curse took her, m'lord's grandfather used to say. She lay like a marble statue in the garden, and the plants would attack those who tried to reach her. He called and called, but she did not wake, and that's how he knew she was dead."

A princess gifted with plant magic, just like her, Rosamond thought, pleased. Not that it had served her particularly well, but even Rosamond's own modest powers were no match for a powerful enchantress, as the evil queen must have been. Margareta had been a much more pleasant monarch.

"Tell me more about the plants in this garden," Rosamond ordered. She only half-listened to the girl's rambling as she trailed her fingers through everything green she could touch, for the plants themselves whispered a far more complex history than any human could.

Sixteen

Siward rode through the outlying villages in a sort of fog, though the air was clear. No, the fog was in his head. Green-eyed and smiling, the mysterious Rosamond haunted him by day and lay beside him in his dreams. Well, not always beside him. Sometimes beneath him and one particularly tantalising time she sat astride him, but…

Siward shook his head. He was supposed to

be listening to petitions from the villagers, making judgements and settling disputes. Not thinking about bedding the beautiful woman who had agreed to be his wife. He had another week or two of this before he could head home to see her again.

It had sat ill with him to leave her alone in his house, with no one but his servants for company, but she had been too weak to even open her eyes when he'd laid her in his bed and kissed her farewell. A chaste kiss, for all he wanted more, because an honourable man did not steal so much as a kiss from a sleeping woman.

He did not doubt that his household would care for her as best they could, but they had not ridden miles with her lolling lifelessly in their arms, as he had. Yet she'd seemed so strong and vital that first night in his arms, crying out for more until he granted her desire.

He refused to regret it. Their one night of passion would allow him to take that beautiful creature as his willing wife. More than he deserved, perhaps, which was why he worried now. Destiny had given her to him, but if cruel fate saw fit to steal her away from him so soon…

Siward prayed that she would regain her strength in his house, instead of wasting away to nothing. Perhaps the place he had found her was magical, granting her strength that waned the further she travelled away from it.

No, that could not be true. She had nearly fallen when she'd first tried to stand up. He could scarcely wait to go home, when he hoped she would fall into his arms again. Not from weakness, but from sheer joy at seeing him again. Siward had to laugh at himself for that foolish thought. How could he bring a girl joy when he'd barely known her for a night? A night where they'd had little time or breath for conversation.

Yet he knew if she asked him to, he would claim the crown for her. There was no doubt in his mind that she would make the perfect queen. Gracious and beautiful, fearless yet soulful…no wonder she was always in his thoughts.

Every glimpse of green reminded him of her eyes. Every time a leaf brushed against him, he thought of the night they'd shared in their bed of roses.

Finally, he made his last judgement at Akos, a tiny village at the foot of the mountains that marked the kingdom's easternmost boundary. Though they offered him hospitality for the night, Siward refused, wishing to sleep in the forest instead. Not that he told the village headman that, of course. He told the man he was needed in the capital, to solve the matter of the succession. An excuse that had the virtue of being true.

He waved to the townspeople as he rode off, his saddlebags filled with provisions he did not need but could not refuse. Siward intended to spend the night in a small dell he had found on his way to Akos, where the soft grass had cushioned him as he spent the night enchanted by vivid dreams of Rosamond.

Soon, he promised himself, he would be home. They would be wed and he could do all the things he'd dreamed about with his very real wife instead of his illusory goddess.

Seventeen

Slowly but surely, Rosamond regained her strength. The garden bloomed as happily as she did. More than once, she had overheard the servants talking about it, but she refused to be deterred by idle talk. When she saw her father again, she wanted to appear as hale and healthful as the day she departed for King Erik and Queen Margareta's court.

After four weeks of spending every day in

the garden, Rosamond decided it was time. On the morrow, she would don her finest gown – or at least the least faded gown in the chest of old clothes Draga had foisted on her – and proceed up to the palace, where she would seek an audience with the king and queen, and explain her plan for the future.

The best of intentions rarely survive until morning, especially when illness sets in. Rosamond's improving appetite disappeared overnight, and what she did manage to swallow she only threw right back up again. She felt dizzy and weak, as she had when she had first arrived.

Rosamond had no more time for weakness, she decided, as she dragged herself outside to the garden. Reaching deep into a bramble bush, she let the thorns pierce her skin as she commanded the plant to help her heal herself.

Her heart beat loud in her ears, as it always did when she attempted magic on herself, deafening her to all other sound. Or it should have, but for an eager thrumming she had never heard before. What was it? she asked the plants as she searched for the source. The answers she received sounded like saplings and seeds, which made no sense. No plant she knew sounded like a rapidly beating heart.

And then she knew. Reaching deep inside herself, Rosamond found the sound's source. A heart so tiny she could scarcely see it, but a human heart nonetheless. Within her, she carried Warin's child – and, after her, the next heir to the throne.

Eighteen

Contrary to his usual custom, Siward left his horse to his groom's care instead of caring for the animal himself. It had been eight weeks…nay, fifty-eight days since he had last seen Rosamond, and he longed for her the same way the first spring flowers sought the sun. He needed her.

Draga greeted him in the great hall, asking inane questions about what he wanted prepared for dinner. Siward waved away her concerns, for he had only one thought in his head.

"How is she? Where is she?" he asked eagerly.

Draga's brow creased. "The sick girl you brought?"

Siward prayed with all his might that she was not still ill. "Rosamond."

"She's in the garden. She's always in the garden," Draga said.

Exactly where she should be, Siward thought as he bolted for the door. It was the height of summer, and everything bloomed so brightly he didn't see her at first. The green gown and white shift she wore underneath blended so well with the leaves and blossoms behind her that he might have missed her entirely had she not moved.

Her face lit up with joy, just as he'd imagined it would. He raced across the garden and swept her into his arms, heedless of who saw as he kissed her with more passion than he'd ever shown anyone else in his life.

Siward wanted more. He wanted to throw her to the ground, tear off her gown and make love to her like he had every night in his dreams, but he knew he could not do such a thing. Not to her. Her body yielded to him so readily even now that he did not dare abuse her trust. Not again. He would not take her to bed until they were properly married, he swore.

"You are home sooner than I thought. Your servants said it would be another two weeks at least," she said, her smile lighting up the morning brighter than the sun.

"I could not stay away from you," he confessed. "I want us to be wed as soon as possible. Tomorrow, if we can."

She drew away from him, bowing her head. "First, I must speak to my father."

Of course! In his eagerness, how could he have forgotten? "I will speak to him. I will ask for your hand and all will be well." No father in the kingdom would refuse him, Siward knew. "What is his name? I shall summon him, and we shall have his answer before nightfall."

This did not please Rosamond, who shook her head violently. "You cannot summon him. Not my father. I must speak to him, and only then can you ask him for anything."

Perhaps her father was a nobleman who thought to claim the kingship for himself. A man with such pride would not agree to Siward's suit until his future son-in-law sat firmly on the throne. So be it. There was nothing he would not do for her, and ruling a kingdom was a small price to pay for happiness with her.

"It shall be as you say," he conceded. "On the morrow, I will go to the castle to attend to some important business, while you speak to your father. Once my business and your conversation are concluded, then I will speak to him. We will be happily wed before this summer is over, I promise."

"I believe you."

She did not leave his side for the rest of the day. Even at supper, they shared a bench, while Draga muttered under her breath. Siward wanted to laugh – surely his housekeeper had been in love before. If she had, she would understand the bond between him and his betrothed.

It felt almost painful to part with her to go to separate sleeping chambers, but he forced himself to do no more than kiss her good night before vanishing into one of the seldom-used guest chambers. After all, he consoled himself, she would invade his dreams the moment his eyes closed.

He did not have to wait long. Sleep stole over him like a magic spell, where the witch was his wife-to-be and he would not have it any other way.

Nineteen

Rosamond refused to sleep alone once Warin had returned. She belonged in his bed, and she'd seen her own desire mirrored in his eyes from the moment he arrived. So she waited until she thought he was asleep, and crept into his bedchamber. Shucking off her shift, she slid under the blankets beside him.

She took his hands in hers and placed them on her body, stroking his fingers along her skin until he took control and caressed her on his own. His soft kisses turned hungry as his hands pushed her legs apart, just like she wanted him to, before he thrust deep inside her.

Rosamond gasped in surprise and pleasure. Tonight, he needed no urging as he drove her to heights of pleasure she had never known before, not just once but over and over until her frenzied cries mingled with his.

When they were both sated, she wanted nothing more than to fall asleep in his arms, but Rosamond knew she must return to her own chamber, at least until they were wed. She needed to be well-rested for her interview with her father on the morrow.

Twenty

"So we are all in agreement, then? Until we find a way to break down the Wall, or another claimant with a more direct line of descent from the royal family makes himself known, Lord Siward shall be king."

Siward blinked, not sure he had heard Lord Vamos correctly. For as long as he could remember, and as recently as the last time the King's Council convened, Lord Vamos had been his most vocal opponent. His claim to the throne had been tenuous at best – a bastard he claimed was a by-blow of the king's, three or four generations into the past. Lord Vamos didn't even have proof of his claim, for the bastard girl had never been acknowledged by her royal father, and the child she'd borne her husband might have been a bastard, too, if the current lord's senescent great-grandfather had not decided to marry her scant weeks before taking to his deathbed. Which begged the question of whether the current lord's grandfather had been conceived in his father's deathbed…

Yet here the man was, turning himself inside out to support Siward's claim to the throne. It almost made Siward want to refuse, for Lord Vamos would as soon hand him a cup of poison as a cup of wine.

Nods and murmurs of assent issued from the men clustered around the table.

Lord Vamos slapped his hand on the table. "It is decided, then. Siward shall be king, provided he can produce an heir within a year of his coronation."

Ah, there was the rub. Siward was the only man among them who did not have a son, or a wife by which he could beget more. Fortune favoured him, for that would soon change.

Siward rose. "With a heavy heart, I accept the honour of being your king, gentlemen. Let us set as early a date as possible for my coronation. The kingdom has been without a king for long enough."

Lord Vamos flashed a smile that reminded Siward of a snake. "It has been without a queen for even longer. Unless you have a wife tucked away somewhere secret, I suggest – "

Siward held up his hands for silence. "I have already chosen my queen, my lords. As your king, I will do everything in my power to ensure the security and the succession in our kingdom. If the Wall ever comes down, though this summer it seemed stronger than ever, our neighbours will find us secure in our monarchy, with no need to look outside our borders for some distant relative of the late king. He named me Regent on his deathbed, as you all know, but I never thought then that I would be safeguarding the throne for myself. I thank you for your faith in me, my lords." He inclined his head, far from the usual bow he would have given these men before today, but a king bowed to no one. He might not be king yet, but in their minds, he must appear to be. With an imperious wave, he dismissed them.

Rosamond's morning sickness returned with a vengeance on the morrow, as if to punish her for spending the night in her husband-to-be's bed. She endured it, as she knew she must, until finally she managed to choke down some small cider that did not immediately come back up.

With Agnna's assistance, she dressed in a pink gown that reminded her of the one she'd worn to the tournament on the day Warin had won the melee. A fitting gown to wear to the palace, where she would do battle with her father for the right to marry Warin.

As it was almost noon, Rosamond decided to attempt to eat the noonday meal before she left. She would feel far better with a full stomach than an empty one, she knew.

Feeling every inch the princess, Rosamond announced that she would take her meal in the garden instead of the great hall. Draga muttered under her breath, then headed down to the kitchen to obey her order.

Rosamond breathed deeply as she stepped outside into the sunshine, where Warin's happy garden awaited her company. She brushed her fingers through their leaves as she passed, drawing strength from their affection. She would need all the strength she possessed to win this encounter, and win she must.

Twenty-Two

Siward stopped at the door to his grandmother's cottage to take a deep breath. She was but a frail old woman, and no threat to anyone, he told himself, but he knew it was a lie. She could flay a man alive with her sharp tongue alone, and every maiden in the kingdom was terrified of her. Some called her a witch, but never to her face, lest Lady Schutz put an evil spell on them.

He knew there was no truth to her being a witch. His grandmother silenced him at the mere mention of magic, for in cursing the princess, the evil queen had cursed her, too. Cursed her to a life where she no longer had a position, for she had no mistress, and no other lady in the kingdom would dare to employ the lady-in-waiting who had served the princess, for how could any woman ever measure up to her? The princess was a veritable paragon of virtue, so the stories said, she had surely become a saint. The queen took pity on her for a time, and Grandmother became the queen's companion, but losing her daughter had broken the queen's heart, and she did not long survive the girl. So his grandmother, without a position once more, had married his grandfather and bore him some children including Siward's own father, which had led to the birth of Siward himself.

Which still didn't help him find the courage to raise his fist and knock on the formidable old lady's door. Luckily for him, the door flew open and Cecilia, a maid from his own household, stepped out. She gave a little start of surprise before she curtsied to him. "Have you come to visit Lady Schutz, master? I shall tell her you are here."

Siward nodded and followed the girl inside. He needed no introduction, after all. He would stay long enough to tell his grandmother that the Council had accepted his claim to the crown, and that he had chosen his queen. Grandmother would be too busy planning his coronation to spare a thought for Rosamond.

Yes, that was the plan.

She greeted him with, "So, have you come to tell me the date of your coronation?"

Of course she already knew. Word travelled fast in a town this size, especially to a woman like her who had spent half her life in the castle.

"On St John's Eve," Siward replied. "Soon, for the kingdom is in need of a leader, and I will not let it wait any longer."

"You must take a bride, too," Lady Schutz

said, nodding. "The sooner, the better. For the naysayers will not rest until you put a babe in her belly. And I know just the one."

"So do I," Siward began, but she didn't let him finish.

"Lord Vamos' daughter, Jolanka. She is young, obedient and definitely fertile." Grandmother beamed. "She will make a good wife for you."

Lord Vamos' daughter? Now Siward knew why the man had agreed to giving him the crown. He had made some sort of deal with his grandmother so that his daughter could be queen. Yet no matter how much he racked his brain, Siward could not recall seeing a young woman any time he had visited the man's house. And the way Grandmother stressed her fertility…

"Is the Lady Jolanka newly widowed?" he guessed.

Grandmother snorted. "The girl is barely fourteen summers old. Old enough to be a bride. Your bride."

But for her to be fertile… "She was his price, wasn't she? You told him I would take Lord Vamos' dishonoured daughter, perhaps even her bastard child, if he would give me the crown."

"Everything comes at a price," Grandmother said sharply. "The girl is a small price to pay. Lord Vamos sang her virtues, swearing that he did not know how the girl had begotten a bastard, for she never left her brother's side, and Fodor would defend her with his life."

Likely Fodor had drunk too much wine and defiled the girl himself, Siward fumed. He knew the man too well, and while Lord Vamos would not have made a terrible king, there was no way he would allow the crown to pass to a rabid dog like Fodor.

"Her brother will, of course, come with her to the castle, to be the captain of the queen's guard," Grandmother continued.

Even if Siward had considered the possibility of marrying the poor girl, there was no way he would tolerate her brother. Not to mention…he would have no way of knowing whether the girl's children were his or the result of incest and rape.

No, Rosamond would make a far better queen, and he could save Jolanka from her family some other way. As king, he could arrange a suitable marriage for her to someone else on the other side of the kingdom from Lord Vamos and his odious son.

"Thank you for your advice, Grandmother. I will consider it when I choose my bride, but I suspect I will prefer someone with a little more experience than a sheltered fourteen-year-old for my queen. I will not keep you or the kingdom in suspense, for I plan to wed the same day as my coronation, on St John's Eve. An auspicious time for fertility, or so I have heard." Siward farewelled his grandmother, telling her he had matters of state to attend to in the castle for the rest of the day, before beating a hasty retreat.

Twenty-Three

Today, Rosamond's morning sickness turned into morning, noon and night sickness. There was no way she could go to the palace in this condition, let along argue Warin's suit. She lay among the cloudberries, with scarcely the strength to sit up. Slowly but surely, her dizziness receded so that she could stare at the nearest cloudberry bush and wonder if it had quite that many blossoms on it when she'd first lain beside it.

When she reached out a finger to stroke the petals, she received a smug burst of satisfaction from the plant. The new blossoms were its celebration of her returning health. Rosamond couldn't help it. She laughed aloud.

"So you are the crazy hedge witch my grandson brought home," a cold female voice said. "They say he plans to marry you, nobody that you are. He could choose any eligible maiden in the kingdom, you know. In fact, he's already all but betrothed to a lady far more highborn than you, a circumstance which he has apparently forgotten. But you shall remind him, when you break the spell you have cast on him."

Rosamond wanted to laugh some more, for the woman's words were surely a joke, yet she sounded deadly serious. Cautiously, she sat up, praying that her morning sickness was done torturing her for today. "I don't know what you're talking about," Rosamond said.

"Don't be ridiculous. Servants talk.

Everyone in this household has seen and heard you talking to these plants. You have done something to them, just as you have magicked my grandson," the old lady snapped. "I demand you take it off."

"Take what off?" Rosamond asked tiredly. "My gown?"

"The spell you cast on my grandson, of course!" The woman glared. "But now I think about it, yes, you should also remove that gown. It is far too valuable for the likes of you. Why, that was worn by a princess to a queen's coronation. Look at it now – covered in dirt by some peasant woman who does not know good silk when she sees it!"

"Tournament, not coronation," Rosamond said absently. "This is not formal enough to be worn to a full coronation in court. This is the style of afternoon gown a highborn lady wears to a tournament. Like the one where Sir Warin won the melee." She rose to her feet, not willing to face this woman at a height disadvantage. No one stood higher than a princess except the queen. Sometimes not even then.

"I…how do you know that?" The woman peered at her.

Rosamond flashed a brilliant, courtly smile that had all the sincerity of cesspool slime. "I know many things. And whatever spells I may have cast, I will not undo. Not for you." The only spells she could cast were healing ones, anyway. What grudge did this woman bear against Warin that she wanted him not to be healed?

"You are a lowborn, ignorant hedge witch who has placed my grandson under a spell so that he believes himself in love with you. You shall remove it, or I shall summon the guards, and you shall be charged with treason!" the strange woman shrieked.

Rosamond drew herself up. "You are a rude, stupid old woman who knows nothing, least of all how to behave when speaking to someone of my rank. Remove yourself from my sight before I summon the servants to do it for you." She was proud of the fact that her voice remained cold and calm to the end, without a hint of her anger peeping through.

The rude, stupid old woman drew her hand back and slapped Rosamond across the face so hard she sent the princess tumbling to the ground.

Twenty-Four

Siward arrived home just in time to witness Rosamond's meeting with Lady Schutz. His instincts drove him to dive between the two women, defending Rosamond, but he held himself back. If she was to be his queen, she would need to know how to respond to courtiers. Plus, he had to admit, he wanted to hear her defence for himself. He knew there had been magic in the air in the ruins, but he would bet his life that it was not of her making.

Interesting. She did not deny the charge of being a witch, or of casting spells. Neither did she confirm Grandmother's suspicions. Her regal response to the old lady's insults made him want to applaud. Oh, Rosamond was born to be queen.

But when Grandmother raised her hand to the girl, Siward did not move fast enough to prevent the blow. When she fell to the ground, his heart felt like it had dropped right out of his chest.

"Rosamond, are you all right?" he asked.

Lady Schutz batted at his shoulder. "Get away from the witch. She will curse you, boy. Worse than she already has. Throw her out of your house and into a dungeon."

Siward had no time for the old woman's hysterics.

"This woman will be my wife, and your future queen. In fact, she's already carrying my child, the next heir to this kingdom," Siward boasted, hoping his grandmother would not spot that this last was a lie. "If you ever attempt to strike her again, I will send you to a dungeon."

Lady Schutz gasped in horror. "Your own flesh and blood! After all I have done for you. You would not dare, boy!"

"Try me, Grandmother. I will marry Rosamond on St John's Eve and there is nothing you can do to stop me. Now get out."

Grandmother drew herself up. "Rosamond, is it? You don't deserve that name just as you do not deserve my grandson. Mark my words, slut: you will never be queen." She turned on her heel, nose in the air, and stormed out of Siward's house.

Siward stared after her for a moment, before he realised Rosamond still lay on the ground where she'd fallen. He hurried to help her up, checking her for injuries, but she assured him she was fine.

She did not look fine, though. She had dirt all over her gown and a frown that made his heart ache.

"Tell me what is wrong!" he implored.

"St John's Eve is so far away," she said slowly. "Almost a year. I would prefer to be wed well before then."

Now it was Siward's turn to frown in puzzlement. "No, St John's Eve is only a few weeks away."

Rosamond shook her head. "I distinctly remember Queen Margareta's coronation was on St John's Eve. The townspeople had bonfires burning in the town square and when I took fright at what I thought was a man ablaze on one, you told me he was made of wicker and not to worry. I refused to continue until I was certain that you were right. You were, but...I had horrible nightmares that night, of how it would feel to burn."

None of what she said made any sense, but Siward chose not to tell her so. She must have hit her head when she fell, scrambling her wits. "I shall take you to bed," he said, lifting her in his arms.

Those green eyes shone as she gazed up at him. "This is why I don't understand your desire to delay our nuptials. Don't you want me in your bed as much as I need you in mine?"

His loins stirred at her words, willing him to say yes, but Siward had long ago learned to control such urges. "To rest," he said softly. "I shall take you to bed so that you may rest."

She struggled in his grasp until he was forced to set her on her feet. "I don't want to rest. I've been doing nothing all day. Now, I need to change my gown so I can speak to my father, to prepare him before you ask for my hand."

Ah, yes. Something else he had to do before St John's Eve. "I shall go with you," Siward said.

She stared at him for a long moment, her lips parted as though she wished to argue. Then she lowered her eyes and nodded. "If you wish."

<h1 style="text-align:center">Twenty-Five</h1>

Rosamond rummaged through the chest of clothes in her chamber. Before, she had given the gowns little more than a cursory glance as she dressed each morning. But now, she laid them out on the bed one by one and truly examined them. What she found frightened her.

Mixed in with gowns she did not recognise were ones she most definitely did. The soiled gown she had worn today wasn't just like the one she'd worn to the tournament – it seemed to be the same gown, only faded from vibrant strawberry to a dusky rose. The gown she'd worn to Queen Margareta's coronation was more peach than pink now, for it had yellowed somehow. Faded, yellowed and, in one case, frayed where the lacings had come apart, as if with age. She did not understand how it was possible. How had Warin brought her things to his home while he was still in the convent with her? Where was Monika, then, and why did he not send for her? And why did he seem to think that it was still June when it was surely July?

Rosamond sank to her knees on the floor beside the empty chest. Only…it wasn't empty yet. A box she hadn't seen before, possibly because it was the same colour as the base of the chest, remained. She lifted it out, and opened it.

Inside lay Queen Margareta's rose crown, as fresh as the day it was picked, though the flowers should be long dead and dried after so many weeks of travel. First the faded gowns and now this. Rosamond didn't know what to think.

She felt bile rise up in her throat that had nothing to do with morning sickness. Not this time.

Rosamond did not know how long she sat there, her mind whirling with impossible explanations. No matter which one she tried to settle on, none of them made sense.

She wasn't sure how long Warin stood watching her before he spoke. "What is that? Did you make it in the garden today?" He nodded toward the crown.

Something else that didn't make sense. "No," she said slowly. "Queen Margareta wore this to her coronation, and afterward, she gave it to me. This travelled with us until we stopped at the convent, where I did not see it again until I found it here, in a box of my clothes."

Warin closed the chest and perched on top

of it. "I never heard of a queen by that name. Was she the one before Queen Maria?"

"No. She was crowned only a few weeks ago. You were there. You fought in the melee and won, before you knelt before her to claim victory. Even though you had a broken arm, you still won." She stared up at him. "That's when I knew you were the only man I could trust to protect me, no matter what happened. And I healed you." Rosamond moistened her lips. "Don't you remember?"

"You must have hit your head when you fell," he said. "Let me help you to bed, and on the morrow…"

"Don't you remember?" she repeated, more urgently this time.

"Rosamond, you're not well."

She jumped to her feet. "Answer me, Warin. Why don't you remember the queen?"

He stared back at her, impassive. "I don't remember a queen because I've never seen one. Queen Maria died soon after her daughter, nigh on fifty years ago now, and

King Almos never really had the heart to replace her. And, what with the Wall and all, he couldn't really go looking for a new wife, now, could he?"

Never seen a queen? Not possible. Unless…

Realisation dawned, turning into horror.

"You're not Sir Warin," Rosamond choked out. "You have all my things, and you look like him, but you're not him. Who are you?"

Twenty-Six

Siward's heart sank. He'd known all along this was too good to be true. A beautiful woman waiting for him, inviting him into her bed, where he was unable to resist her charms. She'd been waiting for someone else.

He rose. "I am Siward, Lord Protector of the Realm and Regent appointed by the king until a suitable heir is found. By my count, for only a few weeks more." Siward bowed low before her.

Her lips moved, but no sound came out. "Regent? But…what is wrong with the king?"

Did she truly not know? "He died," Siward said gently. "Just this spring. He was an old man, and he rarely left his bed. He passed peacefully in his sleep, but not before he named me Regent."

"How long ago did the queen die?" she whispered.

"Almost fifty years ago now. Before my father was born, and after the Wall closed us in," Siward said.

"What of Sir Warin?" Her voice was so quiet now it was barely audible.

"If by Sir Warin, you mean my grandfather, who was the captain of the guard who lost the princess, he died when I was a boy, but not before he told me every story he knew." Siward swallowed. "He had one regret in his life, and he spoke of it more and more as he got older. He wished he'd found a way to save her."

Rosamond didn't seem to be listening any more. Her eyes had a faraway look. "How long did I sleep?"

Siward scratched his head. "I don't rightly know. You were asleep when I found you, just before you woke."

"Did Sir Warin tell you how long ago he lost his princess?" Her voice shook as her eyes filled with tears.

Siward considered his words before he spoke. "She was never his princess. Too high for him, and he knew it. He was just a captain of the guard. He would have given his life for her, if he could. She was his charge, and he failed her."

Tears spilled down her cheeks. "How long?"

He relented. "Fifty years."

She started to sob.

Siward had no idea why she was crying — what was so sad about some princess who'd been dead for fifty years? — but he could at least try to comfort her. He opened his arms to her and held her close while sobs shook her body for what seemed an eternity.

Finally, the storm seemed to subside and she mumbled something into his tunic.

Cautiously, he asked her to repeat it.

"Release me," she ordered.

He complied.

She straightened, wiped the tears from her face and managed to look every inch the queen he wanted her to be. "How dare you," she said, her voice shaking with fury now. "You pretended to be another man to make me feel affection for you, stole my maidenhead, and only now you tell me the truth? Your grandfather was a good man and an honourable one, but he would turn over in his grave if he knew what you have become."

"I stole nothing you did not give me freely," Siward shot back. "You opened your arms and your legs and all but begged me to climb into your bed. You never asked my name, and I never pretended to be anyone but myself. What kind of woman waits naked in the woods, anyway? Not an honourable one, that's for certain."

If anything, this only enflamed her further. "When I took to my bed, I was clothed as modestly as I am now. You know nothing about honour, or what I have endured." Green eyes blazed.

Siward spread his hands wide in invitation. "Tell me, then. Make me understand."

She gave a slight nod. "Very well. The day I went to sleep, I was dying of a plague picked up shortly after King Erik and Queen Margareta's coronation. Two of my travelling companions were struck down with it, too. I managed to heal them both, but not myself, so I barricaded myself in that courtyard and lay down to die. If what you tell me is true, fifty years I lay there, dreaming without waking, as my body slowly rid itself of the deadly disease and everyone I knew and loved died. Until the day you woke me."

No. She couldn't be. If the princess were still alive, she'd be more than sixty years old. Nothing like the stunning beauty before him, who didn't look a day older than twenty. It wasn't possible.

Steadily, she continued, "Then I was Crown Princess Rosamond, daughter of King Almos and Queen Maria. Now…I am your queen."

Twenty-Seven

The strange man who looked like Warin –
Siward, was that what he'd said his name was?
– didn't look particularly impressed by her
announcement. Weren't men supposed to bow
to their queen?

"Well? Aren't you going to say something?"
Rosamond said finally, exasperated.

"You did hit your head," Siward said drily.

She blew out an angry breath. "You mean

you don't believe me? You think instead that I am mad, or making this up? You said it yourself – why would a maiden wait in the woods without her clothes? Well, I gave you my answer. I slept for fifty years, safe until you broke into my bower."

"Even if you are the lost princess, no one will believe you. Even I am not sure if I believe you. You should be the same age as my grandmother, not standing before me, looking younger than I am." Siward shook his head. "If I were to place you on the throne today, the King's Council would declare that I am mad, and give the throne to someone else."

"They would try to steal my throne from me?" The very thought made her shake, though with fear or fury, she was not sure.

Siward laughed. "No, for none of them would believe it's yours in the first place. They would steal it from me."

She bristled. "So you steal not only my maidenhead, but my throne as well?"

"Enough with this this stealing nonsense!"

he snapped. "No matter who you thought I was, you ordered me to make love to you, and I did. Several times. The king has been dead for weeks now, with no clear heir anywhere in the kingdom. I have searched, but still found no one who could take his place." When Rosamond opened her mouth to protest, he held up his hand to stop her. "Let me finish. Until a few minutes ago, I believed no one in the kingdom had a claim to the throne. That is why the King's Council decided this morning to crown me as king on St John's Eve."

"But you believe me now?" she ventured, feeling hope blossom in her chest.

Siward's expression withered that idea. "Heaven knows I would like to, for I don't want the throne. For years, since long before the king named me Regent, we've been talking around in circles in Council meetings, arguing who should and shouldn't be the next king, but never making a decision until today. It might take years before they would be willing to accept you as the lost princess, but even then they would still argue over what to do, for in the end, they would force you to marry the man they chose. Because without an heir, we would be back in the same mess where we started. Stuck behind the Wall, unable to bring in anything from outside the kingdom, with cellars full of fifty years' worth of berry wine that we cannot trade for what we need."

"Why?"

"Because men are stubborn, and they have never been ruled by a woman before. They squawk like chickens if I suggest even the slightest change."

Rosamond shook her head. "No, why this embargo on trade? Did Father insist upon it, or our neighbours? Queen Margareta spoke of war, but only in jest. I can't imagine she or King Erik…"

But Margareta had given her the diseased cloth. Cloth that had nearly cost Warin and Monika their lives. Could she have done so on purpose, to wipe out her people? She weighed the possibility thoughtfully.

No, Rosamond decided. The plague in her body had been a far more advanced stage of the disease than what she'd seen in Monika or Warin's blood. Yet she had been the last of all three of them to touch the cloth. She most certainly hadn't caught it from the cloth but from the dressmaker's girl, Melitta. That laid the blame far from Margareta, who knew nothing of the girl's illness. In fact, that meant all of this was....

"My fault," Rosamond whispered. "Whatever ails the kingdom now is my fault. I thought by isolating myself in that convent, dying away from everyone else, I could save it, but I've only made matters worse. If I had done what my mother and father asked me to, I would have brought home a husband and settled down to have as many children as the kingdom needed to ensure the succession. Instead, I went haring about the palace, looking for a dress. I did not want a throne, but I wanted a dress like Queen Margareta's gown. Even when I realised what trouble I'd brought home, I thought my death would make things right. And now I am awake, I shall mess things up for you even more. Perhaps Warin was right, and I am cursed."

"No. You could not have known this would happen. No one could have predicted the Wall." Siward sounded soothing, but his words were unsettling.

"What wall?" Rosamond asked.

"The wall of brambles that marks our borders, closing us off from the world," Siward explained.

"The berry bushes? I know they're old, but they are hardly menacing enough to be called a wall. Why, they have marked our borders for centuries before my time, and may still for centuries more." Rosamond shook her head. "The world might have changed much in fifty years, but you can't tell me berry bushes have suddenly turned from six-foot shrubs into towering trees."

Siward nodded, his expression serious. "That is almost exactly what I am telling you.

They have formed a hedge more than thirty feet high in places, easily ten feet thick, ringing the kingdom round so that none may enter, and none may leave. Except for birds, and air."

"So cut it," Rosamond suggested. "We are a nation of farmers, labourers, woodcutters. Surely there are enough axes in the kingdom to keep a few bushes from getting out of hand."

"They tried that. For years, every man has tried his hand at chopping through the Wall, but for every blow you strike, it grows back into the breach. If you try to climb it, it sends you back to the ground. I have had swords and axes plucked from my hands countless times, for at the start of every summer, it is my duty as Lord Protector to test the Wall for weaknesses. I have never found one." He stared at her. "That is what I was doing when I found you."

Rosamond shook her head. "It must be magic, but who could put so much magic into miles and miles of bushes? To make plants behave so unnaturally, a witch would have to be constantly manning the Wall, pouring her power into it to keep it from being broken. How long has the Wall stood in its current state?"

Siward's gaze fixed on her. "Since the princess was lost."

Rosamond didn't miss the accusation in his tone. "You think this is my doing? That I would imprison my own kingdom, which I would have died to protect?"

"You're the witch, or so you say. You tell me."

Rosamond's hands clenched at her sides. "Show me this Wall."

Twenty-Eight

It was several days' ride to the nearest section of Wall, but Rosamond did not complain once. She still appeared pale, but she had regained so much of her strength since their first ride together that she seemed like a different woman to the frail creature Siward had carried to his home only weeks before.

Knowing she was perhaps a princess did not change his opinion of her at all. If anything, it made him want her more. If he had to be king, though blood and birth had ill prepared him for such a role, better that he ascend the throne with her at his side. Her father had often said how he'd raised his daughter to rule, or he would never have sent her as an ambassador at such a young age.

If she'd been raised so differently to other girls, no wonder she held his interest so tenaciously. No other woman had ever invaded his thoughts quite so successfully. Even though she remained tucked firmly into her own bedroll on the opposite side of the fire, every night she stole into his dreams and reminded him of their first night together. If that was what it was like to bed a princess, he had no desire for any other woman.

No, that was not entirely true. What would it be like to bed her when she was queen?

Rosamond most certainly owned him, body and mind, even if she didn't know it yet, but she did not completely possess his heart. Not yet. Though he could feel her fingers closing around it…

What did it matter? They had shared one night together, when she'd mistaken him for another man. Now she knew the truth, he would never touch her again.

On the morrow, he brought her to where the Wall blocked the road.

She dismounted from her palfrey – she'd turned up her royal nose at the jennet Siward's groom had tried to give her, to Siward's amusement – and strode right up to the hedge. Like so many men before her, at first all she did was reach out to touch it, to confirm that what her eyes were seeing was true.

Then…she demonstrated how different she was. Closing her eyes, Rosamond pushed her sleeves up and thrust both hands elbow deep into the brambles.

Siward stepped forward to stop her. "Don't, you'll scratch yourself!"

Too late. A thin trickle of blood travelled down her arm before dripping to the ground. She didn't even seem to feel it.

"It's protecting us," she said slowly. "Keeping us from harm."

"How is keeping a kingdom prisoner protecting us?" Siward scoffed.

"They are plants, not politicians. They keep things out to protect us. Because…I wished it." Rosamond blinked. "They did this for me."

No evil queen, no curse, just a princess the plants wanted to protect? Siward wasn't sure what to believe any more. Rosamond didn't seem mad, and then she made such extraordinary statements that no one in their right mind would believe.

"Can you tell them to stop?" Siward ventured.

Rosamond's brow wrinkled. "I could try, but why would I? These brambles have kept us far safer than any castle wall for decades."

"They also stop trade. New knowledge, new stories. We are a small kingdom, and there are things in foreign lands that I can only imagine, for I have not seen them because we are closed to trade. We need metals, goods, food from other climates, somewhere to sell fifty years' worth of berry wine…" If Siward never tasted the stuff again, it would be too soon. He'd heard of something called beer, a drink like ale but with a finer flavour, which he'd always wanted to taste.

"I can ask them to give me a tunnel through which the road could run, as it did when I last saw this spot."

Siward could scarcely believe it. "Could you bring down the Wall?"

Rosamond pulled her arms from the bush. Though blood still stained her skin, there didn't seem to be a scratch on her. "I could, but I will not. A tunnel for the road will be sufficient. One that we can close again, if it is necessary."

Even that would be a miracle. "Do it, then!"

She folded her arms across her chest. "I will. When I am queen, and not before."

Siward's heart sank. This was an argument he sensed he would not win. Inwardly, he applauded the princess and her late father, the king. He had trained his replacement well.

"You would hold your own kingdom to ransom, just for a crown?" he asked heavily.

Rosamond smiled sweetly. "It is my kingdom, and my crown. I've laid down my life for it once, and while I did not die, I still paid a heavy price. If your Council does not want me, then they are fools who don't deserve me, or my powers. I will not touch the Wall until the kingdom is mine."

"You expect me and the rest of the Council to believe not only that you are their lost princess, miraculously alive and not aged a day after all these years, but that you alone can shift an impenetrable Wall that whole armies could not conquer?" Siward wasn't even sure he believed it.

She bit her lip. "Yes." She lifted her hand, tracing a lazy curve in the air. "You see?" Rosamond stared at the Wall with a slight smile on her lips.

Siward forced himself to turn around, both dreading and hoping for what he might see.

Branches twisted and moved, shaping a hole that grew larger as he watched it. The hole ended on the road, arcing up in an arch more than high enough for a mounted man to ride inside. Nay, not inside – through, he realised, as a shaft of sunlight shot through the tunnel from the other side.

Siward fell to his knees. "My God."

"No," Rosamond said sharply. "Your queen." And, with another wave of her hand, the tunnel closed as if it had never been.

Twenty-Nine

Siward said very little for the rest of that day, and most of the next. It was not until after dinner on the second night away from the Wall that he finally broke the silence between them.

"There is only one way you will be queen."

Rosamond sipped from her cup of wine. "Go on."

Siward hesitated. "You won't like it."

She stared at him across the fire, wishing

she could read his thoughts. "I will not condone violence. The King's Council were appointed by my father, which meant he trusted their judgement, or at least their loyalty. I will not have them killed."

Siward looked stunned. "I had not considered that possibility."

Rosamond rose. "Then consider it now. I will not rule a kingdom by fear."

"But you would hold it to ransom with the Wall."

She waved his accusation away. "That is not the same. The Wall is not a threat. I am certain most people regard it as a simple fact of life. If it were to disappear overnight, or open with no explanation, then you will see fear. But if a rumour were to spread that the Wall appeared when the princess was lost, but it will open when she returns, and then you announce my miraculous return…the people will accept me, and the change."

Siward shook his head. "But not the Council. You will waste years arguing with them, and even then, they might not believe you. You might never regain the throne."

Rosamond stamped her foot in frustration. "No matter how stubborn they are, I will not let you kill them!"

Siward laughed softly. "Stubborn as they are, the Council are worth more to me alive. They at least had the good sense to make me king."

She glared at him. "So you're saying I should fight them, for however long it takes, while you steal my throne? I do not think so."

"I cannot steal what is freely given," he said. "And no matter what you do, I shall be king. You won't change their minds before my coronation, and afterwards…they will have their king. What will they want with a girl who claims to be a princess from a prior dynasty? They won't want to give you a crown, or a throne. No, they'll fight to wed you and bed you. Them, and their sons. For it is your blood they'll want, and the heirs they can beget on you. For if I fail, or die without an heir, they will have plenty of children with the right blood to plant in my place. They will never give their throne to a woman they consider little better than a brood mare."

"I am no one's bed toy. I was born to rule," Rosamond hissed.

Siward folded his arms across his chest. "There is a way. A way that will see you crowned queen before Midsummer."

"Tell me, and I shall do it."

Siward looked like he was holding back laughter. "Marry me."

$$Thirty$$

Rosamond looked like she wanted to leap over the fire and plant her fist in his face, Siward decided. But her court manners were too ingrained for her to do anything so uncouth.

"So that I can be your bed toy instead?" she demanded.

In his dreams. "If you wish, or I could be yours." Hastily, he continued, "At least consider it. Not a single man on the Council would question your right to be queen if you are my wife. Save your strength for what is truly important, instead of arguing with stubborn old men. If you care about your people and freeing the kingdom from the Wall so we can rejoin the outside world again, help me. Stand at my side so we can both lead our people into the future."

She looked thoughtful. "Why?"

Because he'd never met a woman he desired more, for both her body and her mind. From the moment he first saw her, he'd wanted her in his throne room. Now, he needed her. "Because you alone can save my kingdom, which makes you the perfect queen."

She slumped. "So you propose a marriage of convenience, then?"

If that was how she felt, then he would accept that she could never love him as she'd loved his grandfather. Siward wished he didn't feel so jealous of a dead man. "That is usually what happens when people pair for politics. Of course, the marriage must be real for appearances' sake."

Rosamond frowned. "What do you mean?"

"The Council will still expect us to produce an heir. They'd be happier with half a dozen, but one would be enough to start with."

If anything, her frown deepened.

He hastened to add, "I promise that every time you share my bed, I will endeavour to ensure you enjoy it just as much as you did our first night together." Siward swallowed. "Even if I have to fill the bed with flowers."

To his surprise, Rosamond laughed. "You would do that for me?"

Siward wasn't sure how to answer. Would she think him weak if he told the truth? Time to find out, he supposed, when no one but she would hear him.

"On that first night, when I first saw you, I thought I had died and heaven had given me a goddess for my own, like the heroes of old. I forgot everything of my life, my responsibilities, for my heart and my mind were full of nothing but you and how best to please you." Siward swallowed, then continued, "You have not left my thoughts for a moment since. Every day and every night, I think only of you. I would give you my whole kingdom in exchange for one more night of bliss with you."

She stared at him for a long time. He hoped she was considering his offer, instead of searching for the most diplomatic way to refuse him.

Then, almost as if she was unaware of what her hands were doing, Rosamond unlaced her gown and let it slide to the ground. Her shift soon followed, so that she stood naked in the firelight. "We have an accord," she said softly, her green eyes burning with desire.

Siward had to force himself to look away. "Good. On our wedding night, when we consummate our marriage, I shall claim my price."

"You drive a hard bargain, Lord Siward. But I accept."

Hard? She had no idea.

Finally, he heard the rustle of cloth as she covered herself, and Siward breathed again. He wasn't sure how he'd manage to wait the weeks until they were wed before he touched her again. But if she only allowed him one night…it would be worth the wait, he promised himself.

In the meantime, at least he had his dreams.

Thirty-One

On their return, Rosamond was caught up in such a whirlwind of activity she barely had time to think, let alone speak to Siward. She needed new gowns for her wedding and her coronation, plus more to wear to court afterwards, and at least a dozen new shifts and veils. Particularly as her newly rounded belly had started to show if her bodice was laced too tight.

What made matters worse was the first two gowns the dressmaker produced were made of scratchy, suffocating wool. And what in blazes had possessed her to make them blue?

"I asked for pink or green silk, not blue wool," Rosamond snapped at the woman. "I can't wear this in court, let alone at a coronation."

The woman dropped a deep curtsey. "I am sorry, mistress, but there is no silk to be had anywhere in the kingdom. Even if we did have some, we have no dye to make it the colours you desire. I have linen and wool, mistress, which I can make white and blue. Unless you can bring down the Wall so that traders can come in, this is all I can do."

All the more reason to get the formalities over with so she could fulfil her promise and poke a hole in the hedge. Unwilling to torment the poor dressmaker any further, Rosamond sent her to work on her new shifts instead. White linen, the woman assured her, would not be a problem.

When her coronation day arrived, Agnna laced her carefully into the same silk dress Rosamond had worn to Margareta's coronation, so many years ago. Mere months for Rosamond, of course, as she had slept through the intervening years, but so much had happened since that day. Rosamond prayed she could emulate Margareta's queenly demeanour today through all the layers of clothing and ceremony.

Once she made it through the day, she'd have the whole night to spend naked with Siward, Rosamond promised herself. True to his word, he had not touched her since she accepted his marriage proposal, and the longer she waited, the stronger her desire for him grew. Not that she would tell him so, of course. The man who usurped her throne could not be allowed to hold any power over her.

Like Margareta, she wore her hair uncovered, crowned in the same roses, though they were tinted a pale pink to match her dress.

This time, it had taken barely a thought to make the flowers change colour, and not a whisper of dizziness. While she'd dreamed away fifty years, Rosamond's power had grown immeasurably. Though the Wall was miles away, all she had to do was touch another plant, and she could speak to them all, every tree and bush in the kingdom. The Wall itself felt like an army of soldiers, standing in formation, awaiting her orders. Tomorrow, she promised them.

Tomorrow, she would be queen.

Her palfrey stood ready outside, though Siward had left early to deal with important business in the palace, or so Agnna had said, so Rosamond rode alone to the city square, the open space between the castle and the cathedral. Today, it was far from empty. A huge bonfire stood in the centre, waiting to be lit, with a life-sized wicker figure tied to a pole at the top. Smaller bonfires dotted the square, and people milled around, chatting and buying food from the vendors who had set up their barrows on the edge of the space. Rosamond's stomach churned at the thought of food – she had no appetite today. Something felt wrong, but she could not identify what. Hooded and covered by her cloak, Rosamond urged her skittish mount through the crowd until she reached the refuge offered by the castle bailey.

There she found Siward, dressed in blue wool that still managed to look regal on him. When traders came to town, she would insist on buying him silks and velvets, as befit a king. For a moment, she forgot he was a usurper, and indulged her fantasies. He should have tunics tailored to show off his physique, widening at his broad shoulders as they narrowed to his taut belly. Cloaks of fur and velvet which would keep him warm even if he rode through the kingdom in the dead of winter. She would have new gowns that fitted her new curves perfectly, so that his eyes were drawn to her every moment she was in the room, banishing all other thoughts from his head. She would rule, not him, as it should be.

Rosamond dismounted and was assailed by a small feminine army, intent on brushing the travel dust from her clothes and making her look as perfect as a princess should on her wedding day. She knew none of them, but she thanked them graciously and swore to learn their names before the week was out.

They scuttled out of the way and Rosamond glanced up to see what had startled them.

Siward stood before her, looking more nervous than she felt. "It is time," he said, extending his arm.

Ah, yes. In the absence of her father, Rosamond was a ward of the crown, which meant the only man qualified to hand her over to her husband was the king-to-be. Some bright spark in charge of protocol had decided that meant she would enter the cathedral with Siward. They would kneel together and say their wedding vows, before they were crowned king and queen. Then they would walk arm in arm through the crowd to the castle, where they would change into rich clothes as befit the new royals, and a feast would be held in the great hall for all the noblemen and women of the kingdom.

Later that night, after the feast, Siward would carry her to the king's bedchamber and make the whole dull day worth it.

To Rosamond's surprise, it all proceeded as planned. Yes, she had stumbled over a broken tile in the cathedral on the way to the altar, and when Siward knelt on her skirt, he'd nearly torn the fragile fabric, but all his grandmother's threats came to naught when they spoke the vows that made them husband and wife. The priest raised his voice to proclaim their union to the assembled crowd, and a smattering of applause swept through the cathedral. Rosamond glanced over her shoulder. It looked like half the kingdom had tried to squeeze inside the vaulted building, and it sounded like the other half were waiting outside to congratulate the new king and queen.

Which brought them to the ceremony she'd

anticipated most.

The priest who'd performed the wedding disappeared, to be replaced by a bishop who adored the sound of his own voice, or so it seemed to Rosamond. He sang, said prayers, and lectured them at length in a language Rosamond vaguely remembered from her childhood, but barely understood now.

Finally, an acolyte stepped forward with an ornate chest that Rosamond recognised, for it held the king's and queen's crowns. The bishop took the king's crown and loudly presented it to the four corners of the earth. Then, he lifted it high above Siward's head and called on the uncrowned king to make his vows of sovereignty.

Siward's voice rolled from his lips like velvet, caressing her ears and her heart as he promised to rule, protect, uphold and all the other things a good king did, casting a spell of his own over the crowd without any magic at all. Even Rosamond believed him. Siward would do all that he had promised, not because this was his kingdom, but because he was their king. The highest in the land, and yet their lowliest servant. She blinked back tears. He truly deserved the throne.

The bishop fussed around him, anointing him with oil and wrapping a fur cloak around his shoulders before droning through another prayer. After this interminable monologue finished, Siward was permitted to rise and take his place at a specially prepared throne on the dais. Then, it would be Rosamond's turn to receive the bishop's attentions.

The bishop reached into the ornate chest a second time.

"We're under attack!" a frenzied male voice shouted, before running feet pounded on the cathedral tiles. "The Wall has doubled in size, and now it is marching inward. It means to wipe us out!"

A man in torn clothing fell to his knees beside Rosamond. He smelled like he had not bathed in weeks. "The Wall, the Wall!" With a wink at Rosamond, the man collapsed in what appeared to be a dead faint.

Even amid the man's appalling stench, she smelled a rat, but in the panic that erupted, he was borne away from her before she could lay a healing hand on him.

She heard Siward and others shouting commands, but she ignored them all and made her way outside to the square. She scanned the space for something green, and found a rose vine that had climbed its way up the castle's outer wall. She grasped it and sent her thoughts winging across the kingdom to the Wall.

Which still waited, obedient to her command. Unmoving. Unchanged. The same size as the day she first touched it. And definitely not attacking anyone.

Whoever the smelly man was, he was a liar, sent to disrupt the coronation. She had to find Siward, to tell him the truth, so they could complete the ceremony. Now, more than ever, she needed to be queen.

Thirty-Two

When people exploded into panic all over the cathedral, Siward prayed for calm. He shrugged off the royal robe and set his crown on the throne he had occupied for barely a moment. What were they but empty symbols, anyway? More important was his promise to protect his people from all their enemies. Even that cursed plant.

Striding through the milling crowd, he

shouted for a groom to saddle his horse, and pack provisions for a journey to the border.

Lord Vamos caught his arm. "The Council will keep the peace until your return."

Siward thanked him, relieved. The Council might not be good at making decisions or agreeing to change, but they excelled at keeping the populace calm. Within moments, Lord Vamos had found the other Council members and led them purposefully toward the castle, like a mother duck with her brood.

His grandmother appeared from nowhere, clinging to him like a babe to its mother. "You will protect us, won't you? You'll turn the Wall back?"

Siward gently pried her off him. "Yes, Grandmother. I will ride immediately and do whatever I must to keep the kingdom safe." He glimpsed Rosamond on the other side of the square, looking lost beside a vine-covered wall. "While I am gone, take care of my wife. See her safely into the castle to await my return."

Lady Schutz followed his gaze, and she nodded. "I will see to her."

"Thank you." He thought for a moment. "What happened to Fodor? I would like to hear more of what he saw of the Wall."

Lady Schutz hung her head. "The poor boy rode day and night to get here to warn us, and it nearly killed him. He is resting, but I'm told it will be some time before he wakes. Time you can ill afford, if the Wall is advancing."

Siward nodded. She was right. Pausing only to ascertain that his saddlebags were full, Siward swung up into the saddle and set off at a gallop for the city gates.

Thirty-Three

Rosamond scanned the crowd, looking for Siward, but by the time she spotted him, he was already mounted and riding away. She screamed for him to come back, but he never heard her. He just kept on going. She slumped against the wall, defeated. Curling her fingers around the vine at her side, she whispered, "Bring him back to me safe, and keep him from harm."

Across the kingdom, a million leaves rustled in their promise to obey her command.

"There she is! The king's whore." Two men seized her arms, and when she struggled, a third grabbed her around the knees, too, lifting her off the ground and out of reach of the obedient vine. Between them, they dragged her to the foot of the cathedral steps.

"Is this the one, Lord Fodor?" the man on her left asked. He was the one who had called her a whore.

"That's the one," the smelly man said. "She's a whore and a witch, as the whole town of Hatar can attest. They saw her communing with the Wall. She danced naked before it, took her pleasure from its branches, before sacrificing the king's own hunting hawk to the devil and painting her wanton body with its blood. Then, still bathed in blood, she seduced the king by his own campfire, and bespelled him, so he would take her as his queen. She is a witch – the evil witch who cursed us with the Wall in the first place!"

Rosamond's mouth hung open in shock. Where had Fodor come up with these lies? It was almost as though he had followed her and Siward to the Wall, and sprinkled the story with the products of his own sordid imagination.

"She's been building an army in the Lord Protector's gardens, too! Tiny berry bushes, grown so huge they could consume a man, they would!" Draga piped up. "She's a witch, all right. Enchanted our poor king, she has!"

Siward's grandmother appeared at the top of the steps. "My poor grandson will not hear of her being tried for her crimes, for she has bewitched him. But now that he is gone, we shall see justice served. You all accuse her of witchcraft, casting evil spells against the kingdom and the king himself. That is treason. Is there anyone who can speak in her defence?" The hateful old woman scanned the crowd. "What, she has no champion? Or is it that there is no one who knows her, for she has travelled from outside the kingdom by magical means, to conquer us from within like the traitor she is!"

Loud cheering greeted this statement. Not just from the men Rosamond could see who restrained her, but from the hundreds, perhaps thousands of people standing behind her.

The old woman had incited a mob, and Rosamond knew there was no place for reason or sense in a mob. Fear's fingers closed around her heart.

Only Siward could stop this.

BRING HIM BACK! she screamed in her head, praying that the plants heard her, though she touched none.

"What say you to the charges, witch?" the crone demanded.

"I am your queen, and you will put me down. When the king hears of this, he will show no mercy." The last part was pure bluff, and Rosamond suspected the crone knew it. The men on either side of her loosened their grip, though, and the third let go of her legs entirely. This gave Rosamond the freedom to stand tall as she finished with, "If you cease telling your lies to my people, I shall see to it that you will not want for food or drink while you are in the dungeons. Perhaps I shall speak to the king, and you will not be executed."

Fodor spoke for them all, it seemed, when he strode forward, stopping so that his foul-smelling face was mere inches from Rosamond's. "Shut up, whore." His meaty fist crashed into the side of her head, sending her to the ground, where the paving stones stole her senses and the darkness gave her a reprieve from pain.

Thirty-Four

As he rode, Siward's head began to clear so he could think. The fastest way to the Wall was to change horses at the first town, and the next, and the next, resting only long enough to ensure he would not fall out of the saddle. He estimated he could make it to the Wall in a little over three days. It would still be another three days back to the city so that he and Rosamond could decide what to do about a

Wall that wanted to attack, but he needed to gather intelligence before a strategy could be formed.

Rosamond knew more about plants and the Wall than he did. Perhaps he should have brought her.

Siward considered this for a moment, then dismissed the idea. Her knowledge should be protected by castle walls and guards, not risked against an enemy none of them understood. If the Wall hurt her…

What could any of them do against the Wall?

Rosamond said it wanted to protect them. The Wall had healed her scratches – he'd seen it. He hadn't imagined the blood, nor the smooth skin she'd showed him afterward.

Why, after fifty years of doing nothing, would it attack now?

She could ask it. Rosamond said she could speak to plants, and in their own way, they responded to her. Protected her. Obeyed her wishes.

What if it only existed to protect her, and not the kingdom at all? What if waking her and taking her to the capital had summoned the Wall to protect her new home instead?

Rosamond would know. If it was necessary, she would take down the whole Wall, now he had fulfilled his part of the bargain and she was queen.

Siward reined in his horse, horrified as realisation struck him. She was not yet queen. Fodor, a rabid dog who had never left the city in his life, had interrupted her coronation before the bishop could complete the ritual.

What did Fodor have to gain out of this? The man never did anything unless it fed his own selfish desires.

His sister, the Lady Jolanka, who his grandmother had promised would be queen.

Who couldn't be queen while Rosamond reigned.

The Wall was right. Rosamond was in danger, and he was sworn to love and protect her.

Time to make good on that oath.

Siward swung his horse around, headed back the way they'd come. He made it a hundred yards before a tree branch plucked him out of the saddle. He hung in the air for a moment, clawing for a handhold, but he caught nothing, so he tumbled into the river that ran beside the road.

He came up spluttering and furious. "What was that for?" he shouted at the offending tree branch. "I'm trying to get home to help her!"

Every tree in the forest shook its leaves as though blown in a mighty storm. With one voice that sounded like an echo of Rosamond, they shrieked, "Bring him home!"

Thirty-Five

Rosamond's head ached. In truth, everything hurt, but her head was the worst. Her arms, from her wrists right up to her shoulders, burned, and so did her calves. Someone doused her in liquid and she spluttered, jerking awake.

She could see the whole city square from up here, for she was level with the cathedral's arched windows, and only a little lower than the castle battlements. That did not bode well, for the only thing high enough to give her such a vantage point was the Midsummer Eve bonfire with the wicker figure tied to the top. Rosamond twisted her head, trying to see if she had guessed right. Indeed she had. She was tied to the effigy, and if she didn't do something, she would burn with it.

From the plague to this. No kingdom deserved to have a princess lay down her life twice for it.

"The witch is awake!" the smelly man shouted.

Fortunately, she could not smell him up here.

"You will rot in my dungeon," Rosamond called back.

"You have no power here, traitor!" the old woman shrieked.

It took Rosamond some time to work out where the old woman was. She stood atop the battlements, half hidden by the roses that had climbed the wall in their quest for sun. They would receive no warmth from Siward's grandmother.

"You are a witch, and a traitor. You seek to rule a kingdom that is not yours!" the woman announced.

Shouts of "Witch!" and "Traitor!" rose from the crowd that filled the square, all of them faceless now in the darkness. A faceless mob had no conscience, either.

"I seek to rule my rightful kingdom!" Rosamond shouted back. "I am Crown Princess Rosamond, daughter of King Almos and Queen Maria. His Majesty King Siward woke me from my enchanted sleep and brought me here so that I might rule by his side. This kingdom is mine, by right of blood and birth!"

The old woman hesitated, but she recovered quickly. "Imposter! I saw the princess's body with my own eyes, buried beneath the roses in a convent outside Hatar. She died fifty years ago, and you cannot be she!"

No. It was not possible. No one had entered

that convent until the day Siward woke her. When Warin and Monika left, she had told the roses to enclose it completely.

That made the old woman…

"Monika!" Rosamond cried. All the people she had known in life had died, except for one – her loyal maid. "Monika, you of all people should recognise me. You were there when Queen Margareta gave me her crown!"

"Liar!" Monika shrieked. "You cannot be the princess, even if you look like she did the day she died. It is a trick of some sort, a spell only an evil witch could cast. And if you are not the princess, then you are the evil queen, who caused this kingdom so much grief. You killed our princess, cursed our land…and almost corrupted our king, but no longer! Tonight, you shall die, burned in the Midsummer bonfires like the devil-worshippers do to their own!"

Desperately, Rosamond tried to tell the vine on the wall to wrap around Monika's feet, to drag her out of sight so she would stop. Stop accusing her. Stop fighting her. Just…stop.

"Light the witch's pyre!" Fodor roared, thrusting his torch deep into the branches.

Stop them! Rosamond screamed in her head. Put out the fire. Don't let me burn.

As smoke rose up, obscuring her vision, she wrapped her hands around the pole behind her. It was green wood, still full of sap. She directed her thoughts into the dying sapling, urging it and all the wood around it to grow, to break the ropes tying her and help her down to the square.

It was no use. No tree could grow fast enough to save her, for all around the base of the pyre, a score of torches dipped to light the Midsummer blaze.

Thirty-Six

Siward rode up to the castle gates, sore, weary and soaked from his dip in the river. In the square, the townspeople were lighting bonfires for St John's Eve, as they did every year. He could even see the wicker man on one, a tradition that had its murky origins deep in the past. Something to do with fertility, was all he could remember. Perhaps that's why it looked so much like a woman, her skirts billowing in the rising smoke.

The bonfire caught, illuminating the figure, who was struggling to free herself from her bonds. Not wicker. A real, live woman.

"Stop them," the leaves on the trees whispered. "Don't let me burn."

Rosamond.

Siward slid from his horse, and shoved his way through the crowd. The flames leaped high above his head, but they had not touched her yet. If he could climb the woodpile and reach her in time, he could save her. A man stumbled into him, grabbing him by the shoulders. "Help me!" the man begged, as something dark trickled from his lips. He collapsed at Siward's feet, nearly tripping him, but Siward only leaped over the man and ran on.

Rosamond was the only one who mattered. The only one who could save his kingdom. Her kingdom. All this belonged to her.

Siward put on a burst of speed. Just before he reached the flames, he leaped, clawing for a handhold. The already smouldering branches burned his hands, but he hardly felt the pain. It would be nothing compared to the heart-wrenching agony of losing Rosamond.

Slipping twice, but climbing ever higher, he reached the top of the pyre. She had stopped struggling now and hung limp and lifeless from the stake they'd tied her to. Whoever had done this would pay with their lives, he swore.

But first, he had to save her. To cut her free and climb down carrying her would take too long. Siward took a deep breath, then charged up to Rosamond, throwing all his weight against the post that held her fast. No, not a post, he realised as leaves showered down on him, but a fair-sized tree. An ominous crack sounded, but the tree did not break. He retreated a few steps further, to the edge of the flames, and charged again.

This time, his aim was true. The tree tilted and tipped, and Siward barely had a moment to wrap his arms around Rosamond to cushion her fall before all three of them tumbled down the side of the lit bonfire to the square below.

Thirty-Seven

"Siward?" Rosamond croaked, then coughed. Too much smoke. "Are you all right?"

His arm stuck out at an unnatural angle, and she could feel the pain rolling off him in waves. Broken ribs, and more besides, she guessed. Much like herself. The soot-smeared man groaned.

Rosamond squirmed around until she could see his face. Yes, he was her husband. His face looked merely smoke-blackened, and his wet, woollen clothes had protected the rest of him from the fire, but his hands...oh, his poor hands. So badly burned there was barely any skin left.

Their tumble had loosened her bonds, so she managed to get one hand free, then the other. Her feet could wait. She took Siward's bleeding, blackened hands in hers and kissed them, wishing with all her might that she had the energy to heal him. But all her magic had gone into the sapling that now lay on the paving, sprouting leaves and roots like it wished to start a forest in that very spot.

Still, she would do what she could. She seized a handful of leaves from the sapling's crown in one hand and lay her free hand over both of his. Closing her eyes, Rosamond drew every bit of power she could from the tree and poured it into Siward. She might not be their queen, but she would give her people back their king.

He let out a wordless cry and arched his

back before another cry escaped, louder this time. Then…"Rosamond?" he said.

"I am here, my king," she replied. Even in her own ears, her voice sounded breathy and weak. "Healing you as best I can. It was…the least I could do. You saved my life."

"But if you heal me, who will heal you?" Siward asked.

No one.

The words seemed to echo around the square, caught by the leaves of the trees and spun into the air.

Siward seized her shoulders. "Don't you dare go back to sleep on me. In fifty years, I'll be dead. Tell me how to heal you, Rosamond. You promised to be my queen, and we have yet to share a wedding night. I won't let you break your word."

Rosamond smiled. "The rose garden. In the castle. Take me there. If anything can heal me, they will."

He lifted her in his arms and followed her directions until they emerged in an unpaved courtyard. It looked nothing like the garden where she'd spent most of her youth, for fifty years of neglect had turned her regimented rose garden into a briar patch more overgrown than the convent where he'd first found her.

"Are you sure this is the place?" he asked doubtfully.

"I am certain. I can smell my roses, welcoming me home," she whispered. "Lay me down among them."

"But the thorns…"

"My roses will never hurt me. You have carried me far enough. I thank you for all you have done." It was a dismissal, but only a half-hearted one. For her heart longed for him to stay.

"I'm not leaving you. I've spent the night with you in a bed of roses before, and I intend to do it again."

Rosamond smiled. "As my king wishes." She coughed again, then said, "I will sleep, and dream, as I work together with the plants to heal myself. If I do not wake with the dawn…"

He sounded fierce. "Then I give you fair warning. I shall kiss you until you do. Even if it takes hours."

Bliss, surely. "You are a brave man, my king. To lie alone and unprotected with a witch where her power is greatest."

Siward lay beside her on the briars, cushioned by roses, and took her in his arms. "I am not alone. I am with you."

Thirty-Eight

Midsummer's Day dawned, and it was glorious. King Siward held his bride in his arms, and though Rosamond's eyes were closed, they fluttered as if she was about to wake. Then she did, and her green eyes outshone the sun.

"Are you healed?" he asked softly.

She laughed. "Yes, and so are you. However did you get all those bruises?"

Siward thought hard. "I was attacked by a

tree."

Amusement sparkled in her eyes. "You mean you weren't watching where you were going, and bumped into a tree?"

"Not this time. It whipped out a branch, grabbed me from the saddle, and threw me into the river. Then it screamed about how it had to bring me back. To you."

"A tree screamed? You must have hit your head."

Siward shook his head, which didn't hurt at all. "No. And not one tree. The whole forest screamed with the same voice. Your voice. Every tree ordering the others to 'bring him home'."

Rosamond wet her lips. "Truly?"

"Truly. And now I am home, I realise my queen has no crown."

Rosamond reached up for Queen Margareta's crown, which her captors had left on her head when they tied her to the stake, in mockery of her mother's gold crown, which she should have worn yesterday. Now she had neither, for the rose crown had disappeared. It was fitting.

"The people called me a witch. A traitor. Not a princess, and not their queen. They don't want me. They want you. Are loyal to you. I am…no one."

"Then we will change their minds. Slowly, at first, but some day soon, you will be more beloved as their queen than you ever were as their lost princess. I promise you." Siward rose from his bed among the roses, and held out his hand. "We have other promises to keep. First, we must go to the cathedral and finish what we started."

"But…"

"I promised you will be queen." The fervour in his eyes brooked no argument.

Rosamond accepted his assistance to rise, and, hand in hand, they walked out of the castle gates.

They did not notice, but if either had turned their heads to look, they would have seen two dead traitors, dangling from the battlements.

No hand had yet touched them, for no one was willing to unwrap the choking rose vines from around Monika or Fodor's necks, or pry out the pine bough that had somehow impaled Fodor so that one end stuck out the bottom of his tunic, while the other jutted from the juncture of his neck and shoulder.

The square was empty but for ashes from the fires and a brittle circlet of dried roses that disintegrated in a puff of wind. Siward led Rosamond through the doors of the cathedral and shouted for the bishop.

Several minutes later, the bishop appeared, looking like he had dressed in a tearing hurry. He eyed the ragged, blackened pair before him. "What do you want?"

"For you to finish the coronation. My queen needs a crown."

When the bishop heard his king's voice, he fell to his knees. "Forgive me, sire, I did not recognise you. Are you certain that you don't wish to wash before…?"

"I said crown her, now."

"Yyyyyes, sire."

In a gown of scorched silk, Crown Princess Rosamond knelt before the bishop. Like King Siward before her, she vowed to rule her kingdom fairly, protect its people and property, and uphold its laws for as long as she lived. She wept as she said the words, for they meant the end of all that had come before. The death of her parents, a goodbye to her childish dreams of freedom, and any desire to throw away duty, even for a day. But it was also a wondrous beginning, with Siward at her side.

Siward placed the royal cape around her shoulders, and the bishop set a crown on her head.

Queen Rosamond took her kingly husband's hand, and, both clad in radiant smiles that outshone the morning sun, they stepped out of the cathedral into a brand new day.

Thirty-Nine

Siward woke Rosamond with a kiss, as he had every morning for the last year since their wedding. "It is time," he said.

She smiled and stretched, still aching from the pleasure of last night's lovemaking. "So it is."

When they were both dressed, Siward opened the flap of their pavilion and led her out into the temporary village of tents that had sprung up beside the Wall.

The road ended where the hedge began, as it had for as long as anyone could remember, except Rosamond. But now it was time to make new memories, which was why half the kingdom had come to see the spectacle. For today, their beloved queen would open the door to the outside world.

Letting go of Siward's arm, Rosamond approached the Wall. She traced a small circle on the hedge, spiralling outward until she had to use her whole arm to span the radius of her circle.

Gasps and murmurs arose from the crowd as Rosamond's magic began to make itself visible. A hole appeared in the Wall, big enough to insert a finger, but no more. The hole seemed to spin, widening as it went, until it could fit first a child's, then a man's hand. Yet still it grew, branches unfolding and undulating until they formed a perfect arch for the sun to shine through from the far side of the Wall for the first time in fifty-one years.

Cheering and clapping erupted, but the show was not over yet. Rosamond took Siward's arm once more, and together the king and queen strode through the arch across the border. Then in view of everyone, they turned to each other and kissed.

On the inside of the Wall, a baby started wailing.

The king and queen returned home.

"The queen commands the Wall, to be our defence when we are in need, but she will open the door for all those who wish to pass through. For it might have been cursed by an evil queen, but she is no match for the power of Queen Rosamond the Fair!"

The wailing baby did not care for King Siward's speech, and the loud cheering from the crowd only made him scream louder still.

Rosamond sighed. "Lady Jolanka, bring him here." She held out her arms, but Siward plucked the baby from her companion's arms first.

"What's wrong, Helios?" Siward asked his

infant son.

"Selene hit him, or pinched him, I am certain of it," Jolanka said, sounding quite proud of the girl as she thrust a beaming baby Selene at her mother. "You'd better name her heir to the throne and not him. She's the fighter, and the elder, too."

"We shall see," Rosamond said. "The king and I have many years yet, in which to live happily ever after. The tale of our twins…is yet to be told."

Fall: Scheherazade Retold

DEMELZA CARLTON

A tale in the Romance a Medieval Fairy Tale series

One

If there was one thing Zoraida hated, it was dragons. Yes, she knew her godson's name was George and that his only ambition was to slay a dragon like his saintly namesake, but when the youth had chosen the biggest, most irritable dragon ever to crawl out of a cave, she'd found herself honour-bound as his fairy godmother to volunteer to be the maiden bait for the beast. Bait, yes. Sacrifice, no. But when silly George had gotten himself knocked out by a blow from the beast's tail, she'd had to decide between fighting the dragon herself or losing her godson.

Whoever had blessed the boy with intelligence had done a piss-poor job of it. They should have endowed him with some common sense instead. The enchanted sword she'd given him lay on the ground, useless, as he put her blessing to use: yes, she'd certainly given him all the swiftness a boy could need for running away.

Her godson was a fool and a coward, Zoraida fumed. Or perhaps the smoke was coming from her skirt, which was definitely smouldering. Damned fire-breathing nuisance.

She lobbed another fireball at the dragon, which splashed harmlessly against his scaly hide, but kept his attention firmly on her and not the fleeing boy. Just a few more seconds and he'd reach the shelter of the city. Then she could leave.

The dragon sent a jet of flame in her

direction and she was too slow to deflect it. This time, her skirt caught fire. Swearing, Zoraida decided George could fend for himself.

Thinking to go somewhere that she might smother the flames, Zoraida opened a portal. She glimpsed snow, breathed a sigh of relief, and stepped through.

Two

Hans eyed his pitiful fire with concern. If he didn't bring more fuel in, the fire would certainly go out and he'd freeze to death. Hardly a cheerful prospect for any night, let alone Yule. He'd planned to be home by now, sitting before a roaring fire with a mug of mulled mead, stuffed full with whatever his cook had created for the feast. He might not be the richest merchant, but he kept a good cook. So what if his hall was bare of tapestries and he didn't eat from golden plates? Good food needed no gold to satisfy his appetite.

What he'd give for a thick chunk of roast pork now, edged with sizzling crackling, ready to dip in apple sauce made from the last of the autumn apples from his own orchards…

Instead, he had stale bread and dried fish for supper, a gift from the fur traders he'd finally struck a deal with. Spending his Christmas Eve in a lonely trapper's hut in the icy northern wastes was worth it for that deal alone. He'd be the sole supplier of the highest quality vair, a fur much prized among the nobility at home, and a single shipload of the stuff would give him the gold to repair the keep so that it once again had all its towers, like it had in his grandfather's day.

But first, he must make it through the night without freezing to death. Good thing he wasn't like some of the men at court, who'd shudder at the very thought of getting their hands dirty. His father had given everything they had, shy of the keep and the land it stood on, to support the holy crusade which had taken his life, and left his son to manage the estate.

So the new baron had chopped wood, mended fences, worked the fields and collected port duties, all the while learning what he could so that when his father returned, he could try his hand at the fur trade. News of his father's death had hit him hard, but it had also given him the push he needed to come out here to see if he could deal direct with the fur traders and not the merchants in the northern ports.

All that was for naught if he didn't survive the night. And to do that, he needed more wood. Grabbing an axe and an empty half-barrel that smelled of fish, he headed outside into the snow.

He soon found the woodpile and fell into a rhythm as the exercise warmed his blood. Nights like this he wished he had a wife to share his bed. One day, he promised himself.

When he was no longer a penniless baron with an empty title and little else.

A flash of light caught his eye. He'd seen the aurora dance across the sky many times, but this was different. It was as though a purple window opened up and a blazing ball of fire shot through, flaming like a comet across the sky before extinguishing itself in a snowdrift on the side of the next hill.

A shooting star. Laughing quietly to himself, he made the obligatory wish, which he hoped one day would come true.

Alas, he knew wishes were merely wind. He would be more likely to improve his fortune by retrieving what remained of the fallen star, if anything. Being a practical man, Hans stacked the wood he'd cut in the half barrel, then headed up the hill to investigate. He'd never seen a star fall before.

Three

The moment Zoraida stepped out of the portal, she realised her mistake. No ground met her feet – the snow she'd glimpsed was a hill in the distance, and she found herself falling through the air to the ground below. Swearing, she angled her descent as best she could for the hill, which held enough snow to smother her flaming skirts three times over.

The snow was deep enough to cushion her

fall, too, she found, for when she hit the ground, the impact only drove the breath from her lungs. No broken bones that she could find, fortunately, for she was not particularly skilled at healing spells. And she'd need all her limbs to climb out of the deep pit she'd created when she landed.

Laboriously, she clawed her way up until she emerged into the open air. As the freezing wind knifed through the shredded remains of her dress, Zoraida wished she'd stayed in her hole. Somehow, she'd lost her shoes in her descent, so her bare feet went numb the moment she stepped out onto the snow. Staggering through the drifts, she made it partway down the hill before she lost her footing and tumbled over and over until her head collided with something hard and everything went dark.

Four

Hans had seen many things in his life, but when a woman climbed out of the hole the star had fallen into, he found himself rubbing his eyes to make sure he wasn't imagining her.

No, he decided, for if he were to imagine a woman on a night as cold as this, he would have wished for one who was warm and welcoming, well-wrapped in furs. Not this stumbling, staggering creature in grey rags who tumbled down the hill and lay lifeless at his feet.

No, not quite lifeless. She still drew breath, though not for long if she was left out here in the cold.

Hans hoisted her in his arms, tucking a fold of his cloak around her to keep out the wind. She was surprisingly warm. Perhaps she'd ridden the fallen star from heaven.

Laughter rumbled in his throat at such a silly thought. But angel or no, the woman needed shelter and the hut was all he could offer her. And at Christmas…all he had, he would gladly share.

So he settled her on the straw pallet beside the dying fire and covered her with a blanket, before wrapping his cloak around himself and heading outside again.

He brought in the half-barrel of wood, then returned to the woodpile for another load. He might not have much to offer, but he could give her a roaring fire to keep her warm tonight.

Hans shouldered the door open, stamping the snow from his boots, and found himself fixed in the sights of a pair of violet eyes.

"First dragons, now a bloody bear. If I'd known fairy godmothering was all about battling huge creatures, I never would have agreed to it. Matchmaking must be easier."

Five

To Zoraida's considerable relief, the tall, shaggy figure she'd called a bear chuckled as he removed his furry hood.

"I'm no bear, lady. I only wear the hide of one. I only wish I had two, for you're sorely in need of warmer garments." He nodded at her.

Zoraida glanced down. Soot had stained the bodice of her white gown grey, and singed the skirt to black-edged ribbons. She must look a sight. "I fancy a dragonhide cloak," she said grimly.

"No dragons here," he said, stacking wood beside a pit of glowing embers fire. "Too cold for them, I'd wager. Too cold for us, too, if I don't build up the fire. If you're hungry, I have food on the table."

Zoraida wrapped the blanket around herself and rose to investigate. Some dried fish, a pouch of oats and some salt were all the man had to eat, yet still he offered it to her. The laws of hospitality were alive and well in this rude hut. She hid a smile. On the morrow, she would conjure a feast to break his fast which would make any nobleman's mouth water, but now she was too tired to summon up a single extra fish.

"If you get the fire going again, and you have a suitable pot, we could share a fine fish pottage tonight," she hazarded, hoping she could manage to make it without burning anything else tonight. Much like healing, cooking wasn't her forte, either.

"That sounds grand, lady."

"Zoraida," she corrected, watching him place the kindling over the embers just right, so flames licked hungrily at the wood. "My name is Zoraida."

He inclined his head. "Mine's Hans. Well met." He clasped her hand between his huge ones, reminding her that though he wasn't a bear, he was large enough to challenge one for the hide he now wore.

"Well met," she echoed.

Six

Some time later, the woman – Zoraida, Hans reminded himself – announced that their supper was ready. He fetched bowls and spoons, then watched as she filled the bowls with a lumpy mess that she said was fish pottage. It looked like nothing he'd ever eaten before, but perhaps the women made food differently here.

"I hope you like it," she said.

Hans smiled politely and stuck a spoonful of the stuff in his mouth. Alternately hard and chewy, it tasted like she'd burned some of it and put too much salt into the pot. He forced himself to swallow and reached for another spoonful. "It's wonderful," he lied.

She smiled tentatively and began eating her own portion. Hans watched as her eyes widened before she struggled to chew and swallow a mouthful that was every bit as bad as his. "On the morrow, I'll make something better. I will – "

More of this? Hans would rather go hungry. "No need, no need, dear lady. This would go better with a flagon of aged mead from my cellars, to be sure, but as we are not in my home, perhaps – "

"This is not your home?" she interrupted.

Hans laughed. "Of course not. This is a trapper's hut, to be used by any traveller or hunter who needs shelter for a night. My home is many miles from here. There, I wouldn't have to offer you the last of my journey rations. Instead, you would have roast pork, a selection of the finest roast vegetables, mulled wine to warm you from the inside, even if it weren't for the roaring fire. And my cook's Yule puddings are worth waiting all year for."

"You would…take me there? To your home?" she asked.

Hans felt sorry for her. The woman had nothing. He might not be rich by most noblemen's standards, but he had far more than she did. "If you wish it, but it is a long journey. We must walk to the next town, where I will procure horses to take us to the port, where we will board a ship to take us to the harbour near my home."

She shook her head. "The distance does not matter. You are offering me the hospitality of your home for a night, yes?"

"If you can make the journey there, then yes," he replied.

Zoraida seized his hand. "Then we go now!" With her free hand, she traced an arch in the air, leaving a trail of light that seemed to ignite when she touched the dirt floor. With more strength than any normal woman should possess, she pulled him through the portal.

Seven

From a falling down shack to falling down towers – yet it was an improvement, Zoraida decided. For one, there was no snow in the keep's courtyard. And while darkness had fallen in the frozen northern wastes, here the sun still lingered above the horizon, though not for long.

"We're home," Hans breathed, touching the stone wall as if to reassure himself that it was real. His other hand tightened around hers. "Right. Time to make good on that promise. You shall have a true Yule supper."

He strode across the courtyard, towing her along behind him. "I have returned!" he bellowed. "And I brought a guest."

Doors opened, letting light and people spill out.

"The baron is home!"

"He brought a lady."

"She looks half-frozen, poor mite."

"Fetch that leg of pork, the baron's hungry!"

"Come, my dear, we must find you something to wear."

Zoraida blinked, finding her hands held by a kind-looking older woman whose hair was neatly tucked under a white veil. She was suddenly conscious of her shredded clothes and unbound hair. She swallowed. "I would…be grateful," Zoraida said.

The woman led her inside to a chamber full of chests, with a bed that didn't look like it had been slept in for some time. A trio of younger women crowded in behind her, bearing cloths and jugs of water. Zoraida almost cried in relief. Between the soot and dragonfire, she was badly in need of a wash.

The older woman pulled various gowns from the chests as the girls helped her remove what remained of her dress. Each time, she glanced back at Zoraida, then shook her head, muttering to herself. After perhaps the fourth gown, Zoraida finally caught a few words: "The colours are too dark!" the woman said.

"White," Zoraida offered. "I usually wear white. It is the mark of a fairy godmother."

"Fairy godmother, hmm? I thought only royalty got those. The baron's father and mother never told me he had such a thing. And you don't look old enough to have been born on his name day." The woman's eyes seemed to read Zoraida's very soul.

"I'm not his godmother," Zoraida said swiftly. "I'm only the godmother to small children and foolish youths who seek to challenge dragons they haven't the wit or courage to fight. Hence…" She grimaced at the remains of her gown. "I think he was some kind of prince, but not all of them are royalty. Some have blood that is destined to become royal."

The woman nodded shrewdly. "So not the baron, but his daughter, perhaps. The queen has just given birth to a second prince, and word is that she might not have long to live. If one of the baron's daughters were to marry a prince…"

Zoraida's heart sank, though she wasn't sure why. "Hans has daughters?"

The woman snorted. "No, nor has he found a suitable woman to bear them. He worries so about restoring the castle, so he has a home to provide for his family. Seems to me he'll do all he can to make the home that he'll forget to find the family."

Zoraida relaxed. "He is a good man, and a kind one. Any woman would be lucky to be his wife."

"I do believe you mean that." She passed

Zoraida a shift. "Put that on, while I find you a suitable gown to celebrate Christmas Eve. Tell me, do fairy godmothers take husbands?"

"Sometimes," Zoraida said, pulling the shift over her head. It was made of fine, soft wool. "There is magic in our blood, so for there to be magic in the world…we must have daughters. Husbands can be quite helpful for this."

The woman laughed. "I'll wager they are very helpful. The baron has no family left. No one. It would be a blessing for him to have companionship. 'Tis Christmas, and I thought…"

"He offered me hospitality for the night," Zoraida reassured her. "I shall stay, and true to the season, I will offer him a gift. What he chooses…will be up to him." And limited by what she could give, but as long as he didn't ask her to cook, she considered herself quite capable of granting his wish. Whatever it might be.

Eight

The woman…nay, the lady who entered the great hall now truly resembled an angel who had tripped and fallen from heaven. Clothed from head to toe in white, she almost seemed to glow in the torchlight. Hans jumped to his feet. "Lady Zoraida," he greeted her with a bow.

She inclined her head regally. "Baron Hans, who is happier to be home than in a hut tonight, I think."

He laughed. "Indeed. I have you to thank for my swift journey. For that alone, you may stay in my home for as long as you wish."

Zoraida blushed and stared at her feet. Hans wondered if Elena had been filling her ears with tales about him while the woman had helped her dress. He opened his mouth to ask, but Elena herself appeared, followed by what seemed like every servant in the keep, bearing food for the feast. For the first time in his life, he was ignored, as every eye seemed to be fixed on Zoraida. Including his.

Elena had set his place at the head of the table, as was proper, but she set a second place for Zoraida at his right hand, instead of at the table's foot. Someone had already shifted the benches so that she had a chair to sit on, too.

Zoraida assumed her seat with all the grace of a queen accustomed to wearing such finery as she ascended her throne. It dawned on Hans that she could well be a queen — he'd assumed that because she wore rags, she was his inferior, but now…

He swallowed. "Lady Zoraida, forgive me if the fare is not what you are accustomed to. I am but a baron, one of the lowliest nobles in the kingdom, and my household had little notice of my return, so if this meagre feast is not enough, then on the morrow, I can – "

She shook her head. "As long as it tastes better than burned fish pottage, I wouldn't even consider turning you into a frog, a fowl, or any manner of beast."

Elena laughed, then smothered the sound with her hand. She evidently knew something Hans did not, he thought. Perhaps Elena had not been the only one telling tales tonight. He felt an unfamiliar pang of jealousy. He wanted to hear the lady's tales.

"I am grateful," Hans said slowly. "What did you turn your last host into? The one who served you bad pottage?"

"Oh, that would be my attempt at supper tonight. I was not taught to cook. I'm also not very good at animal transformations," she said.

"I'm better at elemental magic. Fireballs. Air currents to slow my descent if I open a portal too high up. I think I made it rain once. Oh, and portals, of course. Like the one that brought us here."

Intrigued, he asked, "You mean, you travel like this all the time? Magically?"

She nodded. "It's necessary, what with fairy godmother duties and all. Truthfully, I am an enchantress, but I haven't been one very long, so I tend to stick to the easy tasks. Blessing babies. Looking after children when they hit adolescence, at least as much as I am able. I'm told they require less care once they marry, but none of my godchildren are old enough for that yet. George, the eldest, will not reach marriageable age at all if he keeps challenging dragons."

Hans wanted to ask a thousand questions, starting with whether she'd actually seen a dragon, but the servants began serving the meal and he was soon far too busy filling his plate and then his mouth. His belly reminded him that he hadn't eaten this well in weeks. The pork alone was everything he'd imagined and more.

Gentle laughter brought his attention from his plate to his guest. He was a poor host, Hans realised.

He swallowed his mouthful of roast pork, then washed it down with some cider. "Is the food to your liking?" he asked.

"Yes, of course," she said. "I had thought to conjure a feast for you in thanks for your hospitality, but I see that there is no need now. I would still like to offer a spell in payment for your kindness. If there is anything you want, name it, and if it is within my power to grant it, you shall have it on the morrow."

It was Hans' turn to laugh. "I am home, sharing a Yule feast with a beautiful, charming enchantress. What more could I wish for?"

Nine

What more indeed? Hans might well be the first man she'd ever met who was happy with what he had, Zoraida decided as she realised he meant every word of what he'd said. Granted, he was not a poor man by any means, but he was hardly the richest in the land. And yet…he seemed happy, for all his servants said he was lonely.

She ate her fill of the rich food, which was

quite delicious, despite having different flavours to those she was used to. Just as she was debating whether she could just manage to eat another piece of the sharp, white cheese, Hans rose from his seat.

"I promised the Lady Zoraida some mulled mead! Where is the alewife?" Hans demanded.

"In the kitchens, preparing it, m'lord," a manservant answered.

"Have it sent to my solar. This hall is too draughty when the wind blows from the north." Hans bowed and held out his hand. "If you will accompany me, my lady, I believe I promised you a proper Yule with mead and mulled wine and the finest puddings you have ever tasted before a roaring fire."

Though the thought of more food sounded like madness, she didn't hesitate to give him her hand. Even after a cup or three of wine, the man was still as charming as he had been in the hut.

They reached the archway which led to the rest of the keep, but Elena blocked their way.

She pointed upward. "'Tis bad luck not to kiss a maiden under the kissing bough," she admonished, wagging her finger.

Both of them glanced up. Zoraida saw nothing but a tree branch, wound round with mistletoe. Perhaps this was some unusual northern custom she hadn't yet heard about.

"Forgive me, Lady Zoraida," Hans said. "But my housekeeper is right. I would not let bad luck touch a lady like you. Better to be kissed than cursed."

Zoraida disagreed. She'd never been kissed before, but breaking curses was easy. She'd just…

Oh.

His arms wrapped firmly around her, warm and secure, like he wanted to keep her safe.

His breath smelled of spices and apple as he gently brought his lips to hers. A chaste kiss, no more.

Zoraida breathed a sigh of relief, though he still held her close.

"Must do a proper job of it," he said.

Then his lips were on hers again, more insistent this time, and she gasped at the intensity in his eyes. Not lust. More…determination, she decided. But all coherent thought fled as his tongue teased hers, lightly at first, becoming bolder as she responded in kind. She wanted to taste him, the tart cider on his tongue and the promise of more, if she wanted it. So much more.

When he released her, she nearly swooned – she, an enchantress! To be floored by a simple kiss. Ah, but there was nothing simple about this kiss. There must be some magic in this mistletoe, she was certain of it.

Hans caught her before she fell, and offered his arm as support. "I think that will keep you from being cursed now," he said gravely. "Shall we?"

"Of course," she replied. For the second time tonight, she felt like she was falling – with no snow to cushion her when she landed. If she landed. For her heart beat so fast it seemed ready to take flight.

Ten

For one terrible moment, Hans thought she would faint. Was his kiss so awful? He'd certainly enjoyed it, and he'd thought she had, too, but now he wasn't sure. Her breathing had quickened, as if she feared another kiss. He resolved not to frighten her, and offered his arm instead. He sent up a silent prayer of thanks when her fingers wrapped around his forearm.

Hans took her upstairs to the solar, the room at the top of the keep. It was bigger than the trapper's hut, but infinitely more cosy. His mother had insisted on piling rugs and cushions on the chairs by the fire, so that more than once Hans and his father had fallen asleep while sitting in them. His mother might be gone, but her memory lived on in the soft touches she had left behind. Now he was more glad of them than ever, as it meant he could offer Zoraida more comfort than the shack they'd almost had to share.

As she took her chosen seat by the fire, once again he was struck by her queenly demeanour. As though this was her kingdom, and she belonged here. His mouth turned dry at the thought of sharing his home – his life – with her. But she was no ordinary woman. She might even outrank the queen, for magic was rare in the world these days, and he'd felt her power coursing through him when they'd kissed. Too far above him for a lowly baron to even raise his eyes to her, let alone ask for her hand. But for a night, she had accepted his hospitality, and he would honour her properly. With food, and drink, and what little entertainment he could offer – stories of his travels. And perhaps…perhaps she would tell him a little of what it meant to be an enchantress, so that for one night, he might dream he shared a life with her.

Eleven

"...My skirt caught fire, so I opened a portal, saw snow, and stepped through. And that's how I ended up in the northern wastes on Christmas Eve with my favourite white gown in tatters," Zoraida finished. She expected more questions from Hans, who had proved to have an almost insatiable curiosity for the most mundane things about her life as a fairy godmother, but the only sound he emitted was a snore.

She smothered a giggle. She'd drunk too much mead, she was sure of it, but the sweetness and the spices and the soul-warming heat of it had persuaded her to indulge in a little more than usual. And Hans…the man was such pleasurable company. The way he spoke of his dreams for the future – for his ships, for his home, and for some sort of trade agreement that had made him trek across the northern wastes to where she'd first encountered him. Could a girl fall in love with a man for his kindness and his dreams? Oh, and his kisses. She would like more of those. But not tonight. She would let him snore in his chair, if that's where he chose to sleep, while she retired to the room Elena had assured her would be prepared for her.

As she crossed the courtyard, Zoraida paused to take another look at the crumbling towers Hans had vowed to rebuild. It was Yule, and she'd given him no gift yet. She'd told him her powers lay in the elements, in fire and air and water and earth. What was stone but the mother of earth, after all?

Wrapping her cloak around her, she lifted her arms, and cast a new spell.

Twelve

Hans jerked awake, desperate to find the woman who'd filled his dreams, but he was alone in his solar. Someone had mended the fire while he slept, and removed what remained of the jug of mead he'd been drinking last night, but the beautiful lady proved to be nothing but a dream.

What had her name been? Something exotic. The Lady Zoraida, that was it. An enchantress who fought dragons and could travel miles in the blink of an eye, but who couldn't cook the simplest of meals. Hans laughed to himself. He'd even dreamed up an imperfection in the perfect woman, to make her seem more real.

He should probably head for the hall to break his fast. Smoked fish were what he wanted this morning, with some of that sharp white cheese and fresh bread. He dressed in a fresh tunic and hose, then trotted down the steps to the courtyard.

Hans stopped. If he had dreamed the woman, how had he come home? Was his whole trade agreement a dream, too? Losing the lady was one thing, but to find out he was no closer to rebuilding his home than his father had been would be an even lower blow. Hans glanced out the window, feeling his heart break anew at the sight of the ruined south tower.

Except...the tower stood tall and whole, right up to the slate tiles on the roof. It wasn't possible.

Hans rubbed his eyes, certain he was still dreaming, but the tower did not disappear.

He stumbled down the remaining steps to the bailey, where it had been his daily habit to survey the keep before breakfast, vowing anew every morning that he would restore his family's home. Now, on Christmas morn, his vow died on his lips as he saw the castle as his grandfather must have, its towers rising to the heavens as though nothing had ever toppled them.

He felt tears prick at his eyes, and closed them. Barons did not weep.

"Did I do them wrong?" a female voice enquired. The sweet voice of a dream. "I have never built towers before, but the stone walls seemed to almost shape themselves, they were so eager to be whole again. The walls are sound, but the rooms within are cold and empty. It takes more than shaping stone to make a house a home."

His mother had made this house a home.

How much he longed for someone to help him do the same.

Hans turned, not believing he would see her, for his eyes had played too many tricks on him this morning. Yet there Zoraida stood, wearing a green wool gown today instead of white, with a smile on her face that lit up the whole world.

"You're real," he choked out.

She nodded. "Indeed I am. If you ever doubt it, remember the fish pottage. Enchantresses do not make good cooks." She eyed the towers. "If you wish me to change them, or undo the work I have done, simply say so and I shall. I promised you a wish, a spell, but you would not name your desire, and as gifts are traditionally given at Yule..."

Gifts. A clove orange. A new cloak. A book of hours. Not a rebuilt keep. She had given him far more than he could ever repay.

"I have only one wish," he said. "That you stay under my roof for another night, and tell me more tales of what you have seen."

She began to laugh. "But that will only place me even more in your debt for the hospitality. Tomorrow morning, I will ask you to make another wish."

Hans took a deep breath. "And it will be for another night, and another, and another. Until one morning I work up the courage to ask for your hand, so that you will stay. Last night was…the happiest night of my life. I wish for a lifetime more."

Violet eyes stared at him for a long moment. Finally, Zoraida said, "Then I shall stay. And when you find that courage you say you lack, I want a bower at the top of that tower." She pointed. "For I must teach our children somewhere, and your solar is so cosy, I fear they will fall asleep and learn nothing. But at the top of the highest tower…there, they will see the whole world."

It took Hans a moment before he could close his mouth. "You…will?" At Zoraida's nod, he continued, "Last night, when I saw a shooting star blaze across the sky, I wished I might find a woman, nay, a wife, to grace this keep. I tried to retrieve the fallen star, but you fell at my feet. Now, I find you have done more for this keep in one night than my family have for two generations. How is any of this possible?"

Zoraida smiled. "It is the time of year, I think. The time of mistletoe, magic and kisses. I hope there shall be more kisses."

Hans took her in his arms, prepared to provide a lifetime of kisses for the lady of his dreams.

About the Author

Demelza Carlton has always loved the ocean, but on her first snorkelling trip she found she was afraid of fish.

She has since swum with sea lions, sharks and sea cucumbers and stood on spray drenched cliffs over a seething sea as a seven-metre cyclonic swell surged in, shattering a shipwreck below.

Demelza now lives in Perth, Western Australia, the shark attack capital of the world.

The *Ocean's Gift* series was her first foray into fiction, followed by her suspense thriller *Nightmares* trilogy. She swears the *Mel Goes to Hell* series ambushed her on a crowded train and wouldn't leave her alone.

Want to know more? You can follow Demelza on Facebook, Twitter, YouTube or her website, Demelza Carlton's Place at:

www.demelzacarlton.com